Praise for Two Blankets, Three She█

'The dilemma of the desire for survival set against one's moral compass brings to mind George Orwell's *Down and Out in Paris and London*; Samir's attempts to make the best of his protracted detention has much in common with the plight of the stateless Tom Hanks in Steven Spielberg's film *The Terminal*.'
DUTCH FOUNDATION FOR LITERATURE

'This is an unnerving, ironic book about how lives are ground down by endlessly stretched procedures.'
Leeuwarder Courant

'Al Galidi writes this novel based on his own experiences, but he covers that up so well with his fluent writing style, a sense of humor, and an absence of resentment. A real feat in his case. The lighthearted way in which he writes about tragic experiences makes this a very impactful book.'
KRISTIEN HEMMERECHTS, author of *The Woman Who Fed the Dogs*

'Book of the month? Book of the year! Rodaan Al Galidi has been writing beautiful books for years, but this is his absolute masterpiece. Loose, light, and humoristic—it is precisely for these reasons the book hits home. Stylistically, too, this book is a testament to his mastery.'
Boekhandel Van Rossum

'For all its heavy themes—the tragedy of miscommunication, loss of identity and meaning of life, humiliation, and the incapacity to truly connect—it is also a very light and humorous book.'
Literair Nederland

'A challenging portrait of Dutch hospitality. Absolutely recommended.'
De Correspondent

'You can write emails about refugees until you're blue in the face, but you can also, thanks to the unique power of literature, spend a few hours inside the mind and soul of one of them—by reading this tragicomic masterpiece. It will do you good.'
De Limburger

'"The asylum center," Al Galidi writes, "is a grave where the time of a few hundred people is buried." For this grave he has erected a memorable monument that functions as both a complaint and a mirror. And I, for one, was ashamed of what I saw in it.'
TOMMY WIERINGA, author of *Joe Speedboat*

'Essential reading'
Trouw

'A stunning novel about the experiences of a refugee in a heartless regime. Al Galidi holds up a mirror to us. A mirror that we should all look into.'
ADRIAAN VAN DIS, author of *My Father's War*

'*Two Blankets, Three Sheets* is a valuable and rich novel about fear, uncertainty, arbitrariness and hopelessness, written by someone who was, thankfully, able to use his new language as a lifebuoy.'
Tzum

RODAAN AL GALIDI is a poet and writer. Born in Iraq and trained as a civil engineer, he has lived in the Netherlands since 1998. As an undocumented asylum seeker he did not have the right to attend language classes, so he taught himself to read and write Dutch. His novel *De autist en de postduif* ('The Autist and the Carrier Pigeon') won the European Union Prize for Literature in 2011—the same year he failed his Dutch citizenship course. *Two Blankets, Three Sheets*, already a bestseller in the Netherlands, is his most successful novel to date.

JONATHAN REEDER, a native of New York and longtime resident of Amsterdam, enjoys a dual career as a literary translator and performing musician. Alongside his work as a professional bassoonist he translates opera libretti and essays on classical music, as well as contemporary Dutch fiction by authors including Peter Buwalda, Bram Dehouck, Christine Otten, and Adri van der Heijden. His recent translations include *Rivers* by Martin Michael Driessen (winner of the 2016 ECI Literature Prize) and *The Lonely Funeral* by Maarten Inghels and F. Starik.

TWO BLANKETS, THREE SHEETS, A TOWEL, A PILLOW, AND A PILLOWCASE

RODAAN AL GALIDI

TWO BLANKETS, THREE SHEETS, A TOWEL, A PILLOW, AND A PILLOWCASE

Translated from the Dutch
by Jonathan Reeder

WORLD EDITIONS
New York, London, Amsterdam

Published in the USA in 2020 by World Editions LLC, New York
Published in the UK in 2020 by World Editions Ltd., London

World Editions
New York/London/Amsterdam

Printed by Lake Book, USA

Library of Congress Cataloging in Publication Data is available

ISBN 978-1-64286-045-0

First published as *Hoe ik talent voor het leven kreeg* in the Netherlands in 2017
by Uitgeverij Jurgen Maas, Amsterdam

This publication has been made possible with financial support from the
Dutch Foundation for Literature

N ederlands
letterenfonds
dutch foundation
for literature

Twitter: @WorldEdBooks
Facebook: WorldEditionsInternationalPublishing
www.worldeditions.org

Book Club Discussion Guides are available on our website.

The Netherlands has taught me three things:

1 the difference between a granny bike and a ladies' bike,

2 that you must be at least as wary of Europe as you are respectful,

3 a clever lie is better than the clumsy truth.

FOREWORD

This story was bothering me. It was never easy to write about; I even found it difficult to talk about candidly. Years later, I still didn't really feel like discussing it. I wanted to move on. I started avoiding the subject, so as not to be bogged down by the old memories.

When a certain man asked me, a while ago, about my life in the asylum center, I could tell his question was serious, and that he expected a serious answer. I replied politely that I didn't want to go into it. He asked me to name just one situation. I did, and I think he knew that in my head, I was still actually living in that ASC*. Perhaps he sensed that to get my life going again, I needed to get this story off my chest. Or maybe he didn't want my story to sink into oblivion, the story of that alien world I was forced to inhabit for all those years.

How he managed it, I don't know, but he got me to promise to send him a bit of the story every month. Maybe it was the way he listened, with so much understanding and compassion. Or maybe it was the growing sense of responsibility to keep this story alive.

An email from him on October 15, 2012 got me writing. I started on the first chapter, and as the months ticked by I was afraid I would lose him as my sole reader, or already had lost him, so I kept on writing for two and

---

* Asylum Seekers' Center; see pg. 395 for a full list of abbreviations

a half years, until May 19, 2015, when this book was finished. Without the support of that one reader, it wouldn't have happened. He is without a doubt the midwife of each and every page. I dedicate this book to him. In gratitude that he swept my head clean of those oppressive years.

The narrator in this book is not me. It is someone I've called Samir Karim. This way I can still be the writer, and not the main character.

People might ask me if this is my story, to which I will say: no. But if I'm asked if this is *also* my story, then I will say wholeheartedly: yes.

Go to the Rijksmuseum and have a good look at *The Night Watch*. Do you see Rembrandt? The answer is: no. But you can imagine him behind all those figures, looking out through the dark. Almost invisible.

I have done my best to let Samir depict that unfamiliar world as clearly as possible.

This book is fiction for the reader who cannot believe it. But for anyone open to it, it is nonfiction. Or no: let this book be nonfiction, so that the world I had to inhabit for all those years will be transformed from fiction into fact.

1

I landed at Schiphol Airport at 9 a.m. on the eleventh of February. Or at 11 a.m. on the ninth of February, I can't remember the exact date anymore. I do know that it was 1998.

Some twenty hours earlier I had been walking around Ho Chi Minh City Airport with my forged Dutch passport. The photo had been well-doctored, but there was one hitch: the height of the official owner was 1.73 meters. I am 1.86—thirteen centimeters, almost half a foot, taller. The hand that now writes these words trembled as I stood in line at customs. I could not convince the hand that if its trembling betrayed me, it could mean years in a Vietnamese jail. When it was my turn, I handed the passport, which also trembled, to the customs agent. His narrow Asian eyes bored into me. He examined my passport, looked up and asked, in English: "Where is Curaçao?" His question took me by surprise. I had memorized the information in the passport, spent hours practicing the signature. I knew that its bearer was born in Curaçao, but where that was, I did not know, nor had it struck me as something I should know. The man looked at me, waiting for an answer.

"Near Amsterdam," I said nervously. The man squinted. "About forty kilometers northeast of Amsterdam," I added quickly, feeling the need to provide more details. "A pretty place." Then he smiled. His curiosity had been satisfied, and he stamped the passport.

Landing in the Netherlands gave me my first glimpse of Europe, the origin of all those marvelous books whose translations I spent so much effort tracking down in Iraq, and which I then devoured. Europe might be gray outside, but to me it was more beautiful than any other country I had ever seen. I looked out the airplane window and considered that, for the first time in my life, I could be a person. Here I would shed my fear like an old, torn pair of trousers. Here I would discard my caution like smelly, holey socks. I will never forget that blissful feeling. I waited in my seat until everyone else had disembarked past the smiling Asian stewardesses. As I walked to the aircraft door, I prayed the immigration officials wouldn't be carrying out spot checks, because then they would see where I had come from and send me straight back. Luckily I made it unhindered through the jetway and into the transit hall, where I was relieved to quickly vanish among the other travelers. Some had just arrived, some were just beginning their journey, and others were merely passing through. As for myself, I wasn't sure whether I had arrived, or was beginning my journey, or passing through. First things first: the China Airlines plane had to take off again, and leave Schiphol without me.

Normally a passport is one's most precious possession in a transit hall, but mine was my greatest liability. I had to get rid of it as quickly as possible. If the police catch you with a forged passport, they know which airplane you arrived on, which means they also know how to deport you.

I was a bundle of nerves when a policeman approached me and asked if I needed assistance.

"Toilet," I said in English, and crossed my legs so he would see that I wasn't acting strangely out of anxiety but out of physical necessity. He pointed to the nearest men's room and I thanked him. Once out of sight, I went the other way and ducked into one further up instead. There I tore my passport and ticket into the tiniest possible scraps and dropped them into the toilet bowl. I did the same with the addresses I still had with me, as well as all my Thai, Vietnamese, Laotian, and Malaysian banknotes.

I flushed the global trail that had led me to Schiphol down the toilet. I also threw away the Asian souvenirs I had bought on the advice of a smuggler in Bangkok, who said that travelers to Europe without hand baggage attract attention at the airport, because Europeans always buy souvenirs. So I had filled a carry-on bag with gifts purchased here and there from sidewalk peddlers. The smuggler was right: after checking my bag at Ho Chi Minh City, they zipped it shut with a smile because I had such good taste. Once back outside the men's room all I had on me was ten dollars.

The only thing I regretted was having neglected to bring any warm clothing. I was so busy avoiding getting caught that I didn't consider what kind of clothes would be useful in Holland. In fact, I hadn't the slightest idea of the climate here. Wearing nothing but a T-shirt, I walked through the transit hall and marveled at its enormity. It resembled a city, where everything you wanted could be had.

After an hour had passed, and the China Airlines plane had taken off again, I felt the ten dollars burning a hole in my pocket. Should I drink a nice cup of hot tea, eat a Big Mac, or phone my mother? The photo of the Big Mac made my Adam's apple move up and down, but when I saw people drinking tea, that seemed to me a tastier choice. In the end I decided to call my mother to reassure her. As though I had just left the house that morning, and not seven years earlier.

As far as my mother was concerned, everywhere in the world was safe and wonderful, except Iraq. I don't know where she acquired this positive image of the world, because when I once asked her how old she was—we don't know each other's birthdays—her answer was: "Eight wars."

"I mean in years, mother."

I hadn't spoken to her in more than a year and she had no idea where I was all that time, but when I got her on the line it felt as though I was calling from a block away to say I'd be bringing friends around for dinner. I said I was greeting her from the Netherlands. My mother is illiterate, but she did know that Dutch cows produce lots of milk. In Iraq, Dutch cows have a better reputation than Rembrandt.

"Oh, thank God—Holland," my mother said. "God loves the Dutch, why else would he have made their cows' udders so big? There, among all those cows, you won't go hungry, Samir." I pressed the receiver tightly against my ear to hear her voice better. "Do you remember our Dutch cow? She gave enough milk a day for twenty people." She went on to tell me what had become of the cow, until I was down to my last cent and we got cut off.

I put down the receiver and sighed. Then I started to think about how to get outside. Looking past the other travelers, I could see through the airport windowpanes. I walked along those incredibly long transparent walls and stared at the bare trees in the distance. Not a gap anywhere. Even a needle has an eye—but not Schiphol airport. I paced back and forth like a lab mouse in a glass jar. Every exit had a checkpoint. Exhausted from jetlag and the fear of being caught, I sank into a chair and thought I'd better tell one of the officers I wanted to ask for asylum. My two sisters, both of whom studied law in Baghdad, had often said that nowhere in the world had such favorable laws as Sweden and the Netherlands. This reassured me, somehow. My body felt safe, but my spirit was not so sure. This could have had to do with the faces of the Dutch salespeople in the transit hall shops and the cleaners I encountered. Something in those faces prevented me from feeling relieved and out of harm's way. This did not look like the other countries I had been in, where people smile all the time, even for no reason.

I saw a group of travelers and thought I might be able to slip outside with them, but then they went through a door to another hall to continue their journey and I was left standing alone. If I had just stood there calmly, the officer would probably have walked on, but apparently I was so visibly anxious that he approached and asked if I needed any help.

"I'm Iraqi," I said to the young police officer. Blond locks curled out from under his cap and his eyes were bright blue, like those I had seen on European backpackers during my time in Southeast Asia.

"Come with me," he said, as though the word *Iraqi* was enough for him to know what needed to be done. I followed him. He was big and muscular. He wore boots, as though he was in danger of sinking into a foot of mud, rather than walking through a dry, climate-controlled airport. I was surprised he didn't handcuff me, like other countries' border patrol agents did.

There, behind this burly policeman, among the thousands of travelers who had shielded me, I did not realize

I was walking into the longest wait of my life.

I watched in awe as he opened doors with a card, and not a key. I imagined that Europe was so advanced that people didn't use keys anymore, just their ID card. The policeman opened glass door after glass door with his magic ID card, until the doors changed to steel, erasing the bare trees and the gray February sky. All I saw were corridors and doors and the policeman's muscular back. He ushered me into an office, where a man of about forty-five was sitting at a table. The man swiveled his chair toward me and gave me the once-over. His expression suggested he had been working on something important. The many Post-Its and slips of paper on the board behind him reinforced that idea and made me believe he was doing a good twenty things at once. I noticed that he had soft hands. My young police escort said something in Dutch. This was the first time I heard the language. Of the various languages that came through the public address system at Schiphol, I was unable to figure out which one belonged to the country where I had just landed. The man gave the policeman a quick nod and then turned to me. Suddenly he spoke loudly into my face, in English.

"Why have you come here?" I saw the anger on his face. He asked questions to which he expected no answer. I glanced over at my police escort, and saw that his eyes were glazed over. In Iraq, I would now be tied up as if I'd done something wrong. But here, there were no chains or steel cables on the walls. There was only a portrait of the Dutch queen, with a crown on her head and a gentle smile on her lips. It was an ordinary office, like you'd expect in a bank.

"Why don't you people solve your own problems?" the man asked. "We're not responsible for solving the world's problems, are we?"

The seven years I had spent between escaping from Iraq and now, here at Schiphol airport, shot through my mind. Seven years of hunger, of roaming, and of fear. The immigration police had bitten me at many border crossings, all because I lacked that thin, small book, that book without any poetry at all: a passport.

To this last question, though, the man did seem to expect an answer. My gaze returned to the portrait of the queen behind him, and an answer came to me, from a book I had once read about World War II, about the bombardment of Rotterdam and the evacuation of the Dutch royal family. I said, "Sir, your queen fled during World War II and didn't solve the problems in her own country—even though she had an army, a secret service, a nation, and money. How am I supposed to solve my problems in Iraq when I'm just a civilian without even a kitchen knife?"

The man got up and approached me, his mouth twisted, pressed his thumb against my chest and hissed: "You, you, heh, heh ..." I held my tongue. He sat back down, but kept eyeing me with an ice-cold stare.

"Where's your passport?"

"I tore it up and flushed it down the toilet," I said. At this, the man left the office and returned with another policeman, a large man with short brown hair and a pair of plastic gloves.

"You're to go with this officer and get your passport back," he said.

To my surprise, the man gave me plastic gloves, even though he was mad at me. He even demonstrated that the gloves were long enough to reach your elbows, so I could stick my hands deep into the bowl without soiling them. They apparently hoped a scrap or two of my passport had got stuck in the toilet.

"Otherwise we'll send you back to Iraq," the man added. I dropped the gloves on the floor.

"Pick them up and put them on," the policeman said, but I just stood there.

"Why don't you do what I say?" he asked.

"Sorry, sir, but I fled Iraq so I didn't have to bathe my arms in blood. I didn't come to the Netherlands to stick my arms into a toilet."

The man said something in Dutch to the policeman, who seemed to have been waiting for those words, for suddenly he was behind me, and quick as lightning he tied my hands behind my back, like he'd just nabbed me after a long chase. He pulled the plastic cable ties so tight that they practically cut off the blood to my hands. Then he shoved me toward a small cell. He threw the gloves into the cell, and kicked me in my back so hard that I was thrown against the far wall. My face banged against the cement and I fell to the ground.

"You'll stay here until your passport comes out of that toilet," he said as he slammed the steel door shut. The policeman had not only kicked my back, but my credibility too, because every time I mention that kick, or whenever my back hurts, which it does to this day, no one believes me.

The cell was ice-cold. My face was bloodied from hitting the cement wall, and I was frustrated that I couldn't even wipe the blood out of my eyes. There was nothing to wrap myself up in, or crawl under. My hands were cuffed too tightly to rub them warm. I could only sit down and stand up, or at most take two steps back and forth. All you could see through the small window in the door was a bare white wall.

The officer peered through the window just once.

"Cold," I said, with a quivering voice. I'd wanted to add "please," but only had enough energy for one word. He walked away.

I have no idea how much time passed. When I thought everyone had forgotten me and I'd freeze to death, I screamed, "Open the door! I'll get the passport out of the toilet!" I screamed, but no one came. I sat down, stood up, sat down, stood up, to keep from collapsing from the cold. Not a soul in sight. The thought that the officers had finished their day's work and had all gone home, and no one would know I was stuck in that cell, was terrifying. By the time they found me, I'd have frozen to death. The minutes crept by. After a while I felt the February chill triumphing over my body. My last line of defense was anger. I wanted to get angry at the man in the office, but anyone who could envelope me in such cold was too powerful for me. I thought it best not to be angry at the officer, because what if he did come—I might attack him instead of beg for help, and then he'd leave me to rot in that cell for sure. The only choice was to get angry at myself. With trembling lips, I bawled myself out that an hour ago I opened my big mouth and shouted that the Queen of the Netherlands was an asylum seeker too, and that I did not want to douse my hands in blood in Iraq, nor in a toilet in the Netherlands. I screamed at myself.

"Stupid, stupid!" I banged my head against the wall. I stamped my feet and cursed myself. Flames of rage burned throughout my body. I trembled not only from the cold, but out of anger at myself. I started yelling that I'd even retrieve the passport from the toilet without the gloves. I kicked the cell door and heard the noise it made in the corridor. When I saw the officer's face in the little window, I stopped at once. "I'll go get it, I'll get the passport from the toilet. Please," I said. His face disappeared and the door opened. He came in, undid the cable ties and pointed to the gloves on the floor. With chattering teeth and trembling hands, I struggled to pick up the gloves, and followed the officer.

He took me to a men's room and told me to wash myself. I washed my face, and when I emerged I was told to go back in and wash my T-shirt. Then, in my wet T-shirt, I followed the officer back to the transit hall, where he was transformed into a pleasant man. I saw, beyond the glass walls, European night for the first time. I could only just drag my body, and trudged behind the officer. When he asked where my passport was, I pointed "that way"—not because I knew which men's room I'd left my passport in, but because I did not want to go back to that cold cell. All I wanted was to walk through the heated transit hall. I walked and walked until I felt that my legs could no longer hold me up, and stopped at a rest room. "This one?" he asked. I wanted to answer him, but I couldn't. The world around me went yellow, and I felt my body separate from me.

2

I woke up on the floor of a large room, a sort of ward. I lifted my head. Someone had laid a bag under it. My neck was stiff and I was still cold. The room was filled with travelers caught with false papers, or smugglers, or who knows what kind of folks, sitting on chairs or else on the floor, leaning against the wall. A small television, tuned to a sports channel, hung from the ceiling. In one corner was a vending machine for coffee, tea, and candy.

In the seven years I had wandered around the world without a passport, I had been jailed by immigration police in Jordan, Turkey, Thailand, and Malaysia. Never before had I seen such an orderly, spotless place as this. It looked more like a travel agency than a jail, like we were waiting for our tour guide to arrive. A policeman shook me awake and led me, still half asleep, to an office, where they took my fingerprints. Everything I had with me was searched. Every piece of paper photocopied. Someone dabbed my face with a sponge and warm water, after which they took my picture. Then I was brought back to the crowded room. I lay back down and shivered. I had a fever, and my head nearly exploded from the pain. That cold cell had depleted my body's warmth and energy. I lay there and tried to sleep on the hard floor, feeling the kick in my back I'd got from the first officer, when another officer told me to follow him.

"I'm sick," I said. "I can't."

"You have to follow me," he said. "Now." I tried to get up. "I'll help you."

The officer pulled me up by the arm and led me to another office, where a blond Dutch woman sat at a table. Next to her was an interpreter. I could tell from his dialect that he was Egyptian; since he didn't understand my Iraqi dialect very well, I spoke to him in classical Arabic and explained some words to him in English.

"We are going to take your first statement," the woman said.

"I'm sick," I said, with difficulty. "I've just been in a freezing cold cell, and now I'm sick."

"A cold cell?" I couldn't tell from her expression whether she was curious or irritated.

"Just now, here, at the airport," I said.

"Asylum seekers are not brought to a cold cell, but to the room you've just come from," she said in Dutch, which the interpreter then translated into Arabic, after which she repeated it yet again in English.

"It's true, I was in a cell and it was so cold I nearly froze," I said.

"That's not possible," the woman said. "The airport is a single large building, with a constant temperature. There's nowhere here you could freeze. If I understand correctly, you do not have a passport, is that right? In that case, you certainly weren't brought to a cell somewhere outside the airport, because you're only allowed to leave this airport after your first hearing. Is that clear?"

"I swear I was put in a cold cell."

"I'll tell you something else. Here in the Netherlands you don't have to swear. What you say will be believed if it is credible, and won't be believed if it isn't credible. If you have proof, then your story is more credible. I can't get into a discussion about your being in a cold cell if one does not exist. Is that clear?" I looked at her in silence, and didn't know how I was supposed to respond. She repeated the question.

"Yes, clear," I said, my voice trembling. I felt feverish.

"From now on, no more talk of that cold cell. You'll answer the questions I ask. This is your first hearing. Your second hearing will take place within six months from today. Whether or not you are accepted in the Netherlands as a refugee will be based on these two hearings. Do you have any questions?"

"I hardly have any energy. I've got a headache, a sore throat, and a fever. Can we do this later, when I'm feeling better?"

"We have to carry out this hearing now, to get the procedure started." She began with the first question: my surname. I answered that in Iraq we don't have surnames, but that every person has three names: your own first name, your father's first name, and your grandfather's first name. She handed me a pen and paper, and asked me to write down those three names in Latin script. She told me that without a surname of my own, I would be given my grandfather's first name as a surname. So my grandpa's first name became my family name. Samir Hamza Karim. She informed me that now and forever more, I would be addressed in the Netherlands as Mr. Karim. If I hadn't been so exhausted, I would have chuckled at the idea that my grandfather—dead for thirty years now—would be resurrected in the form of my new surname. And this in an airport thousands of kilometers from Iraq.

"Date of birth?"

"July 1st—" I said, but she interrupted me before I could continue.

"Five other Iraqis I interviewed were also born on July 1st," she said. "Is that your actual birthdate?"

"No," I said. "It is my official birthdate."

"Could you clarity that?"

"I'm so tired. Can it wait until the next hearing?"

"If you're tired, I can get you some coffee." Under any other circumstances, this would have been a kind, thoughtful gesture, but here it sounded like a reprimand. She made a phone call, and a little while later I was given a cup of black coffee with sugar out in the hallway. Actually, I didn't drink coffee, but I took it, it was warm and would keep me awake. I sat down in the hallway and took small sips, my hands still trembling.

The woman came and stood next to me. Her face was different. Softer. She smiled.

"Why are your hands trembling like that?" she asked in English. "Are you that nervous?"

"I'm sick," I said, and eyed her suspiciously because I wasn't sure this was the same woman I had just been speaking to in that office.

"I can tell," she said. She didn't just look different. She *was* different. Someone who wanted me to see that in her office she was just doing her job, and that wasn't who she really was.

"Could you maybe postpone the hearing? I'm totally exhausted." I hoped she would say *yes* this time.

"I'll do my best," she said. "But the sooner we get this hearing done, the sooner you can leave the airport. You can see a doctor at the reception center. That's why it really is important to get this finished quickly." Her voice was gentle when she spoke to me in English. She also sounded tired, which made me think she wanted to get it over with, too, so she could go home. "Were you really put in a cold room?" she asked suddenly. I eyed her cautiously. Was this really the same woman who was sitting at that computer just now, or were they two different women? And which of them could I be honest with?

"I don't know whether the cell was too cold," I said, not so much trying to be truthful as to sound credible. Getting this hearing over with was more important than the price I might pay for it, even more important than the truth.

"Maybe it was cold at first because they still had to turn on the heat," she said. "It takes a while for it to warm up." I nodded, and before she walked off I saw her smile, perhaps more to herself than to me.

We resumed the interview once I'd finished the coffee. The woman was back at her desk and her computer. As a different person. I was amazed at the speed with which she switched between formal and informal in her word choice, her manner, and her facial expressions. What made it especially hard for me was that her manners in the office and out in the hallway were equally genuine. This horrible woman had just been a gentle person who I could become friends with, who I certainly didn't need to be afraid of—and not even ten minutes later, she was horrible again. To this day, I find it hard to get my head around this. "All right then," the woman said in a determined voice. "You said that July 1st is not your real birth date. Do you have two birthdays?"

"I have two birth dates," I said. "The actual one, which I don't know, and this one, July 1st, which the government gave me." Surely a civil servant working for the immigration services should know that among adult Iraqis, half have July 1 as their birth date, and the other half has January 1.

"How did you get your official birth date? Were you examined at a hospital?"

"No, there was no hospital in our village."

"Somewhere else, then?"

"No."

"So how did they determine your age?"

"One day my father and my mother took their ten children, two aunts, my grandparents, my uncles, and my cousins to a tiny one-room building with a window in the nearest village."

"The town hall?"

"No, just a room."

"What was written on the front of the building?"

"I don't know."

"Why don't you know?"

"I was still little, and couldn't read or write."

"How old were you then?"

"I don't know. Back then, I didn't know you were going to ask me this. And that one day my age would be so important."

"I want you to take my question seriously," she said sternly. I wanted to say I really did take her question seriously, but didn't dare.

"All right, then: how old were you the day you went to that building?"

"Five, I think," I said.

"I need you to give me an exact answer, Mr. Karim." I thought this interview could go on forever, and that I might fall off my chair from exhaustion at any moment.

"I know for sure, Miss. I was five years old that day."

"What year was that?"

"I don't know."

"Try to remember." She had them bring more black coffee, probably to jog my memory, and this time I drank it in the office. Coffee on an empty stomach felt strange, and made me nauseous.

"We'll take an hour's break now. I'll see that you get some aspirin," the woman said, and led me into the corridor. "Of course it's a lot to expect for a child to know what year it is," she said, "but everything will be okay after the break." I asked her why the date was so important, and she answered that it would make my story more credible. I could hear sympathy in her voice, which made me even more wary of her. "I'll see you in an hour," she said, and walked off.

A policeman brought me back to the large room, where I immediately lay down on the floor and fell into a deep sleep, despite having just drunk two cups of coffee. After what felt like a minute, I woke up to a policeman calling out my grandfather's name, which had become my surname. He handed me a button-down shirt, still in its plastic wrapping.

"Put this on and come with me," he said.

Two Africans helped me get up, unpack the shirt, and put it on. They walked me to the door. Back in the office, I was still a bit dizzy. There was more coffee.

The woman asked if I could remember the year. I named a year, and she typed it into the computer. Then she asked how I got my official birth date. She looked interested as she listened to my answer. I told her there were ten children in my family. We—my father, my mother, two aunts, my grandparents, uncles, and cousins—stood in line at that one-room building. The man behind the window looked at my eldest brother and declared him to be nine years old. Each brother after that was made one year younger. But at the end the man had a problem, because the youngest brother, by his calculations, should have still been in my mother's belly. So he crossed everything out and started with the youngest, who he pronounced to be one year old, and assigned each successive brother a year more. We were lined up by height, the shortest up front and the tallest at the back. Because I was taller than my older brother and was standing behind him, I was registered as a year older than he. So even though he must have been at least a year and a half older than me, I was now officially a year older. I was proud of this. Over time, what was written on our ID cards became reality. My brother started acting as though I was the eldest. Especially when we took our donkeys out into the fields. Then I was the one who had to say which way to go, when we'd return, and where we would go fishing or swimming. The entire family was assigned the same birthday: July 1.

"So it is not your actual date of birth."

"That's right."

"Then I can't put it in the computer."

"What will you put in, then?"

"'oo-oo'. I'll only enter the year."

"But the year isn't correct either. Why put that in, and not the date?"

"I need it for the computer."

"But Miss, couldn't you just put 'July 1st' in the computer?"

"You just said it wasn't your actual birth date."

"But I also just said the year wasn't right either. Why do you only put into your computer what *you* need, and not what *I* need?" I was angry. The anger made me forget how exhausted and sick I was. All of a sudden I was capable of throwing the computer through the window, jumping after it, and running away.

"Listen, Mr. Karim," she said with a harsh tone of voice. "If you want to continue this hearing, and round it off properly, you mustn't argue so much. You have to realize you're here to give answers, and not to ask questions. Is that clear?" I looked at her, and for a moment I was convinced I'd lost my mind. How on earth did she manage to erase my anger, just like that, as though I was a machine with buttons? She had silenced me in one second flat. I sank deeper into my chair and said yes, it was clear. I answered her questions only to get the hearing over and done with. There was a wall clock behind her. It helped me count the hours. I couldn't say how much coffee I drank to keep awake, but I do know that I was in that office for six hours and fifteen minutes.

Eventually the woman printed out the report of the hearing in duplicate, and I had to sign them. With nothing but the report in my hand, I followed another woman to a parking garage, where the cold hit me once more.

"Are you sick?" she asked as we got into her car.

"Yes."

"Go ahead and lie down in the back." She turned on the car's heating, and a little while later we left Schiphol. The car stopped at a gas station. I looked around, and couldn't believe my eyes. My God, I was free. I was holding a report of my hearing, complete with my photograph. I could simply open the door and run away if I wanted to. The possibility of escape gave me the sensation of safety. *I've been given asylum!* I thought. Finally.

"Where are you taking me?" I asked the woman, in English.

"To an RC*, a reception center, where you'll stay for about three months. Then you'll go to an ASC, an asylum center."

* See pg. 395 for a full list of abbreviations

"And how long will I stay in the ASC?"

"That depends on what you said in your first hearing, and later, what you say in your second hearing. The people from the IND—that's the Immigration and Naturalization Department—will study the report from your first hearing before they conduct the second one. If there are inconsistencies, or if you've given information you're unsure of, you might have to stay longer."

"Weeks?"

The woman laughed, as though I'd cracked a joke.

"A bit longer."

"Months?"

"Wellllll ..." she said. The way she stretched out the "l" made me realize she meant years.

"How many years, roughly?"

"I can't say. Did you say something you're unsure of?"

"Yes."

"What? Why?"

"Because I'm sick. I just wanted it to end."

"Why didn't you refuse to do the interview until you felt better?"

"I asked, but they said that wasn't possible."

"That's not true," she said. "What you're saying is wrong. For one thing, you're not really sick, because you're talking to me now, aren't you. And second, you were informed of your rights, in your own language, and you signed a form."

"No, I didn't," I said.

"Yes, you did. The first thing every asylum seeker receives is printed information, in their own language, about the first hearing and the procedure, so that it's clear what their rights are. Otherwise they don't go through with the hearing. Look in your dossier." She turned on the interior light. The dossier contained papers in Arabic. My signature was at the bottom. It said that if I did not have an adequate interpreter, was sick, or too tired, I had the right to say I was unable to conduct the interview.

"You're right," I said. "Apparently, somewhere along the way I signed these papers without realizing it."

"In that case, the Netherlands is going to be a difficult country for you," she said.

"Then I'll go to Germany. I've heard it's only two hours' drive from here."

"They took your fingerprints. So now you can't ask for asylum in another country."

I lay on the back seat of the car and realized that this woman could only talk like this because she did not live in a dangerous country like Iraq, and did not have a bloodthirsty president like Saddam Hussein. What good was a residence permit, anyway? The hell with it. If you walk into a chic restaurant after not having eaten for years, you don't worry about appetizers and desserts. You just want to eat, and it doesn't matter what. I was safe at last!

3

My story has begun, and you have witnessed my first experience with the system. Now I will jump a few months ahead, to the second hearing, because that is the most boring part of the story, and then we'll be done with it. Moreover, it is the root of the procedure I would be caught up in, and from which, I would learn, there was no escape.

After a month in the reception center in Haarlem, I asked a volunteer if he would have a look at the report of my first hearing and tell me what was in it. This man had once worked in an ASC, so he was acquainted with asylum policy. He read, and translated it into English as he went. After a while he stopped translating, and just read. At the end, he slapped it shut and handed it back to me. "That bitch didn't give you a snowball's chance in hell of getting asylum here."

I was baffled. He told me that the first hearing is actually only meant to register exactly where you came from, and that you're supposed to have an interpreter from your country of origin. My case failed on both counts.

Besides, they had gone much further with me. The volunteer told me that the woman had pieced the report together. She had written down something I had said, and then that I said something else, without explaining why. He looked at me sympathetically and said: "She screwed you." I smiled.

"You're laughing now, Samir," he said. "But this is going to take years. Until you're closer to tears than to laughter."

And now the second hearing.

Three months after arriving in the Netherlands, another woman conducted my second interview. This woman was about thirty years old, smartly dressed, and wore glasses. When her mouth was closed, she looked as though she was holding in a mouthful of air, in preparation for a deep sigh or a loud burp. In her eyes I read boredom, and no trace of encouragement. She looked at me and then at the photograph attached to the first report, to make sure I was the same person. She asked if I had received a copy of the first hearing. I nodded. Then she asked whether I understood the interpreter well enough, to which I replied that I had to talk to him first to find out. So I was allowed to converse with him until I was certain we understood each other. I asked him where he came from. He said this wasn't important. When he confirmed that he spoke the Iraqi dialect, I spoke to him in the Iraqi Arabic I used with my family. From his accent I could tell he was a Kurd, from the north of Iraq. I discovered that he didn't really understand my dialect that well, but that like me, he did speak good classical Arabic. I turned to the woman and said that he understood me.

"You have to take care, Mr. Karim," she said, "this is your future." With the word "this" she picked up the report from the first hearing. I was amused at the idea that my future would be determined by a few sheets of paper, and not by my health, my happiness, or my dreams. Or a never-ending barbecue on the beach, or traveling the world on a legitimate passport.

"He understands my classical Arabic well," I said.

"Then we'll begin the second hearing."

"I would like the second hearing to be conducted in the presence of a lawyer," I said, on the advice of the volunteer from Haarlem, "and that you write down that I've asked for one."

"Mr. Karim," she said, irritated. "You're not here to tell me how to do my job. You're here to answer my questions. This second hearing is part of your asylum application. This is how it works. Do you want to continue with your asylum application or not? You can go through the report with your pro bono lawyer later."

It was difficult to have to be afraid of this woman. I was accustomed to being afraid of a bomb or a missile twenty meters away, a bullet through the window, soldiers and tanks lining the streets, or a hairy-knuckled agent of the secret police. I did not know how to fear a blond woman. But she taught me how. Throughout the interview I increasingly felt like my throat was filled with mucus I couldn't swallow, and that instead, it was turning into bile in my mouth. This woman had the power to send me back to Saddam Hussein's men so they could tear me apart, or to dump me onto the streets of the Netherlands so I could be gobbled up by the cells of the Foreigners' Police. In my three months at the Haarlem RC I had also heard about closed holding centers, where they sent asylum seekers if the authorities doubted their nationality, or if they were suspected criminals, or if they argued with the civil servants who conducted the hearing.

I swallowed and nodded.

"Here, in the first hearing," she said, pointing to the report in her hand, "you said you did not know how old you were when your birth date was registered. Then you said that you were exactly five years old. First you claimed not to know what year you were born in, then later you gave a year. Could you explain how you suddenly knew these things so precisely?"

"I was sick and just wanted to finish the interview."

"Then you could have said you were too ill to answer the questions."

"I tried, but the woman said there was no other choice."

"But you signed these papers in your own language, stating your rights." The woman typed something into the computer, and I couldn't be sure which of the words she was typing were mine, and which were her own.

"Here, too ..." She pointed to a sentence and referred to the page number. "You said you did not know what day you crossed the border, because at that time you didn't know—in your own words—what day of the week it was. Later you said it was August 4th. And here you claim you escaped Iraq to avoid being forced into military service. Then you said you fled because you feared the secret police, because a friend of yours ..."— she studied the page for a moment—"... a Hussein Jawad, had been arrested. A while later you state that you fled Iraq because every Iraqi who is against the system is in danger. Is that correct?"

I nodded.

"Do you have anything to add?" she asked after two hours of going through the report of the first hearing, and requiring detailed explanations of the information I had given.

"Yes, Miss. I'm wondering if this second hearing was necessary. All we did was discuss the first hearing. I had expected you to want to hear new things from me." The woman glowered at me, and reminded me that she knew how to do her job.

She brought me a cup of tea and two copies of the report; one for me, one for her. I signed. Three years later I would receive the results of the second hearing: that I was denied political or humanitarian asylum. The reason for the rejection, after such a long wait, was so vague I did not really understand it. What I did understand was the sentence stating that within twenty-eight days I would be sent back to Iraq.

4

It was evening when the driver delivered me to the Haarlem RC.

"Wait here," she said when we got to Reception. A little while later she returned with a tall, thin man. She spoke with him in Dutch and smiled at me. "Lots of luck," she said as a goodbye. The tall, thin man shook my hand, introduced himself, and led me to a room with a few tables and computers. Behind each table was a bulletin board full of memos, but also the occasional postcard or personal photo of a dog or a child. Dutch people must be awfully forgetful, I thought. Why else would they need bulletin boards full of memos behind their desks?

"You'll be sleeping in the gym for the time being, because all the rooms are taken," the man said. He told me to wait here, and left the room. Then a woman came in. She shook my hand, introduced herself, and asked if I was sick, because my hand was so clammy. I nodded.

"We'll give you a place for special cases, because you're ill. You can sleep there until you're feeling better, and then you'll go to the gym, because all the rooms here are full," she said. "Okay?" I nodded. The walkie-talkie on her belt rang, and off she went. What struck me was the way Dutch people I met shook my hand and introduced themselves. Everybody shook your hand and told you their name. In a government office in Iraq, a civil servant never offered you a hand or a name. The woman returned with a man, a woman, and two children, told them to take a seat, and then left again.

The tall, thin man came back and said to follow him. Our first stop was the supply room, where he gave me two blankets, three sheets, a towel, a pillow, and a pillowcase. Then he asked me to sign a piece of paper, after having impressed upon me that I was now responsible for the two blankets, three sheets, towel, pillow, and pillowcase, and would be fined if I failed to return them. I signed, and followed him to the gym.

"Sir, I was just told I could have a separate room for a few days because I'm sick," I said. The man stopped abruptly.

"Who said so?" he asked, irritated.

"The woman in the office," I said.

"Which woman?"

"The one in the office, just now."

"Didn't she tell you her name?"

"Yes, but I don't remember it. She had short blond hair," I said, but once I couldn't produce her name, the man stopped listening and walked on.

The gym was full of mattresses; on each mattress sat an asylum seeker. We found an empty mattress.

"Here," he said, and walked off. The gym was heated, but it was set so that it was only warm enough if you were actually exercising. The prospect of sleeping in a gym with such a high ceiling only heightened the sensation of cold. On top of it, asylum seekers kept walking in and out, and sometimes did not close the door behind them. Since no one knew each other's name, you couldn't just call out, hey X, close that door. So more often than not, the door stood wide open, letting the cold air whip inside. In my exhaustion, I couldn't get the pillow inside the pillowcase, just tossed the pillow onto the mattress and lay down. I struggled to get the two blankets, the three sheets, and the towel over me. Underneath, I lay shivering.

An hour later I heard a woman's voice.

"Samir Karim?" I was in no state to answer. I felt the blanket being eased back, and I saw the Dutch woman with the short blond hair.

"Get your things and come with me," she said. Shivering, I got up, gathered together the two blankets, three sheets, towel, pillow, and pillowcase, and followed the woman, whose name was Sara. The RC was properly heated. At the end of a hall, she opened the door to a small room with a bed, a television, and a fridge. It was warm.

"You can sleep here," she said. She brought me a glass of water and two aspirins. Later, I would determine that Dutch people are usually large-bodied and have an expression on their face as if to say "lemme check on that," or "keep it short," or "I've had a rough weekend," but not Sara. She had a small, slim build. She moved gently, like someone who had once been very restless but had suddenly discovered eternity. She turned, stood, and sat as if she were doing yoga.

That night I slept like never before, deep and determinedly. I did not wake until the next morning, when someone banged loudly on the door. As I groped for my glasses, the knocking became louder and louder, until I opened the door and saw a woman standing in the doorway.

"Are you Mr. Karim?" I said *yes*. She shook my hand, introduced herself, and walked to the center of the room. Her name was Elly. She was a dry woman. Her voice was dry, her face was dry. She was definitely forty-plus and would surely remain dry forever. She was holding some papers, which, she said, was the report from my first hearing. These papers were proof that I had not been truthful to the staff of the RC last night, she said. She occasionally glanced at me over the top of her glasses as she read.

"Mr. Karim, I have read the report of your first hearing. It does not say you are gay." I was baffled by this woman, who, if there were an Iron Lady marathon, would leave Margaret Thatcher in the dust.

"I am not gay."

"I'm sorry, but this room is reserved for special cases. For gay men only." She told me to get my two blankets, three sheets, towel, pillow, and pillowcase, and follow her. When she decided I was taking too long to collect my things, she bunched them up herself and handed them to me. From the way she did this, I could tell she was more annoyed than she let on. On the way to the gym she told me—I don't know why, maybe to prove she wasn't a hardnose but was just doing her job—that there were only six rooms in the RC for special cases: three for gays or single women, and three larger ones for families. I told her I never said I was gay, but was given the room because I was sick.

"If we gave every sick asylum seeker his own room, we'd need hundreds of them," she snapped. "Then everybody'd be saying they were sick."

There were no vacant mattresses left in the gym. Elly told me to wait, and walked off. I spread a blanket out on the floor, lay down on it, and put the other blanket, the sheets, and the towel over me. When she returned more than half an hour later with two staff members and a mattress, you could read the irritation on her face that I hadn't waited for the mattress. She reminded me that the blanket on the floor was not mine, but belonged to the RC, and that other people would have to use it later.

That evening the woman named Sara saw me lying in the gym.

"Feeling better today?" she asked.

"Absolutely," I answered. I did not want to tell her I still felt sick, because I would rather let the February chill envelop my body than to have another confrontation with Elly's face, which was far worse than the cold.

"I work until ten," Sara said. "If you think you need a room, let me know before then." I told her it wouldn't be necessary.

After a few days, my health started to pick up. I could, however, still feel the sharp pain in my lower back, from being kicked in the cell at Schiphol. The Haarlem RC had a medical clinic, with one or two nurses on duty. If an asylum seeker felt ill, he could go to the clinic. There, he would be given aspirin for most things, and other medicine for infected tonsils, diarrhea, or constipation. If he had something serious that required real attention from a doctor or a hospital, then the nurse said he would have to wait until he was sent to an ASC. (Asylum seekers were entitled to a basic health insurance, which only paid for simple illnesses.) However, when they got to an ASC, asylum seekers needing a more complicated procedure were informed that they had to wait until they got a residence permit, which could take fifteen years. So problems often arose between asylum seekers and staff at the RC and ASC medical clinics. As an official interpreter was too expensive for the clinics and I spoke passable English, I often translated for my fellow residents, and in doing so frequently witnessed this kind of situation.

For example, I remember hearing the man on the mattress next to mine groaning. His name was Farid and he had a toothache. He had already been to the clinic a few times, and each time they gave him aspirin. He wanted to see a dentist, even if the only option was to pull the tooth. But there was a weird regulation at the Haarlem RC, which must have been thought up by an internal staff member, because I've never encountered it anywhere else. It was this: only when *three* asylum seekers had a toothache, and only then, could they all be sent to the dentist together. Farid had heard tell of a Kurdish woman who also had a toothache. So the next day, Farid and the woman desperately scoured the RC in search of a third sufferer, until they finally managed to convince someone that he also had a toothache. He too was given aspirin for several days, until the staff at the clinic decided this wasn't working, and that there were now three people with a toothache. That was good news: they had an appointment with a dentist the very next day, and they all had to assemble at the appointed time. Farid asked me to go along to translate.

The dentist had two consulting rooms separated by a waiting room. First, the dental assistant ushered them, one at a time, into one of the rooms. I relayed which tooth or molar hurt. They got a shot of anesthetic and had to return to the waiting area while the next one had their turn. Then, one by one, they were called into the other room, where the dentist worked. They were out again before you knew it. Some twenty minutes later, all three aching teeth had been pulled, although the Kurdish woman claimed, after the anesthetic wore off, that they had pulled the wrong one. During all this, I asked the dentist why he was in such a hurry. He said that there was a shortage of dentists in the Netherlands, and that even Dutch people spent months on a waiting list if they moved to another city. That surprised me, the Netherlands being such a tiny country. If a Dutch dentist could help three people in twenty minutes, surely a hundred dentists should be enough for the entire population.

At night the pain in my lower back persisted. At the clinic they kept giving me aspirin.

5

After a few days in the Haarlem RC I was told to report at eight o'clock the next morning with the two blankets, three sheets, the towel, pillow, and pillowcase.

I boarded a bus full of other asylum seekers. We were going to be taken to a farm in the village of Veenhuizen, near Assen, where we would stay until more space came free at the Haarlem RC. I observed the Netherlands through the bus window. The first thing that struck me was the lack of soldiers. Nowhere did I see any sign of an army, nor were there any checkpoints. The bus even drove for miles and miles without passing a single policeman. Another thing that struck me was the quiet. There was no honking. In Iraq, cars communicated with one another in the language of honking. A driver could tell other drivers with his horn if he was in a hurry, for instance if he were transporting a sick person or a woman in labor, or if he needed to pee. He could greet someone with his horn, or return a greeting. It was like Dutch cars didn't even have horns, or that it was forbidden to honk. Also, the Netherlands didn't look like a country, but rather like one big city, because between the urban areas there was no desert, no mountains, no valleys. Everywhere, people wore the same kind of clothes, the weather was exactly the same, and it was always the same time. Our new home felt like a suburb of Haarlem.

We arrived at a farm run by the Bouma family. It had

once been a dairy farm, and was now operated as a farm campground. But until the tourist season started, the intake organization for asylum seekers rented the facilities to accommodate the overflow in the reception centers. Mr. and Mrs. Bouma greeted us with a smile. They were about forty and had three daughters and a son. The eldest daughter was eight and she would be my first and last Dutch teacher.

We stayed at the Boumas' farm for thirty-seven days. It had dormitories, a large communal kitchen and dining room, showers, and toilets. I made a very important discovery there: that the Dutch system is not the same as the Dutch people. If I thought about it in a positive light, then the Netherlands was heaven and the Dutch people were angels, and if I let my thoughts turn negative, then it was hell, and its inhabitants coldblooded demons. On our second day there, Mrs. Bouma drove me to her doctor. I said I'd fallen down the stairs. The doctor felt my back and gave me medicine and salve. On the way back I told her I liked to read, and when we got home she gave me a copy of George Orwell's *Animal Farm*.

Those thirty-seven days were my introduction to the Dutch people. One of the things I observed was an amazing clarity of interaction within families. The Bouma children, at least as far as I could tell, were equals. In Iraqi families you always have the most handsome child, the toughest, the strongest, the most clever, the ugliest, the frailest, the favorite, the tallest, the fattest. There are always nicknames. My family's nickname for me was "the big nose" and one of my brothers, who was born back when the family was wealthy, was called "the precious one." But with the Bouma family, I noticed that the parents treated their children the same and gave them equal attention.

After a few days I decided to take a walk in the woods adjacent to the farm. What a terrific feeling that was! After all those wars, misery, and narrow escapes, I could simply walk, for the first time in my life, alone in the woods. Not hurrying anxiously after a smuggler, but just for my own enjoyment. It was a sunny winter day. Just beyond the farm, I overtook a man walking a black-and-white dog. The man had seen which direction I came from. I greeted him, but he looked at me without answering. I walked on. He did too. I heard him talking behind me. Nowadays I'd assume he was phoning someone, but in 1998 there weren't many cell phones. A few steps later I got the nerve up to look back, to judge how fast I'd have to walk to keep ahead of him. He glowered at me. I picked up my pace and veered off the path. About half a kilometer further I heard someone shout. I turned and saw the man with the black-and-white dog. I smiled, but he approached me and shouted something in Dutch. I said I didn't speak Dutch, but that English would be good, at which he spoke an English that fell heavily out of his mouth.

"You live with Bouma?" He was clearly not happy with this.

"Yes."

"Asylum seeker?"

"Yes."

"You know it's forbidden to build a fire here." He said it angrily, as though he'd caught me red-handed. "*Forbidden*," he repeated emphatically. I tried to explain to him that I was just taking a walk, but he stalked off, muttering to his dog in Dutch. He went deeper into the woods, and I returned to the farm.

"Back so soon?" Mr. Bouma said. "Was it cold?"

"I met a crazy man, who yelled at me that I mustn't build a fire in the woods."

"Well, of course you can't build fires in the woods! What did you think, Samir? That's dangerous!" Mr. Bouma was shocked. We were the first group of asylum seekers he had staying at his farm, and I was unable to make it clear to him that the man hadn't seen me building a fire at all.

An hour later the farm was plastered with notices in English and Dutch stating that it was strictly forbidden to build fires in the woods. The next day a woman from the Immigration Services came up to me.

"Mr. Karim," she said with utmost seriousness. "We received a call that a man staying on the farm wanted to build a fire in the woods. I understand it was you. Fire-building is strictly forbidden here. The people in the village are afraid of forest fires." She looked at me sharply with her blue eyes. "Do I make myself clear?"

"Yes, ma'am," I answered. "It's clear." Just like with Mr. Bouma, it would be impossible to get through to her that I did not try to build a fire. She only wanted to know if I understood her, and was not at all interested in whether I had actually lit a fire or not.

That evening I lay on my back in bed, stared at the wooden ceiling, and understood the absence of the army or policemen between Haarlem and Assen.

6

I'll never forget Mr. and Mrs. Bouma and their four lovely children. Their warmth was a great comfort in the face of the countless bureaucrats of the IND, the Foreigners' Police, and the COA*, for whom I was their job, like a cadaver is for buzzards. After a few days at the farm I took a razor blade and opened a top-secret cache: the seam of my trousers. I removed the two hundred dollars I had wrapped in plastic, rolled up and sewn into the pants. I did not cherish the stash as currency, but as a good friend. Rather than spend it during my exodus, I was saving it for the direst of situations. But every time a dire situation arose, I told myself: things could still get worse. So now I took the two hundred dollars from the seam of my trousers and went into Assen. I exchanged them for guilders and went to a music store to buy a guitar. I saw one that cost 175 guilders. I had no experience of buying anything in the Netherlands, so I started to bargain with the shopkeeper.

"This is the Netherlands," she said.

"I know that, ma'am, but could I have it for 145 guilders?"

"This is the Netherlands," she repeated and looked at me with a kind of amazement. "The price is the price. We only lower it if there's a sale, or the product is on

---

* Central Agency for the Reception of Asylum Seekers; see pg. 395 for a full list of abbreviations

clearance. We don't bargain."

"Ah, now I understand. How about 155 guilders?" I don't know, but every time I travel to Groningen and the train stops at Assen station for two minutes, I want to die of shame. There I was, a grown man, begging this blond woman in a music shop to give me a break on the price of a guitar. I'm not ashamed when I play it. I'm only ashamed for those two minutes the train stops at Assen station.

So I'm delighted whenever I can catch a lift with someone to Groningen and avoid taking the train.

One day, Sanne, the eldest Bouma daughter, came over to me while I lay reading on the sofa in the common room. She asked if I could teach her to play the guitar.

"Sure," I said.

"How much does a lesson cost?" she asked.

"Lessons are free," I said. She looked surprised. So I added: "But if you want, you can give me Dutch lessons in return."

"That's better," she said.

"When do you want your first lesson?"

"First we have to make a working agreement."

A working agreement? I had to get my head around this. Here was an eight-year-old talking to me about a "working agreement." Oh oh oh, where in God's name had I landed? In Iraq we'd agree to meet each other in the afternoon—but *which* afternoon? Today, tomorrow, next week, next year? In Iraq, some agreements still haven't been kept, even years later.

"Wait a second, I'll be right back," she said, and returned with a pen and a small book. "My datebook," she explained.

I translated what she said for the other asylum seekers

in the room, and they roared in unison. They gathered around us to witness this wonder: an eight-year-old girl with a datebook.

"Thursday at four, is that all right?"

"Yes."

"For how long?"

"Two hours."

"That's too long. I don't have so much time, and we eat at six. Thirty minutes, would that be okay?" I nodded and she noted it in her datebook. Everyone, me included, watched Sanne write it down. "And when do you want to schedule your Dutch lesson?"

"Whenever you have time," I said. I could barely contain myself and nearly exploded with laughter because I thought it was such a good joke.

"No, you have to name a date."

"Friday at four o'clock."

"Which Friday? This Friday or next?"

"This Friday." She carefully re-opened her datebook and noted it. Then she repeated our dates, to confirm them. What really surprised me was that she showed up on Thursday at exactly four o'clock, and made sure the lesson ended promptly at four thirty.

On Friday Merdaan, one of the other asylum seekers, came to my room. I was napping on my bed. "Samir, man, where are you?" he said. "Sanne's been waiting for you for at least four minutes! And she says she can't wait more than two more minutes." Merdaan and I collapsed in laughter, but soon my two minutes would be used up laughing, so I ran to Sanne with a small black notebook (which I still have) for my first Dutch lesson. Actually, instead of a Dutch lesson, she gave me a lesson in not being late if I wanted to learn something.

In 2006 I returned to the Boumas' farm. I wanted Sanne to see that she was the best Dutch teacher ever, because by now I could write in Dutch—and not only emails and texts, but poems and stories, too. I was disappointed in my own role as a guitar teacher, because I heard that not only did she drop the guitar, she turned her back on music altogether. In the end she bought a motor scooter. I showed her my little black book which contained, in her handwriting, those first lessons. I still regret being the reason she never became a terrific musician. But she did become a first-class scooter driver. She insisted on giving me a lift to the train station, and between the village and Assen station my ass hung between heaven and earth on the back of her bike.

7

I could write an entire book about our stay at the Bouma farm, but this would take too much time. So to make a long story short I'll tell you that it was a learning experience—for me, at least—about what it means for people to have asylum seekers around. What I can say is that our stay there was not easy for the farm, nor for the Bouma family, nor for their dog Rico, nor for the birds and other animals on the farm.

When the asylum seekers concluded that Mr. Bouma was a genuinely kind person who wouldn't hurt a fly, and did not work for the Immigration Services or the Central Asylum Seekers Organization, they went about their own business. They caused no end of problems. The first victim was the Boumas' dog, Rico. Rico was large and pretty scary, but was, as Mrs. Bouma kept insisting, a sweet-natured dog with a heart of gold. Mrs. Bouma told me Rico was an old dog—ten years old, to be precise—which translates to 77 human years. She said he was born on September 3, 1988.

"Where did you get the dog?" I asked.

"Rico, you mean?" Her tone told me it was better to refer to him by his name. She did not answer, indicating I should repeat my question, this time using the name Rico instead of the word *dog*.

"Where did you get Rico?"

"We paid 550 guilders for him. He's a purebred, not from the shelter."

"From the shelter?"

"In the Netherlands you have animal shelters. You know, for homeless animals. Mostly dogs and cats."

"Are the dogs and cats as expensive there, too?"

"No, most of them are too old, too unruly, or have psychological problems."

"Dogs with psychological problems?"

"A friend of mine once got a dog from the shelter. After six months she couldn't keep him anymore, he drove her crazy so she brought him back. He was too much to handle. She thought he had a kind of dog-ADD."

Mrs. Bouma told me things which I doubted then, but later turned out to be true. When she told me that Rico had "papers," I asked if I could see them. This told me something about how wealthy the Netherlands is, compared to me, because Rico had always been acknowledged as a dog. His birthday, right down to the hour and minute of his birth, was registered. Mine was not. From the moment Rico was in his mother's belly he had an address, and after he was born he had insurance. Two things of Rico's that I didn't mind not having, were his leash and his castration. Otherwise he was great.

Rico was a lazy dog, and I don't think he watched TV or enjoyed reading. Therefore he was ignorant about life outside the Boumas' farm. For example, he did not know what "asylum seeker" meant. Before we arrived, he had the run of the place. He took his daily stroll and slept wherever and whenever he wanted. This dog did not know that Muslims do not touch dogs. And if they do happen to touch one, they have to wash their hands, and if a dog touches their things, then those things have to be washed. One day Rico came into our dormitory and started sniffing all our beds. Yasser, an asylum seeker from Yemen, picked up his shoe and threw it at Rico. He screamed at him in Arabic. Rico, who speaks neither Arabic, nor the language of flying shoes, just stood there and looked benignly at Yasser, who then took his other shoe and hurled that too at Rico, hitting him smack on the nose. The dog leapt up and ran outside, yelping in pain. Later, in other dormitories, many more shoes and sandals flew in Rico's direction.

One day a shoe hit him so hard that he went around for days with a bruised eye.

"Today might be another shoe day for him," I said, when Mr. Bouma asked me what had happened to him. Mr. Bouma gave me an inquiring look.

"Shoes?"

"Some of the asylum seekers don't like Rico coming into the dormitories."

"Why didn't you say so before?" he asked. If you didn't know he was such a good-natured man, his voice might have sounded angry rather than disappointed. "If I'd known, I would have told Rico to stay out of the dormitories." I didn't believe Mr. Bouma could actually tell a dog this, but from that day on, Rico didn't set foot in the dormitories, nor in the kitchen or the common room. Rico, who was ten back in 1998, is surely in heaven now. If they were to ask him what the word "hell" means, I know for certain he would answer: "Shoes." Either that, or, "Asylum seekers."

Near the Boumas' farm was a pond with a single white swan. From the small window next to my bed I could see it off in the distance, and every time I looked its way I thought it would be the last time, because it looked so lonely. I imagined he was propelled through the water by an inboard motor, because his body was entirely stationary. Nothing moved: not its neck, its wing, its head, or its tail. He shared the pond with wild ducks, geese, and coots.

One after another, the smaller fowl disappeared. At first I thought they had simply flown to another pond, but when Mr. and Mrs. Bouma also wondered out loud what had happened to them, it suddenly dawned on me, and I realized where all the feathers in our kitchen came from. The wildfowl in the pond had ended up in the pans and then the stomachs of the asylum seekers. When Mr. Bouma asked me about it later, I said I had no idea, because deep down I sympathized with the asylum seekers: wild duck and coot were a delicacy in Iraq. I also didn't want to be a snitch. He seemed to sense this, and didn't bring it up again, but did take me by surprise one day, by asking suddenly why the asylum seekers hadn't eaten the swan too.

"Wasn't there a big enough pan? Or is it just not tasty?" This made me curious, but when I asked around, I got the strange and unforgettable answer: "Aw, he's such a sad creature. And so lonely."

What with the disappearance of the waterfowl and the attack on Rico, it became clear the Bouma family was starting to grow weary of our presence on their farm. The last thing Sanne taught me that day was the phrase "to turn away." I can't remember if I asked her myself, or if she chose it.

The last thing I recall about the farm is that Mr. Bouma built a fence between his house and the dormitories. Or between his family dog and the asylum seekers. The asylum seekers debated the possible reason for the fence. Some thought that something had been stolen from the house, others claimed Mr. Bouma was a racist, or that he was simply sick of us. I asked him. "I saw an asylum seeker throw a rock at Rico, even though he was over here, at the house," he said, disappointed. "If the rock had hit him on the head, he'd be dead."

8

When, after thirty-seven days at the Bouma farm, the immigration services agent came to tell me that I could go back to the Haarlem RC the next day because a bed had come free, I asked if I could stay longer at the farm.

She looked at me and said, as though she hadn't heard my question, that I had to be sure to report there before 5 p.m. She gave me a stack of papers and a day pass for the train and bus. I gathered my things together and put them in a small carryall I had got for nothing at the FreeShop, and left the farm.

"Rico, Rico!" I called, to say goodbye, but instead of trotting over to me, his tail wagging, Rico panicked and ran the other way, as though his name shouted with an accent meant getting hit with a rock or a shoe.

I took the bus to Assen, the local train to Zwolle, and from there, the intercity to Amsterdam. I left the station and walked into town. It was a sunny day. People were sitting at outdoor cafés with their winter jackets on. I can't say why I loved Amsterdam from the very first second. Assen and the Boumas' neighboring village were a constant reminder of being a foreigner. I felt I would be unwelcome even if I lived there a thousand years. But in Amsterdam, to me everyone looked like a foreigner.

After walking around for an hour and a half, I discovered something else: everywhere you looked there was a clock, so you always knew what time it was. So at four o'clock I was back at the Haarlem RC and was once again given two blankets, three sheets, a towel, a pillow, and a pillowcase. Elly brought me to a room with five beds. "This is your bed," she said. "You have to check in every day." She left, but then came back half an hour later and took back one of the sheets because she'd seen in the system that I'd returned one sheet too few the previous time. She added that I needed to bear in mind that I was supposed to return three sheets, not two.

I remember exactly what had happened to those three sheets the first time, because I didn't have much stuff back then. I had folded two of the sheets together, and they got counted as just one when I turned them in. But I was afraid that if I explained this I'd make her angry. And it wasn't worth angering Elly over a sheet, not even over an entire bedroom.

A Somali asylum seeker who was stretched out on his bed told me not to worry. "Sometimes there's a Surinamese guy working in the supply room. He'll give you a sheet if you ask him."

"How much will it cost?"

"He'll just give it to you, free. Sometimes even a blanket too, if you want. He slips a blanket to a lot of the asylum seekers who get tossed out onto the street," he said. "Or else on your last day you can tear it in half and try to pass it off as two."

I shared a room with four other men. The room was small, and all five of us went to sleep at different times and woke up at different times. However, that was just a minor problem. Worse was that two of the others—one fat, the other extremely skinny—snored. The fat one snored softly, let's say *dolce*, in the later hours of the evening. The skinny one snored loudly and constantly. If he lay on his stomach, the volume was tolerable, but if he rolled onto his back, it became amplified to *forte*. It was forbidden to sleep in the hallway, and impossible to sleep in the room. The only solution was not to sleep at all, which was bothersome. After a few sleepless nights I discovered a space behind the washing machines in the laundry room, and I figured my sleep problem was resolved for the time being. But the person on night duty found out and the next day Sieb, one of the social workers, summoned me to his office. When we got there he saw there were new arrivals, told me to wait in the hall until he called for me, and went into the office. So I waited. And waited. Sieb seemed to me to be a polite, pleasant man, but even so, I didn't dare go in and ask whether I should continue waiting, or if I could go. By now I had caught on that an asylum seeker was better off not clashing with a civil servant during his work, because they either panicked, which was bad, or got angry, which was worse. Sieb left his office with a walkie-talkie and even then I didn't dare leave, afraid that Sieb wouldn't find me when he got back. I waited there for more than two and a half hours. When he returned and saw me standing there, he walked over to me and slapped his forehead.

"Oh, sorry, Samir. I'd forgotten you, man. You've been waiting here forever." He ushered me into the office. "What was it about again?"

"I don't know," I said.

"Go on then. I'll let you know if I remember." He clapped me on the shoulder and apologized once more. I was surprised that Sieb felt there was something wrong with waiting in a hall for two and a half hours, and didn't understand why he felt bad about it, but this way I discovered that a two-and-a-half-hour wait in a hall is too long for Dutch people, and this was not a good thing for me to know, considering I would spend the next nine years waiting.

The next day Sieb came to my room and told me that the problem he had called me in for was that the night watchman had seen me sleeping behind the washing machines and not in my room, and that this wasn't allowed. As friendly as Sieb was the previous day, he was now every bit as stern. I didn't understand his attitude then, and I don't know if I ever will.

"But the snoring in the room is so loud," I said.

"What about the washing machines?"

"They stop running at eleven o'clock," I said. "So at least I can sleep from eleven onwards. The snoring goes on all night."

"Snoring is not a good reason to sleep outside your bedroom."

"Then I have another reason."

"What's that?"

"I am allergic to people." Sieb laughed cautiously.

"Then you don't belong in the Haarlem RC, because there are more than seven hundred and fifty asylum seekers living here." He got up, and before he left he repeated, his index finger raised: "No sleeping behind the washing machines." He left, and that night I slept between Dolce and Forte. As I stared up at the ceiling I thought to myself that it was preferable by far to sleep in a room with four washing machines all running at once.

I closed my eyes and mused that my stay in the shelter would probably last three months at most. Then I would be sent either to a refugee center—an ASC, as it's called here—or back to Iraq. As a way to hearten myself I told myself both options were preferable to this.

9

I learned more than two hundred words during my thirty-seven days on the Boumas' farm, either in my lessons with Sanne, or from what I overheard or came across. I made a note of every word I heard, writing it phonetically in Arabic, then reading it out loud to a Dutch person, and if he recognized what I said, he would then write it in Dutch in my notebook, and tell me what it meant. Many hands wrote many words in my notebook. I discovered that while Dutch people like teaching their language to others, they are short on patience if someone doesn't speak it well. My biggest problem is that I spoke passable English. Dutch people had neither the time nor the inclination to deal with my incomprehensible Dutch, to correct me where necessary, and to communicate in their own language. They were always asking, *Don't you speak English?* Not only did this made me feel stupid, but instead of learning Dutch properly, I spent all that time improving my English.

An example: If you say the word "bus" in a country like Thailand, Laos, Vietnam, or Cambodia, people register a foreigner saying the word "bus." If he is far from a bus stop, then they understand he's asking: "Where can I catch the bus?" If he's at the bus station, then he is asking: "Which bus do I take?" If he's standing next to the bus, he wants to know when it leaves. But in the Netherlands, once you've said the word "bus" they look at you peevishly, as though to say: "Okay, so you know the word for bus, but now what?" I learned early on that if you want to communicate with Dutch people, it's essential to speak really perfectly, because there's not much time or patience for guessing games.

During the three months I spent in the Haarlem RC, the reception desk was staffed by a woman named Jeanine and a man named Paul. Two nice people, especially when they were on duty together. I often heard them use the words *Jezus* and *kut*. They repeated these two words often. So one day I got my notebook and asked Paul about the word Jezus.

"Jezus is Jezus," he replied.

"I don't understand," I said.

"Jezus. Bible. God. Heaven. Sunday," he answered, showing me the small crucifix hanging around his neck.

"Ah, now I understand," I said. "But what is *kut?*"

"That's a little trickier to explain," Paul said, grinning.

"Do you have one?" I asked, grinning back.

"No," he laughed. "But my colleague does, that I know for sure." He pointed at Jeanine, who at that moment was on the telephone.

"May I see it?" I asked.

"That depends on her," he said. Jeanine hung up the phone. "This gentleman needs your help," he said to her. She asked politely what she could do for me.

"*Kut,*" I said to her. "Paul here says you have one, and I would like to see it."

"That's not necessary," she said. "Just like everyone else in the world, you came out of one."

On my first Saturday at the RC I went to a bar. I didn't have much money, but I wanted to go out somewhere. Being cooped up with 750 other asylum seekers is not always easy. I went into a bar and ordered an iced tea. I was irritated that the music was so loud I had to shout to make myself understood. And so I committed my first *faux pas* in the Dutch night-life scene: I asked the young man behind the bar, in English, if he could turn down the music. He couldn't even hear my question, and had to bring his ear close to my face, and I yelled my request once again. "Can't," he replied.

"Why not?" I said. "All you have to do is turn the knob to the left, or tap the minus key, and it will be less noisy, just like that." I thought I'd made a pretty good joke, but the guy smiled and repeated that he could not. Then he turned away to pour another customer a drink. I could tell he was irritated, and that he had to do his best to keep smiling when he looked at me. I drank my iced tea, put on my coat, and got up. I wanted to say goodbye to the young bartender, but even though he looked every which way, pouring drinks left and right (and it wasn't even that busy), he did not cast his eyes on me for even one second.

With my first step outside I felt how quiet the world was, and how nice it was to breathe fresh air. I went to a few more bars, but they all looked the same. Dark wood, dark ambiance, loud music, and the same smell: a combination of beer, urine, and smoke. One place I walked past looked nice, it had candles on the tables and it was quiet, and you could see people chatting calmly with one another. That's my place, I thought. I went in, and a pretty young woman who resembled a stewardess placed a small book on my table.

"I'd like tea, please, English tea," I said.

"And to eat?" she said quietly, so that the other tables would not hear.

"Nothing, only tea."

"Sorry," she leaned closer to my ear, "but we're a restaurant." So I couldn't drink a cup of tea. I told this story later, as a joke, but it wasn't funny. To this day I can't figure out why restaurants are quiet, and you can converse there, while you've really come to eat, and that bars and cafés are noisy and stinky, while people go there to converse. Later, of course, I did discover quiet bars and cafés, but only after a few years.

There were various ways to escape the RC and the waiting. A Dutch girlfriend was one such possibility, but for some of the guys there was another option. I found out about it from Adil, a Syrian asylum seeker who was always in the know. For a while now, the RC had been abuzz with news about a lucky asylum seeker from Guinea. Dutch scouts paid regular visits to the Haarlem RC looking for professional soccer players. If someone said he was a pro soccer player, they would take him to the RC's gym, which by now had been cleared of mattresses. They would kick the ball around a bit, and if he was good, they'd go to a nearby field. The lucky African guy was twenty-one. He passed the first test in the gym, and the second one on the playing field, and from then on he no longer slept at the RC. He only checked in in the morning. According to Adil, he had given his dossier to the scouts, who then arranged a lawyer for him, rented a studio apartment for him somewhere in Amsterdam, and gave him an allowance. How the story ends, I don't know, but the guy didn't spend more than a month at the RC.

One of the volunteers at the RC told me that to import soccer players from abroad was really expensive, and that scouting them at the reception centers was cheaper. Pro players went through a shorter asylum procedure once they were adopted by a club. One Iraqi player often complained that if it weren't for his age—he was in his late thirties—he'd have been snatched up by a team, and would have residence papers within a few months. I think a lot of unwritten rules like this existed.

For the women and girls, too, there was a quick way out of the Haarlem RC. Maybe even quicker than for the soccer players. That was prostitution. The pretty girls disappeared out of the RC quickly. Sometimes we only saw them when they checked in. They'd get recruited by guys who cruised around the RC in their badass cars. Whenever a girl or a good-looking woman left the RC alone, these men would follow her and try to strike up a conversation. If that didn't work, someone would get out of the car and follow her, and try to talk her into getting in. It was difficult for these girls to evade the guys with the badass cars. Rima, an Iraqi girl whose mother was sick, didn't dare go out alone, so her mother asked me to escort her to the Aldi to buy groceries, otherwise the guys would harass her. After one incident, she memorized the car's license plate number. I went to Social Services with her to translate; she told them that a guy had tried to push her into the car. The civil servant made a note of the license plate number, but nothing happened, and that same car continued to cruise around the Haarlem RC. When a group of ASC kids took to pelting these cars with stones, a huge problem arose. The kids' parents were summoned, and were warned that their children could be punished if it continued. I remember a group of women making a banner that read "WE ARE NOT WHORES." They demonstrated outside the entrance to the RC, but were not allowed to stay for long. They were asked, politely but resolutely, to roll up the banner and go back inside. When the journalists came, the women were not allowed to talk to them. The Iranian woman whose idea it was to demonstrate was soon thereafter transferred to a different RC. The cars continued to cruise around the area scouting for RC beauties.

Time dragged on, like a ball and chain attached to my ankles, especially after dark and when it rained. Darkness's goal was to eradicate daytime, and rain's was to fall for years and years. Dutch people would say cheerfully, "It won't rain today." Or, "It will be dry this afternoon." Or, "Only a shower in the morning." But they didn't dare say, "It won't rain this week." Or, "There was no rain last year." At the RC I heard a joke, maybe this had really happened and someone had made it into a joke, anyway we laughed about it for a long time: An asylum seeker asks a Dutch child, "How long has it been raining?" and the child answers, "I don't know, I'm thirteen, ask someone older."

10

What surprised me in the Haarlem RC, and later in the ASCS, was that asylum seekers were warned not to discuss their refugee story with anyone. When I brought the reports from my first and second hearing to Social Services and asked one of the staff to translate it for me into English, because my Dutch wasn't good enough to read it, they said, "Are you kidding? No way—that's personal!"

This kind of reaction led many asylum seekers to conceal their reason for fleeing, and unnerved those who had already had their reports translated.

One night, the snoring in my room was so intolerable that I wandered the halls of the RC until 3 a.m. In one of the hallways I saw a small man looking through the glass partition at the empty office of Social Services. Another insomniac. He asked me in Arabic if I spoke his language. From his dialect I could tell right away he was Iraqi. It was an immediate and strong bond: he spoke the desert dialect of my mother, the dialect that had brought shame on our family when we fled the south of the country for Baghdad after Saddam Hussein's rise to power, because it made us sound like bumpkins who didn't know the difference between a camel and an air conditioner.

"Do you know if Social Services will be open today?" he inquired anxiously. His voice betrayed little hope that this would ever happen. He was short and skinny and had an energetic face that had not yet found an outlet in the world.

"Of course," I said. "It's a weekday, so they'll be open."

"Oh, I hope so." He stared at the computers. "Look there. Say we pick the lock or break this window ... we could sneak in and put 'Hollander' next to our names and we won't have to wait for a residence permit. Then we'd be Dutch, yeah?"

"Why are you still awake?"

"Man," he said, "it's impossible to sleep in that room."

"How come?"

"I'm afraid." He fell silent. I looked him over, thought of his small stature, and presumed he was afraid of his roommates, that they might beat him up, or something else, but he kept looking at me and said, as though he'd read my mind, "I'm afraid I'll kill someone if I stay there." He opened his eyes wide, so that I could see the fire in them.

"What do you want from Social Services?"

"Someone translated my report, and now I hear that that's not allowed. And I want to change rooms. Even sleeping in the gym would be better than this. But the cow at that desk there, the one with the computer ..." He pointed to the desk. Behind it, tacked to the bulletin board, was a photo of two white puppies.

"Elly?" I asked.

"Beats me," he said, as though she didn't deserve to have her name remembered. "Every time I find somebody who can translate for me, I come here. And then she sees me and says right away, 'No room change, no room change.'"

"I speak English, don't worry," I said. "When they open, I'll take you to Sara."

"Who's Sara?"

"The woman who sits over there, with the short hair."
I gave him my room number. He told me his name was
Kadhem, and went off to bed. He knocked on my door at
eight thirty. I had just managed to get a few hours' sleep.

"Come on, man, we'll be late," he said. As though he'd
hired me to be ready for him at the designated time, he
beckoned me, turned, and without even checking to see
if I was following him, he marched down the hall. So off
I went, still in my pajamas and slippers. I translated his
words for Sara, explained that he wanted a different
room because one of his roommates stank of old socks,
another of hashish, and the third of dead pig.

"Let me see if there's a spot," she said, and turned to
her computer. He kept looking anxiously at the door.
When I quietly asked him why, he said he was afraid
that "that other woman"—he meant Elly—would show
up. I pitied him. He seemed quite paranoid and that
didn't strike me as a pleasant state to be in. A short
while later, Elly did come in, and sat down at her desk.
She thumbed through some papers. Sara told us there
was no place free, and that the only solution was to
swap with someone. I thought this would be an excellent solution for Kadhem, and that he would be glad,
but when we were back out in the hallway, he said, "Did
you see that? She was looking for a place, but that other
bitch came in and then she quit looking and said there
were no free beds. I swear it, it was because of that cow."

"That's not true," I said. "And besides, I'm sure you can
find someone to trade places with."

For me, Kadhem was like having a cold. Not unbearable,
but irritating. His problems did not all come at once,
but rather one by one. So he was always struggling with
one particular problem, and as soon as it was solved,

the next one cropped up. That same day I returned to the Social Services office with him, to translate. We ended up with Henk.

"Tell him a volunteer translated my interview. And that I didn't know it was forbidden. I really didn't know that nobody could see it except the Immigration Services and my lawyer. Have I blown my chances at a residence permit?" I translated for Henk, who looked at me as if to say, "Is this a question?"

"That's not correct," Henk said, and I translated this for Kadhem.

"Why not? I know for sure I asked a volunteer to translate my interview. So I could understand what it said. He translated it from Dutch to English, and then an asylum seeker from Jordan translated that into Arabic." Kadhem was vexed that Henk did not seem to understand.

"I mean," Henk said, "that he hasn't ruined his chances at a residence permit by having his report translated." I translated this, but Kadhem refused to hear it.

He told anyone who would listen that Henk did not want to believe him, because he was a racist. Nothing I said could change his mind: he insisted that Henk hated asylum seekers.

What amazed me was that Kadhem turned out to have a sixth sense. Only later did I discover that he was often right. He didn't react to what people said, but read between the lines. Before I left the Haarlem RC and moved to the ASC, I learned that Henk was indeed a racist and that Sara was on her guard around Elly, and that this determined everything she did. What also surprised me was that Kadhem—that small, skinny man— was never afraid, except for one thing: that he would murder someone.

11

I found out that I would only stay at the Haarlem RC for three months at most. After that, I would either be sent to an ASC, or to a detention center before being deported. Asylum seekers spent those months praying they would be sent to an ASC. The term "asylum center" was equivalent to "hope." It was like being late to catch a train, and finding out it's delayed. I counted the days, and reported to the reception desk religiously.

I never forgot to sign in, except just one day. I was so sick that I couldn't swallow a single bite of food, and never left my bed.

"Mr. Karim, you did not sign in yesterday," said the woman, when she looked up from her monitor the next morning.

"I was sick, and—"

"No pocket money for a week," she said, without waiting for my explanation. "If you miss sign-in twice, you'll have to leave the RC." She stressed the word *leave*. The way she looked at me is hard to describe. Just "stern" is not enough. But if I say "self-composed and stern" then it misses the mark. Her calm way of speaking, her monotone voice, and her clearly enunciated words made me feel like I'd committed a sin, for which every imaginable penalty was, in fact, inadequate.

"Next," she called, and instead of returning the green reporting card with my photo on it, she lay it next to her keyboard and looked at whoever was behind me. The way her powerful blue eyes looked past me forced me to step aside and let the next person approach the window. As I walked through the hallways of the RC I thought, "Should I go back and retrieve my card, or not? And will they be angry if I don't?"

The window always closed at five o'clock. So before closing time, I stood in line and when it was my turn I told the staff member, a man this time, that I came to pick up my card. He looked at the card, and at the computer.

"You didn't report yesterday," he said, without looking up. I did not reply; I was waiting for him to ask why, but he kept on typing. His large face bobbed between the keyboard and the monitor. Then he slapped the green paper through the gap in the window with the words, "Wait there." I looked back, knowing he had gestured to a corner of the hallway. I took a few steps toward the corner, and stopped. I looked at him questioningly, to see if I was standing where he wanted me to. When he returned to the computer, I stayed put. I wondered what the punishment would be, but could not understand why he didn't just tell me, and instead made me stand in the corner.

Only later did I get a grip on the Dutch respect for regulations. A Dutch criminal follows regulations more conscientiously than an Iraqi lawyer. Dutch law has a variety of penalties for whoever does not obey the rules, but even those are not enough. Therefore some civil servants in some RCs and ASCs thought up the "stand in the corner" rule. They applied this when an asylum seeker had, in their opinion, committed an error; then he was told to stand in the corner.

So there I stood, in the corner. The man made a few

phone calls—I was anxious that he was calling someone to come take me away and put me in a cell. Meanwhile I looked at the man and at the wall clock behind him. Time ground to a near-halt. One by one, other asylum seekers came to sign in. The man behind the window typed, looked at his monitor, jotted something down on a piece of paper, telephoned. I kept looking at him, so that if he happened to glance up at me I could respond immediately, but he did not look my way. I didn't dare ask him what I should do.

What I discovered at Schiphol airport, at the RC, and beyond, was that while they are at work, Dutch people conceal their aggression behind an official kind of respect. If you cross the line with disrespectful behavior, you have to accept that Dutch people transform into official wild animals, backed up by other official wild animals. The lower the status of the official wild animal in the system, the greater the aggression. Civil servants are empowered to vent their aggression in a variety of ways. Power of the keyboard, power of the mouth, power of the hands. When a Dutch civil servant loses his patience, he can turn a person's life into a living hell.

At exactly five o'clock—I could still see the wall clock in the office—the civil servant who had sent me to the corner got up, looked at me for the first time in an hour, with pinpointed harshness, as if to say: I haven't forgotten you, and you're doing exactly what I want. He turned off the light and left. I stood there and heard his footsteps die out. I thought he would come back, but he did not. I wanted to leave, but I didn't dare, because wouldn't he have given me permission to? When the light in the office went out, I could no longer see the wall clock. Now I did not know how quickly or slowly time progressed.

The longer I waited, the deeper the hallway embedded itself in my memory. Now, all these years later, I still stand waiting in that hallway. My knees began to shake, and I was thirsty, but I stayed there until someone from the night staff walked by while doing his rounds.

"You can't stand here after five," he said.

"Can I go, then?"

"Didn't you hear me?" the man said, irritated. "Yes, you can go. YOU. CAN'T. STAND. HERE." I turned and headed, knees stiff, off to bed. I groaned as I lay down. Not only my back was in pain, but my spirit too. It was eight o'clock in the evening.

12

"Congratulations, Samir," Sara said with a smile. "You're on the list for an ASC." She explained that this meant the IND*, the Immigration & Naturalization Service, did not doubt that I was Iraqi, and that there was a chance I would be eligible for a residence permit. "Bring the two blankets, three sheets, towel, pillow, and pillowcase back to the stock room, and bring your receipt back here." I did not snip the sheet in two. The Surinamer who worked in the stock room did not make a fuss if an asylum seeker came up a sheet or towel short. He greeted me in his cubicle with his pearly smile. I placed the two blankets, two sheets, towel, pillow, and pillowcase on the counter, and he tossed them into a hamper behind him.

"Where's the third sheet?"

"I ate it," I said. He laughed so hard that he almost fell over backwards, chair and all.

"Funny, man. You're leaving today?"

"To an ASC."

"Better than Afghanistan, right?"

"I'm from Iraq."

"And certainly better than Iraq." He handed me the receipt, walked around to the front of the counter, and gave me a goodbye hug.

"Give me some advice," I said to him.

* See pg. 395 for a full list of abbreviations

"Don't eat too many bedsheets. They'll give you indigestion."

Back in my room, I stuffed all my belongings into an Aldi shopping bag and left the Haarlem RC without saying goodbye to anyone or looking back. I walked to the station in my first Dutch spring, past the branches that had been frozen but were now in bloom. Before I went into the station I heard someone call my name.

"Hey, Samir, wait! Guess what! We've been assigned to the same ASC!" I turned and saw Kadhem come trotting up. Oh, God, I thought, I'd rather carry fourteen Aldi bags than this.

"Can't you go there on your own?" I said.

"Man, what do you think? You'll get lost for sure. You're better off coming with me."

"But I'm stopping in Amsterdam to see Van Gogh."

"Who's he? Another asylum seeker?"

"Yeah, and a painter too."

"You're nuts. Come with me to the ASC. If the Social Services window is closed when we get there, we'll be stuck without a bed for the night."

Because of Kadhem, I put off meeting Van Gogh for nine years. We went to the asylum center together, arriving at three in the afternoon. And that is where my story actually begins, a story that had to wait—my apologies—for eleven and a half chapters.

The ASC was a large building. People said it used to be a prison, after that a hospital, and then it stood empty for many years until it was refurbished as an asylum center. People also said—but I don't know if this is right—that it had also been a police academy. The walls were thick, the corridors were narrow and long, and resembled tunnels. The building had two entrances: a door at the back, which was open until eight in the evening, and a door at the front, which was open 24/7.

Inside the building there was an amazing smell. A smell I had never smelled before, and will never forget. And nowhere else in the whole world could you observe, at least not so clearly and for so long, what happened here: *waiting*. If waiting has a smell, then it is the smell that permeated the ASC. The make-up of the approximately five hundred residents changed sometimes monthly, sometimes weekly. People came and went. Some vanished, others appeared. And they all waited.

Upon entering the building, you first came to Reception, a counter that was staffed by two receptionists, day and night. After that, you went through two large glass doors into the first corridor. To the right, there was a hallway with some offices, one of which belonged to the Foreigners' Police. This was the scariest one. It was manned by police officers who intervened whenever there was a problem. Then there was the Social Services office, the largest office. Behind each desk sat a social welfare worker. On any given workday there were at least four of them present, sometimes five. They tried to keep everything on an even keel, helped everyone as much as possible, acted as middleman in case of problems, and organized activities. Most of the offices closed at five o'clock; Social Services closed at eight.

If you took a left after Reception, you saw a small room with the letters VVN* on the door, which stood for *Vereniging Vluchtelingenwerk Nederland*, or the Dutch Council for Refugees. This is where the asylum seekers' dossiers were kept. This cubby-hole was open on weekdays until noon. There was one paid staff member and a volunteer,

* See pg. 395 for a full list of abbreviations

who prepared the asylum seekers for the hearings and the subsequent court cases, explained the legal aspects of each person's case, and offered support. Their perpetual problem was the asylum seekers who came to ask how long they would have to wait. The answer was always: "We don't know. That's up to the Immigration Department." The only thing they could do was call the lawyer and ask if there was any news.

I walked up to Reception; Kadhem followed. We each handed our papers over to the receptionist. This gave him the impression that we belonged together.

"Are you family?" the man asked.

"No," I answered, "we traveled together because he doesn't speak any English." The receptionist looked through the papers again, made a phone call, and a few minutes later someone from Social Services came to get us. She offered her hand and introduced herself. Her name was Lily Vanderhaeghe. She was a bit chubby and had a cheerful, freckled face.

"Come with me," she said in a loud voice. She could have been an opera singer instead of a social worker. It must have been awful for her parents to have to hear the volume of their child's voice.

I walked behind her, and Kadhem behind me, to the social services office. We were each given two blankets, three sheets, a towel, a pillow, and a pillowcase, for which we had to sign. Lily Vanderhaeghe took me to my new quarters, a room with four beds. She told me I had two roommates, and that the Foreigners' Police had sent the fourth to a closed center as punishment. No one knew if or when he would return. She first knocked on the door, and when there was no answer, she opened it.

"This is your bed, Samir," she said. I sat down on the edge of the bed in room O-139. Orange 139.

This particular ASC had three sections, each of which consisted of three floors, and was named after a different color. Rooms in the Yellow section had a Y in front of the number, those in the Blue section got a B, and so mine had an O for orange. The walls in the three sections were painted in the corresponding color. To be honest, after spending nine years walking through an orange hallway, waiting behind an orange door, looking through orange window frames out into the cold, faraway world, I now become sick to my stomach at the sight of the color orange.

Before I forget, now that I'm on the subject of the color orange, I remember that we were given free orange T-shirts. I don't know how they ended up at the ASC or who had brought them, but once, a table full of orange T-shirts appeared in the hallway, surrounded by asylum seekers looking for their size. An older Iraqi woman had asked the Dutch man, who was there to make sure no one took more than one T-shirt, if he had any other colors.

"Black, or gray?," she said. "I'm too old for such a bright color."

"What, don't you like it?" he asked, smiling.

"I don't know, but just look around you. The hallway looks like it's been filled with oranges." The woman was not aware that orange was the Dutch national color, and that the T-shirts were given away not as articles of clothing, but as a color.

Okay, so there I was. Sitting on the edge of a bed in room O139. I looked at the walls, the window, and the trees outside. The view I would have for nine years. Day in, day out. Week in, week out. Month in, month out. Year in, year out.

From the moment I walked into the ASC I saw facial expressions I had never seen before. Not during the four wars I had seen in my life, and not in any of the countries I traveled through after fleeing Iraq. It did not resemble an expression of intense grief, nor one resulting from a deadly illness or paralyzing fear. It didn't resemble anything. Only after years and years did I realize what it was: *waiting*. People sometimes waited there for years. Ten years, some of them, or five, or eight. The one who waited longest in that ASC had been waiting for more than sixteen years.

13

On the first day in that strange-smelling building, my residence for the time being but one that still felt strange and certainly not homey, I left room O-139 and heard something out in the hallway that gave me a good feeling. Jamal, an Iraqi who I would later become friends with, was dancing down the hallway with his hands in the air.

"Good news from the immigration office?" I asked.

"No," he said, "from my wife's belly!" He was married to Najat, a Tunisian. Their son Milaad was born in exactly my first hour in the ASC. This felt like a good sign. I congratulated Jamal and decided to buy that new little life a gift with my first weekly allowance.

That same evening, a brief conversation in the same hallway soured my sensation of hope. After all the staff except the receptionists went home for the night, people would start coming out of their rooms. It was as if they'd been in hiding, or were otherwise invisible. People who, for some reason or another, did not show their faces during the day. One of them, a man of about fifty, spoke to me in English at the end of the hall.

"When did you get here?" he asked.

"Just now, a couple of hours ago," I said.

"Go away! Don't sleep here! Go! Soon you won't be able to. Do you understand me? Soon you won't be able to!" His eyes bugged out as he yelled this at me.

"Why not?" I asked.

"Because!" he barked, as though I'd insulted him.

"Tell him what you told what's-his-name a few weeks ago," said another man of about the same age, who came over to stand with us.

"How do I know what I said a few weeks ago," said the first one. "God damn it, I don't even know what I said yesterday. God damn it."

"Remember what you said about a bird, a cage, the woods, all that stuff?" continued the second man, trying to jog the other's memory.

"Oh yes, that. Now I remember." He looked straight at me, squinted a bit, which made me think he'd forgotten it already, but then he started speaking, softly at first, his voice gradually getting louder.

"Now you are like a free bird who has just been put in a cage. Go away, right now. While you can still fly. Go back to your life. But if you stay in the cage, your wings will wither and die. You'll never be able to live outside this cage. DO YOU UNDERSTAND ME? You'll be afraid that the cats outside will gobble you up." He kept looking at me.

"But I don't *have* a life outside the birdcage to go back to," I said to him. He glanced at the other man, irritated.

"Just look what we've got here. God damn it." He turned to me. "And now you want to argue with me, heh?" Suddenly he got really angry. "You want to fight, don't you? Goddam. Come on, fight, then."

"Why are you yelling like that?" the other man said. "He's just got here, and you're babbling to him about sparrows and cages and birds. A lot of nonsense."

"Nonsense? So suddenly it's nonsense? You're the one who asked me to tell him the story. Typical of you. For *years*." They started to argue, and were clearly very angry with one another.

I grabbed my chance and walked off. Maybe, I thought, Sara in the RC was a tad too enthusiastic in congratulating me on being admitted to an ASC.

After I arrived, I wanted to go out and get something to eat, but one of the receptionists called over to me.

"You're from Iraq, right? Come here. Do you speak Dutch? Or English?" A woman was standing at the counter. From her black clothing I could tell right away that she came from southern Iraq. She had a stack of mail, some open and some still unopened, in her hand. The receptionist asked me to tell the woman that there had been no letter today from the IND. He enunciated the words "NO LETTER TODAY," and looked at her while he said it, because he knew that she knew what it meant.

"The IND, what is that?" she asked. I translated her question for the receptionist. He told me to tell her that last year alone, he had explained it at least fifty times, but when I translated this, she stood silently as though she hadn't heard. As if the receptionist was talking to and about someone else. She resumed her questioning, affecting, I assumed, the most pitiful voice possible, but this was apparently just the way she talked.

"And you, can you explain to me what the IND is?" she asked me in Arabic. I started explaining in my southern dialect, until the receptionist exploded. He held his hand over the mouthpiece of his telephone and yelled at us, as if this was the umpteenth time he had had to reprimand us: "Hey, hey, hey!"

"What?" I asked, genuinely taken aback.

"If you two want to chat, do it over there, okay?" He waved toward the hall outside the nook where the reception desk was. "Not at reception, yeah? It's not allowed for asylum seekers to chat with each other at reception."

I apologized, we went out into the hall, and I explained to the woman what I knew about the IND. She went back into the ASC and I went outside. That was my first clash with the system in the ASC, of which I had involuntarily become a cog.

Zainab was her name. She was a middle-aged woman from a village near Nasiriya, in the south of Iraq. Zainab's entire family had fled over the border with Iran at the end of the Gulf War, when America pulled out of southern Iraq and Saddam Hussein struck back mercilessly. Her family reached Canada in 1994. Zainab was a simple, uneducated, and illiterate woman who had spent her entire life in that village near Nasiriya. The only three trips she ever made were to Najaf, to visit the grave of Imam Ali; to Karbala, to visit the grave of Imam Hussein and his brother Imam Abbas; and to Samarra, for the graves of Imams Ali al-Hadi and Hassan al-Askari. She had not changed from the person she was back in her village near Nasiriya, where she was born and where many years later she would have died if her life had been allowed to progress normally, without Saddam Hussein's wars.

In 1992 she married her cousin, who was murdered during the Iran-Iraq war. She did not remarry, and wore black to this day. She looked perpetually on the verge of tears. I always thought she had either just finished crying, or was about to. It was impossible to insult her, to teach her anything, or to frighten her. For fifteen thousand US dollars her family had wangled her a fake visa to Canada, and since there were no direct flights from Damascus, they opted for a transfer at Amsterdam. This was the advice of the visa-fixer, who rightly said that the other option, via Istanbul, was not a good idea, because it was better to travel via a country where one could ask for asylum. So they bought her a ticket for Damascus—Schiphol—Quebec. The first leg of the journey went smoothly, but because Zainab had trouble negotiating the transfer, she lost her way, and herself, at Schiphol airport. Her flight to Canada left an hour later without her. When she went to buy a new ticket, they asked her which country's Canadian embassy had issued the visa.

"Canadian Embassy?" she asked. "I've never been there." That is how they discovered her visa was forged. They couldn't send her back to Iraq either, because the Iraqi passport she had with her was also forged, and she was considered a refugee. And so she ended up in an RC and, later, in the ASC.

Before ten o'clock every morning, you could find her in the corridor outside the door to the Social Services office. She stood there holding the reports of her first hearing, her second hearing, and the letters from the Immigration Services and the Justice Department, and stared through the glass partition. She did not dare enter the office, because the personnel had been telling her for years, hundreds of times, that there was no news for her. And that if there *was* news, they would go to her room, B-24, and tell her. She would stand there until one of the staff members came out and looked at her, or became irritated with her, and told her there was no news today. Then she could return to her daily life in the corridors.

One day I went to a thrift store with her, where she bought a Brother sewing machine and some fabric shears. They gave her some sewing things, too, for free. Then she started taking in, letting out, or otherwise altering clothes that the asylum seekers bought at the thrift store. Even if she bought a zipper or buttons, she never asked for any money. The only money she accepted, after much persuasion, was for the food she cooked. I gave her the bank ATM card that I got from Social Services so she could withdraw the money for when she fed me, which was every day. One day I asked her if she had withdrawn the money. She said she'd forgotten the PIN-code, and when I went to the bank I saw she hadn't withdrawn a cent. So every Wednesday, as soon as the money was deposited, I would take it out, and give her the entire weekly sum—if I remember correctly, it was eighty-six guilders, and later, forty-five euros.

One day, Pieter Oomen, a difficult man from Social Services, approached Zainab. Pieter always had the air about him of a man who was busy with a million things at the same time, which he wanted to solve all at the same time. Sometimes he was sweet-natured and gentle, and other times a tyrant. He thought Zainab was selling food to the other asylum seekers, and that she earned extra money illegally with the sewing machine. We told him that she did so voluntarily and never charged us, but he would not be convinced. He couldn't very well take away her pots and pans, but he did confiscate the sewing machine. He pulled the plug out of the socket, and picked up the machine with the trousers she was letting out still in it. She looked at him benignly and silently, as if she herself had asked him to take the machine away and repair it, or some such thing, and when he was gone she took up her post outside the glass partition, looking in at his desk. She stood there every day, with an expression like she was glad to have something to do, and if we asked her what she was doing there, she would always answer enthusiastically, "I am

14

On my first night in the ASC I was up until the first
blackbird began singing. The ASC was like a faraway
world where I had landed, floored by jetlag. The difference being that jetlag from air travel is over in a few
days, but jetlag from the ASC has lasted to this day.

Imagine a building with five hundred people inside.
Some of them have become exhausted or crazy from the
endless waiting. The interior of this building then
becomes an enormous grave, in which time is buried.
In my years there, I never slept more than an hour or
two without waking up, because there was something
in my body that always stayed awake. The hallways were
the worst: a constant stream of people anxiously mill-
ing around, as though they had been committed against
their will. Especially after ten at night. From that part-
slumber, part-waking, I began to feel sluggish when I
slept and sluggish when I was awake. A bit like what you
see in the faces in the doorway of an Amsterdam coffeeshop.

I shared room O-139 with two other asylum seekers.
Fouad was from Yemen and had been in the ASC for five
years, while Walid was a Palestinian whose procedure
had been going on for some thirteen years already.
Sometimes they mentioned "the Fourth," and gestured
at an empty bed. When I arrived, he had been gone from
nearly two months, and no one knew where he was or

when he would return. The Fourth's procedure, I heard from my roommates, now stood at seven years. Fouad, Walid, and I all spoke Arabic. Usually they put asylum seekers from the same country together in a room. Women and girls were never assigned to a room with men. There were hardly any women or girls on their own here anyway.

The first conversation between Fouad and Walid I heard that evening, one that I would continue to hear over and over for years to come, began with a discussion of the lengthy wait for a residence permit. Then it turned to the other residents of the ASC, then it was about their families, about asylum seekers they had met over the years, and especially about the asylum seekers who had gone crazy or committed suicide. What surprised me was that they would burst out laughing when the subject of crazed asylum seekers came up, as if they were telling jokes. They showed little respect for failed suicide attempts. Their take on it was that the person did it to attract the attention of the Immigration Services, in the hope of shortening the procedure. But when they talked about asylum seekers who successfully committed suicide, their voices became subdued and earnest.

"There are asylum seekers who kill themselves?" I asked.

"Sure. During the first five years of the procedure, people hardly think of suicide, but after that, they do." Walid paused to count. "Let's see, I'm in my thirteenth year. So, ripe for suicide eight years now." He roared. So did Fouad.

"I've only just ripened," Faoud said, at which point they brought up an Iranian asylum seeker who had committed suicide a year ago.

"Who'd have thought that he, of all people, would snuff out his own life," Fouad said. "He was so positive and optimistic. The children loved him, because he spent half of his food money on candy for them. But one day he got a letter from the IND that he would be sent back to Iran within twenty-eight days, and—"

"It was from the Justice Department, not from the Immigration Service," Walid interrupted. "That kind of letter comes from the Justice Department."

"No way, it was Immigration. I know for sure. You might be here for thirteen years, but my Dutch is better." He got up, pulled open a drawer from under his bed and took out a thick stack of papers fastened with a rubber band. Instead of bringing out the relevant proof, he started thumbing through the hundreds of sheets of paper he had received from the Justice Department, the Immigration Services, his lawyer, and his family. Then Walid opened the drawer from under his bed, too, and produced a dossier more than twice as thick as Faoud's. In this way I learned how thick a dossier is for someone who has been in the Netherlands for five years, and how thick it is for someone who's been in the Netherlands for thirteen years. Within a few months I was able to guess from the thickness of a person's dossier how long their procedure had been going on. After a while I could even narrow it down from years to months. I got up quietly. Not letting on that I was upset, I walked into the hallway and hurried to Reception, as though the door could slam shut at any second and I would be stuck here.

No amount of cheerful activity from a big, lively city could dispel the somberness of that building. I went outside and, as though I had escaped from a prison cell, strode to the street that I'd heard led to the small city center, hoping to vanish into the bustle. After a while I asked an old man the way to downtown, and he answered me in English.

"You *are* downtown." I looked around and saw a few shops, all of them closed. Yes, I had seen other dreary places in my life, but never anything quite as dreary as a Dutch town. You feel as if time has long stood still. Through the windows you see elderly, solitary people sitting under soft, elderly light, and at their feet an elderly dog. Solitude more solitary than all solitude. Only the gas heaters and the furnaces give off warmth; don't expect an ounce of warmth from a face. I walked from the town center to the sea. There, I watched the waves. Ah, I believe that whoever understands the sea never needs a psychiatrist. Those endless waves and the distant horizon. The sea is the only visible eternity on Earth. I breathed deeply. The sea air—washed for thousands of miles with blue, freedom, and sails—entered my lungs.

In wartime 1991, during the bombardment of Baghdad, when heaven and earth had become one great hell, I once watched a father try to convince his frightened child of about five that what he saw was really just fireworks. Instead of reassuring the child, he actually reassured *me*. In thorny situations, the way you look at things is sometimes the only chink through which you can escape from reality. Ever since that day, whenever I experience difficult situations I think of that father, of that trembling child, of the quaking ground and shattered windows, and in my mind I alter what is happening in my life at that moment. So there on the beach I shut my eyes, smelled the sea air, and changed the ASC into a free hostel. My breathing gradually returned to normal, and I felt better as I walked back to spend my first night in the ASC.

From that day on, whenever possible, I would go every day to sit at that very same spot on the beach.

15

Each hallway in the ASC had a kitchen. Since the asylum seekers all came from different regions, the building did not smell all that pleasant. Like standing next to the ventilation hood in a cheap restaurant. You smelled onion, garlic, and burnt oil. No matter how often the staff from Reception opened the kitchen windows to air the place out, the smell hung there permanently and crept from the kitchens to the corridors, and from the corridors to the rooms. Pretty clever of me to have transformed the ASC into a free hostel that first year, and not a cheap kitchen. But oh, wouldn't it have been a joy to have a cave, or a hole in the ground, where I could be alone. Don't ask me how, but as soon as men are made to share a room with other men, that place becomes a prison.

That first night was horrible. I wished I wasn't a human being, but an apparatus with an ON/OFF button, so that I could just disappear from the world with the flick of a switch. It wasn't so bad sharing a room in the RC because you knew it was temporary, three months at most, and that it would soon be over, but in the ASC I might have to share that room for years, and have to listen to the same discussions for years on end—the same griping, the same snoring. So that night I sat in the kitchen and opened a book an Iraqi asylum seeker had left behind in the RC. It was a book about the torture in Iraqi prisons. Maybe the asylum seeker wanted to use it as proof that the situation in Iraq was not good, and that he deserved a residence permit. Now I used it to get through my first long night in the ASC. The book was full of stories told by people who had experienced Saddam Hussein's prisons firsthand. Even though the information was not new to me, I read it page for page. And with every page I read, the ASC became no longer a free hostel, but a five-star hotel. I figured I should count myself lucky to share a clean room with two men, instead of a cramped cell full of men who could only stand, not lie down to sleep, because there was no room, and who were only allowed to go the toilet twice a day, and sometimes not even that.

Suddenly, a large white man was standing in the kitchen holding a walkie-talkie. He saw me sitting in a corner on the floor, said something in Dutch I didn't understand, and then walked off. A little while later he came back, stood akimbo in the doorway, and this time gave me an angry look. Again he said something I didn't understand, switched off the light while I was sitting holding a book, and left me there in the dark. I didn't get it. I closed the book and went out into the hall, where I saw John, one of the African asylum seekers.

"I don't speak Dutch," I said. "Do you maybe know what he said?"

"He said that he just told you to turn off the light and read in the hallway."

"What's the difference where I read?"

"Who knows. Maybe it's the money? He's a son of a bitch, that receptionist. He's always like that. Not the other ones. But now you can go back in the kitchen and turn on the light, because no one will come check for a while. They only make their rounds once an hour." I preferred to sit in the hallway rather than see that big nasty man again, but it was as if he switched off the light with every sentence I read. I got annoyed and shut the book. Just then, a woman walked past. If I hadn't looked up I wouldn't have noticed her. I had never seen a face like hers before. So pale. It looked like she was sleepwalking. She held an empty bottle, went into the ladies' toilet, and came back out with a full bottle of water. My God, I thought, what a cadaver.

In the end, I couldn't read any further and wandered through the hallways of the ASC. Everywhere I went, there were people—sitting, walking, standing—who couldn't sleep either. People who lay low during the day, and only came out in the quiet of the night. That night I discovered that the Yellow wing was for families with children, and for the rest I saw all the kitchens, emergency exits, and ghosts of the ASC until I heard birds singing outside. I opened a window, and sure enough, they were singing loud and clear. Even though it was still pitch-dark. I'd never heard a bird sing in the dark. The night air wafted inside. Exhausted, I trudged back to O-139 and opened the door.

"That's true," I heard Walid say.

"What's true?" I asked softly, but got no answer. He was talking in his sleep. I lay down on my bed and was out like a light, and soon thereafter—it seemed like just a few minutes—I heard Walid and Faoud talking. Exactly where they'd left off the previous evening: first about the too-long wait for a residence permit, then about the other residents of the ASC, about their families, about asylum seekers they had met over the years, and the asylum seekers who had gone crazy or committed suicide. This is how my first night in the ASC ended, a night that would be repeated hundreds and hundreds of times, and would change me for good.

The next morning I left room 0-139 and walked out into the orange hallway. What at night had been a serene brook had now turned into a surging river. I heard children running and shouting, and people chatting or calling out, as if the building had been transformed into a market or a schoolyard. Life started early here. I remember wondering, that first day: what do I do now? I went to the kitchen and noticed that every asylum seeker had their own utensils and cooking pots. A man from Sudan advised me to go to the thrift store. There I bought a teakettle, which must have boiled a lot of water since World War I and made a sound like the sirens in Baghdad during the Gulf War; a pot from World War II; a frying pan dating from the Cold War; and a cup and spoon. All those generations of kitchen things together cost me less than five guilders. I went to the Aldi and bought my first sugar, salt, tea, and eggs. I went back to the ASC and slowly began to figure out what life was like there. I got to know people in a way I'd never done before. How strange life is in an ASC, so bizarre how people made friends there: you leave your room, stand in the hallway, and don't have to actually meet anybody, because you are immediately one of them.

I was frying an egg when Kadhem entered the kitchen. He also had a room in the orange wing. We were like Laurel and Hardy, except that we were both thin. I was— and still am—six foot one and 168 pounds. Kadhem barely reached my shoulder and was even skinnier. He appeared silently, out of nowhere, like a cat, and disappeared just as quietly . And this is irritating, if you live in the same building for years on end.

16

I'm not sure how to explain life in the ASC. You could compare it to the Titanic, except that life here sails on an ocean of waiting for an answer from the authorities. The asylum seekers are icebergs, and how big each underwater chunk is, you don't know. Some asylum seekers are gashes in the ship's hull and many are treacherous storms. Once in a while they sink the ship. Then the police are called in, who dredge the Titanic up to the surface again.

Sometimes I forget I'm telling this story to people who are not asylum seekers themselves and don't know what an ASC looks like. So let me explain in a bit more detail. The ASC where I was housed consisted, as I've said before, of colored wings: yellow, blue, orange, and one last wing, in green, that they had to knock together because the stream of asylum seekers required more and larger centers, and whose room numbers were preceded by a G. Each wing had, in addition to the rooms, a large communal kitchen, a shower room for women and another for men, and a room for the washing machines. Families lived in Yellow; Blue was usually for asylum seekers who had been there for more than six years; and the rest were put in Orange or Green. On the ground floor there was a social or recreation area, where for twenty cents you could drink coffee or tea at the bar, or buy chocolate bars and bags of chips. There was a pool table and a place to play cards. Also on the ground floor, across from the office of the activity team, who organized film evenings, bingo afternoons, or soccer tournaments, was a nursery, which was manned by volunteers.

In the ASC the day did not begin when the rooster crowed (I believe that in the Netherlands, roosters are not allowed to make too much noise), nor when the sun rose (because it is so often overcast in this country). In this building, the day started when mail was delivered to Reception. Then, five hundred asylum seekers would throng to Reception to see if the Immigration Services or the Justice Ministry had sent them a letter that day. Every asylum seeker waited for mail, even the children, because they heard their parents talk about it every hour, sometimes every minute of the day. Every day. Except Sundays, because then there was no mail delivery.

Every asylum seeker handled it differently. Some sauntered nonchalantly past Reception, to cast a glance at the receptionists in the hope that they would call them over. Asylum seekers who were afraid the receptionists wouldn't know who they were would repeat their name every day, which irritated the staff.

"My name is Habib."

"We know."

Others would pass by every hour and ask the receptionist: "Mail?" and if the person behind the counter shook their head no, they would walk on, only to return an hour later with the same question, or they would stand there for a while to make sure there had been no oversight. Once it had been confirmed there was no mail for them that day, they waited for tomorrow's mail. Everyone hated Sundays—I did too, and I still do—

because there was no mail delivery. But even on Sunday, there were asylum seekers who would go to Reception to inquire about the mail. As if the day could not begin without this question. You would often hear the ASC receptionists say: "It's Sunday." Not: "It's Sunday, and there is no mail delivery on Sunday," because they had been saying this not for days or weeks, but for years. For most asylum seekers, the day began by asking about the mail. For some, it *was* their day. And for Abdulsalaam, it was his life.

The most bothersome asylum seeker for the receptionists—and for the other asylum seekers too, by the way—was Abdulsalaam from Yemen. He asked for his mail every day for sixteen years. He was twenty-five when he arrived in the Netherlands, and turned forty-one in my last year at the ASC, still waiting for a letter from the IND. You could ask every asylum seeker how long Abdulsalaam had been in the Netherlands. An asylum seeker who had been here for ten years said that Abdulsalaam had been living in the ASC for ten years; an asylum seeker who had been there a year, said that Abdulsalaam had been in the ASC for a year; an asylum seeker who had been in the ASC for three years would say he'd also been there for three years. Every asylum seeker counted the number of years Abdulsalaam had been there according to the first time they saw him.

I remember deciding one day that I wanted to hear from Abdulsalaam himself how long he had been in the ASC.

"Phew, how long has Abdulsalaam been living in the camp?" was his answer. Many asylum seekers referred to the ASC as "the camp." After thinking for a moment, he said the date of his arrival was notated in his second hearing, and he went off to his room in Blue and returned with a large black garbage bag full of papers. He tossed the bag at my feet. "Here, the date I arrived is in this bag." He seemed curious too, about how long he had been in the ASC; he opened the bag and started fishing out and inspecting dossiers and folders and papers. He opened letters, smaller plastic bags filled with papers, envelopes, and yet more letters. From the IND, from lawyers. There were also receipts from stuff he'd bought at the Aldi and elsewhere. After about twenty minutes I offered to go to his room so we could take our time figuring out how long he had been here, but in the end I didn't. It was a hopeless case.

Abdulsalaam was the asylum seeker most occupied with waiting, not for a residence permit, but for a letter. He often complained that the IND had surely forgotten him, for he hadn't received a single letter in three years. Not even a deportation order, the form letter the IND regularly sent out, in which they inform the asylum seeker that he is expected to leave the country within twenty-eight days. I myself received many such letters.

Abdulsalaam was not so much afraid of being sent back to Yemen as of having been forgotten altogether: that a civil servant somewhere had made a mistake and erased his name from the computer and that the IND didn't know he was still waiting. No matter how often the Social Services personnel, the receptionists, and the volunteers assured him that this was not the case, he asked every time why he had not received a letter from them yet. Whenever you bumped into Abdulsalaam in the halls of the ASC, where he drifted day and night like a ghost, the first question he always asked was whether today was Sunday. Sometimes children would yell "Sunday! Sunday!" when they saw him way down the hall, and then run away. Abdulsalaam's manner of speaking was irritating, especially for Dutch people. To this day I have not yet met anyone who could irritate Dutch people the way Abdulsalaam could. Unfortunately he was not aware of it himself.

As soon as he woke up in the morning he would hurry to Reception, as though his letter would be returned if he didn't fetch it in time. He would ask, gesticulating wildly, if there was mail, and would add that his name was Abdulsalaam. If they replied that the mail had not been delivered yet, his eyes would open wide and he would utter the few Dutch sentences he'd learned in all his years in the ASC.

"No mail today? My name Abdulsalaam. Why not mail? Today no Sunday, really?" The receptionist—it did not matter who—would become irritated and repeat the same exact thing to Abdulsalaam, because he only understood a few sentences, and changing even a single word would mean Abdulsalaam no longer understood.

"No. Today is not Sunday. The mail will come, but is not here yet." The receptionist spoke slowly and enunciated every syllable.

"But why no mail today? Is not fair. I wait. And today is no Sunday and no mail."

"That's right. Today is not Sunday, Abdulsalaam. The mail will come today. Before five o'clock. Maybe earlier. The mail will come today, but is not here yet."

"Aha," Abdulsalaam would sigh, turn, and walk off, only to return every hour to ask if the mail had arrived yet.

I remember not being able to sleep one night, and sitting in the hallway outside room O-139 when I saw Abdulsalaam approach. He stopped in front of me.

"Was it you I told I'd come back in half an hour, or someone else?" he asked.

"Someone else."

"So not you?"

"No, not me."

"Do you remember who I was talking to half an hour ago? Or where: in Yellow, Orange, or Blue?"

"Where what?"

"I told someone I'd come back in half an hour, and it wasn't you. You weren't there, and you didn't hear me. You really don't know who I was talking to, and where?"

"I really don't."

"You don't. Then I'll ask someone else. But you don't know, right?"

"No, I don't." Abdulsalaam went on his way, and when he was out of sight I hurried back into my room, in case he walked in circles and would soon show up again with the same question.

So every day, Abdulsalaam and four hundred and ninety-nine other asylum seekers waited for the mail delivery. If no letter arrived, then the asylum seekers would wander through the corridors like passengers trapped in a transit lounge. Some went grocery shopping, others went in search of clandestine work. Some stood in line for the daily check-in, or tried to fish or to read, but most didn't really like walking around outside the ASC. You discovered pretty quickly as an asylum seeker that most Dutch people looked at you askance. Even I, who spoke reasonably good English and quickly learned the Dutch language, played guitar a bit, enjoyed concerts and literature, had traveled and experienced things—even I, in those first years, was never once invited to a Dutch person's home. So I too felt more comfortable in the ASC than on the Dutch streets. At least, in an ASC located in a small town. In a large city, you can disappear into the crowd. For that reason, asylum seekers always hoped they would be placed in an ASC in a big city. But you had no choice in the matter, unless you had a family member in a certain ASC. In theory, you could request a transfer to another center, and they made a note of it, but in practice it was almost never granted. And if you missed signing in even once without a reason—that is, without a reason that fell within the civil servants' definition of "valid," and with confirmation from Social Services or the medical clinic—then the requested transfer might take even longer. At least, that's how it went in our ASC.

The daily sign-in was an unvarying obligation and a constant humiliation. For goodness sake, how many times did we stand in that line without anything happening. We could talk quietly among ourselves, but beyond that you were at the mercy of the civil servant on duty, how quickly he or she felt like doing their work, or whether there were "urgent matters" like chatting with a colleague or fetching coffee; these things were more important than the people in line being allowed to get on with their daily routine. At times I got the impression that signing in was a way to lull asylum seekers into submission. Talib and I often went to sign in together. I'll tell you about Talib later. He was someone who could turn everything, even that endless waiting, into a joke.

There was also a school and a library in the ASC. The library was open from ten till five, except on weekends. The librarian was Mieke, and I think she was a volunteer, because she did not attend the daily Social Services meeting between twelve and one o'clock. She did have an office, upstairs at the end of the hall. If you were to take an X-ray of her chest cavity, you would not see a heart, but a kilo of gold. There wasn't a single asylum seeker who did not adore Mieke. There were only three Dutch dictionaries in the library. The asylum seekers went there often, to borrow books or read newspapers in a variety of languages at the large communal table, but also to go to Mieke to arrange an appointment with the lawyer, or to find a way to get an appointment with a medical specialist in a hospital, which was usually only possible if an asylum seeker was nearly dead.

As I mentioned earlier, the clinic at the RC told a sick person that he had a better chance of getting a more involved procedure, or more expensive medicine, at an ASC, and in the ASC they said that the insurance did not cover it, or at least not until you had a residence permit. I wanted to see a specialist or a physiotherapist for the pain in my back, but I could not convince the medical services that this was absolutely necessary. The last time I asked, the nurse snarled at me: "You don't have to keep coming back with the same problem. Who doesn't have back pain?!" And she gave me some aspirin.

The school in the ASC was open to everyone, from whenever you wanted until whenever you wanted. Therefore the classroom was almost always empty. A volunteer named Albertina gave Dutch lessons. Asylum seekers under the age of eighteen were sent to a real school on the outside. If you were older than eighteen you went to Albertina. You often saw Albertina, her gray hair let down and in one of her colorful dresses that would more suit a girl of sixteen than a woman of seventy, walking down the hall with an armload of chocolate, in an attempt to convince the asylum seekers that the Dutch language was more important than a green card. I had the chance to eat seven of her chocolates, the equivalent of seven Dutch lessons.

Someone would always walk past the classroom during the lessons, and would see through the window that there was a box of chocolates on the table, and that students were talking and eating chocolate. When they came in, the first thing Albertina would ask is, "Are you a new student?" She enunciated the words clearly, one by one. At the word "you" she poked her index finger into the chest of the asylum seeker, to let them know that the word *you* meant "you," and at the same time would reach into her bag. Then she would take out, for instance, two slippers. One of which was totally ragged, and the other brand-new, adorned with little flowers, and still wrapped in cellophane. Then she would say, "New slipper," holding up the plastic-wrapped one. The asylum seekers munched their chocolates, gave each other surprised looks, and repeated what she said. "New slipper!" Then she'd take the ragged one, hold it up and say, "Old slipper!" The asylum seekers took another bite of chocolate and chanted in chorus, "Old slipper." At the end of the lesson, everyone knew what kind of chocolates they had eaten, and how many, but beyond that, not much about what kind of lesson they had just had. Anyone who had an old and a new slipper at least knew they were slippers.

Back to the lesson. I remember Albertina once writing the word "I" on the board. A good way to start learning Dutch, I thought. She stretched out the sound of the word, pointing to herself as she uttered it, and then back to the word. Then she wrote "you" underneath it, and pointed at one of us. After that, she wrote "we," came and stood among us, and got us to stand up and all say "we" in a sort of spiritual, meditative tone. As she said the words "I," "you," and "we," she gestured with her arms and breathed deeply, as though this was not a Dutch lesson but rather a yoga class. At the next chocolate—er, lesson—she asked if there were any new pupils. This time she took out a used sponge and one wrapped in cellophane, and repeated the "old" and "new" lesson. A female asylum seeker tried to explain that that was just what she needed, a new sponge, so Albertina reverted to the previous "slipper" tutorial.

The lessons often elicited some amusing misunderstandings. People would confuse pronunciations, like turning *kettle* into *cattle*, or *pedal* into *paddle*. But the funniest—and I have to explain the Dutch here—was the word *gastvrij*.

In Dutch, *gastvrij* means "hospitable," or "welcoming"; *gast* = guest and *vrij* = free, more or less.

"I am *gastvrij*," Albertina said, pointing at herself. No one understood what she was talking about, but Albertina kept pointing at herself and rubbing her hand over her chubby stomach, as though she'd just enjoyed a delicious piece of cake.

"Gas?" asked one of the asylum seekers, biting off a piece of chocolate.

"Free," called out another.

"Albertina gas-free?" joked Esmat, one of the pupils, in Arabic. "She has enough gas in her stomach to inflate a bicycle tire!" Everyone laughed.

"And you?" Albertina continued, thinking Esmat had understood her explanation. "Are you *gastvrij*?"

"I gas-free? Madam Albertina, since live in camp I not move, like pig. Eat wait, that all. Eat wait, eat wait. I not gas-free. I enough gas to blow up Social Services."

17

One day, the best thing to happen in the ASC in years occurred, and in our very own wing, too: the arrival of Yelena, a young Russian woman. She was gorgeous. She looked like Julie Christie in *Doctor Zhivago*. At once, the ASC turned into the most sumptuous palace in the world. Her beauty immediately softened everything. I would often stand in the kitchen, right next to the door to the corridor, and wait until she came out of the shower room. I had just seen her vanish into the ladies' showers like a blond lightning bolt carrying a toilet case, when an irritating voice behind me called out my name.

"Pretty, isn't she?" I did not want Kadhem to see that I was spying on the women's shower room, because that was disrespectful.

"Yeah, she's pretty," I shrugged.

"Very pretty?"

"Very pretty." It felt like Yelena had been jammed into my throat, and I had to either swallow her or spit her out. I got all worked up. Yelena was like a pressure cooker, like the last bottle of water in the desert, like a dentist who works weekends, or a corkscrew in the woods. A liberation. She had Russian good looks: a round face, thick, red lips, and blond locks. All the asylum seekers were amazed: how did she manage to slip out of the clutches of the pimps, the loverboys, the human traffickers who hung around the Dutch RCs?

The men and boys in the ASC followed her around. All manner of stories about her made the rounds: she had a sexually transmitted disease, she would go to bed with anyone who gave her twenty euros, she was the girlfriend of the biggest hash smuggler in Rotterdam. Many asylum seekers claimed to have been in her room. She spoke English with a thick Russian accent, over-using certain English words, like "incredible." Sometimes the English syllables came out of her mouth like a jigsaw puzzle, and you had to piece them together to make any sense of it: "I want deep in my chhheart hap penis and I need cre dit fordat."

Yelena had everyone's respect, at least when she was physically there. Then she was the most powerful, the most beautiful, the most blessed, the sweetest. But in her absence, she was a dirty whore. Not only the asylum seekers, but the Dutch people working in the ASC were in awe of her. They never treated her like an asylum seeker. With my own eyes I saw a man from Immigration smile at her, greet her, and stop to have a chat with her. This was unheard of. She opened the door to her room between 8:30 and 9:30 in the morning, and would emerge with sleep still in her eyes. Fortunately her room, O-124, was just across the hall from the kitchen. So between 8:30 and 9:30 I would go to the kitchen, just to witness her walk from her room to the showers wearing her zebra pajamas. Over time, I had to reserve the stove nearest the kitchen door earlier and earlier, because more and more asylum seekers wanted to fry eggs or make tea between 8:30 and 9:30 in the morning.

"You're waiting for her, aren't you?" Kadhem asked. "You'd better turn your omelet before it burns, just like you're doing inside at the thought of that Russian bombshell." I nodded as I flipped the omelet. "You're waiting for her. Zainab is waiting for the civil servant from the IND who is in charge of her dossier. Everybody's waiting," he said smugly, as though he did not belong to those who were waiting.

"What about you, Kadhem, what are you waiting for?" I asked.

"Money from my brother in Dubai, so I can hire the best lawyer in Holland. I'll wangle that green card and get out of here, and you'll come live with me, Samir. Not only you, but that Russian bombshell in O-124, and that African in room B-80 with the best ass ever, and that Romanian chick in G-31 with the most delicious tits, and the Chechen girl in B-27 with the nicest ... eyes, the Chinese in Y-43 with the smoothest legs, and the Iranian, oh my god the Iranian woman in Y-50, ahhh. Too bad we can't take the Afghani woman from B-65 with us, because then her brother will come butcher us both." He listed all the young women and their room numbers, one by one.

"If you take all these women home with you," I told him, "you'll need another whole asylum center, and a nursery next door." He laughed out loud. Whenever he laughed, he became smaller, because his pride drained out of him.

18

So Kadhem was waiting for money. You should know that there are two categories of asylum seekers in the Netherlands: rich and poor. Rich asylum seekers can afford a lawyer. Poor ones can't.

Every asylum seeker in the Netherlands is provided with a *pro deo* lawyer. His first and second hearings, and the documents pertaining to his asylum request, are sent to this lawyer. Some of us wondered if we even had a lawyer, because the appointments were so short. An asylum seeker who spoke passable English or Dutch got to speak with his lawyer for a bit longer.

The pro deo lawyer was more a sort of postman who forwarded, or briefly explained, the letters sent by the Immigration Department. If an asylum seeker had new documents to present, for instance to show that his brother had been imprisoned by the regime of their home country, then the pro deo lawyer made copies, keeping one for in the dossier, and sending the other to the IND. Sometimes all the asylum seeker had to do was hand the document over to the secretary, without even seeing the lawyer. The lawyer would in turn forward the IND's confirmation of receipt to the asylum seeker. And so on and so forth.

I'll share with you a little about my own experience with lawyers. When I was admitted to the ASC, I was given the name of a lawyer. They sent him the reports of my first and second hearings, and gave me his address and phone number. I had bought a prepaid telephone card for ten guilders and called the office often, but each time, the woman who answered said he was in court or was busy with a client. Whenever I told the secretary who I was and what I wanted, she would say, "Just a moment." I stayed on the line and hoped that the ten guilders would not vanish from the card before she got back. I stared at the little screen where you could see how much money was left on your card. The guilders melted away and the lady's "just a moment" was followed by another "just a moment." Then she came back and said "thanks for waiting" and told me the lawyer couldn't come to the telephone, and that it was not possible to make an appointment for the near future, because he was busy. She asked me to call back another time. I kept buying prepaid phone cards, and kept on calling, until I was finally given an appointment for two and a half months later. I could always call in the meantime to see if there was an earlier opening. Later, I learned that you had to have a Dutch person with a Dutch name do the calling for you. I can't explain why this is so, but it is. Maybe a Dutchman doesn't dare to be mean to another Dutchman, or he knows that a Dutchman is acquainted with the laws of his country, and knows what the other one can get away with, and what not.

There are asylum seekers who are satisfied with their appointed lawyer. They were lucky enough to get a brilliant, humane lawyer who takes asylum cases seriously, and sends the asylum seekers letters, and agrees to talk to them. But those lawyers, passed along the asylum seekers' grapevine, are so completely booked that they often have a waiting list of four or five years. As a poor asylum seeker, you just have to make do with whoever you're given.

But for a wealthy asylum seeker who can pay for his own lawyer, it's an entirely different story. The lawyer goes through the first and second hearings with him and an official interpreter, who comes from the same country and speaks the same dialect. If the interpreter at the first hearing was from another country, then the lawyer can snooker the Immigration Department and say there were lots of misunderstandings between the interpreter and the asylum seeker.

The interpreter at my first interview came from Egypt. He barely understood my Iraqi dialect, and his classical Arabic was rusty, probably because he'd been in the Netherlands for so long. Getting him to understand me was an arduous undertaking. Whenever I used an English word with him, the woman from the Immigration Department reprimanded me, saying I had to speak in my native language, and asked if I was speaking English because I wasn't really from Iraq after all. She blamed my using English on me, not on the interpreter.

If I reread my hearing now, I see so many comical misunderstandings. For instance, I had told her that I was once smuggled over the border by a shepherd. In the report it said that I was the shepherd, and instead of being smuggled by a shepherd, I was a shepherd who smuggled sheep. Hilarious—but this could mean years in an ASC.

When, years later, I was assigned a different lawyer, it turned out that my first lawyer neglected to point out the many mistakes in my first and second hearings. And then they said that unfortunately it was too late to fix it. A paid lawyer has every sentence from a hearing translated. The asylum seeker can then say whether the document is correct or not. I heard a story of an Iraqi asylum seeker who paid ten thousand guilders for a lawyer, who shot down every attempt to find flaws in his case by arguing that the Moroccan interpreter had completely misunderstood his client's words.

In addition, the paid lawyer corrects the first hearing reports, and if the person's story has some holes in it or needs to be fleshed out here and there, he presents new information and says that the asylum seeker had not said such-and-such because he did not feel well, or was under mental duress. These were the techniques used by paid lawyers, which is why Kadhem was waiting for money from his brother in Dubai. He was hoping for six to ten thousand guilders, because he had heard from other asylum seekers that with this sum you could definitely hire a good lawyer, and would quickly be offered political or humanitarian asylum in the Netherlands. It's too bad details like this are so boring, because I could go on about it for hours. For instance, about the asylum seeker who paced the halls of the ASC waiting for his sister to sell her wedding gold and send him the money. Or another, who was waiting for help from an uncle who'd been living in America for the past twenty years. The funniest one I heard was about an asylum seeker who no one knew and who came from a poor family. He was waiting for the lawyer's beautiful daughter to fall in love with him, so her father would take his case for free.

Oh, how gentle the Netherlands is for the asylum seeker who can pay. Dump gasoline in a car and the engine keeps on running. For hundreds of miles. With more gas, thousands of miles. Dump money in the system that is the Netherlands, and the system's humanity keeps on running until you can prove everything.

I remember Edhem, an asylum seeker who was really from Jordan, but had applied for asylum as an Iraqi, because he would never get asylum as a Jordanian. He paid 7500 guilders for a lawyer who could convince the Immigration Department that he was Iraqi, but spoke with a Jordanian accent because he lived in a village on the border. The name was made up, and there had never been a village there, only sand. He told me his story after having asked several times for information about Iraq. Because he was interested, he said at first—but after a while, he confided in me that it was to give his story a more plausible slant. He was given political asylum after two years and three months. He asked if I had a fat wallet, so he could give to me the address of his lawyer, but back then my wallet was—and still is—even thinner than Gandhi.

There are some situations I'll never forget, and although they are trivial, they still make my memory throb with pain. I remember having secured an appointment with my lawyer, after having a Dutchman make the call for me. I had been given a day ticket to go there by train. When I arrived, I showed the secretary my dossier. She said that if I had new documents, I could just mail them, and she handed me the office's business card, even though I obviously had the address, because I was there.

I told her I had an appointment with my lawyer. But she said he wasn't in the office and that I would have to make a new appointment to see him in person. I replied that it would be difficult to convince the ASC to give me another day ticket for the train.

She responded sourly, "So pay for it yourself! You've got a free roof over your head, food and drink, and a clean toilet. Free health insurance and a free lawyer. Surely you can find your own way here? There are people working hard so that you can get things for free." The woman did not shout. No, she said it in a gentle tone of voice. I felt my face break into an ice-cold sweat. I hoped she didn't see the effect her words had on me. And then she continued, not directly at me this time, but to the world in general: "Asylum seekers pay thousands of dollars to smugglers to get here, and if this fails then they'll pay it again and again. They wait in hotels here and hotels there, spend thousands of guilders on forged passports and visas, but once they get here they won't pay a few guilders to go see their lawyer." The telephone rang, she answered, and started chatting. I concentrated on my knees, so they wouldn't buckle and make me collapse onto the office floor. I touched my forehead and felt how wet my face was. I saw her smiling amiably on the phone, and when she had finished the call she apologized, her voice now calm, not stern at all. "Sorry for the interruption," she said. "You're welcome to make a new appointment." Normally, Dutch people are diplomats at their workplace, but this woman was different. She could emit, with immense power, clarity, and sureness, from a mouth just two inches wide, words that delivered a punch that would make an Olympic boxer jealous. I never bothered her again.

19

Yelena, the Russian beauty, had a room to herself. When she woke up, between 8:30 and 9:30 in the morning, she only emerged from her room if there was no one in the hallway. She probably listened carefully at her door to check whether the hall was empty. If the coast was clear, she darted out, quickly closed the door behind her and locked it, and went down the hall to the women's showers. She did not look straight ahead, but toward the wall, until she disappeared behind the door to the showers. This scurrying made her resemble a frightened rodent. As though no one was allowed to see her, as though someone like her had no need for a shower or a toilet. Dressed and with make-up, her whole posture and look was different. Then she would walk erect and facing forward, her chin raised just a little. She looked like a model, with one difference: Yelena was prettier, for she was not too skinny and not too fat. She was exactly right, a miracle.

At the beginning, she was most irritated by John, who I'll tell you about now. John, the African asylum seeker who had helped me when I wanted to read in the kitchen, always had public transportation day tickets for sale. Asylum seekers were given them for free if they had an appointment with their lawyer, or were being transferred to another center, or for various other reasons that did not fall into any special category. How much

John scalped a day ticket for depended on how long it was still valid. The cheapest were those tickets valid only on the day itself, until the last train and the last bus.

John hit on every woman inside and outside the ASC. If he had a woman, he called her a good friend. Otherwise he called her a filthy whore. Even the women at Social Services and Reception were not exempt from his advances. When you talked to him, he answered every question with "Everything is the same." As long as he lived in the ASC, everything stayed "the same." John had a lot of contact with Dutch people outside the ASC, mostly hash addicts or alcoholics. He also had the strangest method of cooking that I saw in my nine years there. He would take his empty pan to the kitchen at the busiest time, and bum a bit of potato from this one, some onion from another, from him a piece of meat, from her a dab of tomato puree, and a dash of oil from wherever. Then he would put it on the stove and ask one of the other asylum seekers to turn off the flame when they left the kitchen. He would come back later with a spoon, take the lid off, and eat it straight out of the pan. Sometimes he would leave the pan there and find it washed the next morning, or else still full of rancid food stinking up the whole kitchen, or sometimes even filled with new food. So John never complained about life in the ASC. He never referred to the others as "asylum seekers," but as "brothers and sisters" (when he was drunk or stoned) or "sons of bitches" (when he was sober).

I couldn't tell you where he came from exactly, because he only used the word *Africa*, as if that entire continent was his home.

John was the first asylum seeker to discover that Yelena listened carefully at her door before venturing out into the hall. So he stood at her door and spoke quietly, contrary to the way he normally spoke. This was difficult for him, but he managed, his face tense, which made him look even angrier. As soon as she came out, he would corner her and start talking. Everyone except John could see that this annoyed her. Especially when he leaned against her door, so that it swung wide open and anyone who walked past could look inside. Whoever saw him leaning against the doorpost like this would think he had something going with her, which was exactly his objective. He wanted it to be clear to all the men in the ASC that Yelena was taken. By him. Eventually that's what happened: everyone thought they had something going. Sometimes I saw her standing there with her legs crossed because she had to pee, but he just stood there talking. This went on until one day when I left my room and saw him leaving hers at the same time. It was clear that this time, he did not want anyone to see him.

A few days later I was standing in the kitchen frying eggs, hoping to catch a glimpse of Yelena, when John came in.

"She's a whore," he said to me.

"Who? Someone from Social Services?"

"No, the whore in O-124." Without waiting for me to ask, he told me he'd given her twenty guilders but did not get his money's worth. From that moment on, John left her alone, but after him there were other men. Even the children cheered up when they saw her, because she did not look like an asylum seeker. From the first time I saw her in the hallway, that hallway became beautiful.

Even my roommates' snoring became a Mozart sonata, and the endless, tedious discussions about residence permits and other asylum seekers turned into the gentlest poetry. When I lay in my room, I mused on the distance between my bed in O-139 and hers in O-124, which was ten meters at most. Then I closed my eyes and heard nothing, felt nothing, and dreamt that I melted like ice and flowed off my bed, under our door—quietly, so that no asylum seeker would step on me in the hall—and under her door and into her bed, where I would turn back into a person.

One day I left my room at about eleven in the evening to walk to the sea before going to bed, which had become a routine of mine. All of a sudden she opened her door. There she stood. She was wearing glasses I'd never seen before, and she smiled at me.

"You go out every evening around this time," she said. I was surprised. It was the first time she had spoken to me, I'd never really met her properly, and already she knew my habits.

"How do you know that?" I asked.

"I just know. You walk like an old man and your shoes make lots of noise." She laughed, to let me know it was a joke and not a put-down.

"Your ears might be ugly, but they work pretty well," I said.

"Really?" She touched her ears.

"Yes, really," I said.

"So where do you go?"

"To the sea," I said.

"Can I join you?" she asked, and without waiting for my answer added, "Give me five minutes." She closed her door, I heard her turn the bolt, and I waited in the hallway.

"How much did she ask for?" John whispered, when he passed a few minutes later.

"A lot."

"Forty?"

"More."

"How much?"

"Five minutes," I said, and he laughed.

"She gives great blow jobs," he whispered. "Good luck, man." He slapped my shoulder and walked off.

I waited. I felt stranger by the minute, nauseous from the excitement, insecurity, and such amazing luck. Then, as I stared at her orange door, I felt a wave of anxiety wash over me, as though she might reappear as a witch. But half an hour later the door opened, and she emerged into the hall dressed to kill. I knew all her clothes and pajamas, but this time she was wearing a dress I'd never seen before, like she was going to a party. She had applied soft make-up to her face.

"Sorry to keep you waiting. I decided to freshen up," she said with a smile.

"Being late in an ASC is like a fart in a bubble bath," I said, and laughed loudly, but she didn't get my joke. We walked down the stairs from Orange to the ground floor, past the closed Social Services counter, the office of the Foreigners' Police, and Reception. Being in the open air was a relief.

"Wait up! Wait!" we heard behind us, so loud that, at once, fifteen lights went on behind fifteen windows and fifty asylum seekers looked outside. I turned and saw Kadhem hurrying toward us. He stopped maybe twenty meters away, and motioned for me to come. I gestured apologetically to Yelena, went over to him, and he slid twenty guilders into my hand.

"You might need it," he whispered, turned, and walked off.

"Why did he call you over?"

"I don't know, but I'll ask him tomorrow if you want."

"Never mind," she said. "What did he give you?"

"Condoms."

"Oh, so he thinks that I ..." She sighed and appeared irritated. My joke did not go over well.

We walked side by side to the sea. She struggled to walk comfortably in her high heels.

"Look at those Dutch windows," she said, nodding furtively at the houses. "Big and beautiful. And you can see everything that's going on inside."

"Do you want to live in the Netherlands?" I asked.

"Maybe," she said, and took a few steps. "I don't think so," she continued, and after taking a few more silent steps: "I don't know ... what about you?"

"I'm waiting for a passport, and then I'll fly to Indonesia," I said. "To Makassar."

"Dutch people are so polite," she said, maybe to let me know what I wanted didn't interest her. "They're sweet and safe, but terrible dressers. Have you ever had a good look at the staff at Social Services, or the clinic, or the IND? They always wear the same thing. Boring, isn't it? Horrible." The more she talked, the happier she seemed.

"How do you like life in the ASC?" I asked.

"Fine, but I don't know if I can stay more than a year." Another few silent footsteps. "A year, sure. No longer than that. You?"

"I don't know," I said. "Other people count the years. I count the hours. Time goes so slowly." I told her about the ASC before her time, but stopped short of telling her how the ASC had changed after she arrived.

We reached the sea. She stopped and stared at a tiny light on a faraway ship. I looked at her.

"Incredible," she said, and breathed deeply. Her entire

face breathed. "Incredible," she repeated. "Imagine if they locked the doors of the ASC and no one could get out. Then, all the asylum seekers would think of the sea, but now nobody does except you. You're clever."

"Oh yes, I'm very clever and very intellectual," I said, and exploded with laughter, because the way she said *clever* suggested she doubted whether I really was clever—or, for that matter, if any asylum seeker could be.

"I also think you're important," she said, and before I could reply that yes, I was indeed important, she asked if I had killed anyone.

"Not yet," I said, laughing even harder. Two old people with an old dog passed us and looked up, startled by my loud laughter.

"Some men feel guilty if they have killed someone, and then they go to the sea every evening, or to church, or they feed the birds," she said with doubt in her big blue eyes. "The ASC is full of strange people," she pronounced, as though she and I hadn't just come from there.

"I could invite you for a drink," I said.

"In your room? With three other men there?" she asked with a smile.

"No, in a pub."

We drank tea in one of the cafés and after an hour or so we walked back to the ASC. During that hour, she talked quietly about the few people at the bar, their clothes, the pub's decor, the glasses, the bartender, and especially about a woman with tattoos who was leaning against the bar. After all these years, I still think back on that hour as a pleasant one. I was having a warm drink with the beauty of the world. That hour was the finest one, after years of fleeing, of forged passports, smugglers, Foreigners' Police, customs agents, borders it sometimes took years to cross, and jail cells here and there. A shiver ran down my spine, but a good one, the best one after all those shivers of fear, fear of being caught or having been caught. Or shivers of cold, until you're let out of the cell, or shivers of not knowing where they'll send you, now that you've been captured.

Just as we reached the ASC, another asylum seeker cycled past us at top speed. He swerved through the entrance gate, dumped the bicycle on the lawn in front of the building, and sprinted off, leaving the bike behind. Behind us, a Dutch man came running through the gate, out of breath. He picked up the bike and walked it to Reception. When we walked in after him, Tobias the receptionist called out to us.

"Stop!" We did, and he pointed at me.

"Him?" he asked the man with the bike, who then looked at me.

"I don't really know, it was dark and ... he cycled away so quickly and ..." He scratched his head. Yelena and I looked at the receptionist and at the man.

"You can go," Tobias said to Yelena, and she scurried off, without looking at me or saying a word.

"And you, wait there." He pointed at a corner.

"Sorry, but why?" I asked. "What's happened?"

"Just wait over there and keep quiet." He sighed exasperatedly, as though I'd been arguing with him for hours about not wanting to stand in the corner. Tobias consulted a list of phone numbers posted on the wall and dialed. I looked questioningly at the man with the bike. He shrugged his shoulders and raised his palms, as if to say, I don't know either. Soon enough, a squad car with two policemen pulled up. I heard the story. An asylum seeker had taken the man's bicycle, which wasn't locked, and rode off with it. The man who hadn't locked his bike, because he was chatting with a friend behind a fence, had shouted that it was his bike, and ran after the thief.

"Him?" asked one of the policemen, pointing at me.

"I didn't steal the bicycle," I said to the policeman.

"You only need to say anything if I ask you," replied the policeman.

"I don't know for sure," the man said. "It was dark and the asylum seeker was fast." The policeman took down the man's name in a small book, and told me to come with him. We went back outside. At the police car, he told me to put my hands behind my back. He bound them together with plastic cable ties, opened the back door and pushed my head down so I wouldn't bang it. Suddenly I was being driven off in a police car. I could have protested that they had the wrong guy, I could have yelled and struggled, but it wouldn't have made any difference. I had long known this much. After about twenty minutes we arrived at a police station, deserted save just one duty policeman working at a computer behind a pane of glass. One of the officers ordered me to follow him, so I did. He stopped at a cell and told me to go in.

"May I use the toilet, please?" I asked, but got no answer. I went into the cell and heard the door close behind me. I only turned around after the sound of his footsteps had stopped. He hadn't said a word. Not why I was brought to this cell, or how long I'd have to stay there. He hadn't even checked my pockets, nothing. After a while I was prepared to exchange all of Iraq for five minutes in the men's room. My insides held half a liter of urine like a bomb ready to explode.

So this is how my first date in the ASC ended: not in the bed of a gorgeous Russian woman, but in a police cell. A few hours earlier, my thoughts were only of beauty, but now all I could think of was a toilet in which to empty my bladder. I discovered a closed-circuit camera, and asked it if I could go pee, and showed it the plastic cable ties. Eventually a female police officer came and released the cable ties and led me to a rest room.

The next day they let me go. No one asked me about the bicycle, who I was, or what I had or hadn't done. Once outside, I hurried through the quiet Dutch streets past patches of grass of every color except green and under a sky that appeared nothing but black and gray. When I checked in at the ASC they didn't ask why I was late. Everyone knew I had spent the night in a cell.

Back in O-139, I was empty. Drained. Physically and emotionally.

"Hey, Samir, is it true, what I heard?" Kadhem asked me that evening. I stood at my whistling water kettle.

"What did you hear?"

"The police brought you in, because you …"

"Because I what?"

"Never mind," he said. It was clear that there were words stuck in his throat that refused to escape. Later, I discovered that the gossip that had traveled along the asylum seekers' grapevine was that I'd been arrested because I was trying to sell Yelena's body in the city center. Better a bicycle thief than a pimp, I thought. The story grew and grew, until everyone believed I had offered to sell Yelena to a Dutchman, who went to the ASC reception desk to lodge a complaint.

In the end, it turned out that it was Djabir who had stolen the bicycle that evening. Djabir was a professional bicycle thief, who stole expensive, high-quality bikes and within an hour had transformed them in his room (where bikes were officially not allowed, but he

20

My life in Iraq? I'll share an important moment with you. The moment I was introduced to the war. During my childhood years, there had been so much talk of the war in the north and the soldiers who went there, but for me, that wasn't a war; those were just stories. One afternoon, I met the real war. The conflict with Iran had already begun in 1980, far away, on the border. In our town, oil and gasoline became scarce, and there were long lines at the gas stations. So one afternoon I was standing in line with my father, and I noticed soldiers patrolling the scene to keep order. They carried machine guns and cables, which in Iraq were used not only for electricity but also for the soldiers to vent their anger.

At a certain point, one man complained loudly about having to wait for so long for just a few liters of gas, whereupon the soldiers pulled him out of line. In a flash, they circled him and began whipping him with their cables. A terrible silence descended over the on-lookers. It lasted for maybe a few minutes, this circle of soldiers around that man. When they stepped back from him, he was all red. He did not move. The soldiers left him lying there and returned to watching the line from a short distance, as though nothing had happened. My father held my hand firmly. I remember that his hand started to tremble, and when he felt this, he let go of mine and began gently stroking my head. He took me to the other side of the line so I didn't have to see that bloodied man on the ground.

"Is he dead?" I asked my father. He bent over to my ear, perhaps more to let me know I needed to be quiet than to answer me.

"Not dead," he whispered. "They didn't shoot him."

I stole a glance at the man. "He's not moving," I said softly.

My father bent back to my ear and gave me an answer I will never forget.

"Because he hasn't had breakfast."

I looked at my father. His face was pale and he was sweating. This was the first time in my life I had ever seen my father afraid, and I became afraid too.

When it was our turn, we bought gas in a jerrycan, and my father and I walked back to the car. He seemed more relieved to get away from the pump than pleased to have bought gasoline. I saw that the man was still lying on the ground, and that flies crawled over his blood.

"The gas station attendant said they've called an ambulance, and that it's on the way to take him to the hospital," my father said on the way home.

I lost my innocence that afternoon, learning that in the blink of an eye, war can change everything: the earth, the sky, man, the birds, the insects, the walls, the trees, the gas pumps, and my father.

Not long after that, the sirens began to wail for weeks, for months on end. They filled the air in Baghdad, where we lived, with their screaming. Of course, our dog had never been allowed in the house, but when the sirens began to wail, and Iranian missiles fell on the city and the ground shuddered and glass shattered from its frames, he ran inside, terrified. My mother had more trouble with the dog being indoors than with the missiles or the sirens. She would wash all the carpets and cushions with water every time he came in, everything that she suspected the dog might have touched. As the dog fled into the house more and more, my mother changed the rules. She decided that every time the dog came inside, she would wash just one sheet or blanket. And after that, when she got tired of the missiles and the dog running in and out, she would ask us—having seen him indoors with her own eyes—whether the dog had been in. We would answer "No, Mother" as one.

The war has its own little family jokes. I remember once when the dog lay in the corner quivering because a missile had just hit. My youngest brother called out to my mother, "Didn't come inside!" to which my mother replied, "The missile or the dog?"

I'll stop talking about Iraq now, because otherwise it will be too much for me. To be honest, it's painful to talk about it. But I'll tell you why I fled Iraq, because that has to do with my stay in the Netherlands.

When I fled, Iraq had a population of eighteen million. So I had eighteen million reasons to flee, because every Iraqi was a reason—myself included.

Another reason is that after I finished my degree in civil engineering at the university in Erbil I was supposed to go into the army, and I didn't want to. I did not want to go to war and have to shoot in the air or in the dark, and always be afraid that I had killed someone on the other side. That responsibility was too much for me. That was the reason I did not join the army, and ended up in an ASC seven years later.

I still remember my flight from Iraq. Everything was dangerous, even your name. I did not have a passport. In Saddam Hussein's day, you only got a passport in Iraq if you could show several documents. One document from the army saying you had fulfilled your military service, one with a stamp of approval from the secret service, one from your neighborhood saying you were a decent citizen, and one from the Ba'ath Party testifying that you were a reliable member. Getting each of these documents was a major hassle. For instance, I was never a member of the Ba'ath Party. Obtaining a document stating that I was a reliable member, without actually being one, was certainly possible, but very expensive. The forged document I bought had a fake name, so I would be untraceable and not endanger my family should I get arrested.

In those days, under Saddam Hussein, things were terribly chaotic. You could get arrested and sent to prison, and be stuck there for years without anyone asking why you were there. Later, lots of people gave a made-up reason for their imprisonment. For instance that they couldn't show an identity card when they were picked up, while in actual fact they had been caught trying to flee the country, which was seen as treason, and was punished severely.

After obtaining the document with the false name, I went in search of money. But I had no idea how to go about it. My family could scrape together one thousand dollars for me. That thousand dollars is another story. In those days it was the equivalent of one hundred thousand euros for a Dutch postman today. Many families had put aside a bit of gold, in case one of their children wanted to marry, or to dip into in difficult times. My mother sold her dowry gold, as well as the dowry gold she had inherited from her mother.

When I accepted those ten American sheets of paper and held them in my hands, I saw them as my ticket to freedom, to the wide world, which I had read and heard so much about. Even now, the word *dollar* has a special, magical ring to it for me. Because that word came to my rescue in many situations in Thailand, in Vietnam, in Hong Kong, and in Laos. Every day, I took those ten little sheets of paper out of a drawer. I counted them and looked at them. Then I imagined using one to get myself smuggled to Turkey, the next one to get to Greece, yet another to stow away on a ship to Italy, and from there, one more bill which would take me to Berlin or Paris. That's what I thought. What I didn't know was that in fact I would end up disheveled and penniless on some nondescript street in Jordan, because human smuggling is a world unto itself, and I was still a novice.

After my many failed attempts to get to Turkey, a friend of mine fixed me up with a smuggler who could get me to Jordan. This smuggler wanted to know how much money I had. The friend had told him I had two hundred fifty dollars; I would pay the smuggler two hundred, so I still had fifty dollars to survive during my first few days in Jordan. But this smuggler was clever. He didn't believe that I had only two hundred fifty dollars. I traveled to his city near the border and met up with him. We agreed that he would smuggle me over the border that very night, but he left me waiting in his house with his mother and family for a few days, until he came back and said it would cost me not two hundred dollars, but five hundred. I would pay him fifty up front and the rest when we got to Jordan. But since I only had hundred-dollar bills, this was impossible. This way he figured out I didn't have any fifty-dollar bills, and that I therefore couldn't have just two hundred fifty. He left me waiting for another couple of days. Once he came by to say someone from the Ba'ath Party knew I was hiding out at his place and wanted one hundred dollars to keep quiet. I paid. Then he said the police knew where I was, and they too wanted one hundred dollars. I paid. His mother, his younger brother, or his father assured me each time with a poker face that it was true. Fear, naiveté, and stupidity kept me from wondering why everyone, from policemen to members of the Ba'ath Party, demanded exactly the same price to keep quiet: one hundred dollars. Nobody asked for fifty, or one hundred and fifty. This kept me in that house for longer and longer. One day he came and asked me for one hundred dollars, this time to keep the neighbors quiet, but I told him I was flat broke. An hour later he came back all wound up, and said that the police were sure to come looking for me tomorrow. So come nightfall, I said goodbye to his old mother and younger brother, who were home alone, and left the house. I asked around for advice on where to go, until I arrived at a deserted bus station, hoping to find a truck, bus, or car that could take me back to Baghdad. Hardly two hours after I left his house, the smuggler found me at the bus station.

"What are you doing here?" he asked anxiously. "Are you crazy? They'll see you!"

"But everyone knows about me anyway, don't they?" I said. "The police, the Ba'ath Party, the army, the secret service, and—"

"Come with me," he hissed. It was clear he had no time to argue, so we ducked into the shadows and slipped back to his house. His fate, apparently, was tied to mine: if he hadn't been afraid that my getting nabbed would also get him arrested for trafficking, he wouldn't have tracked me down even after my last dollars were gone.

That same evening, I was sitting in the back of a truck in the company of some forty sheep, on a Jordan-bound highway full of checkpoints. This was the last thing I expected. I was sure the smuggler would take back roads, not a busy highway. Now, I can assure you that sheep have a keen sense of fear, because when I tried to hide among them, they kept shifting to the far side of the cargo hold. I crept over to them, to disappear into all that wool, and again they all shuffled away from me. When the truck stopped, my heart was in my throat: surely this was a checkpoint. I wished I were a sheep. I kneeled in a corner at the very back of the hold, expecting the soldiers to appear any second. They would spot me at once. In one horrible moment that I will never forget, a flashlight shone in my face. I froze with fear, but heard the voice of the smuggler calling out to me above the drone of the engine.

"Why don't you hide between the sheep?"

"Don't ask me, ask the sheep! Or do I have to pay them a hundred dollars too?" I'm not sure if I really did say that, or if I made it up later to jazz up the story, but I do recall what the smuggler answered. It made my flight easier, not only there in the truck, but also in the seven years that followed, until that cold February day when I landed at Schiphol.

"Don't let the sheep know you're afraid!" I don't know why he stopped the truck and came to have a look, but he was right, because from that moment on I lay on my back on the floor of the cargo hold and tried to breathe calmly. With each deep breath I trembled less. I slid myself slowly toward the sheep, until I could touch them, and wriggled further among them until I reached a corner. I stayed put, and tried to wedge my body, my thoughts, and my fear into that corner. I stopped thinking about why I was there, how I had gotten there, and where I was going, because if I did I'd start trembling from fear, and frighten the sheep all over again. To this day, whenever I'm in a difficult situation, I shut my eyes and go back to that truck. Me in one corner, the sheep in the other. And then I repeat what the smuggler told me at the side of that highway: "Don't let the sheep know you're afraid!" It eases my nerves.

Each time the truck slowed down, my fear increased and the sheep ran away from me. Then I'd put aside my fear, and hide among the sheep again. I've crossed many a border since then, but none was like that first border between Iraq and Jordan. When the only way a person can cross the border of his own country is hidden between nervous sheep, then that country is definitely a cage.

And then I was released from that cage. Smelling like sheep. The first thing I noticed was that there weren't photos of King Hussein of Jordan everywhere. It wasn't necessary to check the license plates or traffic signs to know you were in Jordan. The absence of Saddam Hussein's photos made it clear. After that long, awful journey I stood at the side of the highway to Amman with empty pockets. Once fear stopped gnawing at me, hunger took over—but hunger is far easier to tolerate than fear. I ambled here, sat there, walked a bit further, hid here, reappeared there, and ended up at a vegetable market. I started slipping overripe fruit and vegetables into my pockets. An old woman with a small vegetable stall saw what I was doing and called me over. She gave me a bag of produce and a piece of bread. I ate all the fruit and vegetables out of the bag as I left the market. Coming upon a cemetery, I lay down and fell into a deep sleep. I stayed there among the graves until sundown, then returned to the old woman's stall and helped her pack up her wares. She handed me another bag and asked where I was planning to sleep.

"In the cemetery," I said, and walked off. She called me back in and gave me a bottle of water. Back in the cemetery, I sat down between the graves and ate. At that time I only had one problem: my life. Because I didn't know what to do. Where to go. I did not know anyone in Jordan except the king, but unfortunately not personally.

Sleeping among the deceased relaxed me. To be honest, lying there on my back, I felt the earth and it was hard, and my body was so exhausted that on my first night outside of Iraq all I wanted was for the graves to open up and swallow me whole, the earth would close above me and I would vanish from this world. That's how desperate and defenseless I felt. I slept long and soundly, for in the smuggler's house I slept poorly out of fear and because of the family's pale faces. I awoke to the call to morning prayer and walked toward the mosque. I washed my face there, and sat. After prayer, someone came over, spoke to me briefly, and slipped something into the pocket of my trousers. So now I had enough money to travel further. By two in the afternoon I was on Al Hashemite Square in Amman.

21

From there I will jump directly to the city of Zarqa just northeast of Amman, where after a few aimless weeks I got a job in a bakery. From three in the morning until nine at night I worked in the oven room, where I also slept. It was a sauna in there, because fires burned the entire day to bake Arabic bread. After closing the shop in the evening, I slept and sweated, with a large bottle of water next to me, which I drained every hour. The worst part, though, was that the place was infested with mice. They crept into your clothes and scurried over your body. There were too many to count. I earned fifty cents a day, so fifteen dollars a month. You needed at least three thousand dollars to get smuggled to the Czech Republic—if it went well the first time. A complete smuggle to Germany (because the Czechs did not offer asylum at that time) cost you another thousand. I wanted to save up for it, but every twenty or fifty dollars I had went to buying medicine or was sent to Iraq, which thanks to the American embargo had nothing except hunger, sickness, and Saddam Hussein.

After a few months, more experienced in the bakery, I was the one who would stack the bread and clean the premises. I started at six in the morning and got a dollar a day. The owner of the bakery was an army officer, which was a stroke of luck, because both times I got picked up for being in Jordan illegally, he managed to get me released. His mother and father stopped by the bakery often to make sure everything was running smoothly. His mother was blind in her right eye, and his father was blind in his left eye. The mother came in the morning, so I swept all the rubbish to the right side, so she wouldn't see it. Then at midday I swept it all over to the left side, so that her husband wouldn't see it. (Every time I tell this story, people think I'm kidding. I'm not.) I also tutored two of the owner's sisters and one of his children in math, physics, chemistry, and English for free.

Around that time I bumped into an old acquaintance from the university in Erbil. I had shared an apartment with him and two other students for three years. He had come to Jordan on an official passport, so it seemed safer to give my money to him for safekeeping instead of hanging onto it myself. By that time we had rented a room with two other Iraqis in an old house full of our countrymen. After three years, when I had saved enough to escape from Jordan, I came home from the bakery and he was gone, along with all my money. I still marvel at how stupid I was to consider him a friend.

The next day, as I dragged myself to the bakery on what should have been my last day of work, I collapsed out of pure misery, right on the sidewalk. A young Jordanian named Ibrahim sat down next to me and asked if I was dizzy. I told him what had happened, and he smiled and told me not to worry. He brought me to his father's office supply store where he occasionally helped out, and made tea for me. Ah, isn't it wonderful that there are people who will help you out when you have no one else. Ibrahim was a lantern that gave light to everyone he knew. He became a good friend.

A few months later Ibrahim told me he was going to

Sint Maarten, the starting point of the smugglers' route to America. He would write me from there. We said our farewells, and after about three months a man came to the bakery and asked for me. He handed me a sealed envelope from Ibrahim. He wanted me to open the envelope in his presence. So we walked to a teahouse around the corner.

In the envelope was a videotape and a letter. It read: "On this videotape, many birds fly, and you are one of them. Ibrahim." I knew immediately what he meant. I didn't bother to look at what was on the videotape, but rather what was in it: a stolen Dutch passport. The photo of a blond, cheerful-looking youth was fastened with two metal rivets, and the stamp on the photograph was not regular ink, but embossed. I thumbed through the passport. It gave me a new dream. "There is another envelope inside," the man said. I opened it and found two hundred dollars with the message from Ibrahim: "To get the photo changed."

Now I had another problem. How was I to travel on a passport that had no Jordanian entry stamp? I started asking around among other Iraqis in Amman, and in doing so found out how Iraqis left Jordan with a forged European passport. First they bought an Iraqi passport from someone who had traveled to Jordan legally. Then they changed the photo in that passport with one of themselves, and used it to fly out of the country, their forged European passport hidden in their luggage. I decided to fly to Bangkok because, alongside Libya and Yemen, Thailand was the only country whose embassy would give a visa to Iraqis. After obtaining the visa in the Iraqi passport I'd bought, I went from travel agent to travel agent in search of the cheapest flight.

So there I stood, a month later, in line for customs at

Bangkok airport: on my ticket a fake Iraqi name, in my hand a stolen Dutch passport, and in my heart the fear of the Iraqi border. I had thrown away the Iraqi passport in an airport trash can. There was a whole row of customs officials, and I chose the one who yawned just at that moment, in the hope that his drowsiness would make him a bit more lax. The line moved slowly, and I became more and more nervous. Unfortunately there were no sheep at that airport to hide behind. But I did have that smuggler's words in my head: *Don't let the sheep know you're afraid.* Just as my turn approached, I realized I had made a stupid, fatal mistake. On the plane they had given us an immigration form, and I'd mistakenly filled in the information from the Iraqi passport instead of the Dutch one. Idiot! There was no way to leave the line, and anyway, the stewardesses had handed out the forms in the airplane and I wouldn't be given a new one here. My knees began to tremble, and even now as I write this, they are trembling again. I had no idea how long I could stay standing. I saw the customs agent glance at me, expecting me to take a step forward. I silently repeated the smuggler's words and approached the counter.

"Passport, please," he said in Thai English. I lay the passport on the counter with the ticket and the immigration form. *Don't let the sheep know you're afraid ...* The man thumbed through the passport and glanced up at me once or twice. *Don't let the sheep know you're afraid ...* I expected him to summon the police any minute, once he noticed the discrepancy in my papers. It felt like time stood still. Then a miracle happened, a wonder that played out before me in slow motion. He picked up the rubber stamp, pressed it onto the ink pad and then twice onto the immigration form, once at the top and once at the bottom. He tore it along the perforation, stuck one half in the passport and tossed the other half nonchalantly into a small basket next to him. He stamped the passport and returned it to me with a faint smile. I took it, nodded, and walked off in disbelief. I disappeared as quickly as possible into the throng and left the airport. Bangkok's air was humid and hot. I took a deep breath, as though I had not just landed in Thailand, but in heaven itself.

I'm able to tell you this now, all these years later, but even after so much time, when I look back on it, the fear is still palpable. Anyone born with an "acceptable" passport will never know how sharp the teeth of this world are, and how hard they can bite. The teeth of this world: policemen, Foreigners' Police, customs agents, receptionists at cheap hostels. The worm and the bird move effortlessly throughout the world, but the man without a passport ...

So that was Iraq and Jordan, in a nutshell. If I were to tell you more details, my life now would be even more difficult, my nights shorter, my nerves even more shot, and for you, reading these pages would be no fun. I'll certainly bring it up again occasionally, but only now and again, because that's less difficult. Bitter medicine should be administered in small doses. But remember that I am now standing outside Bangkok airport. Because, first, I'll take you back to the ASC.

22

In a place like the ASC, with so many residents, you meet a whole range of characters and personalities, many of whom I will introduce you to in the chapters to come. Take Fatima, for example, a Syrian woman who was so fat that she looked like a Japanese sumo wrestler wearing a head scarf. She was a simple woman, was illiterate, and had no idea what was going in the world a few hundred meters away. But Fatima was a fantastic cook and had a heart of gold. She baked biscuits and cakes; she could cook Syrian, Lebanese, Iraqi, Egyptian, and Palestinian specialties. All you had to do was mention a particular dish and she'd say, "Get a pen and paper." Then she would dictate the ingredients for that dish and the shop where you could find them the cheapest. After you returned with the groceries, she would disappear into the kitchen for several hours and bring the result to your room: a filled pan and a smile.

Now let me tell you about a certain Iraqi man. This man lived in Yellow with his wife, their daughter of thirteen, and their fifteen-year-old son. Whenever I saw him, he was always dressed in a suit and tie and patent leather shoes. He walked perfectly erect. At first I thought he was an interpreter or a lawyer, but Kadhem told me he was also an asylum seeker. Because his English was good, he never needed another asylum seeker to translate for him, so in the beginning no one knew what his story was. He remained a mystery, and did not seek contact with the other asylum seekers. His wife was two women: when she was with her husband, she was also well dressed, but when he was outside the ASC she wore sandals and was more relaxed in her behavior, and chatted and laughed with everyone with or without a reason.

One day I was at Social Services translating for someone, when the man walked into the office. At once I could tell that he enjoyed a great deal of respect from the staff. The woman who he had an appointment with was on the telephone, and when she saw him she held her hand over the mouthpiece, smiled at him, and said, "Sorry, but I just have to finish this phone call." He smiled at her and said he would wait in the hall. I could hardly believe my ears! A staff member being so polite to an asylum seeker, and even *apologizing*—this, I had never seen.

"No, no, you can go back to your wing. I'll come get you when I'm finished," she said. He smiled a thank you and walked off. Ah, I thought, so that's why I never saw him waiting at Social Services. I was amazed: this was more like a banker talking to a customer than a civil servant talking to an asylum seeker.

What also amazed me, and the rest of the asylum seekers, too, was that he had been given a second, separate room in Yellow for his son and daughter. I never saw this happen with any other family in the nine years I spent there. Families with one or two children got one room. A family with three children got a bigger room. Families with more than three children got an even bigger room. A family with *two* rooms—this was a first. I remember an Armenian couple with one child who got divorced. They asked the man if he wanted to stay in the same room with his ex-wife and child, or share a room with three other men. He preferred to stay put in the room with his ex-wife than to have to sleep in a room with three other men—and then he started renting out his spot in the room belonging to the three Chinese (I'll tell you about the three Chinese later, who had a room in Orange. That is a whole other story.)

The mysterious Iraqi man piqued the other asylum seekers' curiosity. Who was he? What had he done to earn such respect? He would surely be given political asylum before the year was out. One day a new Iraqi asylum seeker arrived at the ASC: Ridha, from the city of Samawah. After about three days, he started telling anyone who understood Arabic that the man was a general from Tikrit, one of the cities most loyal to Saddam Hussein. Ridha told us that back in 1991 he had seen, with his own eyes, the general take a pistol and execute men whose hands were tied behind their back. He asked many of the other asylum seekers to go with him to Social Services to tell his story, but no one would go. Ridha's mantra, in all the halls and all the rooms, was that the general did not belong in an ASC, but in a prison. One day there came a knock on O-139. It was Ridha. He said he needed an interpreter. I was still in my pajamas, and asked if he could just wait for me to change into my trousers, but he was in a huge hurry, so I just put on my sandals and followed him to the office. Ridha's face and entire body trembled with emotion.

"I want to register a complaint against the pig in Yellow," he said.

"Pig? In Yellow?" I asked, as I followed him to Social Services.

"A filthy pig. In room Y-19. I'm talking about General Abdul Galik al-Tikriti. That filthy pig thought he could escape justice and start a new life in Europe, but God sent me here as a witness against him." Ridha was hurrying down the stairs ahead of me. Anneke Hamelinck, the duty staff member, asked us to wait in the hall until she called us. I saw Ridha's face quiver with tension. "Now I know why I never got caught, why I was never robbed and left for dead by smugglers, from when I fled my home until this very moment. God was protecting me, he delivered me from my house to the Netherlands with just five hundred dollars in my pocket. One hundred to get to Diyarbakir, another hundred from Diyarbakir to Ankara, a hundred fifty from Ankara to Greece, another hundred fifty from Greece to Italy, and finally, in the back of a Polish truck to the Netherlands for free. I often wondered who was protecting me, an angel or a devil? But now I know that God wanted me to come here, so that that general would get his just deserts."

Ridha talked and I listened. I couldn't tell if what he was saying about the general was true or not. My first impression was that he was a professor or ambassador, and anyway, even if he was a general, I still thought his wife and children were nice.

But Ridha said, "Can you imagine? In 1991, that unarmed man in Y-19 behaved like he was God in Samawah. He decided who lived and who died. When Saddam Hussein's army recaptured the cities, one by one, we were put behind barred windows, hundreds of us. One morning that general came in with some soldiers. He pointed at someone, who the soldiers then grabbed, and then someone else, and someone else. Then he ordered the soldiers to shoot the ones he'd pointed at, on the spot. They left the bodies there with us." Ridha talked, and the more he told, the more believable his story became, and the more despondent he got. A Bosnian woman who was standing next to us with her child shifted a few meters away. Then Anneke called us in.

Anneke Hamelinck was certainly pushing sixty. Of all the staffers at Social Services, she had the most experience with asylum seekers. She was always crabby, not only to the asylum seekers, but also to her colleagues, the policemen, and herself. Fortunately I know nothing of her private life, but I can assure you that all those years of working with asylum seekers broke her, both physically and emotionally. She would speak to us in the most unofficial manner, saying, for instance, "Don't be so pathetic," or "What a big fibber you are," or "Are you gonna act normal, or do I have to call the Foreigners' Police?" She is the one who taught me the Dutch fake swear word *gadverdamme*. Even though she was crabby, Anneke was not particularly hard on the asylum seekers. She did not punish anyone immediately, but only threatened to. She often said she herself was a European mongrel, because rather than having a quarter or a half non-Dutch blood, she had little percentages of all kinds of backgrounds. Five percent Chinese, ten percent Surinamese, a splash of Czech, a dash of Macedonian, and ten percent German, which was the cause of her hay fever (in May, she always said that her ten percent German blood had now taken over her body, and she became even crabbier). Her last ten percent was "unknown." She would say that you'd have to take DNA samples from at least five billion people to find out where that ten percent came from. Anyway, what it boils down to was that she wasn't really a typical Dutch person. At work the Dutch tend to adhere to the motto "the rules are the rules," but Anneke would occasionally make an exception whenever she thought the situation demanded it, or if she really liked you.

"You," she said to Ridha. "Why do you look so angry?" She had no idea that he'd just been crying.

"Tell her what I just told you, out in the hall," Ridha said to me in Arabic.

"No, you tell and I'll translate."

"Do I have to go through it all over again?" Ridha looked even crabbier than Anneke.

"It's your story. You tell it, and I'll translate. Yes or no?" I said, crabby myself now, too.

"Listen," Anneke interjected firmly, "have you got a problem with each other?"

"No," I said.

"All right then. I haven't got the time to sit here listening to you two argue. Get going," she said, and pointed to the door.

"I coming here telling from that dog in that Y-19," Ridha said in broken Dutch. Anneke had enough experience with asylum seekers to understand not what they actually said, but what they were trying to say. If necessary, she delved directly into a person's mind—don't ask me how—and read his thoughts. Sometimes, though—I don't know why—she pretended she didn't understand.

"Dog? Is there a dog in Y-19?"

"He doesn't mean dog, he means pig, but maybe he doesn't know the Dutch word for pig," I said.

"Ja, pig. I wanting talk you from pig that living in Y-19."

"Pig, dog, rabbit ..." said Anneke. "You know it's forbidden to keep animals here."

"What's *mudjrim* in Dutch?" Ridha asked me.

"Criminal," I said.

"He is ..." and looked at me again.

"A criminal," I said.

"Criminal! Criminal! Pig! Filthy pig!" he shouted, and then continued ranting in Arabic, "Down with the Netherlands, that gives rooms to criminals in Yellow!" Ridha screamed and yelled, until Anneke yelled back even louder.

"Quiet, now! Mouth shut!" She looked ready to eat him alive. Taken aback, Ridha shut his mouth at once. He was suddenly no longer facing a woman, but a tigress. She looked at me and asked me to explain what was going on. I repeated what Ridha had told me out in the hall, because it was impossible to interpret for him without a whole lot of confusion. Then Anneke looked at Ridha. She asked him for his W-document, the asylum seeker's proof of ID. He gave it to her.

"You can go," she told us.

"What about my ID?"

"You'll get it back later."

This all took place during the walk-in hour at Social Services, between eight and nine in the morning, when you didn't need an appointment. That very same day, Ridha's bag was packed and ready to be moved to a different ASC.

"Did they give you back your W-document?" I asked.

"Yes, and a train ticket," he said. I walked with him to the station. He talked and I listened. This time it wasn't about General Abdul Galik al-Tikriti, but about the Hollanders. He went on about what had happened at Social Services, as though I hadn't been there with him.

"Can you believe what assholes these Hollanders are? I tell them that a pig is living in Y-19 and they say to me I have to learn to respect my fellow asylum seekers, and not to call them pigs. I tell them that there's a criminal in Y-19, and they say you're not supposed to call another asylum seeker a criminal. I tell them one of Saddam Hussein's henchmen now lives in Y-19, and they say you can't give any information about other asylum seekers, only about yourself."

23

This story about the general reminds me yet again of how unfairly things can go during an asylum procedure. Yes, the general was also just a human being, and his wife and children had nothing to do with his choices or his past, but still. It's not always fair. And I wasn't the only one who thought so.

After Ridha was gone, the story of General Abdul Galik al-Tikriti kept banging around in my head. Was what Ridha said true? It made me curious about this man. I once asked the son what their family name was.

"Al-Hassan," he replied. That was the official surname the general had given his children. I asked where they originally came from. "From Tikrit." So "Al-Tikrit" was right, because in Iraq, if people don't live in the city where they came from, they often add their hometown in this way. Sometimes this method of naming gets used more often than one's official surname.

At one of the translation sessions offered by the VVN (an NGO that defends the interests of asylum seekers in the Netherlands) I met Tamara, a volunteer in her early twenties. She worked there every Wednesday. The volunteers were usually older people, retirees, so it was unusual to see such a young woman. Tamara spoke perfect English. On the one hand, she was fearless, even visiting asylum seekers in their room, but on the other hand she was introverted and quiet. When you met her in the ASC she was outgoing and open and personable, ready to help you out, or to come drink something in your room, but if you saw her in town, she was an entirely different person. Closed. She would ignore asylum seekers on the street, and look away so she didn't have to greet them. Once I asked her if she was ashamed to speak to asylum seekers outside the ASC.

"Why do you ask?" was her answer.

"Because here, you're cheerful, but outside the camp you pretend you don't know us."

"That's because I'm uncomfortable with the whole asylum seeker situation," she said. "Here, I can deal with it, but not out there." When I told her her answer did not convince me, she invited me to go for a walk outside. Many more such walks would follow.

When we spoke, she would correct my English and teach me Dutch words. Tamara was a treasure chest, and the treasure itself could talk to me and explain things during those dark, doubt-filled days. She referred to the Social Services staffers as "the dog trainers" and to the Foreigners' Police as "the blue monsters." Most importantly, Tamara was a two-way mirror, allowing me to see both the humane aspects of the ASC and the inhumane ones. No matter what the ASC staff did, I felt, it was nothing compared to what happened to the Iraqis in Iraq under Saddam Hussein. For me, everything, including the Foreigners' Police and their occasional crackdowns, was necessary to keep those five hundred people in the ASC under control. Five hundred people with different languages, religions, backgrounds, and values. But Tamara would still compare the rigid treatment of the asylum seekers with the mild way the police treated Dutch people on the outside. Whenever I told her that the Foreigners' Police were a million times better than the police in Iraq, she would immediately blow her top. She'd stop dead in her tracks, look me in the eye, and start yelling.

"Don't be so stupid! That's a ridiculous comparison!"

"Why?"

"Because you are a person, Samir. And the Dutch people are too. The police have been taught to treat everyone the same: Dutch people, asylum seekers, illegals. Right?" Her face looked ready to explode.

"Believe me, Tamara, here in the ASC I get more respect than in Iraq," I said.

"If you think like that, then you're a real asylum seeker."

"That's right, I am."

"Then you'll have a rough time in Europe, because in that building they treat you like a wild dog that needs to be broken. If you don't see that, life outside the ASC will be impossible."

"Are you always so negative?"

"Since I started volunteering at the ASC, yes. Look, I was born and bred here, and never gave all those rules a second thought. But since I've been working at the ASC, I realize how inhuman the system can be."

"What's inhuman about the camp?"

"Just think, living somewhere for years without your own room or your own shower. No vacation, no right to have a dog or a cat. Not even allowed to work and earn your own money. Even prisons are better organized."

This is how our first conversations during walks outside the ASC went. Tamara never invited me to her home, even though she visited my room many times. Nor would she ever allow me to treat her to a drink in a café or bar.

Once, I was translating for an elderly Iraqi woman

whose basic health insurance did not cover an operation for carotid stenosis, the narrowing of the aorta. She hoped the VVN could help her find a charitable organization that would pay for the operation. As I was translating, my eyes glided over all those drawers full of dossiers, and I thought of Abdul Galik al-Tikriti. A few days later I saw Tamara leave the ASC and walked with her for a bit. I told her the story of the bloodthirsty general, as Ridha called him, and I asked Tamara if I could perhaps have a look in Abdul Galik al-Tikriti's dossier, to see if he really was a general. She said in a stern voice that this was forbidden, adding that she worked at the ASC to help asylum seekers, not to spy on them. I told her that if Ridha was right, then the man was not an asylum seeker, but a war criminal. She walked off without answering.

A few days later she told me to meet her at the dike at three o'clock that afternoon. At the appointed time and place, she opened her bag and handed me a stack of photocopies.

"Read this and don't tell a soul," she said. I paged through the papers then and there, standing on the dike. It was Abdul Galik al-Tikriti's dossier.

"Was he a general?" I asked.

"Yes, in the Iraqi army," she replied. She said he came from Tikrit, had studied in the Soviet Union, after which his career took off in Saddam Hussein's armed forces. I stood there blankly thumbing through the papers without really taking anything in. After a while she asked for them back, turned, and walked off.

The general became an eternal headache for me. Now I believed everything Ridha had said about him. But what baffled me was that I could be so bothered by this one unarmed general in the ASC, while in Iraq I had encountered thousands of soldiers and hundreds of generals. In an attempt to do something with this uneasy feeling, I went—like Ridha—to Social Services. Not to Anneke this time, but to Mark Douwes. He was one of the more easy-going staffers.

"I have information about the man in Y-19," I said. "He was a general in the Iraqi army. I know an asylum seeker who was an eyewitness to his war crimes."

Mark looked at me. "Do you mean Mr. A. al-Hassan?"

"Yes, him." Mark turned to his computer and asked for the name of the asylum seeker who claimed to be a witness. Then he got up and asked me to follow him to a separate room.

"Listen, Samir," he said, after I'd sat down at the table. "It's important to remember that in the Netherlands, an asylum seeker is only responsible for himself, and for his own story. No more than that. No asylum seeker in the Netherlands has the right to get involved with another asylum seeker's story."

"But this man is a war criminal, a murderer. He has no rights, not in the ASC or anywhere else."

"That's not for you or me to say. It's the job of the Immigration Department and the Justice Ministry. Mr. A. al-Hassan in Y-19 is their business, not ours."

"Could you please transfer me to another center? I can't live in the same building as a war criminal," I said, doing my best for it to sound like a polite request, and not as a demand.

"No, I can't," Mark said. "You can put your name on the list. The wait for a transfer is about three years." Seeing that this did not satisfy me, he added, "But you're not obliged to stay here. You can leave, if you like."

"With pleasure. Can I have my fingerprints back from the IND's computer, then? So I can ask for asylum in another country."

"You know that's not possible," he said, getting up. "I hope there won't be any problems between you and the man in Y-19?" It wasn't a question, but a statement, and that was the end of my conversation with Mark.

I did not cause any problems with A. al-Hassan, but Kadhem did. Ridha had, in his short time at the ASC, infected Kadhem with his ire. When Ridha left, Kadhem took over where Ridha left off. At first he would say, "Before that cow Anneke sent Ridha to another camp, he told me ..." and would go on to describe Ridha's anger and desperation. There wasn't a single Arabic-speaking asylum seeker who had not gotten an earful from Kadhem, and after that he proceeded, with the smattering of English and Dutch he had, to repeat everything he knew about the general in the halls of Orange, Yellow, and Blue. Not only to the asylum seekers, but to the volunteers in the canteen, the bicycle repair shop, and the library. After a while, when he talked about the general, it wasn't Ridha who was angry and desperate, but Kadhem himself. Eventually his story began with, "I saw it with my own eyes." Once everyone in the ASC had heard Kadhem, except the general himself, the problems between them started. It was more of a problem for Kadhem than for the general.

Kadhem was constantly on the lookout for the general by himself, without his wife and children. As soon as he caught sight of him, he would start spewing curses, or hissing and shouting. The general ignored him, and pretended not to have heard. Some asylum seekers tried to get Kadhem to stop, but then he would just repeat what he had heard from Ridha. In his tirades, the general was responsible for more and more victims, until all the wars, disasters, and rage in Iraq were the fault of that one general in our ASC.

One day I was in line to sign in with the Foreigners' Police. Kadhem was in front of me.

"Well, look who's there. The murderer," Kadhem said loudly in Arabic. I turned and saw the general join the back of the line. He was alone. He never signed in together with his wife or children. The general must have heard what Kadhem said, but he did not react, as though it wasn't about him. "In Iraq they made our lives a living hell. And now that we've fled they come here to make our lives hell all over again," Kadhem said angrily, staring straight at the general, who busied himself with a sheaf of papers and appeared not to hear. "The criminal, the general," Kadhem said in Iraqi dialect. "He stands here pretending not to notice or understand anything, because his Saddam Hussein, the bastard, isn't here." He started to raise his voice. The quieter and calmer the general became, the more it wound Kadhem up.

"You," said the officer behind the counter, pointing at Kadhem. Kadhem pointed both thumbs questioningly at his chest.

"Me?" he asked, surprised.

"Yes, you," answered the officer. "Keep your voice down." The man turned to talk to someone else, and Kadhem continued, just loud enough for the general to hear, but not the officer.

"Me? Did I say something? Saddam Hussein's general spoke, not me." He kept at it, repeating all kinds of swear words that cannot be translated with the same effect, but were the basest words you could use to insult someone with.

"You there," the officer shouted from behind his window. Kadhem glowered at him. "In the corner." By then, Kadhem was so angry that no corner in all of the Netherlands, or in the entire world for that matter, could intimidate him.

"No corner, mister," Kadhem shouted back. "He general corner sit!" he yelled, pointing at the general. "Murderer! Murderer!"

Two policemen came out into the hallway. They ordered Kadhem to stand facing the wall, but he started screaming, "Murderer! The murderer corner sit general murderer! Corner general murderer Saddam corner Hussein!" One of the policemen wrestled Kadhem to the ground. Blood dripped from his nose. His hands were pulled behind him and he was held down while the other policemen cuffed his hands behind his back. We stood in line and watched all this out of the corners of our eyes. They pulled Kadhem upright, but he wouldn't stand up on his own, so they dragged him down the hall and outside.

After signing in, I would check Kadhem's room to see if he was back yet, but he only reappeared a few days later, early in the morning. A few days in the custody of the Foreigners' Police seemed to have tamed him, because for a while he did not utter a word about the general. The saddest thing I heard in my whole nine years in that building is what Kadhem said to me one rainy day. We were sitting at the window in the orange hall, looking out at the grayness.

"Just imagine," he said, and looked at me as if he had thought long and hard about what he wanted to say. "I have more respect for Saddam Hussein now."

"Why?"

"Whoever works for him has power. Even here." It was

painfully simple logic. Those words wounded Kadhem's throat as they came out, like rusty nails. We stared outside, and after a brief silence he suddenly said, as though he regretted saying something good about Saddam Hussein, "But maybe the Dutch authorities don't know that Abdul Galik al-Tikriti was an Iraqi general."

"They know," I whispered.

"How do you know they know?" The question mark was more evident in his eyes than in his words.

"I got a look at a copy of his first interview," I said.

"Stolen?"

"More or less."

"The bastards. They know." I immediately regretted telling him.

24

One person I will not forget, but certainly won't miss, is Sayid from Mosul, Iraq. The asylum seekers suspected Sayid of spying on us and telling everything he knew to the director of the ASC, to Social Services, and to the IND. I knew for sure the Dutch people did not ask him to, but rather, he did so of his own free will, because this was just the way he was. He was simply a blabbermouth. Sayid was in his twenties, with his hair combed up in front. He spoke Dutch and English in addition to Arabic. In those days I didn't know yet what the internet was, but now I can assure you that Sayid was the Google of the ASC. He knew everything, wanted to know everything, and was prepared to pass everything on. Whether this was his way of getting attention, or whether his soul was poisoned, I don't know. You can only comprehend Sayid if you're an Iraqi, because in Iraq there are a lot of people like him, well trained by Saddam Hussein. I'm sorry, but I have to tell you a joke now that explains the new Iraqi spirit, which Saddam Hussein created between 1968 and 2003 to pit Iraqis against one another, and to begrudge each other everything: Two Iraqis are given the death sentence. They ask the first Iraqi what his last wish is. He says, "I want to see my mother before I die." Then they ask the second Iraqi what his last wish is, and he says, "That he does not see his mother." If you understand this joke, then you're halfway to understanding Iraq's problems.

If you didn't know him well, you'd think Sayid was a good guy. He got along with all the asylum seekers, with all nationalities. Being open, but also being a crafty sycophant, made it look like he fit in. The Dutch people, too, were always overly friendly to him, and there was an air of special treatment. It was for this very reason that the asylum seekers assumed he was spying on them.

Residents often saw Sayid leaving the director's office, a place off-limits to any other asylum seeker. He would often chat with the Social Services staffers, but so did other asylum seekers who spoke good English or Dutch. At first there was some doubt as to Sayid's connection with the Hollanders, but after Serdar decided to sew his lips together, that doubt evaporated, and everyone's suspicions were confirmed.

Serdar, a Kurdish asylum seeker, had been in the ASC for thirteen years when he decided to sew his lips shut. He definitely had help doing it, but only a few people knew that it was his friend Arshad. Serdar himself was obviously in no position to say who it was. The situation was tricky for the staff at the ASC, because when Social Services called in the Foreigners' Police, and they went to Serdar's room, they were surprised to see a woman there who had been brought into the ASC posing as a visitor. Their hands were tied, because the woman was a journalist. She showed them a slip of paper Serdar had given her. On it was written, in Serdar's handwriting and in Dutch, that he had sewn his lips together so he would die of hunger, because that was better than waiting any longer than the thirteen years he had already spent in the procedure. The journalist was removed from the ASC, but there was already a television crew waiting at the gate. So Serdar's story trickled into the media, and there was nothing Social Services, the IND, or the Foreigners' Police could do about it. Serdar had organized it well.

That day, I heard Sayid say he couldn't possibly have sewn his lips together himself, but on the day it happened, Arshad had been looking for a small needle to mend a shirt. So less than an hour later, Arshad was summoned to Social Services, and later we heard he'd been punished: his W-document was confiscated and his pocket money withheld for a month.

I'll never forget Serdar's sewn-up mouth. It looked gruesome, and the children in the ASC thought so, too. At first they got close to him and stared in amazement, but when his lips started to swell and his face took on a strange look, they avoided the orange wing, for fear of bumping into him. If they saw Serdar coming, they would run away or dive into the nearest room.

Dorine Janssen, Serdar's contact person from Social Services, visited his room regularly in an attempt to open a dialogue with him. And although Serdar spoke good Dutch, Dorine asked one of the other Kurds to translate what she said into Kurdish, and asked me to translate into Arabic, which he also spoke fluently.

"I don't think it's wise to keep your lips sewn shut," Dorine said in her pleasant, compassionate voice. Her face seemed to mirror the pain his lips must have been in. Serdar wrote something in Arabic on a scrap of paper and gave it to me, so that I could read aloud. I let my eyes fall upon the paper, but didn't want Dorine to see my reaction, so I did not look up right away. She asked me what it said.

"For thirteen years you people have sewed my lips together in this place, and that was never a problem. Now I've done it myself, and you don't want me to. Why?" Then Serdar added to the note that he would only allow them to remove the stitches if the IND would act on his asylum request, and that if they did so forcibly, his Dutch friends outside the ASC would contact the media. He pulled out a newspaper from the drawer under his bed and handed it to Dorine. In it was an article with a photograph of his maimed face. Dorine looked at the photo, and with a serious expression she got up and left.

Shortly thereafter, instead of someone from Social Services, a woman from the medical clinic started coming by. She always brought a scale with her, to weigh him. She was perplexed by the fact that Serdar did not lose any weight, even though he was unable to eat. When she asked him about it, he did not reply by note, and from that moment on, he refused to get on the scale. Soon enough, Sayid started spreading a rumor among the asylum seekers that he'd seen one of the Kurdish men buy little straws through which Serdar was able to drink soup. Sayid was careful about the way he spread this gossip, because he had seen first-hand how violent Serdar could be if you riled him.

A few days later, a man with a necktie and briefcase— he was from the IND—came, together with an interpreter, to have a word with Serdar via written notes. The interview, which lasted for more than two hours, took place in his room, because Serdar refused to go anywhere else. After that visit from the IND, Serdar finally agreed to go to a hospital, but he wouldn't tell anyone why. At about four o'clock an ambulance drove up, and to our surprise, Serdar had all his belongings with him.

25

Kristi was a beautiful African woman. I can't remember which country she came from. She had a son, Jimmy, who was at least five, because he went to school. Kristi was a twenty-three-year-old woman when she wasn't talking, but when she did talk, she was a volcano, or an earthquake. The way she spoke was like boxing. When she spoke English, she often repeated the words *fuck* or *fucking* or *ass*. She had similar favorites in Dutch, many of them based on private body parts. Kristi usually started talking in Dutch, and when her command of the Dutch language petered out she would continue in English. But first she would briefly summarize in English what she had just said in Dutch. Kristi was the only woman in all those years who went to the shower room in her underwear, as though the ASC was her own house. And in the summer, she was one of the very few who went to the beach (she would go with Yelena) in a bikini to swim and sunbathe. She was perhaps the only woman who believed that the ASC was not only a place to wait or to go crazy in, but also to live.

Kristi always managed to get a line moving. Once we were waiting to sign in, and as usual, the officer behind the window was chatting with a colleague—sorry to be repetitive, but this situation, or a variation on it, happened a lot. So up comes Kristi, like a black tigress, joining the line at the rear. But when she noticed the line wasn't moving, she addressed the asylum seeker in front of her, as if it were his fault the line wasn't moving.

"What are you standing there for? Why aren't you moving?" The person in front of her gestured to the person in front of him.

"And you, then?" she would shout at the next in line. "Why isn't this line moving? I haven't got all day." He in turn would point gingerly at the person in front of him. That was me.

"Hey, how long you been standing in this fucking line already?"

"More than twenty minutes," I mouthed, so the man behind the window wouldn't hear me, and my afternoon wouldn't end "in the corner" or in a cell.

"More than twenty minutes?!" she said loudly. I gestured for her to come stand in front of me, and the asylum seeker in front of her did the same, and so it went with each person in line. In less than thirty seconds she was standing right up front at the window.

"Sir! Sir!" she called. The officer turned to see who was addressing him. As soon as they made eye contact, she screamed, "I want to sign in. I've been standing in this fucking line for more than twenty minutes. And on top of that I'm having my period and I have a headache. And I have a child that has to be picked up from school and I have to do the grocery shopping and cook for him. I'm busy, not like you, just sitting here all day at that fucking computer." When she realized she was spending more energy searching for Dutch words than being angry, she became even angrier and switched to half-Dutch, half-English.

"I wanna sign in, I have a child. I have my period. And the money I get from this fucking country is not enough to buy him and me food. And the other children in school make fun of him because I cannot buy him normal clothes. I cannot even buy *maandverband* for my period. If I stand here any longer, blood will start dripping on the floor and that is not healthy. Is it?" Her voice filled not only the office, but the hallway and the entire ASC. The officer checked her W-documents and signed her in, and the dead line came to life. That was Kristi. Don't get the impression that she was ill-humored. It's just how she was. There was not a system on earth that could tame her.

One summer day, while I was walking down the hall in Yellow, I heard her call after me from her room.

"Hey, hey, Iraqi, come in here." Only her head and her hand stuck through the door opening. I went over to her, but at the last moment I didn't dare go in. Kristi was wearing only a yellow bikini bottom. Her bare breasts in her room made me nervous. I was not prepared for such a situation. This was Yellow, the wing where families live. Usually all you heard were crying children or the clatter of cooking pans. My head was in her room, and my body in the hallway, and she was looking at a box full of bikinis on the floor.

"Come in," she said. "What, are you afraid I'm going to fuck you or something?" I went in and left the door ajar, as though I might need to make a quick escape. She dug in the box for the yellow top, put it on, and looked in the mirror—the same mirror I had carried here myself for her, after she'd bought it at the thrift store.

"Nice?" she asked, turning in front of the mirror. "Yeah, nice. But it reminds me of all that yellow in this fucking building. Ah, from the minute I set foot in this fucking building, I hate this fucking yellow." She took off the yellow bikini, I looked the other way, and when I turned back she was wearing an orange bikini, taken from the box she had bought for three euros at the thrift store. "What do you think, is this one nicer?" she asked, without looking at me. I looked at her body and felt a fire starting to burn inside me. Soon, smoke would be coming out of my ears.

"Please, Kristi, no orange bikini. Ever since I've been living in the orange wing of this building, I hate everything orange, including the Dutch soccer team and Valencia oranges. That's why I have a vitamin c deficiency." She laughed out loud and did another spin in front of the mirror. Without wanting to, I fantasized that she was posing for me, and not for the mirror. Suddenly she turned to me and yelled, her face taut with anger, "What are you doing in here? In my room? I'm changing and need a little privacy and you come on barging in here! You really are a fucking asylum seeker!"

"You called me," I said. "I was just walking down the hall and you called me."

"I did?"

"I don't know why, but yes, you called me."

"So why are you here without knowing why I called you? Why didn't you ask me from the hall why I called you and what I wanted? Why do you just charge into the room of a single woman who's changing? And furthermore, you live in the fucking orange wing. What are you doing in Yellow?!"

"I don't remember," I said, and thought how totally out of place her beautiful body was with her angry face.

"And now?" she said with a suddenly dramatic intonation, as though I had made her life an unbearable hell for two unhappy decades of marriage. "And now ... Pleeeeease get out. And don't disturb me anymore. Just because I live in this fucking building doesn't mean that everybody can come waltzing into my room while

I'm naked." I grabbed my chance, and left. I was afraid she'd start hitting me, or would scream and attract the attention of everyone in the wing.

Back in the hall, two opposing feelings bounced between my ears, and it hurt. On the one hand, I wanted to throw myself on top of her and make love to her, and on the other hand I wanted to run like mad and never lay eyes on her again. I hadn't taken more than a few steps when she called me again. I did not answer. She ran after me in her orange bikini, grabbed my hand, dragged me back to her room and shut the door. I nearly exploded, thinking she wanted to have sex with me after all, but then, why she had just chased me out of the room? Now that her expression had changed from angry to adorable, naive, and needy, I suddenly felt as if I had a thousand tons of nerve. Now all I had to do was summon that last ounce, to touch her, to kiss her, or throw her to the floor and make love to her. But before I had scraped together that last little ounce of courage, she told me with a sweet voice that she remembered why she had called me.

"Can you please pick up my son from school and bring him to the showers at the beach?"

"Sure, but will the school allow it?"

"Just say you're his father."

"That's impossible, it's obvious that his father is black, too."

"You're right," she said, handing me her W-document. "Take this to the teacher and tell her I've got a broken arm."

"And what if the teacher sees you lying on the beach tomorrow in your orange bikini?"

"These Hollanders are crazy," she said. "Crazy and dumb. I've seen that teacher so many times in town, and she doesn't recognize me and doesn't say hello." So I took her W-document to school and brought Jimmy to the showers at the beach.

26

Kristi managed to turn me into a father. At first she asked me to pick Jimmy up from school "once in a while." Then, once in a while became regularly, and regularly quickly turned into often. She not only wanted me to fetch Jimmy from school, but also to pose as his father. When I told her that this was impossible, that the teacher wouldn't believe me, she would go along with it for a bit, only to turn around and ask me again to pretend to be Jimmy's father. Dutch people, she claimed, did not look at a child's color, and anyway, there were plenty of blond Hollanders walking around with black children. Jimmy himself didn't seem too interested in having a father. If it were up to him, he would not have a mother either. But Kristi kept begging.

"Pleeeeease, will you pick Jimmy up from school? I'm too tired." So I did, because I liked having something to do outside the ASC. It wasn't long before she stopped asking, and started ordering me to fetch Jimmy. Once she saw me leaving my room holding a toiletries bag.

"Hey, Iraqi!" she yelled. "No shower now! Go pick up my son first, then shower."

One day she asked Jimmy, when we got back from school, if he had called me "Papa" at the school gate. When he said no, she smacked him and started yelling.

"Listen! From now on, when he comes to pick you up, you shout 'Papa! Papa!' and run over to him. Got it?" Later, I told Jimmy he didn't have to, but he could tell his mother that he did. Lying to his mother was better than getting smacked, and better than lying to himself. This is how I became Jimmy's father. Eventually I figured out her reasoning behind all this. Having a child at a Dutch school is a huge hassle, and now Kristi could send me to school whenever anything was up with Jimmy.

Jimmy's teacher, Miss Nanda, wasn't all that bad; in fact, she was great, and very pretty. I often sat alone with her in the classroom, discussing Jimmy for a quarter of an hour. She talked seriously about Jimmy, with responsibility and compassion. I gazed at her, and watched how she brushed her bangs out of her eyes. If what I could see of her was so marvelous, I thought, how delicious must the rest be? It also occurred to me that Jimmy being at a Dutch school saddled him with a big problem: he was stuck between an African mother who wanted to make an African man out of him, and a Dutch teacher who wanted to make a Dutchman out of him. Pretty soon he'd be neither. What would Jimmy become? This thought vexed me, but I also hoped Jimmy would continue to be a troublemaker, so that I could have many more of these quarter-hours with Miss Nanda.

Miss Nanda's looks excited me so much that I started offering to fetch Jimmy from school. I was prepared to be not only Jimmy's father, but his mother, too, if it meant being able to see Miss Nanda.

About seven months later, Miss Nanda informed me that it was her last week at the school, and that Hans would be taking over Jimmy's class. When I asked her if I could invite her for a cup of tea, she smiled.

"That's not a good idea, because you've got a beautiful wife and a beautiful child."

I thought it was nice of the Dutch parents in the schoolyard not to ask how come I had a black child. But it was the mini-dates with this unforgettable woman that taught me that there was more to the Netherlands than the ASC.

27

One day, I was walking outdoors and saw Najat pushing the baby stroller towards our building. I looked at little Milaad, who was born the same day I arrived at the ASC. Now he was already big enough to sit up in the stroller.

"Look at this one, will you," I said with a lump in my throat. She thought I was talking about her son, instead of about my own wait.

"How old is he now?" I asked her, because I wanted to know how long I'd been here.

"Do you want to know when his birthday is, so you can buy him a present?" she asked in Tunisian Arabic. I stared at the little boy, who smiled and fidgeted with his hands. "In three weeks and one day he'll be a year old," she said, and headed for the entrance, because it had started to rain. I stood there. So I'd been in this building for almost a year without hearing anything from the IND or the Justice Ministry. It was starting to eat me up. I had to get out of here.

"Want me to bring you some shampoo, Samir?" Sayid joked as he passed me on his way inside. I followed him in.

I don't really know how to explain what happened to me then. It was like I'd been asleep for months, and had woken up in a world I didn't know. I looked around me, confused. Like when you spin around in circles, and suddenly stop, but your head wants to keep on spinning and escape from the rest of your body. Little Milaad became the symbol of my waiting. It was like I could look my wait straight in the eyes.

Zainab, the Iraqi woman with the sewing machine, was standing in her black clothes at the counter, while Wouter, the receptionist, tried to make it clear to her that there was no mail today. Then he explained for the umpteenth time what the IND was, to which she replied, with her pathetic voice, "What? What? What?" over and over. I walked further and saw Fatima with a plate full of snacks, trudging from the Social Services office to the Foreigners' Police, then to Reception and after that to the Dutch volunteers, offering everyone a taste and hoping to maybe get a residence permit in return. At O-139 I stuck my key sluggishly into the lock. My room-mate Walid was lying on his back, wearing only his trousers. His belly was a hairy bulge. I lay down on my bed and wished it would sink through the orange wing deep into the earth.

"Are you sick?" Walid asked.

"I'm not sure," I said. "Maybe." I was sweating, and my body was on fire.

"You look pale. I'll go get you some aspirin from Reception." Walid put on a shirt and his slippers, and returned with a glass of water and two pills. I swallowed them and draped a towel over my face. I heard an unfamiliar voice say, "Do you want another aspirin?" Was it the Fourth, back from lockdown?

"No," I said.

"What?" Walid asked. I removed the towel from my face and saw Walid standing over me. "You were talking in your sleep." I put the towel back and fell asleep. I dreamt. My brother and I were on our donkeys, riding under the date palms on our way to school. Not to take classes, but to stamp out the ashes, because we had burned down the building the day before.

That's how it went in our village. The villagers had built the school out of reeds, clay, and date-palm leaves. During lessons we sat on a carpet of palm leaves. The blackboard was tall and narrow, and the teacher would use the top half, while the bottom rested on the ground. My brother and I were first-year students but also last-year ones, because you learned everything from the other students, and nothing from the teacher.

But now it was harvest time, and just like every other year, the blackboard and palm-leaf carpet were removed from the school, and the students and parents then set fire to the building. This practice started after the government instigated compulsory education, including during harvest time. The villagers had a problem with this new rule. Their solution was to burn down the school, so the children could help out with the harvest, simply because there was no school to go to. Once the harvest season was over, everyone got together and rebuilt the school in a single afternoon.

Our donkeys knew the way through the date palms, and my brother and I looked forward to seeing a layer of ashes on the site of our school. Emerging from the palm grove, we could see the hill where the school once stood. There was a new teacher that year, and he stood there with a few students and fathers.

"Don't worry," one father said to the teacher. "After the harvest, we'll rebuild it."

"But the children will miss so many lessons," the teacher fretted.

"But not their brains," another father said. "It'll be fine."

"Fortunately there were no children inside."

"What do you think?! That we'd burn down the school with children in it? We even removed the blackboard and carpet."

"Does this happen often?"

The fathers looked at each other, surprised.

"Of course. Every year."

"But why?"

"Because of the harvest. Only then," said a father.

And my brother and I turned our donkeys around and disappeared back into the palm grove. The sun shone high in the sky, birds chirped, and the clear water of the Euphrates flowed and sang at the same time.

I awakened from a deep sleep. I was sweating. It was six in the evening.

"You were talking in your sleep," Walid said.

"What did I say?"

"The only thing I could understand was *donkey*," he said. I tried to sit up, but my muscles were frozen. I closed my eyes, fell back to sleep and woke up four hours later. I went to Reception, took two aspirins, and paced up and down the hallways among the ghosts of the ASC. I tried to convince myself that I only had a fever and wasn't losing my mind.

"I'm not staying here," I told myself. The idea of leaving felt like a cool breeze blowing into a stuffy cell. If staying in the Netherlands was so difficult, it should make leaving all that much easier.

28

I tried in vain to reach my lawyer, to see if he could help
me leave the Netherlands. I asked Albertina to call him.
She did get through, and told me he said his job was to
help me stay in the Netherlands, not leave it. I went to
Social Services and talked to Anneke, because she was
the one with the most experience. She said my only
option was to return to Iraq. Then she said she could
give me a day ticket for the train, so I could get to the
Dutch border for free, because she secretly did want to
help me. She advised me to go to the VVN. There, Wim
told me it was impossible to have my fingerprints
removed from the IND's computers. If I wanted to go
back to Iraq, the Dutch government would give me a
plane ticket.

At the IND they said I couldn't approach them directly,
but had to go through my lawyer, Social Services, or the
VVN. So I ended up back at Social Services, this time
with Annelies Vos. Annelies said she hadn't been working with asylum seekers for so long, and that I would be
better off asking Anneke, so back to Anneke I went. She
said that I had just asked her the same thing two months
earlier, and that I shouldn't keep coming back with the
same question, and that maybe I should try the VVN or
the IND or my lawyer, or maybe the United Nations, the
UN. That "UN" was a new word in the closed circle I had
been running around in, like a hamster on a treadmill,

for more than two months, and so it felt like a way out. Albertina told me there was an expression for this: *being sent from pillar to post.*

"Are you the pillar or the post?" I asked Anneke, who directed me to the vvn with a smile and a nudge. At the vvn—Wim was there, as always, and this time Tamara, too—I asked if they could call the United Nations for me, to get my fingerprints back from the IND. Tamara said she could try, but doubted they would be able to help because the UN had its hands full with millions of refugees who didn't even have a tent, a blanket, or a hunk of bread. My problem was, you might say, a luxury problem.

"Can I ask you something?" Tamara said. I nodded. "You haven't been in the Netherlands for very long. Why do you want to leave?"

"To keep it that way," I replied.

On the way back to O-139, I felt I needed to recharge my spirit in order to be able to stay in this building. A while later I went to take a shower. I closed my eyes and turned on the cold faucet. The water hit me like whips.

"Aaaaaaahhh," I screamed.

"Is the water too cold?" someone called back.

"Not the water. This country," I called back. Fifteen minutes later I was standing in line to sign in.

29

Before I can go further with my story, there's something else important that needs to be explained: the workings of an ASC is one huge misunderstanding between the asylum seekers themselves, and between the asylum seekers and the Dutch people who work there.

For example: making friends with Dutch people outside the ASC was impossible for asylum seekers, because they rarely spoke Dutch well enough to make contact. This is why the asylum seekers taught the locals their own language called "Asylumseekerese." This language is, in a nutshell, a few words of Dutch and a few words of English, all jumbled up and put back together in the grammar of the asylum seeker's mother tongue. Russian, Arabic, Romanian, Persian, Kurdish, Portuguese, Turkish, Somali—you name it. If an asylum seeker wants to say he saw an old man sitting on the grass, then you won't understand him if you don't speak Asylumseekerese. Then you would think he said "old grass with sitting man on the gray hair," or "old grass saw man sitting," or "the sitting on an old man is grass." If you spent a week at an ASC and noted down what you heard, you could publish a collection of modern poetry. Communicating with an asylum seeker is simple if, instead of trying to understand what he says, you try to understand what he is trying to say.

Additionally, you should know that most asylum seekers—I shouldn't say all—are putting on an act.

Because the people-smugglers say that Dutch immigration officials purposely make asylum interviews more difficult for educated people, and therefore diminish their chances for a residence permit, many think they'll be better off by claiming to be uneducated.

The result is lots of highly educated asylum seekers claiming to have only finished primary school, and hoping that this will facilitate their procedure. Most say they were laborers or farmers, with the exception of the few who could verify their story with official papers, or those who, like me, just didn't know to lie about their background.

I know a professor at the University of Baghdad who said in his asylum interview that he had been a concierge at the university. He made this up because he knew the university well, and walked through the front door every day. To say he was a professor would have made his interview far too complicated, but for a concierge the report would only be a page or two.

When I confessed to this professor that I had told the immigration people I was a civil engineer, he groaned, "Then the IND has it in for you." This proved to be correct: my first and second hearings were a good twenty times longer than his. We were asked the same questions, so that wasn't it, but in my case it was like running an obstacle course in the dark. As though an engineer was expected to know and remember every detail from the moment he fled to the moment he sat there across from the immigration officer. But not so a concierge at the University of Baghdad.

So the fact that many asylum seekers were putting on an act was amusing for the asylum seekers themselves, but tricky for the Dutch staffers. If someone had told the IND that he had been tortured in his home country and consequently suffered from PTSD, then he kept up the charade in the ASC. Among ourselves he behaved normally, but as soon as there was a Dutch person around, even a volunteer, he would act crazy. You would often see an asylum seeker look over his shoulder, and change his behavior if he saw a Dutch person coming. Someone who claimed to be terrified of the secret service in his own country would pretend to wake up terrified at night in a cold sweat. In time, however, asylum seekers actually became what they were pretending to be.

There was a Syrian asylum seeker named Zuhair. He had told the IND that the Syrian secret service had tortured him by forcing him to bang his head against the wall, and that even now he still heard the secret service in his head, screaming at him to bang his head against the wall. You wouldn't believe how often Zuhair stood banging his head against the walls of the ASC. At first he only did this in his room, but his roommates told him to stop because it was bothering them. Zuhair insisted that he really did hear the screaming of the secret service, but they didn't believe him, and said he should go do it in the hall outside Social Services. So he did, but Anneke came out of the office, angry, and said that he was welcome to bang his head against a wall, but not against the glass partition.

Then there was Nabil from Iraq. He had told the IND in his first and second hearings that he had been beaten on the head, and since then had terrible headaches. He never asked for mail at Reception, only for aspirin. And he was constantly bothering the staff at the medical clinic. Whenever there were Dutch people around, he would groan from the pain, press a tablet out of the blister pack and swallow it with a bottle of water. But when there were no Dutch people in sight, we would see him toss the aspirin into the garbage. After a few months, however, Nabil began to get genuine headaches, and started to take the aspirin even when there weren't any Dutch people around.

The best actor of all was Baback, an Iranian who had applied for asylum as an Iraqi. I have no earthly idea how he managed to convince the IND that he was an Iraqi, seeing as he didn't speak a word of Arabic, let alone the Iraqi dialect.

Baback did have an incredible command of Asylum-seekerese, though. In the eight years he lived in the ASC, he learned a bit of Dutch but also a few words of Arabic, a few words of English, and a smattering of Chechen, Romanian, Chinese, Russian, French, and Portuguese. This was the language mix with which he communicated with the world. With Iranians and Afghans he spoke fluent Farsi, and his face would change—it softened, as if speaking Farsi gave his facial muscles time to relax. The Iranians said that even though he spoke their language, he was not Iranian, and the Afghans likewise said he was not one of them. Since he had claimed asylum as an Iraqi, and I came from Iraq, Baback was eager for the Dutch people in the ASC to see us in conversation together, so they would believe his story. So I would always have to listen to Baback and pretend to understand what he said. I would nod as he babbled in his unintelligible language. But the upshot was just the opposite of what Baback intended, because instead of assuming Baback came from Iraq, the staff at the ASC assumed that I spoke Farsi.

30

One day I saw Tobias, the receptionist, run toward the front door, followed by a slew of asylum seekers. Doors started to open, more asylum seekers ran outside; some thought there was a fire, some ran simply because the others were running. I also hurried to Reception and went outside, and saw what all the ruckus was about: a man was standing on a window ledge on the fourth floor.

I had never seen him before. Not while signing in, not at Social Services, not in the hallways. A hermit.

"He's gonna jump out of the window!" a child shouted. I looked back up at the man standing on the ledge and holding onto the window frame. He was looking up calmly at the sky. He did not want to jump, but rather to fly away.

Everyone's eyes were glued on the window of room B-51. Half the ASC, the entire Social Services, the receptionists, and the Foreigners' Police. Passersby peered through the tall gate. A police car arrived, three officers got out and spoke to the Social Services people. Shortly thereafter, a second police car with two more officers pulled up.

"He won't jump," I heard one asylum seeker say. "He did this once before, and when the police went to his room, he let them take him away."

I looked up at the man in his black jogging pants and white T-shirt. It seemed like he was planning to stay there for a while. When Yvonne from Social Services went into the building with three police officers, all went quiet. This lasted about seven minutes, and then the man jumped. There was a scream. I don't know if it was the man himself, or someone else. Then a thud on the ground. We all ran over and stood around him in a circle. He lay on his stomach, his face cocked to one side. I looked up. Yvonne and the three police officers were looking down from the window.

In the nine years I lived in the ASC, eight asylum seekers committed suicide. This one affected me the most, because it was the first, and because it happened in front of my eyes. It was probably even worse for the children who were standing right in front of the building. I will never forget the silence that reigned in the ASC after that. A terrible silence, as if nothing, not even shoes in the hallway, could make a noise. Not even a faucet that someone forgot to turn off. For days, you didn't hear a single child laugh, a woman call out, or a man shout.

Everyone was surprised that the man, who was named Dagel and came from Iraq, actually jumped. His procedure had only been going for four years. Normally, asylum seekers only start committing suicide after the fifth or sixth year. Even long before he jumped, Dagel kept to himself, coming out of his room only to shower or use the toilet. He did nothing. He no longer signed in. He no longer bought groceries. Mr. Van 't Zijde, his contact person, often went to B-51, and he made an appointment for Dagel at Social Services. But Dagel never went. Mr. Van 't Zijde would then go back to B-51, this time with a different interpreter, to make sure Dagel understood that he had to go to Social Services to explain why he had stopped signing in as we were required to do. Again Dagel did not show up. So then Mr. Van 't Zijde took away Dagel's bank card (where his weekly pocket money was deposited), made a new appointment, and told Dagel his W-document would be confiscated if he didn't come to Social Services, and that he'd get his bank pass back at the meeting. Dagel didn't go, so Mr. Van 't Zijde took Dagel's W-document as well, and ordered him to come with him right then, otherwise he would call the Foreigners' Police. Dagel wouldn't go, and Mr. Van 't Zijde called the Foreigners' Police. Before they arrived at the ASC, Dagel stepped out onto the ledge of room B-51 for the first time, and looked up at the sky. They dragged him back inside and took him away with his hands cuffed behind his back. A few weeks later Dagel returned from the lockup. From that day on, he stood at the counter at eight o'clock sharp to sign in, so he was always the first in line.

I was curious about Dagel, who I saw for the first time just before he jumped. So a few days later I walked from Orange to Blue, and went to B-51. The room had been cleared out and someone was repainting the walls, even though everything looked white and clean. Dagel's three roommates had been called to Social Services, where they were told they did not have to sign in for a month, and after that they could be transferred to another ASC, or another room, if they wanted. They would also be given two train day-passes per week during that month. I wanted to talk to one of them about Dagel, but no one saw them again. After B-51 had been repainted, the doors and windows were left open for a few days, and then the room was sealed off for the rest of the month. After that it was filled with four new asylum seekers.

Seeing Dagel jump made me realize I had been in the ASC for too long, and I had to get out of there soon. I was shocked, because in Iraq, with all the wars, pain, resentment, and fear, I'd never once met anyone who considered suicide. But here, in a building with an open door and surrounded by a grassy lawn, a man threw himself from a fourth-floor window.

My apologies for telling you about so many different asylum seekers. But their stories in the ASC are inextricably linked to my own. Every one of their stories is also my story. We are like the principle of communicating vessels: when I talk about them, I am talking about myself.

31

Yelena was standing outside the door to her room. She was wearing glasses. "Do you still go the sea sometimes?" she asked.

"Only to steal a bike," I replied. It was meant as a joke, but she turned and marched back into her room. When the water kettle whistled, she came out and went to the kitchen.

"So when do you go to the sea?" she asked, as though I had just told her I went there every day.

"After I've had my tea."

"I'll go with you," she said. Later, after I'd drunk my tea, I was leaving the ASC grounds and saw her sitting on a bench near the gate. I walked past her, and she called out for me to wait.

"Life in the camp is becoming unbearable," she said. "The four Russian books I own, I've already re-read a thousand times. I thought of going to a hostel, but it was too expensive and besides, they asked for my ID card. As soon as they saw my W-document, the receptionist looked at it suspiciously, front and back, and then called someone over to explain what it was."

We had arrived at the sea before I knew it.

A few weeks later, I saw Yelena in the kitchen, smiling. She told me she had a boyfriend. A Dutch guy named Maarten. It was like she'd finally gotten a residence permit. At that time I was planning my escape from the Netherlands. So while I was trying to make

Yelena a long-ago memory, she kept finding me in the ASC and talking about Maarten, a blond beanpole more than six feet tall. She started sleeping at his place, and after a while only showed up at the ASC to sign in. Sometimes Maarten dropped her off, sometimes she came alone. She carried a small snapshot of Maarten in her wallet, and showed it to everyone. The other asylum seekers regarded Maarten's photo as Yelena's residence permit.

I remember the first time I saw Maarten in real life. We were standing in line to sign in, and as usual it was not moving. Yelena joined the back of the line. Every once in a while she checked the wristwatch Maarten had bought for her. Suddenly the real Maarten appeared.

"Good morning," he greeted the line. And to Yelena: "I thought you'd be done already." She said she'd been standing there for a while. We watched as Maarten walked up to the counter, and leaned his head close to the window. He asked the officer if Yelena could sign in. The officer, for whom we had been waiting for a good twenty minutes, smiled back.

"Just a sec," he said, and called the first asylum seeker in line, and then the rest of us. Within two minutes everyone, including Yelena, had signed in. She strutted proudly, hand in hand with Maarten, out of the ASC.

Shortly thereafter she offered to let me sleep in her room whenever I wanted to be alone.

"All my things are in the cupboard. It's locked."

It was wonderful, after such a long time, to be able to sleep without other people's snoring, nightmares, and breathing, because since landing at Schiphol I hadn't experienced this, except in a cell. I was happy. I could roll over in bed as much as I wanted. I could sit the way I wanted. I looked at the walls: they surrounded me, and me alone, and for that reason they were, for that moment, my personal property, and not my prison.

A few days later, Sayid asked me how much I paid Yelena to sleep in her room. How he knew I was sleeping there, I don't know, because I sneaked there late at night when no one would see. Some days after that, Mr. Van 't Zijde told me it was forbidden to sleep in another room, and that he'd told Yelena this too. Sayid had obviously snitched on me. So I enjoyed her bed for only a few days. But even without her in it, Yelena's bed had made the ASC a heavenly place.

32

The hope of requesting asylum in a country other than the Netherlands was rekindled by the story of three asylum seekers—two brothers and an acquaintance of theirs—who had gone to Germany. The friend, Kawan, had been sent back because they could tell from his fingerprints that he had already requested asylum in the Netherlands. But not the brothers. The reason for this, said Kawan, was that the brothers had used cement to harden their fingertips, which made the fingerprints undecipherable. You applied the cement, let it dry, and then peeled it off. So the computer did not recognize the brothers' fingerprints, and therefore did not discover they had already been in the Netherlands. Kawan was unlucky. Because I had trained as a civil engineer, and cement was part of my study and job, I knew this could work, in theory. Cement became my ticket out of the Netherlands.

From that moment on, life in the ASC became tolerable again. I talked to various asylum seekers who had tried to claim asylum elsewhere, but were sent back because of their fingerprints, so I knew where your chances were better or slimmer. London would be my first choice, because they rarely deported asylum seekers. I also heard that it was possible to get casual work to support yourself, even before you had a residence permit. And I spoke English. But getting to London was complicated:

to fly, you had to have a passport; to travel by boat required a smuggler; and to go by bus without a passport you mostly needed luck. So I scratched out London and moved on to the other possibilities: Oslo, Stockholm, Berlin. As for Norway and Sweden, I had heard mostly awful things about the snow and the dark. That if you spat on the street, you could hear your frozen spit clatter over the asphalt. And the only way to travel there was if you had either a tiptop passport and an ID card or bank pass with the same name, or else a reliable smuggler. The trouble with smugglers within Europe was that they never take the risk of traveling with you. All they do is provide forged passports, and these are expensive. So that left Germany. I only had to get information about the border, two hundred guilders cash for the trip, and a handful of cement. I sold my guitar for forty guilders. A hundred and sixty to go.

I enjoyed those days, while I was busy saving that 160 guilders. My hope outweighed the strength of the IND and the Justice Department combined. As I walked down the halls of the ASC I thought: not much longer and I'm out of here. Then I'll turn the "Netherlands" page and never look back.

I bought the smallest possible bag of cement, poured out a handful, and mixed it with some warm water. I stuck my hands into the pan of cement, and repeated this a few times a day. My skin began to change. I took sample fingerprints with an inkpad to see how it was progressing, and despite my inexperience in reading fingerprints, I could see that it was going well. The lines had become thicker—and the pain of the dry skin more acute.

After doing a lot of research, I decided it was best to go via the Dutch border city of Enschede. From there, you switched trains to Germany, where you could ask for asylum. There, I had heard, the asylum procedure is much quicker and more thorough than in the Netherlands.

I wanted to say goodbye to Tamara, Kadhem, and Zainab before I left, but when I found Kadhem he said he would see me off from Enschede. The next day I was surprised to find him carrying an overnight bag.

"What's that bag for?" I asked.

"Man, this place is terrible. I'm going to Germany too." He hurried down the hall and called to me over his shoulder, "Come on, or we'll miss our train. Germany's far, man." I ran over to him, so the whole ASC wouldn't hear where we were going. He looked up at me. "I haven't sat here all this time just to let you go alone, you know. And now we'll go to Germany together. Fantastic, man. Bye-bye, Social!" he called out and waved as we walked past the glass partition. "Bye-bye, Foreigners' ass!" he said as we passed the counter. "Bye-bye hallway, bye-bye Reception!" Outside, he took a deep breath. "Jeez, man, how did we survive this place for so long? Man, man, man. It's just like Saddam Hussein's asshole."

"But listen here," I said. "I don't want you to come with me."

"Quit wasting time, man, the train will leave without us." We walked toward the station. "So why don't you want me to join you?"

"Because I don't know where I'm going, or what I'll do. I've got an idea ... How about if you stay here, and I'll write when I get there, and fill you in."

"But I've said goodbye to everyone. I can't go back to

the camp, man. I told everybody I was going to Germany, and this was the last time I'd see them." Half an hour later we were sitting in the train.

In Enschede we bought tickets to Germany. Not two minutes after the train crossed the border, two policemen entered our coach and started walking down the aisle. One looked at the right-hand seats, the other at the left-hand ones. I nudged Kadhem.

"Don't worry, they're just conductors," he said. "Ticket-checkers."

"Oh really? Checking tickets with guns and handcuffs? They're police." Kadhem glanced their way.

"Hm, you're right, man, they're police. And you said to me: Come on, let's go to Germany! Didn't occur to you that they might check the trains ... Man, we should have walked. There are no land mines along the border." For once, I was not irritated with him, because I had other things on my mind, like what to do if we got caught.

"Tell them we wanted to go to Amsterdam but got on the wrong train," Kadhem said.

"And bought the wrong ticket? Are you crazy?"

At the next station, the two policemen led us out of the train, and escorted us back to Enschede, where two Dutch policemen were waiting for us.

"Traveling without a passport?" one of them said. "Why's that?"

"We have no passports," I said.

"Asylum seekers?" We had no choice but to say yes, and were taken to a police station. Everything we had with us was photocopied. They told us we were lucky we got caught immediately, otherwise things would have been complicated. Now they could just let us go, so we could return to the ASC on our own. One of the policemen gave us a lift back to Enschede station.

"See that one, just pulling in? It's the international train, they nearly always check it. But that other one is a local heading to Germany. It stops in every town. Good luck."

Kadhem and I looked at each other. We couldn't believe our luck, but soon enough we were sitting in the local train the policemen had pointed out. It made a brief stop every ten minutes or so. At first, most of the passengers were Dutch, but after a while it seemed like more Germans were getting on, although without speaking to them, we couldn't be sure. We looked out of the window. All you could see were trees, but once we rode parallel to a highway we could tell from the license plates that we had left the Netherlands. Station by station, that Dutch police officer gradually transformed from policeman to angel, with wings instead of a gun.

"Look, Germany! And without a smuggler! Great, isn't it?" Kadhem exclaimed. "Maybe we should become smugglers. What do you say?" He roared with laughter.

The German train stopped and pulled out, stopped and pulled out, and we waited until it arrived at a big station. At each slightly bigger station, we decided to hold out for an even bigger one. But suddenly, two policemen came walking toward us.

"Throw your ticket under your seat," I whispered to Kadhem, and did so myself. Kadhem rifled through his pockets, patted his entire body, as though he had pockets everywhere, or as though the ticket could jump from pocket to pocket.

"Where'd I put that damn ticket ..." he hissed, without realizing the two German policeman were already standing there looking at him.

"May we see your bags?" one of them asked in English. I thought maybe he was only searching for drugs. I nodded. "Passport or ID card first, please." When they figured out we didn't have any, we had to get off the next station, where they searched us and our bags. From head to toe and back, from right to left and left to right. The German police should take a course in the difference between frisking and boxing.

"When did you leave Enschede?" one of the officers asked.

"We didn't come from Enschede, but from Copenhagen," I said.

"Denmark?"

"Yes, Denmark, and we were on our way to Enschede to ask for asylum there, but we decided to do that tomorrow. We wanted to go to a bigger city, so we could find a cheap hostel."

"Are you traveling together?"

"Yes."

"But his ticket," the other one said, pointing at Kadhem, "says you got on in Enschede." He held out the ticket he had found in Kadhem's pocket.

"What did he say?" Kadhem asked in Arabic.

I told him to shut up.

"Sir, we want to go back to Denmark. We only want to pass through Germany. We're not after anything here."

"Not without a passport." Then they escorted us on the express train back to Enschede. This time there were no policemen to meet us on the platform. The two Germans waved and got back on the train. We stood on the empty platform and first decided to find a shawarma joint before coming up with a good excuse about why we hadn't signed in that day.

33

Kadhem and I got back to the ASC at about midnight. I trudged off to O-139. I thought I'd said farewell to this building for good, and here I was, not even twenty-four hours after I left. I walked past the sign-in window. Tomorrow, I'd have to stand there with a pretty good excuse.

At nine the next morning Kadhem and I reported to Anneke Hamelinck at Social Services. Anneke had heard, maybe from Sayid, that we'd tried to go to Germany, and smiled when she saw us come in.

"Back so soon?" she asked. "Did you miss us?"

"Sent back," I said, glad that it was Anneke and not any of her colleagues, because despite her moodiness, she was generally more flexible than the other staffers. "Could you do us a favor?"

"Smuggle you into Germany?" she joked. But my sense of humor at that moment was overshadowed by the IND and the Foreigners' Police.

"We didn't sign in yesterday. Maybe if you could tell them …" I was at a loss for words.

"Are you planning to try again? Germany, I mean?"

"They didn't take my fingerprints," I said, "so yes, sure."

"And him?" she asked, pointing at Kadhem. I translated and he nodded.

"I'll do my best about yesterday." We were off the hook, for now.

I went to the canteen and sat there pondering my options. Sayid offered the solution. He knew another resident who had been sent back after being in Germany for a few months. He would know the best way to get there. Sayid wasn't sure which room the man was in, and he knocked on countless orange and blue doors until we found him. The man, still in his pajamas, told me how I could easily get into Germany.

We would have to go back to Enschede, to a coffeeshop near the border, where a lot of Germans went to smoke marijuana. Some came from just over the border, but others drove from further away, and these were the ones you had to ask for a lift. The only thing we had to do was drink tea in a coffeeshop and chat with a German with a car.

Kadhem and I went back to Anneke and asked her for two train day-passes. The more rules Social Services had, the more exceptions there were. Exactly when the exception kicked in wasn't always clear, but when Anneke realized we wanted to take the train to the border, she did not hesitate for even a moment. She handed us two tickets.

"Good luck, and I hope never to see you two again," she said with a smile, and shook hands. The next day we took a taxi from the station to a coffeeshop near the border. We drank tea, and sure enough, most of the customers were Germans who came here to smoke pot. We bounced from table to table, and I chatted with the Germans in Dutch or English. I discovered that a coffeeshop is the best place to make small talk with people, because usually the spirit is on a higher plane than the body. Everyone I spoke to lived in a small town just over the border. Kadhem went outside for some fresh air, but soon came hurrying back inside to say that the German who would be our smuggler had arrived. A lean man dressed in leather had stepped out of a Bordeaux-red Volkswagen Passat with German license plates. Kadhem saw him open the back door and let out a large black dog. They walked to a tree, which the dog peed against. After taking the dog for a brief walk, he tied the leash to the door of the coffeeshop and went inside. Judging from the amount the dog had peed, the man lived far away, and that was a good sign.

We went back inside and sat at the man's table, where he rolled a large joint. He spoke good English. When I asked why, he said he learned it during his many trips to Southeast Asia. So the conversation turned to Thailand, and to Khao San Road, the street in Bangkok where all the Western tourists slept, ate, and bought souvenirs. And to the Friendly Guesthouse, where I had also stayed. Two hours later we were sitting in his car back to Germany.

The nice part about him was that he didn't ask what our plans were, but where we wanted to go. I looked at him and smiled.

"A city far from the border."

"Trouble with the police?" he asked.

"Yes, but not here. In Iraq," I said.

"I'll help you guys," he said, and didn't question me any further. After about twenty minutes he said that the Netherlands was far behind us now. He drove, and we listened to the country music he put on.

At a certain point he pulled over and said, "I could drop you at a train station, where they only check tickets until Berlin. But maybe it's better if you stay overnight at my place, and I can take you further tomorrow." So we spent the night in a detached house in a German town. The man opened the train timetable and said we should be ready to go the next morning at five thirty, and that he would bring us as far as he could. He rattled off a list of cities, and we nodded at each name, none of which we recognized or could remember. His refrigerator was full, and he filled our stomachs with bread, jam, and cheese, and then we sat on a black leather sofa in this house that resembled a wonderful cemetery of music. There were cassette tapes, LPS, CDS, record players, recorders, cables, electric guitars, and microphones everywhere. I always think back fondly on that house. There are houses that give you a warm feeling in your heart the minute you walk inside. This was one of them. Later that evening, a woman came home who looked exactly like him, thin and dressed in leather, but with two breasts and no facial hair. We slept in separate rooms full of stuff that belonged to their children, who had long moved out. At 5:00 a.m. the man woke us with a knock on the door. There was coffee, tea, bread, and cheese. Then the man drove us along the back roads, provincial byways, and the *Autobahn*. He drove and drove, and when we arrived at a good-sized city he stopped at countless traffic lights, until we reached a large train station. Among all those thousands of people coming and going, the police were unlikely to stop and question us.

"Good luck," the man said, and he waved as he drove off. We watched as the Bordeaux-red Volkswagen disappeared, and then stepped into the crowded train.

Later, we got out at an even bigger station. It looked like the transit hall of an airport. We started looking around for an asylum seeker. How do you spot an asylum seeker? His clothes don't fit any given period or style, but are a mishmash of periods and styles. Do you see a man wearing 1980s shoes, a hippie shirt, and gabber-house jogging pants? Then he's definitely an asylum seeker. On top of it, his hairstyle will tell you how long he's been here. A guy with an Elvis Presley hairdo is a recent asylum seeker, the Mick Jagger look tells you he's been denied asylum, and if "Zarathustra" comes to mind, then his procedure has been going on for more than fifteen years. We accosted an Iraqi guy. The first thing we wanted to know was the name of this city, and his reply confirmed that he was an asylum seeker.

"I have no idea. But you guys are in West Germany." We looked at him questioningly: "West" Germany—did the train go back in time, or what? But the man, whose name was Shaban, explained that asylum seekers preferred to request asylum in the western part of Germany rather than the East, because, he said, it was "a million times better."

This is how we discovered that, for asylum seekers, the Berlin Wall hadn't yet fallen.

Outside the station, Shaban bought us a shawarma at a Turkish restaurant, and two tram tickets.

"In fifteen minutes we'll be at the *Heim*," he said.

The Heim was a German ASC. There was a small office near the entrance, where I told the receptionist that we wanted to request asylum. He said it was too late for that today, and we'd have to wait until tomorrow. We assumed that meant on the street, but he told us to follow him, and led us to a storeroom. He opened the door and said we could take whatever we needed for the night. There were sheets, towels, blankets, pillows, shampoo, toothbrushes, and toothpaste. Kadhem and I took a bit of everything, like we were at an all-you-can-eat buffet. This was the first difference between Germany and the Netherlands: we could take what we needed, not what a regulation form *said* we needed. The second difference: we didn't have to sign for anything. We were taken to a communal bedroom, where a Russian man was sleeping, and were given money for dinner in the Heim canteen.

We did it!, I thought, as I stood at the buffet with my tray. The lady dished up for me and asked, "Enough?"

"More," I said. Third difference between Germany and the Netherlands. Once, we smuggled a Palestinian into the RC in Haarlem, where he would stay a few nights before moving on. When I asked for some extra food to share with him, the man who was dishing up said, "No, that's enough."

The next day we had to give our names, and they took our pictures and fingerprinted us. In the coming days, they would take our statements, and a couple of days later I was sitting in an office, next to an interpreter and opposite a German at his computer.

"Is your real name Malik Amien?" he asked.

"Yes," I said.

"Have you ever requested asylum in another country before coming to Germany?"

"No."

"You're sure?"

"Yes."

"Could you come around here?" The man pulled a chair up alongside him, and the interpreter said he wanted me to sit down at the computer with him. At first I didn't understand why, but the interpreter repeated it, so I did. On the monitor I saw the picture of me that had been taken at Schiphol airport.

"You applied for asylum in the Netherlands in 1998," the man said. I stared at the monitor, and then at the man's face. It wasn't the face of someone who had just been lied to, but rather a face with "Why?" written on it. He sent me back to my chair on the other side of his desk, and asked that question.

"Sir," I said. "I am losing my mind in the Netherlands."

"Why?"

"There are people there who have been waiting in that ASC for sixteen years. Many of them have lost their mind. I was there for a little more than a year, as you can see in the computer. I asked for asylum, they took two statements from me, and since then I haven't heard a word. If I ask why, they say that the Netherlands is a little country, and that there are lots of asylum seekers."

I hoped my words would change his mind, but all he said was that, as far as he knew, the Netherlands had an excellent asylum program. "And a year isn't even that long."

"Isn't there any way I could stay here?" I asked.

"I'm afraid not. Your only choice is to return." I opened my hands and looked at my fingertips, at those thin lines which had become a big fat problem.

"How long can I stay in Germany, then?"

"Until the return procedure has been processed," he said, and began typing something into the computer. I could feel that I had been changed from a person into a package that needed to be sent in a hurry, not because the recipient is eager to receive it, but because the sender is eager to get rid of it.

34

We—Kadhem and I—ended up in a Dutch detention cell. Whether other asylum seekers who had gone crazy or had psychological problems ended up in a place like this, I don't know, but this was a secure unit. The doors were shut behind us, personal data was noted, belongings were confiscated, and we were taken to a long corridor with cells on both sides. A more dismal place was hard to imagine.

Kadhem was terrified. He breathlessly asked me if the agents were going to lock us up. Kadhem's fear surprised me: was he claustrophobic? I was brought to a small cell; the man closed the door behind me and walked further with Kadhem. As another cell door was opened, Kadhem started to scream and curse. I think it was more to drown out his own fear than to intimidate the policeman, but nevertheless two more agents came running. I was able to get a glimpse of the tussle through the small window in my cell door. The policemen grabbed Kadhem, which only made him thrash more wildly, and wrestled him to the ground. From the shouts it sounded like he bit one of them. They kicked Kadhem in the stomach, and I heard some heavy thuds.

Eventually the ruckus subsided. No more noise from Kadhem, only some shuffling. Through the corner of the window I could just see Kadhem, his head bleeding, being dragged into a cell. I was worried: Was he badly injured? Was he even alive? I hoped the agents would check on him, but all was quiet. As far as I could tell, we were the only detainees.

Some time later, I'm not sure how long, my cell door opened, and an officer brought me to a washroom and ordered me to fill a bucket with water and mop up the bloodstains in the hallway.

I hurried to Kadhem's cell and peered through the window. He lay on his back, and his bloodied eyes were open.

"Kadhem," I whispered. I tapped on the window, but he didn't move. He didn't even blink. I ran to the end of the hall and banged on the door.

"The floor's not clean yet," the police officer said.

"Kadhem, there, in his cell ... He's dead," I panted nervously.

"You've got five minutes to clean that hallway," the police officer said.

"But Kadhem is dead," I said.

"Mop. The. Floor." He said it firmly and slowly. My blood rose to my head, which felt like it might explode any second.

"He's dead!" I yelled.

"Come with me," the policeman said, and brought me to another hallway. He opened the door to a space the likes of which I'd never seen before and can't easily describe. Not in Iraq, not in Jordan, not in Laos, Thailand, Vietnam, or Malaysia, where I had seen plenty of jail cells. I'd never even seen such a thing in Hollywood films. It wasn't a cell, nor a place, nor a space. It was nothing. It made me think of the inside of a ball. The walls, ceiling, and floor were padded, like mattresses covered in heavy leather. The only other thing was a very strong lamp, which gave off heat as well as light.

The officer closed the door. The inside of the door was padded, too. I stood in the middle of that thing, without any idea of where or what it was. If I so much as moved my feet, I sunk into the mattress. I walked from wall to wall, from mattress to mattress. I turned in circles. Every inch of it was exactly the same. No beginning and no end, no up and no down. I turned and turned, but it was as if I wasn't turning, because everything was the same, except the tiny window in the door and the lamp.

Later, when I told someone about this experience, he said I had been brought to a place where I couldn't hurt myself. It wasn't a cell, but a place to calm down aggressive prisoners. But you know, in that space where I supposedly couldn't hurt myself, I was worse off than if I had been able to bang my head against a steel wall.

That padded cell tortured my spirits with a thousand hands. A thousand hands with a thousand whips. Without the art of dreaming and the capacity for complete submission, this cell would destroy you. It would throttle not only your body, but your spirit as well.

I had no idea how long I'd be kept there. The place was removed from space and time. In a country like Iraq, the cell is not the problem, but the people who put you there. In the Netherlands, the cell itself is the problem. What did I do in that space? I sat and I stood, I sat and I stood, I sat and I stood. When I got tired, I either stayed sitting or standing, then I stood up and sat down again, sat and stood. I turned in circles, and before I got dizzy, I stopped and turned in the opposite direction. Then I sat and I stood some more. Food did not interest me. Hunger distracted me from the cell. I recalled that years ago, during Ramadan, I would be dizzy and headachy the first few days, and after that my body became weak, but my head clear. I could remember things better. So now I closed my eyes. I felt my body become colder and my thoughts clearer. I thought of my travels over the past years, starting with the moment I left home, up until I was locked in this cell. I remembered thousands of everyday situations and relived them, minute by minute. So in that padded cell I recalled that the girl from Stuttgart named Katie who I met in Bangkok had different colored eyes. One was blue, and the other somewhere in between blue and green. And that the small tattoo on her lower back was not a pair of wings, but two small feathers. And I hadn't read out the subtitles to the Western *Two Mules for Sister Sara* for my mother, who was illiterate, but for my aunt. These were the kind of things that passed before my eyes.

Bangkok airport. I saw a blond guy and his girlfriend, who had also just arrived, hail a taxi. They put their bags in the trunk. I asked if I could ride with them. They said they were going to Khao San Road. I nodded, fine with me, because all I wanted was to leave the airport.

Bangkok was huge and noisy. Everywhere there were cars, tuk-tuks, motor scooters, people pushing hand-cars, traffic jams, honking. All the hubbub calmed me down, because in this enormous city I could melt into the crowd. Khao San Road was almost a kilometer of souvenir shops, travel agencies, hostels, hotels, and massage parlors. I did not see a single policeman, only Western tourists. This was exactly where I needed to be.

I decided to set aside the few dollars I had, and live rough. The Thais placed food and drink at the many statues of Buddha as an offering—sometimes the drinks even came with a straw—so for a while Buddha kept me fed. Sleep was a more pressing problem. It was impossible to sleep outside, because every square inch was taken up by passersby. I couldn't find a single undisturbed corner in which to curl up. Later, when I had more experience finding a place to sleep, it was the mosquitoes that plagued me. They protected Bangkok better than the Thai police.

When it rained, I tried to find some sort of covered place so my forged passport and migrant documents would stay dry.

One day I found a hostel, quite possibly the filthiest I had seen in my life. It was a wooden building, and what you rented was basically just a roof above your head. The walls were thin planks, maybe half an inch thick. A room cost fifty US cents a night. During the day it was empty except for the man at the reception desk and, since there were no clients, the mice and rats had the run of the place. They gnawed like rusty saws through the rotten wood partitions. But once twilight fell, the rodents disappeared and the sex workers arrived. Mostly either prostitutes or something that, prior to my stay in Bangkok, I never imagined existed: ladyboys. In those days I regarded them as women with a penis.

Those first nights, I thought there were earthquakes, because as soon as it got dark the walls started shaking. Behind every wall you heard an orgasm. Orgasms to the left, orgasms to the right. If there were a World Cup of Orgasms, Bangkok would win for sure. Above and below, left and right—in total, four pairs of copulating men and women (with or without a penis) surrounded my room, which was only slightly bigger than a holding cell at Schiphol airport. The activity started quietly and cautiously, but soon turned into wrestling matches, and then into kickboxing, followed by shouts of *"I'm coming!"* These shouts were then followed by more of the same in Chinese, French, German, and in other languages I did not understand, but which undoubtedly meant the same thing. Sometimes the shout was preceded by a woman's voice saying in Asian English, "You must finish now."

I tossed and turned in my bed as those orgasms bounced at me from all sides. There would be a lull, and then one wall would start shaking, and then the next, and the next, and another lull, and the whole thing would start all over again. I wasn't living in a room, but in a drum. This went on until about five in the morning, at which point things quieted down, and the rats and mice were no longer disturbed by the orgasms and could start making noises of their own. Fortunately, I could tolerate this, and would sleep until seven, when the din of Bangkok began anew.

Finding work in Thailand was very difficult, so I decided to go to Malaysia. But I had a problem: my migrant documents showed the name on the Iraqi passport I no longer had, and not the name on the Dutch passport which I did.

I met an Algerian guy who took me to Soi San Street, or San Soi Street, which was the place to get a passport, an ID card, a driver's license, a bank pass, you name it. You walked down that street with a couple of hundred dollars and you left it as anything you wanted: Swedish, Portuguese, American, or Qatari, and complete with a license to operate a car, truck, bus, train, or cargo ship, or to fly an airplane. I left the street four hours later and fifty dollars lighter with migrant documents that matched the data on the forged passport and with "official" airport stamps. I slept one last time among other people's orgasms and left Bangkok the next morning.

I boarded the train to Malaysia. The doors of the old Thai trains did not shut properly, even when the train was moving, but we rode so slowly through some villages that you could easily step in or out. Passengers would get out to stretch their legs, amble a bit, and get back on; boys and girls would jump on in one village to sell fruit in plastic bags, and then hop back out at the next. The journey took thirty hours. I wasn't afraid, because having evaded capture at the airport made me confident of the passport in my pocket. I remember the old train's windows, which were hard to get open when they were shut, and hard to shut when they were open. I also remember the enormous tropical trees outside, and the various landscapes that passed by. I sat in that train not as a refugee, but as a traveler. I had seventy US dollars in my pocket. Bangkok vanished behind me, and Kuala Lumpur came ever closer.

35

Every piece of metal on that train made noise. Every screw, nut, and bolt. Every window and all the doors, which kept sliding open and shut while the train was moving. My entire body hurt. I lay my head down on my bag and slept. When I woke up, I couldn't take the racket anymore, so I got out and caught a bus for Kuala Lumpur. It drove and drove, as though Kuala Lumpur was at the end of the world.

Traveling on a forged passport makes the word "border" the most awful word in any language. On the one hand, you're eager to reach the border and cross it, so you can rest easy, and on the other hand it's terrifying. All the other passengers on the bus were sleeping. Only the driver and I were awake.

At the border, the Thai official quickly stamped our passports, and then we proceeded to the Malaysian side. I handed my forged Dutch passport to the Malaysian official. He examined it and asked to see my ticket as he paged through the passport.

"Sorry, do you have any other identification besides the passport?" he asked.

"How do you mean?"

"A driver's license or something?"

"I don't drive."

"Bank card? ID card?"

"My passport is all I take with me when I travel," I said.

He eyed me warily and asked me to get my bag out of the bus for inspection.

"I'm sorry, sir, but I have an appointment in Kuala Lumpur."

"Don't worry, after we've checked it, you can go." He looked me straight in the eye. "May I ask who your appointment is with?" He reached for a pen and paper. I was taken aback by this unexpected question.

"Who do you have an appointment with?" he repeated, looking me straight in the eye again, making it clear he expected a direct answer. The only Dutch names I could think of were Van Gogh and Rembrandt, but I couldn't possibly have an appointment with either of them in Kuala Lumpur that day. I had to think fast.

"Marco van Basten," I said. My younger brother was a fan of the Dutch national soccer team and had lots of posters of this player. The official handed me the pen and paper.

"Could you write it down for me?" Again I was taken by surprise. I knew how to pronounce it and write it in Arabic, but I had no idea how to write it in Latin letters, let alone in Dutch. So I spelled it phonetically: *Markufan Barstin*. He asked me to take a seat.

"Do you have Marco van Basten's address in Kuala Lumpur?" he asked. I said I didn't, but that I was to meet him at the bus station, which was why I didn't want to miss this bus. He asked me how I knew Marco van Basten, and then he handed me another piece of paper and asked me to write it down again. I'd forgotten exactly how I had written it the first time, and spelled it differently. The official compared the two sheets of paper in a way as to let me know he was comparing them. Then he looked at me with a question mark on his face.

"Do you have money with you?"

"Yes," I said.

"Can I see it?" I showed him the sixty dollars I had left, plus a few Thai banknotes.

"Is that all?"

"Yes."

"And you don't travel with a bank card or traveler's checks?" He counted the money, gave it back, and asked if he could search my bag. In the breast pocket of one of my shirts he found a slip of paper with the telephone number of a friend of mine named Mohammed. Written in Arabic.

"So you're Dutch?"

"Yes," I said. The Malaysian border was turning into a noose.

"And you speak Dutch?" I nodded. I had meticulously studied the information in the forged passport, but it never occurred to me that it's a good idea for a Dutch person to speak Dutch, and that a Dutch person shouldn't write notes about a person named Mohammed in Arabic. I knew I was in trouble. He picked up the phone and said something in Malay.

"Don't worry, we'll bring you to KL. Kuala Lumpur, I mean," he said with a reassuring smile. That smile of his was definitely worth fifty dollars, because it gave me hope that he would not be angry or aggressive and might let me go. Another official came, they spoke in Malay, and the other man picked up my Dutch passport.

"Listen, mister, if you tell us the truth, we'll try to help you, so if you're not really Dutch, please say so. It's easy enough for us to find out, but it takes time. If you tell us now, it will be better for you. Are you Dutch?"

"No," I said.

"Why do you have a Dutch passport?"

"So I can travel."

"Where are you from?"

"Iraq."

"Oh, Iraq." And then: "Follow me," as though the word *Iraq* suddenly transformed me from a person into a dog who had to follow his master.

I was made to wait in a small office. I was like a stone that someone first thought was a precious gem, until they realized I was just an ordinary pebble and tossed me onto the ground. If the Malaysians put the dreaded "red stamp" in my passport, the Thai border officials would also red-stamp it, and that would mean a one-way ticket back to Iraq, where it would not be my passport that was stamped in red, but my body, and I would end up in one of Saddam Hussein's mass graves. A single color can change a world full of continents, mountains, oceans, and deserts into the eye of a needle.

Of the three or four Malaysian officials, there was one who was always smiling. Every now and then he brought me a bottle of water, which I drank and immediately sweated back out. He kept saying "don't worry," and asked what part of Iraq I came from, what I did there, and why I did not have an Iraqi passport. It felt like he was showing a personal interest. He was still young, maybe he was inexperienced at border control. After a while he asked if I was a Muslim, and I nodded.

"Don't worry, Allah will help you," he said. I wanted to say I'd prefer that *he* helped me, but the way he uttered that sentence made me believe him.

"Do you know what will happen to me now?" I asked.

"You can't enter Malaysia with that passport. But don't worry. We won't send you to prison, just back to Thailand."

"Can I ask a favor?" I asked.

"What?"

"Let me stay here a little longer before sending me back. Because if you send me back right now, the Thai border police will get suspicious. And could I go back without a red stamp?"

"I don't know," he said, smiling, and then left. This time his smile was absolutely worth a thousand dollars. Shortly thereafter, he returned with the same smile. "Don't worry. My shift ends at eight o'clock, and you can take the bus back to Thailand just before then."

"And the stamp?"

"I can't say."

At seven thirty the smiling man said to follow him. He clapped me on the shoulder and shook my hand.

"Allah will help you," he said as he handed me my passport. Trembling, I opened it. No red stamp. I decided right then that I loved Malaysia.

But what would happen at the Thai border? Would they ask why I only spent a few hours in Malaysia? How would I answer? The anxiety came rushing back—my apologies to all of you who are sick and tired of hearing about border control and trembling hands. At the end of the day, border control is no more than an official and a tally counter. Beyond it is a country, with mountains and rivers and lakes. Highways, dirt roads, hospitals, restaurants, museums, hostels. With a forged passport, your freedom either ends with that counter, or it begins.

The Thai official stamped my passport without even looking at it, or at me, and tossed it in a nonchalant arc onto the counter. At the next small town, I got on the train back to Bangkok. Now I didn't have a cent on me. Literally. And once hunger knows you're flat broke, it bites harder.

36

It was raining, so the statues of Buddha did not offer much solace. I asked a worker at an Indian restaurant if he could give me some leftovers for my dog. Every day he gave me a black plastic bag full of bones and half-eaten bread, which I took to a quiet corner to eat. I spent my days looking for that invisible dog. Daytime meant filling my belly, nighttime meant hiding my body from mosquitoes and the police. The more it rained, the less Buddha provided. I wandered the streets, sat under trees, looked at walls, went to the market—time passed without purpose.

After a few days of sleeping in deserted corners, I found myself once again on Khao San Road. This was good. The more Western tourists there were, the fewer the spot checks by police.

My experience at the Malaysian border reminded me, to my surprise, how much power Europe had.

In the hope of understanding this power, I spoke with many Western tourists, but discovered that most of them were traveling "to find themselves," as one of them put it. That sounded strange. A person who has to find himself? Had he misplaced that self somewhere? And if he was traveling to find himself, why did everyone have so much respect for Westerners, while all I wanted was to protect my body from Saddam Hussein and got no respect from anyone? It turns out that most of the Western people I met were not that worldly at all.

They confused Iraq and Iran, Khomeini and Saddam, Baghdad and Tehran. That's just as uninformed as saying Hitler was the leader of the Soviet Union and Stalin was the Führer of the Third Reich.

The other thing that surprised me about Western travelers was how dirty they were. There was one young woman with a European passport and a whole assortment of plastic cards from insurance companies, banks, and I don't know what else—and there she was walking around barefoot, with three and a half inches of armpit hair, scratching her scalp, and smelling disgusting because she hadn't showered in ages. She told me she was traveling for a few weeks to do exactly what she felt like, something she did not dare to do in her own country. She wanted to be herself.

If I wanted to discuss literature with one of them, it could only be about books that had been turned into Hollywood films. Everybody knew Bob Marley and how many hairs he had on his ass, but no one knew how many CDs he'd recorded. I know I shouldn't generalize about Europeans, but this was my first impression.

I remember one of those travelers, who I'll call Oscar. He was about thirty and would sit at an outdoor café drinking beer and pondering which restaurant he would choose for his next meal. He was often in the company of two German girls and a blond Danish guy. I would join them occasionally to take a break from my fear of the police, because even if they were on patrol, the policemen would just walk past our table without taking any notice. Oscar held that all people were equal and that borders, visas, passports, and money should be abolished, so that the world would belong to everyone. I once asked him where he came from. He got angry and gave me a half-hour lecture about how he was a citizen of Earth, and that where he came from was irrelevant, because his birth country was not his choice.

"But a few days ago you asked me where I came from," I said.

"Did I?" he said, surprised. "Then I sincerely apologize."

Time and again I listened to Oscar's lecture about how everyone was equal. "You and me, too," he said.

"Sorry, but you and I are not equal, and we never will be," I replied once.

"Oh, but we are!" he exclaimed. "You're a person, I'm a person."

"Well put," one of the Germans chimed in.

"You don't believe in borders, nationalities, money or passports, right? Then give me your passport, your bank card, and your traveler's checks. I believe more in them than in myself," I said, and I meant every word. I would have accepted the whole lot, too, but he was never going to give them to me.

This is how I spent hours listening to the unique philosophies of Western travelers to avoid being checked by the police.

Because Thailand was one of the few countries that issued visas to Iraqis, there were a lot of my countrymen in Bangkok, all of them trying to get themselves smuggled to countries that offered asylum. Many of them lived in hostels on Khao San Road. A strange mix. All ages, all religions, all colors and dialects. The common denominator was the fear of Saddam Hussein and the hope of getting asylum somewhere. For some, the smuggling option had failed and they had no more money to try it again. Others were in the process of organizing a smuggler or were waiting for friends or family to send money.

If you had a false passport, getting onto an airplane to a European country that offered asylum required a smuggler. In Bangkok there were more smugglers than there are kinds of cheese in Holland. Four of them were considered the most reliable: an Iranian, a Pakistani, a Palestinian, and a Jordanian.

I got to know the Palestinian, who we called Galileo. I had heard of him, and met him, through Shakir. Shakir was a tall Iraqi guy, about twenty-five but on the inside still a child, and was so naïve that he had lost all his money to shady smugglers and ended up on the street when his family in Iraq ran out of things to sell. He was my guide in Bangkok. Having been there for so long, he knew exactly where to find edible refuse and knew the places with fewer mosquitoes. He told me about the four reliable smugglers and said that if, by some miracle, he should ever have enough money, he would want to be smuggled by Galileo. Galileo's waiting list was long, because his policy was to accept money only once, and keep trying until he succeeded, no matter how many times the person was captured. He would get them out of jail by bribing the police.

One day Shakir came up to me with a broad smile. That smile was not for himself, but for me.

"Your big chance!" he said, hugging me tight. "Just like that! And it won't cost you a cent!" I didn't realize he was serious.

37

Smuggling fees for an Iraqi in Bangkok: a minimum of four thousand dollars if you spoke English. Between seven and ten thousand if you did not speak English. Having blond hair simplified the process and thus lowered the price to about two and half, because it was easier to pass off someone with a light complexion as Scandinavian. The most expensive passports were the European ones with an Arabic or Turkish name. Spanish, Portuguese, Italian, and Greek passports were worth a fortune. A Dutch passport, to be honest, was the cheapest: since soft drugs were legal in the Netherlands, they were liable to suspect you of being a drug smuggler, and therefore the passports were not so popular. I managed to travel on a Dutch passport twice: first to get out of Jordan and later to fly from Vietnam to the Netherlands. And I was never once suspected of smuggling drugs.

Apparently there was an Iraqi woman who spoke only Arabic and wanted to be smuggled to England. She had been caught at the airport many times and it had cost Galileo stacks of money to keep getting her free. Shakir had told Galileo I spoke English and would accompany her to England.

"This is your chance! You can go to England and they'll give you asylum and a passport, and then you can go wherever you want!" An hour later I was sitting across from Galileo. I had learned his Palestinian dialect from the Palestinian refugees in Al-Zarka in Jordan, so this established an immediate rapport.

"I have a cow and I want to smuggle her to London," he said, exhausted. "It goes wrong every time, and it's already cost me half my head." He took off his cap to show me he was half bald.

"So what do I have to do?" I asked.

"I hear you speak English. I'll arrange a passport and a plane ticket. You go with Nahida to the airport and do all the talking. You check in with her, get on the plane and"—he snapped his fingers—"that's that. What do you think? Schmooze for five minutes in Bangkok and a few hours later you're in London."

"Sounds interesting," I said. "I have a Dutch passport."

"Perfect, then it will only cost me the ticket. If you get nabbed I'll bail you out and fix you up with a new passport." I showed him my Dutch passport, but after looking at it for less than a second he threw it onto the floor.

"That's no passport. That's nothing."

"Nothing?"

"Look at the photo!" I picked up the passport and looked. "Don't you see?" he asked as I studied the photograph. "Not how it's been doctored, but the picture itself. You."

"...?"

"Travel on a Dutch passport with a picture like that, and you may as well announce 'Arrest me!' to every border agent in the world."

"How come?"

"Look at the mustache on that photo!" I had a thick mustache: a typical southern Iraqi. "Search the Netherlands from north to south, and you won't find even one mustache like this!" Now that he mentioned it, I'd never met a Western tourist with a mustache. They were either clean-shaven or had a full beard. Suddenly that passport had turned from a lifeline into a liability.

"But they let me in here with this one," I said.

"The problem is not getting into Thailand. Really, it isn't. You could get in with a photo of a donkey. The problem is getting *out*." Now I realized why they had spotted me at the Malaysian border. I said goodbye to my mustache, flushed it into the Bangkok sewer, and swore never to grow one again.

Ali al-Karbala'i was an Iraqi in his late twenties and came from the city of Karbala. In Bangkok he was known as Ali Taxi, because he organized taxis for refugees. He was also the one who kept track of who was next in line to be smuggled, which brought him in extra money from refugees wanting to jump the line. He was always well dressed, and chose his words carefully. He made a trustworthy first impression. Later, though, I found out that under his slick veneer he was a monster. He took me to get a picture taken for the new passport Galileo was arranging for me. As soon as we were alone, he turned into a different person, someone who thought only of how many cents he could slip into his own pocket.

"Did you bring money for the photo?" he asked, even though Galileo was supposed to pay for everything. To avoid getting into a tiff, I paid for it with the little money I still had. Then Ali said I had to sleep in a hotel until I left. I told him I had no money for a hotel. Only when we got back to Galileo's place did he hand over the one hundred dollars that Galileo had given him for my daily expenses and in case the police picked me up. I didn't accept the money, because it felt that rather than being smuggled, I was working for them. But I needed the accommodation and shower that Galileo offered me, so at least I could sleep in a proper bed until Ali al-Karbala'i had arranged a taxi to the airport for Nahida and me.

We each had a British passport. The name on her passport was Turkish, and on mine, Moroccan. In the taxi Nahida constantly repeated the name in her passport, to be able to say it from memory. The taxi driver, amused, asked what my wife was doing.

"Repeating her name," I said.

He laughed. "Why?"

"Because she forgets it. She's crazy," I said, and he laughed even harder.

We had two suitcases, because Galileo wanted our stay in Thailand to look plausible. They contained English books, souvenirs from Bangkok, bottles of shampoo and massage oil, condoms, and even a vibrator. Everything an English woman could need in Thailand.

We joined the check-in line. Every time the line shifted, Nahida got the jitters, as though I might abandon her there. So I stood closer to her, but now she was afraid I might hug or kiss her. She begged and begged, with tears in her eyes, that I not abandon her before she boarded the airplane. I begged her in turn to keep quiet. She was in such a state that even an airport staff member came over and asked in English if everything was okay. She looked at me in panic, as if she'd never heard the word "okay" before. I reassured the man, and he smiled and walked off. She stopped begging, but started to tremble. She pleaded with Allah to help her. I whispered in her ear that Allah was not the god of the English, but of the Iraqis, and that if she wanted to call upon Allah or recite the Koran, she had to do that to herself and not out loud, not with that British passport in her hand.

"Everything okay?" the woman at the check-in desk asked. Nahida gave her a frightened look.

"Yes, everything's okay," I said. "It's just that she's a little tired, she's two and a half months pregnant and it's her first child."

The check-in lady smiled. "Great! Congratulations!" she said. This maneuver worked wonders in getting us through the check-in, but I knew we would need an even bigger wonder to get us through passport control.

Once we were in line, Nahida kept turning around nervously to make sure I hadn't run off. Other travelers eyed us warily. The closer we got to the counter, the more uncontrollably she trembled. What an idiot I was not to just walk out the airport exit and back to Galileo, how stupid I was to be standing with her in this line, not to board an airplane to London, but to be thrown into a Thai or Iraqi jail. The line moved forward, and Nahida turned to me, her face pale, and whispered, "That man there at the counter is looking at passports."

"Yes, what else would he be looking at? The passengers' backsides?"

"Isn't there another way to the airplane?" she asked out loud in Arabic.

Galileo had neglected to instruct Nahida how to behave at the airport, or at least not explicitly enough. And Nahida herself, like so many Arabic women, was not at all world-wise. Galileo had just handed over the passport and told her to learn the information in it. All Nahida managed to memorize was the Turkish name, and none of the rest. I whispered to her that she needn't say anything, only hand over her passport to the official and smile. But when it was almost our turn, she suddenly had to go to the toilet. I pointed to where it was, but she was afraid I would abandon her, so I let her hold both passports and boarding passes. She was hardly back when she suddenly had to go to the toilet again. We were next in line, but she insisted that her bowels were in a spasm from the anxiety.

"Not now, just wait. In a few minutes we'll be through passport control, and you can sit on the toilet for hours."

"I can't, I'll explode," she said, so I joined the back of another line. After waiting an eternity for our turn, the official gestured to us that we had to approach the counter separately. I handed her her passport and nodded to go ahead. She did, but turned facing me, her back to the official, as though he was supposed to check her ass and not her passport. She looked at me in desperation, and I hissed in Arabic for her to turn around and look at the official. He was taken aback by this strange performance. He asked something I couldn't catch, she turned and beckoned me. The official was trying to talk to her, but she kept insisting I translate for her. The line behind us got longer and longer; some passengers shifted to another line. Now the official beckoned me himself.

"Are you traveling together?"

"Yes, she's my wife."

He asked how long we had been in Thailand, and why we hadn't bought a round-trip ticket in London, but in Bangkok. I replied that we did buy one, but that due to unforeseen circumstances it was no longer valid. He wanted to see this other ticket, but I said I had thrown it away. He looked from the one passport to the other, at the entry stamps, and at his computer. He asked if we had traveled to Bangkok together. I nodded, at which he gave me a skeptical look. Maybe it was something he saw on the monitor. At this point I knew there were only two ways for us to get through passport control: if he was a fool, or by a miracle.

We were brought to a room where they searched our things and told us we could only travel if we had a document from the British embassy confirming that we were the rightful owners of the passports.

They kept the passports. "But we need them," I said, not because I really wanted it back, but rather to mask my urgent desire to get out of there.

"If you don't want to leave the passports with us, then you have to stay in Thailand." Twenty minutes later we were back outside.

I looked at the sky, and we got in a taxi with the money Galileo had given us in case things went wrong, and after sitting in a traffic jam we found ourselves back at the hotel. All I wanted was my Dutch passport back so I could disappear. Ali al-Karbala'i told me Galileo had the Dutch passport, but that he had left it with a Chinese guy who would replace the photo with a better one, without a mustache. After a few days without a passport, he did give me an Iraqi passport—from a man who had meanwhile been smuggled—with my photo. The visa was good for a month. So instead of arriving in London as an Englishman, or walking around Bangkok as a Dutchman, for one month I was a legal Iraqi. A few days later I saw Galileo again, and asked him for the Dutch passport back. He said he'd smuggled someone else with it already, but he would fix me up with a better forgery, including a driver's license and ID card. He invited me to eat at his place, and I jumped onto the back of his scooter. An hour later we took the stairs up to an apartment he shared with his English girlfriend, Amy.

"You know I trust you now, right?" Galileo asked, as he and Amy smoked a joint. "I trust you more than Ali al-Karbala'i." I didn't answer. "You could have dumped that poor woman and gone to London on your own, but you stuck with her."

"Did you really smuggle someone else with my Dutch passport?" I asked, because I heard a different story every time.

"You'll get your passport back, but if you just sit tight, you'll get a better one."

"I'd rather have it back now. I'm an Iraqi for just two and a half more weeks, and then I'm nobody."

Galileo went to another room and brought back my passport. I went to return the Iraqi one to him, but he said, "Not necessary. Hide the Dutch one somewhere and carry the Iraqi one with you, even after it expires. You can always prove you're Iraqi, even with a fake Iraqi passport, but with that mustache picture you'll never pass yourself off as Dutch, even if it were true. What do you think, will you give it another go with Nahida?"

"Give me a hundred cows with French or British or Danish passports and there's more chance of getting them on that plane than Nahida. I pass."

"How come?"

"I made it through Bangkok airport once on a fake and Dutch passport and now I almost made it through with a British one. I don't trust my chances of leaving that airport a free man a third time." I said goodbye to Galileo. He wanted to take me back to Khao San Road himself, but I said I would manage. So there I was with two passports, which was complicated, because if you got picked up with two passports it was clear that at least one of them was fake.

38

Sometimes the brain stops working, and a person becomes a boat whose captain is either dead or asleep. A boat adrift with neither direction nor destination. This was me in Bangkok, trudging aimlessly through the busy streets and simply waiting until I couldn't take another step, and then falling asleep somewhere. From the moment I had left my home three years earlier, I hadn't had a single week of rest.

Fortunately it wasn't long before an Algerian who was also wandering the streets asked me in French, and then in English, if I was looking for work.

"Work? As what?"

"See that American there, in that van? He's looking for extras for a movie." Non-Asian-looking extras, to be exact. So I went over and offered my services, and waited in the van until the American told the Algerian he had enough extras. The van drove off. The American talked to the driver, and occasionally turned to us to say what a lot of fun we were going to have. Miss Thailand would be there, too. He passed out cold drinks from a cooler, and a few hours later we arrived at a wooded area full of trailers, tents, and more cables than branches. They were shooting a Vietnam War film. A "bush war," with soldiers, generals in conclave, dead bodies, guards, and whatever else you needed for such an affair. There were trailers full of make-up and clothes in all sizes, and rails on the ground, on which the cameras rolled. They brought us to the tents for the extras and gave us each a towel, shampoo, razor blades, and mosquito repellent.

I took a long shower, and smeared my body with bug repellent. For two full days I did nothing but eat, drink, shower, and rub my skin with bug repellent. In the evening we—about twenty or thirty men and women—sat around a campfire, where we danced, sang, and drank. I hoped the film shoot would go on for the rest of my life.

I remember once ducking into a tent with the Algerian, named Bakr, two Moroccans, a Thai girl, and a Thai man during a cloudburst. The rain hammered the roof of the tent. I asked about Miss Thailand.

"Haven't you seen her yet?" asked one of the Moroccans in English.

"No, in fact I haven't seen a single pretty woman here yet," I said. The Thai man and girl laughed out loud.

"What will you do if you see her?" he asked.

"Hug her! Then for the rest of my life I can boast that I hugged Miss Thailand." Everyone laughed.

"This is her," the man said, pointing to the skinny girl.

"That can't be," I said. "She hasn't got any breasts." To this day, I'm ashamed of having said that, and still don't know why they just laughed and didn't get angry, because she really was Miss Thailand. I didn't dare hug her, or even look her in the eye after that.

The real work started on the third day. A scene in which Vietnamese troops captured a group of American soldiers, and were preparing to beat them to death. One of them would be rescued by a Vietnamese girl—played by Miss Thailand—who would then take him under her wing. I hoped, as did all the extras, that I would be the soldier Miss Thailand would rescue, but a blond Russian guy got the role.

"It's because he's blond," Bakr, the Algerian, griped to me in Arabic. Bakr and I, together with two Africans and a Chinese, played the American soldiers who got beaten to death. A Vietnamese actor was instructed to grab me by the hair and slam my head against the ground. They had set down a pillow made to look like a rock. Before they started shooting, I pointed to the pillow and said in English to the man playing the Vietnamese soldier, "Here."

"Okay," he said with a smile, but once the camera was rolling he forgot he was a Thai actor and not a real Vietnamese soldier. He grabbed me by the hair and bashed my head against the ground, not the pillow.

"Cut!" the director shouted, and the scene was repeated, but despite the director's instructions, the Thai man who grabbed my hair kept forgetting he was acting in a movie.

After a two-hour break, we were given torn clothes and were brought to a make-up trailer. I was made black and blue, as if I'd been beaten everywhere, and was given wounds with blood and flies. The other extras were made to look equally awful. Then we were hung from a tree by our ankles and were told to let to our arms dangle. This scene also had to be shot several times.

My first day as a movie extra. We were paid in Thai money: a thousand baht. And that day we were paid double, because of the hanging, which really hurt.

One minute I was a soldier with weapons, bombs, knives, and binoculars. Sometimes with a beard, sometimes not. The next minute I was covered with blood, lying in a muddy ditch. In total I played ten different dead bodies. With or without an American flag. With or without a Thai playing a Vietnamese fighter holding his fingers against my neck to see if I was still alive. Sometimes with bullet holes in my head, sometimes not. The time I had to hang from my wrist was the most painful. I was a wounded Vietnamese (with my face to the ground, thus unrecognizable), an American general (at least, disguised as one, so I could play the general during a staff meeting), an American GI, a corpse, a soldier, another corpse, and then another soldier, sometimes all in a single day. The entire Vietnam War was fought in those few square meters of woods.

On one of the first days there were explosions, and we were supposed to act frightened. The director, a guy named Will, came up to me after the shoot.

"Why weren't you afraid? Seen war before?"

"Yes, the real thing."

"Where are you from?"

"Iraq."

"Iraq? Oh, sorry, man," he said, and continued with the shoot, shouting above the bombardment. I thought I'd made a mistake by telling him I was from Iraq; maybe he had a thing against Iraqis because of the Gulf War and now I'd lose my gig in the Vietnam one.

But this turned out not to be the case. That evening he came to the tents where the extras slept, and spoke to Bakr.

"I am really sorry for what happened in your country." Bakr gave him a puzzled look. "The war in Iraq, I mean." Bakr pointed to me and said that I was the one from Iraq, not him, so Will came over to me and offered his apologies.

"Where is your family now?" he asked.

"In Baghdad."

"Has Baghdad been completely destroyed?" he asked anxiously.

"No, just a few neighborhoods here and there," I answered truthfully. He picked up his enormous mobile telephone—they hadn't been around for so long in those days, and had to be carried on a belt—and asked Brad, his assistant, to come over.

"He's from Baghdad," he said to Brad, who stood facing me. "He managed to flee Baghdad just before it was obliterated." Will walked off to make another phone call, leaving Brad standing there with me, and never came back to tell Brad why he'd called him over in the first place, or who he'd just been on the phone with. I had no idea either. Will must have had a robust mind, because he was occupied with a thousand things at once. Brad left and I went to lie down in my tent, because in an hour I had to get strung up again.

39

Bakr and I did not look at all alike. The difference was bigger than between a burka and a bikini, but Will, whose mind was always on the go, kept getting us mixed up. He would see me and ask, while talking on his enormous mobile phone or shuffling through a stack of papers, if I had seen the Iraqi. He kept calling me "the Iraqi" even though I'd told him my name at least a hundred times, and when he finally learned it, he started calling Bakr by my name.

"Yes, I've seen him," I would reply. "Right here. I am Samir the Iraqi." Then he would laugh and thump me in the stomach.

"That's a good one, man." Then he would suddenly stop laughing, and look at me with dramatic intensity. "But how did the Marines manage to destroy all of Baghdad in just a few hours? Is that possible?"

"No, Will, that's not possible," I said.

"But didn't you say they did? ... Forget it, maybe I saw it in a movie. Sorry, man."

One day he was walking past with one of the famous Thai actors, and pointed at me. I was lying in a pool of mud and blood for a scene where a few ambushed American soldiers were about to be rescued by helicopter.

"He's a special one," Will said to the Thai actor. "He's one of the few survivors of the bombing of Baghdad in 1991, before Saddam Hussein pulled out of Kuwait." He said it with the confidential tone of someone who had inside information. The Thai actor smiled tenderly, came over, and gave me a sympathetic slap on the shoulder. "Great, man," he said.

I didn't know how to respond. I did survive the bombardments in 1991, but so did a few million others. And besides, I was certainly no hero.

Not long after that, a scene in which I was an American soldier with a machine gun got held up because of rain. Will came over to me.

"Your whole family wiped out?"

"No," I replied as he examined his printed scenario. Then he shouted to Brad that everybody had to be ready for when the rain let up.

"Did you see them get killed?"

"No."

"You're lucky you didn't see it. I mean, you're not lucky that they all got murdered, but that you didn't have to witness it. Y'know, that would really be cruel, if you had to see it happen. Horrible."

"They're still alive," I said. "Lots of people did die, but fortunately not my family." Will was still looking through his papers.

"Yeah, yeah, I know, but you're really lucky."

A few days later he told Brad to pay me in American dollars rather than baht.

"The Marines wiped out his whole family." He winked at me, and Brad started giving me twenty dollars a day, every morning. At the end of each day Will asked if I'd been paid yet. I said yes, and he gave me another twenty dollars, for the next day. Every evening I signed two receipts and got forty dollars. If he had wanted, I would have signed receipts all day long.

Once, Will gave me a fright when he approached me

with three men in police uniforms. I couldn't tell whether they were real Thai policemen or film extras.

"C'mere," Will called. I was worried that the Thai police were checking the extras' papers.

"Just imagine," Will said to the policemen, "the American Marines tied up his whole family and executed them in front of his very eyes. If he hadn't been sick as a dog and lying on the ground half-dead himself, he'd have been murdered too. It's a crime, you know, the things we do in other countries."

I wondered how the Marines could have done all that to my family in 1991, considering the Americans weren't in Baghdad at all. Not on the ground, anyway, only in the air. The next day, Will asked how it happened that the Marines had shot my whole family, but not me.

"Were you sick? Did they take pity on sick people?"

"The Marines murdered my entire family," I said, but Will was engrossed in his scripts and did not hear me.

Later, there was a scene that had to be shot in the rain. The cameras, protected by large umbrellas, rolled over their rails; various colors of smoke filled the air. After shooting the scene Will whispered to me, "Did they suffer?"

"No, they didn't suffer," I answered.

"Did they go down with the first shots?" His facial muscles quivered.

"Yes, Will, with the first shots."

"What about the child in your sister's arms?"

"Him too. He fell to the ground, because they hadn't tied him to the wooden beam."

"Fantastic! I've got to write that down! I've really got to write it down! They hadn't thought of tying the child to the beam. Because he was in his mother's arms. Fantastic. The child fell, not because they hit him, but because they'd hit his mother. I've got to write that down." He called Brad over and asked him if he'd already said to pay me in dollars.

"Yes, Will," said Brad.

"Pay him in dollars. His fucking life is in tatters. We killed his whole family and he's got no one, except his sister's child, who he has to support."

He appeared to be occupied with two different movies at once: one about Vietnam, in a few square meters of woods in Thailand; the other about Iraq, in his mind. I was fine with that, as long as I got paid twenty dollars twice a day. I hoped Will's movie would never get finished, because I ate, drank, showered, slept, and smeared bug repellent on my skin, and all I had to do was dangle from a rope, get shot at, be murdered a couple of times a day, and nod my head at a staff meeting. I will never forget the Vietnam War, or Will. His warm, dramatic, sometimes melancholy voice. And his dollars.

I also think back fondly on the day when I came out of the shower wearing only jogging pants and a towel, and Will pulled up alongside me in his jeep.

"Get in!" he said.

"I'll just go get dressed."

"No, man, we'll be right back." I sat up front next to Will, who drove and talked at the same time. And when he talked, he looked at me and not at the road.

"You know, anyone who's seen war first hand has a different take on it than someone who's only heard or read about it, or seen it in a movie. The real thing is another matter altogether ..." He made it sound like a profound philosophical insight that he exclusively owned.

"So where are we going?"

"Just there. Bangkok." He thumped the steering wheel.

"If I don't get away from that fucking film sometimes, I'll go crazy." I said nothing, but thought: how was I supposed to go to Bangkok dressed only in my pajamas and without my fake passport.

Finally I said, "But I don't have anything with me, not even my passport."

"Don't worry, man. Just say you're an American."

"I'm not sure they'll believe that."

"Then I'll tell them. Don't worry." He stopped at a market stall, bought a colorful shirt that went with my pants, and we drove into Bangkok. He took me to a place I never imagined existed. Everything there smiled: the people sitting at the cafés, the people who worked there—even the cats walking under the tables to keep the place free of rats and mice.

"I've got that story of your family in my head. It makes me think of the film we're shooting. It's really important for people to see war, and to realize it's not a vacation, but murder. How much does it cost you a month to support your sister's son?" Without waiting for my answer, he called over a waiter and told me to order whatever I wanted. "Fifty dollars a month isn't much," he said, even though I hadn't named an amount. "But how did you manage to bury your whole family after they were executed, while you were so sick and probably scared out of your wits after seeing them murdered in cold blood?"

"I didn't bury them," I said.

"You were probably dead too. Inside, I mean. That's why you left them for the rats to devour instead of burying them." He was angry, as though this had happened to his own family. "And the boy? You probably crawled over to him." I nodded. Will continued: "He was covered with dust and ashes and his mother's blood."

"Exactly," I said.

"And when you got to him, you turned his face toward yours."

"Yes."

"And his eyes were wide open, but the expression was dead."

"Yes."

"And when you saw this, your face sank to the ground, as though now they'd killed you too."

"Yes."

"But you didn't die. You just couldn't bear the dead look in that boy's eyes. You looked into those wide-open eyes, and the camera zooms in closer and closer, until the screen is filled with the child's eyes. And then in that child's eyes we see a sky full of smoke and brutality. That's how everything ends. Great, great!"

"Yes, Will, great."

"You, dying inside," he continued, gesturing to show how the screen would be filled. "But then the boy's eyebrows start to move. He's still alive!" He repeated how great it was, and we ate and drank. Will took a wad of Thai banknotes out of his pocket and tipped everyone who smiled. He stroked the cats under the table, and then we walked for half an hour to another place, this one full of women in short skirts and European men, most of them over sixty.

"If you see a woman you like, just tell me. My treat," he said, and grinned. A Thai woman came up and hugged Will, and before I knew it we were sitting at a bar surrounded by six Thai women. Will went off with one of them and came back forty minutes later. That felt like a long time to me, because without a passport or money, all I had was Will's mouth and his wallet. He told me the woman was very good, and that I could have her too, but I said no thanks and stayed seated at the bar. Then he went off with two other women, and returned an hour later, exhausted.

"Can you still drive?" I asked.

"No," he said. "You give it a try. It'll be a great experience, for sure. A scene in the first movie I directed was with a man on the run from the police, in a stolen car, and he'd never driven before." I said I'd rather not drive. So he drank a large bottle of Coke to stay awake, got into the jeep, and started telling me about the three Thai women. Whenever he stopped talking or looking at me, I checked to make sure he was still awake. I was relieved to get back to the Vietnam War alive. My life in the American movie was better than my real life.

On the last day, Will called me to his trailer and gave me a stack of papers to sign. I got richer with each signature. He told me to put a different date, name, and signature on each receipt. Then he took a wad of dollars out of his pants pocket and started counting out hundred-dollar bills.

"You've done good work," he said. I tried to refuse the money. Not out of pride, but simply to make it clear to him that he'd given me more than enough. "Take it, you've worked hard for it," he said, then he stuffed the bills into my pocket and thumped my stomach hard. It was nine hundred dollars.

Shortly thereafter, the tents were packed away, the cables rolled up, and the fake walls torn down. By the end of the day the "war zone" in the woods was vacant. Once back in Bangkok I had the feeling it was a ghost town, despite all the traffic jams and the honking and the noise. I was waking up from a dream in which I was murdered, strung up, tortured, and shot dead, over and over. I had enough dollars to rent a room in a hostel and think about my next move. I had left Iraq to avoid having to fight in Saddam Hussein's army, but after all those border controls, all that wandering, and the constant fear of the police, I was convinced that I'd be better off returning to Iraq. I phoned my family to tell them of my decision, but they said this was impossible. They had just paid a civil servant a huge amount of money to have me declared dead, and even officially buried, so that the bureaucracy would stop asking where I was.

"What would it cost to be resurrected?" I asked.

"A lot," my brother answered.

"What would it cost?" I asked again, thinking of the nine hundred dollars.

"Your life."

So returning to Iraq was not an option.

40

I wandered through Southeast Asia. For three years. It was like scratching your way through the wall of a cell only to find another cell on the other side, and then scratching through the next wall and ending up in yet another cell—this was my life. I don't think anyone has ever bought as many nationalities as I did. Dutch, Portuguese, Spanish, Greek, German, British, Czech, French, Swedish. Each time, I memorized my new name and height and practiced the signature. Fabrício Oliveira, 1.82m. Werner Dachwald, 1.74m. Christian Lefèvre, 1.89m. Lars Lindfors, 1.91m. For more than three years I was the most international person on earth. Since I didn't have much money, I kept buying nearly-expired passports. I was a Spaniard for three months. The expiration date on that passport had been changed so many times that the ink had bled through to the next page.

Twice, I had a Dutch passport: the first one, Ibrahim had given me in Jordan, which I used to travel to Thailand, and the second one had the Antillean name of a man from Curaçao. I went to Soi San Road and for fifty dollars I bought a fake driver's license with the same name, and for another fifty dollars a Dutch student ID. My odyssey without official documents could finally end. I decided to request asylum.

From Bangkok, I traveled via Laos to Hanoi, Vietnam, and discovered that having a Dutch passport was a real blessing, because since they were on the lookout for drugs, everywhere I went they inspected my clothes and bags and everything I was carrying, but not what I was most afraid they would check: the passport itself. First I took the bus to Laos. I wore the filthiest clothes I had, clothes I had intentionally worn a lot and sweated in and never washed, because I'd heard from an Iranian refugee in Bangkok that border officials would stamp your documents quicker if you stank. At the border I gave the Thai official my passport and saw how put off he was by the smell of my dirty T-shirt. He stamped the passport, returned it to me, and I left Thailand for the last time. The same thing happened at Laotian border control.

Three days later I bought a plane ticket to Vietnam. At Vientiane airport, two men herded the cows and sheep off the runway, and the small plane took off for Hanoi. There, I handed the official my passport, and he smiled at me and looked at the passport and smiled at that, too. I smiled back. He stamped it and I walked into Hanoi thanks to his many smiles. I took the train to Ho Chi Minh City, because I had heard from one of the smugglers in Thailand that this was a naïve city as far as forged passports go, and they were therefore quite lax in checking them.

I was sitting in the cheapest compartment of the train. That night I was awakened by two men in uniform. One of them told me to come with them. "And take your bag with you." I followed them, convinced I was going to be searched, but was surprised when they escorted me into the first class compartment, where you could lie down and sleep properly, and it was quiet, even though it was the same train.

"Here," said one of them. "Five US dollars." I only had a ten-dollar bill, which he accepted with a smile. "Ten is okay too," he said, as though in Vietnam, ten was less than five. This would be a good thing, because then I could easily get to Sydney from here. He wished me a good night and I slept in a wonderful bed and thought to myself that the real Vietnam was even better than the Vietnam in Will's movie.

I rented a room in the home of a Vietnamese mother and daughter. The mother spoke French, and the eighteen-year-old daughter spent all her time listening to ABBA and trying to learn English, which the mother regretted, because she preferred French. I had a key to the house and to my room, though I never locked it. If I went out, it was always cleaned and tidied up by the time I got back, and the mother left fruit out for me. I wasn't planning to stay long, because I wanted to go to Australia. But things turned out otherwise. I went to a travel agent, where the woman at the desk also smiled at my passport. Apparently in Vietnam a passport is also a person who must be smiled at. The woman took the passport to a small office and returned with a man who was now holding the passport. And, naturally, smiling.

"Chidnie?"

"Excuse me?"

"You go Chidnie?"

"Yes, I want to go to Sydney." He smiled.

"You go Chidnie," he repeated. Just to be sure, I added that it was in Australia. "Yes, yes, you go Chidnie. You need pisa."

"Pizza? No thank you, I'm not hungry, I want to buy a ticket to Sydney."

"Yes, yes, you go Chidnie. You want pisa."

"No thanks, I don't want pizza. I want ticket."

"I know, I know," he grinned. He called over another man and said something to him in Vietnamese, at which the second man laughed loudly. Then he called over someone else, who also laughed, then yet another colleague came over to ask what was so funny. Maybe the man could tell I had a forged passport, I thought, but he took a sheet of paper, wrote something on it, and showed it to me: *Mr. Holland, you need a visa to go to Sydney.*

He returned my passport, smiled, and thumped me on the shoulder. "Mr. Pizza, Mr. Pizza." The whole office laughed. He gave me the address of the Australian embassy for a visa, and said to come back once I'd gotten it.

"I will come back with an Australian pizza," I said, and this time I laughed along with them.

I left the travel agent. Do I dare go to the Australian embassy with a forged passport? No. A few blocks further there was another travel agent. I went inside and half an hour later I came out with a plane ticket to Amsterdam.

41

So here I was in solitary confinement in a Dutch police station. When they brought me back to a normal cell, it felt like I'd been moved to a five-star hotel.

I was anxious to know if Kadhem was still here, or if he was even still alive. I peered through the small window and saw that his cell was clean and empty. Meanwhile, people came and went. Some were locked up for a few days, others just a few hours. One day a Christian Iraqi was put in the cell across from mine, and we talked through the little window in the door. He had been sent back from Sweden, where his family lived. He told me he wouldn't be spending the night, because they were going to move him from here to an ASC. His family had arranged for a lawyer to take care of it. I asked if he could help me, too.

"Not to worry," he said.

Now, it is generally known that the Christians in Iraq do not lie, do not exaggerate, do not curse, and when they say something, they mean it. He promised to remember my name, but just to be sure, I took a slip of paper left over from Germany with my personal information on it, tore off the bit with my name, wadded it up, and covered it with snot. I threw it out the little window into the corridor and told him to step on it when he left his cell, in the hope that it would stick to the sole of his shoe. Two hours later they let him go. He bent over, picked up the wad of paper, made a disgusted face, and stuck the wad in his pocket. Two days later I was let go. When I called the lawyer to ask how much I owed him, he said that the bill had been paid. From Sweden.

When I returned to the ASC, both my body and spirit were at the end of their tether. I felt like a wild animal that had been tamed. I eyed the Dutch staffers warily, including the volunteers, and did my best to avoid them. If a Dutch staff member asked me to translate something or do them a favor, I did so perfunctorily, and waited until they said I could leave the office again. They thought I was taking things too far: surely I had no reason to be afraid of them? But I had been broken. I don't know what animal to compare myself with. An animal that once had a free spirit, a wild heart, but that now only does what the tamer's whip tells him to do. I was empty. Broken. Kaput.

Upon my return, I stopped by Zainab's room to ask after Kadhem before going to my own room, O-139. She told me he was not back yet. Then I asked at Social Services, but they said they could only tell me if I was family. Was Kadhem really dead, after all? If not, where was he? I eventually called the Red Cross and gave them his name and all the information I had about him. I found out he was still alive, but was now in jail for trying to stab a policeman. I told them what I had seen, and they said they couldn't do anything but that he would be set free soon, because he had calmed down. All I could do was call back if he hadn't turned up in the next three days.

A couple of days later he did indeed turn up. I saw him standing in line to report. He was skinnier than ever. His clothes looked empty. His eyes were deep, dark holes. Extinguished.

"Kadhem!" I cried. He glanced at me, and then turned back to face the counter. He left right after reporting. I went to his room, and one of his roommates opened the door. Kadhem was sitting on the edge of his bed.

"Where have you been all this time?" I asked, to get the conversation going.

"Not important," he said.

"Is there anything you need?"

"No." He kept scratching his neck. His skin was all red. "Some cream for your neck, maybe?" He did not answer, but took a piece of paper out of his pocket and stared at it.

He only left his room to go to the Aldi or to report or to shower, and spoke to no one except Zainab. I asked her about him, and all she said was that he'd gone crazy after returning from Germany.

I remember once seeing him at the front of the line to report. He searched nervously in his pockets for his W-document, the ID paper an asylum seeker gets while his process is still pending. The man at the counter watched him as he fumbled through the pockets of his jacket, his pants, his shirt.

John, the African asylum seeker, walked over to him. "It's right in your hand, man. Don't get crazy on us." Kadhem thrust the document to the agent behind the window and feverishly scratched his neck. It was like he'd slipped into some sort of waking coma, oblivious to his surroundings and doing everything automatically. This neck-scratching was an uncontrollable tic. Zainab told me she had his bank card and PIN code so that she could buy him food, but that he hardly ate anymore and since he got back from Germany she had already taken in his clothes twice. Aside from Zainab, no other asylum seeker could make contact with him, but if a Dutch person spoke to him, he would pay close attention, wide-eyed, and tried to understand every word.

There was a room in the ASC where you could get secondhand clothes. An older Dutch lady volunteered there once a week.

"Are you from Iraq?" she asked me one day. "Do you know what happened to that Iraqi man who ... wait a second, what was his name again? ... Kadim? He's acting so strange. Do you have any idea why?"

"Kadhem. Yes, I do. They made him crazy in a lockdown," I said without thinking.

"Made him crazy? In a lockdown?"

"Yes, every asylum seeker who acts strangely has either been waiting forever or has spent time in a lockdown."

For days, my conversation with the old lady bothered me. I regretted opening my mouth. I was afraid she might tell Sayid, and that he would blab it to Social Services. Or that she would tell them herself. I spent an anxious week until the following Thursday, when the lady would be working in the secondhand clothes room again. I asked her if she could keep last week's conversation to herself.

"What conversation?"

"About the lockdown."

"Oh, now I remember!" Her laugh was more like the cackle of a chicken. "This isn't Iran, you know. You don't have to be afraid of something you said. You're from Iran, right?"

"Iraq."

"Oh yes, Iraq. But we're in the Netherlands now. You don't have to be afraid anymore." The woman did not know that I had discovered by now that the Netherlands was more dangerous than Iraq. The only difference being that Iraq is dangerous for the body, and the Netherlands for the soul. She launched into a lengthy monologue in which she tried to impress upon me that I was in a safe country, and that one needn't be afraid, and that they have laws here and no dictator, et cetera, et cetera ... I nodded sheepishly, as though to admit I was wrong and she was right, and that only now, after our little talk, I could begin my life in the Netherlands, without fear.

Later that afternoon, she spotted me in the social hall. Pieter Oomen from Social Services was with her. She cheerfully called out to me, "No more of that being afraid of the Dutch, hey, Samir?" She smiled and her voice sounded friendly. Pieter looked at me and at her, surprised, and this scared me to death. "He thinks his friend went crazy in a lockdown," she said, "but I told him that we don't torture people in prisons in the Netherlands, and that only hardened criminals get put in jail." The old woman told Pieter how she'd rescued me from fear, while on the inside I was more frightened than ever.

"But ma'am," a voice said. "I went crazy in a lockdown. Just look." It was Firaas. He started dancing like a monkey with a clownish grimace.

Time marched on, but I seemed to be marking time, and had no other choice than to do so. The other asylum seekers offered a touch of diversion now and again. Especially Firaas and Abdulwahid. They were polar opposites. Abdulwahid was a respectable, decent gentleman, and Firaas was a sneak and a brown-nose. Two extremes, a welcome change of pace. I know for sure that if I hadn't lived in the ASC, I would never have got to know either of them.

And while Abdulwahid and Firaas were complete opposites, they had one thing in common: they gave me insight into the system and into the Dutch. Abdulwahid was more like the Dutch. He was honest, direct, and sincere. Firaas, on the other hand, was a compulsive liar and a conniving phony. He always knew how to get whatever he wanted. I was always fascinated (and still am) by how deftly Firaas worked the system and Dutch society, and always got what he was after, and how Abdulwahid absolutely could not. And how Abdulwahid eventually left the country because he just couldn't hack it in the Netherlands, and how at this moment Firaas is walking around Middelburg somewhere as a naturalized Dutchman.

42

One of the receptionists would lock the back door of the ASC every evening at eight o'clock sharp. Then you could only enter or exit the building via Reception. I did not use the back door that often, but once it was locked, the ASC turned into a prison. So I made a habit of using the back door before eight in the evening. Even if I didn't need to go anywhere, I would check the door to make sure it was still unlocked, just to have used it before the staffer came around with the key. Sometimes I would try to open the door after eight o'clock in the hope that they had forgotten to lock it.

The most painful part about the ASC was that it was open 24/7. This actually heightened one's sense of powerlessness. Because here I am wandering around in a building with open doors, waiting for a civil servant somewhere to let me start my life. Sometimes I think it would have been easier if the ASC doors had been kept locked all the time.

Picture yourself waiting at a station or a bus stop with a few people, and not knowing when the next train or bus will arrive. Within fifteen minutes you'll start feeling restless and will look around at the other people, who are getting restless too, and will also look around or at their watch. Now imagine a building with a few hundred waiting people, not for fifteen minutes, but for year after year. Not waiting for a bus or a train, but for their life to begin again.

I paced through the orange halls, back and forth, upstairs and downstairs. Then I walked through the ground-floor hallway past Reception and the offices, to Yellow. In Yellow I paced the halls, back and forth, upstairs and downstairs, walked backed through the ground-floor hallway to get to Green, where I paced the green halls, back and forth, upstairs and downstairs, and then did the same in Blue before returning to Orange, where I went through the whole routine all over again. Sometimes I had to make a conscious effort to look at the color of the walls to know where I was.

At first I tried to avoid the other asylum seekers so as not to have to deal with their problems, but later I started intentionally seeking them out, in order to deal with *their* problems, and not with my own.

Firaas lived in Green. He was new in our ASC, but he was no rookie, that much was clear. The music he listened to in his room betrayed the route he had taken to get to the Netherlands. He listened to Italian music, so he'd been in Italy; there was also Greek music, so he must have also been in Greece; and the Turkish music he played completed the picture: from Kurdistan to Turkey to Greece to Italy, and finally to the Netherlands.

Firaas carried around a small green book in Arabic, which he studied and from which he recited lines as he walked through the halls. I once heard him say, "Our Father who art in Heaven ..." and then burst out laughing. I asked him why, to which he replied that he had to laugh, because all he could think of with "Our Father" was his own father in heaven, and not God.

"Just imagine: my father, who's sleeping up in heaven and snoring so loudly that the people on the next cloud can hear it." Then he exploded with laughter and waved the little green book in his left hand. "The solution will not come from the IND, but from this." And then he broke out laughing again.

Firaas strutted so proudly with that green book and repeated, loudly and calmly, the words from it, that you would almost think he was a preacher himself. But when he couldn't contain himself any longer, he would burst out laughing and roll around on the floor. With him, you never knew whether or not he was acting. One day I asked him when he became a Christian.

"I have never been a Muslim, and will never be a Christian," he said. His father had been an old-fashioned Iraqi Communist, and he himself had grown up in the Soviet Union before his family returned to Iraq. In the end, he fled.

"So what's with the Bible?"

"Not for the Son or the Father or the Holy Spirit, but for the IND official who is handling my dossier." He laughed.

Only later did I understand what he meant: churches in the Netherlands help refugees, especially families with children. A lot of asylum seekers who had exhausted their possibilities of getting a residence permit but also could not be repatriated were simply put out onto the street. These were people, for instance, who had not reported their home country truthfully, and the embassy of the country they claimed to be from denied their existence. Or people who had given a false name, or had invented a name that didn't exist in any country at all. Or people from a country where the situation is unsafe, but to whom the IND nevertheless refuses asylum. This category of asylum seekers was assisted by the church, which was nicknamed "Jesus's ASC." Asylum seekers might get a little money for food, or if they were sick they would be sent to a doctor for free, and in many cases Christians (often older ones) would take an asylum seeker into their home no matter if they were Christian or not.

There was an Iranian asylum seeker named Hussein Aga Hussein. His procedure had been going for ten years, and he looked exhausted and desperate. But suddenly the other asylum seekers saw a transformation in Hussein Aga Hussein. He started to smile and started wearing a suit and necktie and polished shoes. Iranians are usually Shiites, and they do not wear a necktie, because it is shaped like a cross—according to the Shiite Iraqis, at least. No one, not even Sayid, knew why Hussein Aga Hussein wore a tie. He himself was very secretive about his situation. After a few months the letter arrived from the IND that Hussein Aga Hussein had been waiting for all that time. A residence permit. The other asylum seekers started spreading gossip about Hussein Aga Hussein's girlfriend, who was a lawyer. But Sayid insisted there was another secret, that only Hussein Aga Hussein and the IND official knew. The day he left the ASC, everything became clear, to Hussein Aga Hussein's regret.

A green Volvo station wagon carrying three elderly Dutch women and a man of about fifty pulled into the forecourt of the ASC. Hussein Aga Hussein said good-bye to the staff of Social Services and the Foreigners' Police, and to the volunteers. He hastily loaded his belongings into the back of the green Volvo, but the man and the three older women themselves were in no great hurry. They made jokes with the children and handed out candy. As I walked past, the man greeted me kindly and shook my hand.

"Do you know Hussein Aga Hussein?" he asked.

"Yes, he's from Green," I replied.

"What does that mean?"

"The green wing, room G-15."

"Ah, now I understand. I'm so happy for him. He's never missed a Sunday in church. He has found the path to Jesus." This man's name was Jens van Munster, and he was a pastor. He asked me if my Dutch was good enough to read a book.

"Not really," I said. He asked what my first language was, reached into the inside pocket of his blazer and took out two small green books.

"Is this Arabic?" he asked.

"No, Persian, I think," I said. He opened the tailgate of the car and took another book out of a box. "And this one?"

"Yes, Arabic."

"Here, take it. Perhaps you will also find the path to Jesus." he smiled, and I took the book. It was the Bible in Arabic. The same little book that Firaas had been walking around with. I asked him if he had any other books in Arabic, and he took out an illustrated children's book with the stories from the Old and New Testament. He also gave me the address of the church and started talking about the light and the truth. More and more asylum seekers gathered around the car, and the three older women passed out books and the address of the church. And before long, everyone had figured out where Hussein Aga Hussein went every Sunday in his nice clothes.

"Did Hussein Aga Hussein get a residence permit because he became a Christian?" I asked the pastor.

"The residence permit is irrelevant," he replied, smiling. "It is the path to Christ that matters."

"Does that path go through the IND?"

"Not through the IND, but through the heart. It is the path to love, peace, and light."

Up walked Mirko, a Kurdish asylum seeker whose Arabic, Dutch, and English were very poor.

"Did Hussein Aga Hussein get a residence permit because he became a Christian?" he asked me.

"I have no idea, but this man does," I said, pointing to the pastor, who was listening attentively.

"Please ask him for me," Mirko pleaded.

"Mirko would like to know if Hussein Aga Hussein got a residence permit because he became a Christian."

"I don't know," was the pastor's mellifluous answer. He continued, enunciating carefully so that Mirko would understand, "But he did find the way to Jesus. What language do you speak?"

"I Mirko my name seven year thurree months one weeks two days in camp," Mirko said.

"Would you like the Bible in Arabic? Or in another language?"

"Yes mister. Me want residence permit. I Mirko seven year thurree months one weeks two days. Mister look here: one hair black, one hair not black. One hair white, other hair also white. One hair falling. One hair waiting for falling. Soon Mirko bald. Mirko seven year thurree months one week two days in camp. Wait, wait ... No, not two days." He turned to me. "What today is it today?"

"Thursday."

"Wait wait, mister Jesus, I Mirko seven year thurree months one week *thurree* days in camp. One hair black, one hair white, one hair fall in shower, one hair fall in bed of seven year thurree months one weeks thurree days. Waiting, IND, waiting, minister justice, waiting lawyers, waiting ASC."

"What language do you speak?"

"O-107. Seven year thurree months one weeks thurree days. Hair not good. Mirko not good. Mirko letter IND. Mirko letter Jesus. Mirko letter mister. Mirko sick. Mirko waiting. Mirko ASC."

Jens van Munster asked me what language Mirko spoke.

"Kurdish," I said, and he got three boxes of books from the back of the car.

"One of these is Kurdish."

"This," Mirko said, and took the book without looking at it. "Hussein Aga Hussein. Iran. Residence permit. No war Iran ... Mirko Iraq, Saddam, very bad war, no residence permit. Mirko O-107." When Mirko noticed that Jens van Munster just stood there smiling, he turned to me and said in Arabic: "I heard that a Dutch man with a Volvo station wagon is handing out residence permits at the gate. He just gave one to Hussein Aga Hussein. Is this him?"

"More or less," I said. He turned back to Jens van Munster and repeated his story about how long he had been in the ASC and that he should have been the first to get a residence permit, because there was a war in Iraq. Then he asked me to tell the pastor that maybe the IND had confused Iraq with Iran, so that now Iranians were getting residence permits instead of Iraqis.

The rumor that Hussein Aga Hussein had gotten a residence permit via the church spread like wildfire. Whoever got a book from the Volvo station wagon and studied it well, the story went, would take a test at the church and if you passed you would be given a residence permit on the spot. The fact that the story made the rounds in various languages only heightened the misunderstanding. It spread through the windows, doors, and air. Like a bolt of lightning, it zipped through the yellow rooms, to the orange beds and along the blue and green corridors. Asylum seekers thronged the car, with Hussein Aga Hussein, who had not wanted the asylum seekers to think he had converted to Christianity, sitting in the back. In less than an hour, all the boxes in the back of the car were empty. Some asylum seekers had a copy of the book in a language they did not even speak.

Jens van Munster stood among them, speaking in a gentle voice, and the asylum seekers gazed at him as though he were some sort of knight in shining armor who would rescue them from captivity. He said there were no more books, but promised everyone they would get one in their own language. He spoke about the miracle of Jesus, while the asylum seekers thought of the miracle of Hussein Aga Hussein, who had been buried in G-17 in the ASC for more than ten years and had just been resurrected. They believed every word Jens van Munster said, because now they understood why Hussein Aga Hussein had been transformed from a somber, depressed man into one in a suit and tie and gleaming shoes.

"Jesus is the way to the light," Jens van Munster said, his hands in the air.

"What's he saying?" Fatima gasped. She had hurried outside as best she could with her hefty girth once the news had reached her, and now she stood next to me sweating and panting.

"He says that Hussein Aga Hussein has been given a residence permit because he became a Christian," I whispered.

"Jesus is the way and the light. "

"What is he saying now?" Fatima whispered.

"He says they sent a letter to the IND."

"What was in the letter?"

"I don't know."

"Why not?"

"Because I can't listen to him and translate for you at the same time."

"Pay attention now then, and translate it for me later."

"… And what did Jesus say about his enemies? Forgive them! Love them!" The asylum seekers listened in silence.

"What was in the letter?"

"That he went to church every Sunday in decent clothes."

"Now I understand why his shoes were so shiny." Fatima took a deep breath. "Whoever goes to the mosque gets sent to the jihad, and whoever goes to the church gets a residence permit. I think the church is better."

That was Fatima's conclusion. Now I will give you Mirko's take on all of this, and what he tried to make clear to three Afghani women from Yellow and two Iranians, one of them with a wooden leg. Remember that Mirko's Dutch had not improved in all the years he had spent in the ASC, in fact it got worse as a result of hearing all those other languages flying around the place and getting added to his Dutch as though they were real Dutch words.

Mirko said: "This Dutchman. Look. This Hollander man give books to everybody. With Hollands, with Arabic, with Kurdish, with Persian, with Turkian, with China, with African. You take book. You open book. You read book. In hallway camp. Walk back and forth book read. Then buy new clothes and black shoes shiny. Study study. Then every Sunday shaving, shower, new clothes, shoes shiny, walking to exam in church. Eight months. Then open-end residence status. I swear it to Allah."

I heard one of the three older Dutch women call to Firaas, who went over to them. Apparently he knew her and Jens Van Munster. Later he told me exactly what had happened with Hussein Aga Hussein, and what Jens van Munster had done for him. Mirko turned out to be right.

43

Firaas was the world's biggest sneak. He hardly ever slept in his bed in the ASC, but where he did spend his nights, only he knew. Whenever you listened to Firaas, you never knew if he was telling the truth or making it up on the spot. He never told a story the same way twice.

One time I was sitting in the laundry room. He had tossed a few of his shirts into my load of washing. He stared at the whirling drum of the washing machine.

"My head's spinning just as fast as that. Maybe even faster," he said. "Do you remember that Dutch woman I told you about?"

"Which one?" I said. "You tell me about so many women."

"The older one. I was so stupid. Really, really stupid," he said, slapping himself on the forehead. "I met her when she was out walking her dog. I said what a nice dog it was, and that I had always wanted one of my own. I squeezed out a few tears, and whimpered that pets weren't allowed in the ASC. She hugged me. What a horrible rule, she said, everyone should have the right to have a house pet. She invited me to her home. When I made a pass at her, she said she was too old for me. Of course I said that wasn't so. I visited her often and she let me walk her dog. One evening she opened the door wearing beautiful clothes, made up, new haircut. I couldn't wait to get to the bed, and so I screwed her right there in the front hall." He heaved a sigh and turned his gaze back to the washing machine.

"So why are you so sad? Your story ends with an orgasm behind the front door, and is sure to be followed by an orgasm on the sofa, on the stairs, in the bedroom, and in the shower."

"No, but I was really stupid."

"How come?"

"Because today I saw her daughter. And ahh, was she pretty!" He looked at me as I removed our clothes from the washing machine and tossed him his shirts. "What do you think," he said, "should I try for the daughter, too?"

"Don't ask me. Ask Social Services, they're bound to know." It was meant as a joke, but he took it seriously.

"Good idea. Why didn't I think of it myself!"

Later, I was lying on my bed when suddenly Firaas was standing next to me. He exclaimed that the Dutch people are the best in the world. He had been to see Annelies Vos at Social Services.

"I told her I had a problem, and started with, 'May I ask you about it?' I said it that way on purpose, because it flatters the Dutch if you start with 'may I' when you ask for something. It warms them up. Haha. Oh, how happy you can make a Hollander by starting your question with 'may I.' It makes him feel like he can decide whether or not you can have sugar or milk in your coffee. Or watch TV. Or whatever." He guffawed and beat his hands against his chest, as he always did when he laughed. "Annelies Vos said I could talk about anything and everything. This was the Netherlands, wasn't it? I acted surprised." By now I was sitting up on my bed and could see Firaas demonstrate how he acted surprised. "And she said: 'Really! This isn't Afghanistan, you know!' I said: 'Thank you, thank you. In Afghanistan you can't talk about things, but I guess here you can.'"

"But Firaas, you're from Iraq," I said.

"Never mind. It was all about being emotional. If I had to go into the whole story about being from Iraq and not Afghanistan, and that we had Saddam Hussein and not the Taliban, I would get distracted and couldn't be emotional." He laughed even harder, and continued, "Anyway, I whined to her about my problem, and really thought she would think I was a dirty, oversexed jerk, but she seriously advised me that if I really was in love with the daughter, it was only fair to tell her I was also involved with her mother." At this, Firaas nearly doubled over laughing.

"Annelies Vos said that?"

"Yeah, man. And then she said: 'If I were you, I would take some time out from both of them. Then you'll know how you really feel.' And then …"

"Well?"

"She gave me two day passes for the train! And said I didn't need to sign in for a week." He took the train passes out of his pocket as proof.

"I don't believe you," I said. "Two day passes and not signing in for a week, just to decide whether to have an affair with the mother or with the daughter?"

"If you know how to talk to Dutch people, earnestly and with plenty of emotion," Firaas said, "then you can screw not only the mother and the daughter, but Social Services, too."

I would never have been friends with Firaas outside the ASC. He was somebody who was only your friend when he really needed you. Because I listened to him seriously, and never tried to contradict him, he liked talking to me. For instance, when he started a secret affair with the receptionist Tabitha, he told me everything about the staffers at Reception.

Firaas also told me the story of Hussein Aga Hussein and Jens van Munster. He, and he alone, had known for a long time why Hussein Aga Hussein polished his shoes and where he went on Sundays. Firaas had snuck after him one day on his way to church. Apparently Jens van Munster had given him a letter for the IND saying Hussein Aga Hussein had found Jesus, that he was a good Christian, and that as a convert he would face the death penalty if he were sent back to Iran.

Hussein Aga Hussein begged Firaas to keep it under his hat, and bought his silence by promising he could get such a letter, too, and from that moment on, Firaas marched around the ASC with that small green book and learned its verses by heart. Hussein Aga Hussein was worried that if the secret got out, before you knew it five hundred asylum seekers would show up at the church at once, all wanting to become a Christian and get a letter from Jens van Munster. And then he would have to wait another ten years for that sheet of paper.

"And? Did you get one, too?" I asked.

"Of course, it's being processed by the IND now."

"How long until they let you know?"

"No idea. Hussein Aga Hussein got his answer after three months."

"But he's been in the Netherlands longer than you have. One little sheet of paper from the church won't speed up your procedure that much."

"You really don't understand the Netherlands, Samir," he said. "Do you believe this Jens guy personally went to the IND with Hussein Aga Hussein?" I shook my head. "But you do believe that the Iranian spent ten years in the ASC and after he started wearing a necktie and polished shoes he got a residence permit, right? How long I've been in the system doesn't matter. My future in the Netherlands has nothing to do with my story, but with Jens van Munster's. That's what counts for the IND. The bottom line is that the Hollanders trust each other. For ten years they didn't believe Iran was too dangerous for Hussein Aga Hussein, but as soon as Jens van Munster said so, suddenly it was. Wake up, Samir!" he said, and shook me by the shoulders.

I did not believe him, or maybe I did not want to believe him, because if what he said were true, then it would make my life in the ASC even worse than it already was.

44

One day Abdulwahid and I rode our bikes into town. Abdulwahid did not really ride, he zigzagged back and forth over the bicycle path. But he himself thought he was a pretty good cyclist.

When you move to the Netherlands, something changes in your life: cycling becomes more natural than walking. Ask a Hollander how far it is to the station, and he'll say, "Ten minutes by bike." But how far it is on foot—this, he has to think about. Most asylum seekers started learning to ride a bike within a couple of months, even before they learned to speak Dutch. There were three ways for an asylum seeker to get their hands on a bicycle: 1. Steal. 2. Buy. 3. Fish out of the canal. I did not believe number 3 either, until I saw it with my own eyes. An Armenian asylum seeker went fishing with a large U-shaped metal hook attached to a rope. I thought for sure he was one of the ones who had gone crazy from waiting, but there he was, bike-fishing in the canal with his homemade fishing rod. The first one he hauled in was rusty and muddy, so he threw it back and kept fishing until he caught a new bike. I also caught my first bike that day. It was a woman's model, which I still to this day prefer to a man's bike, because you don't have to lift up your right leg like a dog peeing against a tree.

Asylum seekers learned to ride a bike on the ASC forecourt. The slowest learner by far was Fatima, because of her weight: if you helped her onto her bike from the right side, she'd fall over to the left, and if you helped her on from the left side, she'd fall over to the right, and the time a sturdy Chechen and I decided to help her onto the bicycle from both sides, it cost me three ribs.

In second place for slow learning was Parishad, an Afghan woman in her mid-fifties. Because of her head-scarf and billowing Islamic dress, she totally forgot she was on a bike at all. Before she sat down on the saddle, she would take a deep breath, recite a few holy verses so that Allah would not abandon her, and as soon as she said "now" (the only Dutch word she knew, and this she had only learned in order to learn to ride a bike) we would push her off. Right away she'd start screaming "Allah Akhbar!" as though she was not on a bicycle in the Netherlands, but on a tank in Afghanistan. Her attempts to ride always ended dramatically, because either her headscarf blew off her head, or one of her many skirts flapped up, which she then tried to push back down with both hands, forgetting about the han-dlebars entirely.

In third place was Zainab, who wanted to learn to ride a bike so she could do her daily shopping at the Turkish market, where the meat was halal. Her problem was that she was terribly unsure of herself, and despite our constant instructions to look ahead, she always forgot where she was. We would point forward, to illustrate that "ahead" was not under her feet, but the minute she started moving she shrieked as if the saddle were a wild animal that might bite her, the handlebars a snake winding its way around her hands, and the pedals two scorpions. When the bicycle fell over, she would hop off it and watch from a safe distance as the wheels spun.

But the most difficult case of all was Abdulwahid.

Abdulwahid loved horseback riding and could also ride camels and donkeys. If the dinosaurs had not become extinct, he would have ridden them too. He could drive a truck, a tank, or a bus, so you would think riding a bicycle would be a breeze. He learned quicker than the three ladies, but his problem was that he didn't really ride, he swerved.

So the Dutch people who passed us that day became irritated, because we rode very slowly, and if Abdulwahid had soaked his tires in white paint, the line he left behind would resemble a cardiogram. Sometimes they would shout, "Hey, watch out!" or just give us dirty looks, although they could just as well have had a little chuckle about the Yemeni man trying to become a Hollander.

When a young couple passed us, and the woman had to swerve so much to avoid Abdulwahid that she almost ended up on the sidewalk, she cursed loudly.

"*Godverdomme!*" She cycled on. Abdulwahid started pedaling furiously, and set off in pursuit.

"Where are you going?" I called to him.

"She's angry," he called back in Arabic, and I could feel trouble brewing. The couple was unaware that Abdulwahid was cycling after them. They stopped at a house and went inside. Abdulwahid stopped, too, and knocked on the door. A woman opened it. Her expression said she would rather watch ten horror films than stand face-to-face with this panting, strangely-dressed man on her doorstep.

"I seeing girls boys seeing also them here coming. Girls says then me and my bike, girls says ..." Abdulwahid wanted to repeat her swear word, but he had forgotten it, and asked me in Arabic what it was. At the sound of Arabic, the woman recoiled even more, as though there were an al-Qaida terrorist on her front porch.

"Godverdomme," I said.

"Yes, *gatwerdoomie*." Just then, the young couple appeared at the door. Now, six fearful eyes gazed at Abdulwahid, and then a gray-haired man also appeared. The four Hollanders stared at us without any idea what we were doing on their doorstep, and Abdulwahid stood there repeating himself in his unintelligible Asylumseekerese. Inside the house, a dog barked, two cats eyed us nervously from behind the living room window, and if I'm not exaggerating, a parrot shrieked. Neighbors peered out from windows and doors.

"Sorry, but what do you want?" the woman asked.

"We were just wondering if you had any old bikes for the asylum seekers at the ASC," I said, and Abdulwahid nodded, because he thought I asked the woman why the girl had cursed at us.

"No, we don't have any old bicycles. Not in the shed, either. Nowhere."

"Thank you, ma'am," I said, as I made to turn and leave with Abdulwahid.

"Could you not come to the door anymore?" the woman said. Her voice sounded cautious and irritated at the same time.

"We won't be back again, ma'am," I said, and led Abdulwahid by the arm to our bicycles.

"Did you tell her the young one was rude to us?"

"Yes."

"Did she apologize?"

"The woman said that girl was in a hurry, because her grandmother is lying upstairs on her deathbed. She was cycling so fast because her granny could die at any moment." When Abdulwahid heard this, he turned and called out to the foursome, who were still standing in the doorway, "Sorry girls, sorry boys, sorry parents, sorry dogs, sorry cats, good life granny upstair."

We set off on our bicycles, and I tried to keep the tempo going, in case they had called the police.

"Not so fast. They didn't call the police," Abdulwahid said, "because grandma upstairs is dying." We swerved our way back to the ASC.

45

It was a well-known fact that gay people were quick to be given asylum, sometimes within a year, and that they always got a room to themselves in the ASC. Firaas, as expected, made good use of this.

The day Firaas got his own room it was raining cats and dogs, as it had been for days. He came and sat down next to me in the social hall and dangled the key in front of my face.

"Know what this is?" He dangled the key even closer to my eyes and leaned over, his mouth close to my ear. "Deep sleep, Samir ..." he whispered. "Liberation from snoring and farting." He laughed out loud. "The ASC has just turned into a free five-star hotel. Just got it. Can you believe it?"

"But how?" I asked incredulously.

"I was afraid Annelies Vos would see me, because I had already asked for advice about the older woman and her daughter, so she knows for sure I'm not gay. I waited until Wednesday, because that's her day off, and went to Hilde." He had put on his most pitiful voice and told Hilde he had a secret to share with her, and even the other staffers mustn't find out. When she wouldn't take him to a private room, he broke into tears.

"Real tears?" I asked.

"Of course, what else?" he replied. "I can cry on command. Didn't I ever tell you what happened at the Turkish border?" I shook my head. "A bunch of us got picked up by Turkish soldiers. I cried and kissed their boots, and they let me go. Then I cried and begged until they let us all go. We ran away. Later, one of the guys I was with asked if I wasn't ashamed to whimper like a woman. Now the Turkish soldiers would think that all Iraqis were crybabies and bootlickers. I had to laugh, because he was the one who had begged me to do something to get us off the hook. I rescued him, he ran off like a rabbit, and now he was trying to act like a lion. Haha!"

"And then?"

"Well, Hilde patted me on the shoulder and—"

"I meant at the Turkish border."

Firaas had cried and begged his way from Iraq to Western Europe. On his second attempt to get into Turkey, he succeeded in reaching Ankara, where he cried for an elderly Greek lady, and did such a good job of it that she paid for his trip to Greece. He never saw her again, but had begged enough money to get from Greece to Italy, and finally to the Netherlands.

"Okay, and the single room?"

Firaas explained his tactic: if you cried and altered your voice every now and then, it gave the impression that you had been bottling it up for years and this was finally your chance to come clean. Hilde brought him to another small office and got a box of tissues. He sat wiping the tears from his cheeks until she started looking at her watch. This meant it was enough, because, he explained, there's no point in crying for a Dutch person who is pressed for time.

"I said I was gay and that no one knew, and in fact I hadn't known either until now, but here in the Netherlands, where everything is possible, I finally dared to give in to my true feelings. Sleeping in a room with three other men gave me nightmares, I said, I was afraid they would rape or murder me. I said I was so happy to feel free and safe in the Netherlands, and was finally ready to come out of the closet."

"And then you asked for a room to yourself."

"What? Of course not! I'm no fool! Now listen good, Samir. Let the Hollander decide for himself what you need. Then he'll do his best to arrange it, and feels like he's rescued you. That he has solved your problem. If you tell him what you want, he gets annoyed that you're telling him what to do, and he'll doubt your honesty. I thought Hilde would need to discuss it with her colleagues first, and then Annelies Vos would find out I said I was gay, and would blab that it wasn't true, because I had come to her earlier with that mother-daughter dilemma. Or that that Pieter Oomen guy would throw a wrench into the works. That's why I thought I would never get the room to myself, and forgot all about it, but last week Hilde asked how I was doing. I told her I was sleeping poorly, and she understood. This gave me hope, but still nothing happened. Until this morning, when I heard she was looking for me. And now ..." He dangled the key again. Then he whispered, "For three euros you can sleep in my room when I'm not there."

For weeks, Firaas tried to keep his private room a secret. Not because he was afraid the others would think he was gay, which they knew full well he wasn't, but rather that Social Services would find out that it wasn't true. There was a woman, whose name I won't mention, who would sleep with an asylum seeker for ten euros. She had three children, and her husband had become an alcoholic in the six years they lived in the ASC. He hit her if she did not bring him alcohol. At first she borrowed money from the others, but since she was unable to repay it she started sleeping with them. Later, she rented Firaas's room to sleep with men, with the free condoms from Reception.

I might have already mentioned that asylum seekers were allowed a maximum of three condoms per day and two aspirins per eight hours. This meant an asylum seeker had the right to three orgasms and six headaches per day. Name and time were taken down, and if you returned too soon for your next aspirins, you went away empty-handed. In the case of a really serious headache, you sent another asylum seeker. I remember once asking John to get me some aspirin. I had just been talking to Yelena, and John returned with three condoms. When I said I had a headache, he replied, "Sorry, man, I thought your pain was lower down."

John, incidentally, was the one who was always asking people to pick up three condoms for him at Reception, because he had already used up his daily quota. One day I told him he must be a rabbit, needing so many condoms. He laughed and said he didn't use them himself.

"So what do you do with them?" I asked.

"I smoke them," he said. This was more or less right, because I later found out he sold them at the entrance to a coffeeshop, and used the money to buy marijuana.

46

The asylum seeker we called Yellow got his nickname because on the day he arrived at the ASC he was wearing a yellow shirt and was given a private room in Yellow. He had been sent to us from Utrecht, where he had spent three weeks in an RC. He immediately got a room to himself, and within nine months he had been given political asylum. Technically it should have been humanitarian asylum, his lawyer said, but a residence permit is a residence permit. He was friendly, and I heard he came from a wealthy family. Zainab once asked me if the person in Y-3 was a man or woman, because he always looked timidly at the floor when he walked through the halls. No one knew his real name, everyone called him Yellow. He didn't mind, and always answered with a smile if someone called him by his nickname. When people congratulated him on getting the residence permit, Yellow reacted awkwardly, as though he had swiped it from someone else. In fact, everyone was happy for Yellow, except Abdulwahid.

An asylum seeker who got a residence permit usually tried to keep it a secret from the others. And when he or she was subsequently assigned a house or apartment, the address almost never got shared with anyone in the ASC. This was because the person with a residence permit did not want other asylum seekers showing up on his doorstep if they were evicted from the ASC or wanted to go into hiding to evade deportation. And there was a good chance of this, because who else could asylum seekers turn to? The only asylum seeker I ever saw hand out his address was Yellow. He wrote out many little slips of paper with his address on it and gave one to every asylum seeker who said goodbye to him. He said they were welcome and that his door was always open should they be evicted from the ASC. Before Yellow left, Sayid spread the rumor that the Justice Ministry had tested Yellow's ass to make sure that he was gay. I'm sure he meant it as a joke, but people took it seriously. Talib joked vulgarly that getting a residence permit in the Netherlands wasn't so difficult. It simply involved having your ass tested, and if you passed—he snapped his fingers—you got asylum.

Abdulwahid and I were walking down the hall when I mentioned that Yellow was leaving.

"Is he being deported?"

"No, he got a residence permit."

"How long has he been in the country?"

"Nine months, I think. They gave him political asylum."

"Come with me," Abdulwahid ordered, and pulled me along like a sheep. He was in a hurry, and at first I thought he wanted to go to Social Services, but he led me to the yellow wing, knocked on Yellow's door, and when he answered, Abdulwahid pulled him along, too.

"Let's go, and bring that political asylum of yours."

"Huh? My what?" Yellow was so taken aback by Abdulwahid's fierceness and haste that he grabbed his letter from the IND and went with us to Social Services. Abdulwahid marched up to Mr. Van 't Zijde's desk, as he was the only one in the office.

"Mister!" Abdulwahid said.

"Make an appointment first," Van 't Zijde said curtly.

"What did he say?" Abdulwahid asked me.

"That you need to make an appointment."

"Ask him why I need to make an appointment. Aren't we all in the same building? Does he make an appointment with his wife at home if he wants to talk to her? Does he make an appointment with an asylum seeker if he wants something from him?" I translated. Van 't Zijde asked what the problem was.

Abdulwahid grabbed the sheet of paper with the residence permit out of Yellow's hand.

"Translate for him: Why does an ass get asylum in the Netherlands, and a head doesn't?" he demanded. Spittle flew off his lips. Mr. Van 't Zijde did not answer. "Look!" Abdulwahid shouted. By now, more staffers had come into the office to see what was going on, so I translated for everyone. "The Ministry of Justice tested this man's ass to see if he was a political refugee. Why don't they test even one head of the hundreds of other asylum seekers?" Van 't Zijde went as pale has a ghost. He did not dare look at Abdulwahid. Anneke stepped forward and took the paper out of Abdulwahid's hand.

"Listen here," she said crossly, "don't talk to us like that."

He brought his face closer to hers. "How am I supposed to talk, then? With my ass?" he shouted. Anneke took a step back.

"Tell him that if he doesn't leave our office immediately, I'll call the Foreigners' Police." I knew that Abdulwahid would attack and strangle Anneke if I translated this for him.

"Oh, Abdulwahid," I said, "aren't you ashamed to shout at a woman like that?" because I knew this was the only way to calm him down. It worked; he went silent at once.

I led him out of the office and to his room, where he sat wallowing in shame for having shouted at a woman.

A few minutes later, Anneke came to me.

"That's totally out of order, that kind of talk. And he can't force another person to come to us with his asylum papers. If he doesn't watch out he'll end up in a cell." It was as though she were making me the guilty party. She waited for an answer, but I didn't know how to respond.

"I think Abdulwahid is stronger than a cell," I warned her. "They'll let him out after a few days or weeks or months. Then he'll calmly sharpen a knife in the kitchen and decapitate someone from Social Services." Anneke could tell I was serious.

"Come with me," she said. I followed her, and she gave me two day passes for the train, one dated that same day, and another without a date.

"Go give these to Abdulwahid, and say he can come back when he has calmed down."

"Where is he supposed to go?"

"I don't care. He's been given train passes before, to go to see a friend in Nijmegen or somewhere."

"What about reporting?"

"I'll take care of that. He doesn't have to come back until he's calmed down."

I brought the two train passes to Abdulwahid, but he didn't believe he'd been given them just like that. He thought I had begged Social Services for them, so he insisted on giving me one.

"Do you think the woman from Social Services is still afraid?" he asked. His shame had not worn off.

"Maybe you should try to be less angry when you talk to Dutch people," I said. "They're always so soft-spoken."

"Me, angry?" he exclaimed, surprised. "Have you ever

seen me angry? I've never been angry, not in my entire life."

"So you weren't angry back there?"

"Of course not. If I had been angry, I'd have broken his neck and taken that bitch's computer and smashed it on her head."

But of all the situations involving Abdulwahid, the one I think back on most was his attempt to finagle a letter from Jens van Munster saying he had become a Christian. This was after Firaas also got asylum as a Christian convert. I saw the letter Jens van Munster had sent. The pastor's name was printed at the top, and at the bottom was his signature. It was a brief, official-sounding letter. Firaas read it out to me and exploded with laughter after every sentence. Especially the part that said Firaas had "found the way to Jesus" and that there was no doubt that "Jesus lived in his heart."

47

Hussein Aga Hussein's residence permit was one thing, but when Firaas also got his papers there was no doubt in the minds of the asylum seekers that every Christian convert would be automatically given asylum. So on Sundays in the ASC you saw more and more asylum seekers putting on nice clothes and polished shoes and going off to church.

One day Abdulwahid came to O-139 and asked me if I thought this was really a way to get a residence permit. "If it is," he mused, "then it must be a miracle. God isn't even capable of it. Ali Mohammed in B-17 has been begging God for a residence permit for eight years now, and it still hasn't happened."

"Well, Jesus can do it in six months," I said. "He walks on water, raises the dead, restores sight to the blind, and now has a new task: giving residence permits to asylum seekers. If Jens van Munster could rewrite the Bible, I'm sure he would put that in."

"I'm not joking."

"Neither am I. Jesus gave two residence permits to two asylum seekers. Both of them within a few months. If that's not a miracle, then I don't know what is."

The following Sunday, Abdulwahid woke me at 6 a.m. and insisted I go to Jens van Munster's church with him, to ask for a letter saying he was a Christian. I was still half asleep, and asked him to come back in a couple of hours.

"And besides, Abdulwahid, it's not that simple. He won't just give you a letter. You have to convince him you've become a true Christian. That takes years."

"It took Firaas only a few weeks."

"Firaas could convince not only Jens van Munster of it, but Jesus himself. You can't."

"I'll tell the man from the church that I believe in Jesus, but don't want to become a Christian. That I only want that letter. I'm sure he'll give it to me."

"You believe in Jesus, but don't want to be a Christian?"

"Of course! Jesus is in the Koran, too. And Mary. I'll tell that to the man from the church." Abdulwahid couldn't remember his name, and kept referring to him as "the man from the church." "I believe in Jesus. And my aunt's name is Myriam—that's Jesus's mother, who got pregnant without a husband. I've known about Jesus for a long time. As soon as the man from the church hears this, he'll give me that letter."

Abdulwahid and I got on our bicycles and swerved our way through the deserted city to the church. Abdulwahid entered a church for the first time in his life. He gazed upward and all around him.

"Big place," he said. In the pews were a few Dutch people and several asylum seekers. At the back there was a table with white porcelain coffee cups placed upside down on their saucers, two large Thermos flasks, milk and sugar packets, and cookies from the Aldi. Jens van Munster came over and greeted us warmly. I stood a few steps behind Abdulwahid, to make it clear I was only here to translate for him. I would have felt a little warmer with a cup of tea, and pretended to try to figure out which of the Thermoses contained hot water.

"Sorry, that's for after the service," Van Munster said. I expected him to ask us something, but he only shook our hands and smiled benignly.

Abdulwahid looked at the tall, stained-glass windows.

"What a huge place," he said. "They're bound to have plenty of letters here, not just for a couple of asylum seekers, but for all of us ... But where do they hand them out?" He had expected a table where the papers were already laid out, waiting to be stamped.

"This gentleman writes the letters," I said. Jens van Munster smiled when I gestured at him.

"But where are they?"

"That's not important. When it's your turn, he'll know where to find you. So do you want me to translate, or not? He's waiting."

"Look, mister church," Abdulwahid began, in Arabic. "They did not crucify Mary along with Jesus. But in the ASC they are crucifying five hundred people. A mother with her children, a father with his children, a child with his parents, and an old man with his sons. Everyone gets crucified along with everyone else." I translated, and Jens van Munster listened calmly. Abdulwahid pointed to a text on the wall and asked what it said. It was, Matthew 27, verses 45 through 47, the pastor replied.

Now from the sixth hour there was darkness over all the land unto the ninth hour. And about the ninth hour Jesus cried with a loud voice, saying, "Eli, Eli, lama sabachthani?" That is to say, My God, my God, why hast thou forsaken me? Some of them that stood there, when they heard that, said, This man calleth for Elias.

Abdulwahid nodded, slowly surveyed the entire church, and then turned to Jens van Munster, looked straight at him, and took a deep breath. He reached into his pants pocket and took out a crumpled piece of paper. I thought it would be his personal information, but I was mistaken.

The sheet of paper was so crumpled that Abdulwahid must have had it in and out of his pocket a thousand times. On it was a numbered list from one to I-don't-know-what, and next to each number was a name written in Arabic script and a year in Roman numerals. Both sides of the sheet were filled; the handwriting started out large, but got smaller as it reached the bottom edge of the page, so that it would all fit.

Abdulwahid looked at the sheet of paper and solemnly straightened his posture. He spoke in Asylumseekerese. A few sparrows were chirping noisily, the church acoustics amplifying the sound, but when Abdulwahid began speaking, they went silent.

"Here, mister. Name asylum seeker. Here, mister, years wait in camp." Jens van Munster's face remained unmoved, but friendly, as Abdulwahid read off the list of names. The church's acoustics accentuated the solemnity of his delivery.

"Salim Ali al-Shumari, eleven years waiting. Don Karoma, eight years waiting. Samu Biru, five years waiting. Karo …" He tried to decipher the last name, but couldn't. "Karo Karo, ten years waiting."

"Why are you reading me all those names?" Van Munster asked calmly.

"Just wait, I have to say them all." Van Munster listened in silence. The Dutch churchgoers and the asylum seekers in the pews also listened attentively, and turned to look at Abdulwahid as he recited the list. "Akram

Isfahani, thirteen years waiting. Bagdjaar Ali Amien, seven years waiting."

Jens van Munster repeated his question. Abdulwahid looked at me.

"He asked why you're reciting that list of names."

"I promised I would get each of them a letter for the IND from the man from the church," Abdulwahid said, "stating their name and that they are good Christians." I translated.

"But this is a place of worship and reverence, not for letters for the IND," Van Munster said gently, and I translated. Abdulwahid's eyes widened.

"Tell him he gave letters to two asylum seekers, and they got a residence permit. He did that. Why not now?"

"Because this is a hallowed place, it is the house of God and not a place to ask for immigration papers," Jens van Munster replied. I did not translate this, because I could tell from Abdulwahid's face there was no point.

"Why not?" he yelled.

"Sorry, but there's no need to shout."

"And why not shout? Am I at City Hall? Or in the ASC?" Now Abdulwahid was shouting for real. "People are rotting away in the ASC!" He pointed to his list. "For years and years. You can save them with one sheet of paper. You did that for two already. There are families there, old people, children, sick people who cannot go to the hospital without a residence permit." I tried to translate all of this, but the pastor kept repeating—still with his calm, serene face— that this was a church, a place of prayer and contemplation, and not for immigration papers.

"Liar!" Abdulwahid shouted. "You went to the ASC and handed out little books to give them a ticket to Heaven. And here in your church, you won't give them a piece of paper? Where are those letters?" Van Munster stood there, and did nothing. All he said was that maybe it was better if we left now, and came back another time to have a quiet chat.

"You want me go?" Abdulwahid screamed in Asylum-seekerese. "You calling police then? Go ahead, call police." His face trembled, and he turned red. "Police work for Jesus? Call police then!" When he paused because no one reacted to his tirade, I saw my chance to take him by the arm and slowly lead him out of the church, but he shouted all the way outside that they should go ahead and call the police.

On this quiet, gray Sunday, my greatest wish was to cycle out to the sea under the gray sky, but I was afraid that Abdulwahid was still angry enough to turn around and go back to the church and shout some more. So I stayed with him until we reached the ASC. I asked him why his own name was not on the list.

"Oh, you're right," he said, his eyes wide, as he placed his bicycle in the bike rack. "I guess I forgot."

This is how my life went in those days. I allowed the days to pass, and watched the lightning that struck other asylum seekers. But lightning struck me, too, when Kadhem committed suicide.

48

He hung himself by a rope from a tree. He had come to my room earlier that week to repay the twenty euros he said he had borrowed from me in Germany. I couldn't remember lending him money, but figured he saw it as an excuse to resume contact. This was probably not the case, because he'd lost all interest in the goings-on at the ASC: Abdulwahid and the church, the General, who I'd heard had been given a residence permit, Yelena and her boyfriend Maarten. It was clear he preferred to be left alone.

Zainab kept saying that the Hollanders had made Kadhem crazy, and that now he wouldn't even touch the food she made for him. He spent the last three or four months of his life more or less secluded in his room. I once saw him at reporting time, and he was trembling so much out of fear for the man behind the window that I went to Fedde de Vlieger at Social Services and said I was worried about Kadhem. But he told me to let Social Services do their job, and to worry about myself instead of the others. I waited until Thursday, which was Fedde de Vlieger's day off, and went to Patrick Schepenmaker. Patrick looked in the computer and said I had previously been to Social Services with the same thing, and that Fedde had already given me an answer. The subject shifted from Kadhem's mental health to me wasting Social Services' time with things that were not my business, and to how I mustn't go approaching different staffers with the same question. On a day when both Fedde de Vlieger and Patrick Schepenmaker were free, I expressed my concerns to Ruth Bleeker, but she too said I should mind my own business, and that she knew full well which asylum seekers needed help, and that Social Services personnel all followed the same protocol. And since there wasn't a day when Fedde de Vlieger, Patrick Schepenmaker, and Ruth Bleeker were all free, I did not go back.

The day before it happened, Zainab knocked on my door, accompanied by Akram, an Iranian woman. Since it was "not done" for a woman to knock on a man's door, she had brought Akram with her as proof that she didn't visit my room alone.

"I looked for you in the social hall, and in Yellow and Blue and Green, and couldn't find you," she said, "which is why I'm here."

"What can I do for you?" I asked.

"Kadhem," she said with a meek smile, as if it was something that was embarrassing, but still needed to be said.

"What about Kadhem?"

"I think he's gone crazy. He's trembling like he has a fever, and he said, 'I can't sign in tomorrow. I'm afraid they'll lock me up.'"

The next day, he hung himself.

In addition to Dagel and Kadhem, I knew six others who committed suicide during my nine years in the ASC. I really hope I can find a path through this story that bypasses their deaths. Kadhem's death sliced open my heart, and it bleeds to this day whenever I think back on it. Maybe because I knew him better and longer than the others.

In the days following his suicide I felt like I couldn't breathe, and spent as much time as possible outside the ASC. When it got chilly and dark I'd go back inside, but the minute I passed Reception, I felt the noose around my neck tighten. I went to Patrick Schepenmaker and asked if I couldn't get transferred to another ASC. It didn't matter where.

"Why?"

"I can't live here anymore. I'm claustrophobic."

"The Netherlands is a small country. You'll be claustrophobic wherever you go."

"I can't sleep. Things have happened here that make me claustrophobic."

"Like what?"

"Kadhem's death."

"Oh, was he a friend of yours? Sorry to hear it. But you weren't his roommate, were you? Then I'm afraid there's no grounds for a transfer. You can request one through the normal procedure, but there's a long waiting list." Further attempts to get a priority transfer were also in vain. I sat on the stairs leading up to Orange and heard myself wheeze with every breath. Edith, a nurse at the clinic, came up to me.

"Are you okay?" she asked.

"Kadhem."

"I didn't ask your name," she said with a smile, "I asked if you were okay. You look so short of breath. Maybe you need Ventolin."

"Not Ventolin. Another ASC," I said. She shrugged her shoulders and walked on, but two days later she showed me how to use the Ventolin inhaler.

"When it's finished, you can get another one," she

said. Every time I thought of Kadhem, I reached for the Ventolin.

Zainab had been the keeper of Kadhem's bank card for some time. She'd withdrawn his weekly allowance, but did not use it for groceries; instead, she saved it for him, €118 in total. But she didn't know what to do with it now that he'd taken his own life. Kadhem's remains, too, worried her. What had become of them, what had the Hollanders done with his body? She would start her day by inquiring at Social Services. Someone always went along to translate for her, and they would give her the exact same answer every time: that they could not tell her what had happened to Kadhem's remains because she was not a relative of his. Some residents who had already translated for her repeated Social Services' answer even before she asked them to accompany her. Then she would claim to have a different question for them, but once at Social Services it was again: what had happened to Kadhem's body? Since I never refused anything she asked, she latched onto me as her regular interpreter. The first time we went, Edwin Bunskoek said as soon as we walked in, "If she's here to ask about the body, the answer is the same." Then he opened his red notebook and said she had already asked about "Kadim's" body eleven times. I translated this for her.

"Today, I'm not here to ask about the body." I translated.

"What, then?"

"I was just wondering ... If an asylum seeker commits suicide, what do the Hollanders do with the body?"

"We are not a cemetery, we're Social Services," Edwin said, more to me than to her, and demonstratively changed the number 11 to 12 with a red pen. We left the office, but Zainab waited in the hallway. Two hours later she was still there, gazing forlornly at the staffers' faces through the glass partition, hoping someone would call her in and tell her something, anything, about Kadhem's remains.

She once asked me what the Arabic word *jutha* was in Dutch.

"Corpse," I said. "Or *body*—easier to pronounce." She asked me to repeat it every time she saw me in the hallway, in the kitchen, in the social hall, until the word stuck. She would look at me with utmost concentration and say: "Body."

"Perfect," I would say. From that day on, she went to Social Services every morning and waited at the door until walk-in hour started at 8 a.m., and recited the sentences she had taken so much trouble to memorize.

"Good morning, sir. Good morning, ma'am. Body Kadhem where?"

Just as she used to go to Reception every day to ask whether there was mail for her from the IND or the Ministry of Justice, now she went to Social Services to ask after Kadhem's remains.

"The Hollanders are Christians, they have no idea how to give Kadhem a proper Muslim burial," she fretted. "His soul will never find peace."

When she heard from another asylum seeker that Dutch people sometimes cremate a body and scatter the ashes in the ocean, this nearly drove her crazy.

"I can't sleep anymore," she sobbed to me. "Kadhem visits me every night. He knocks on the door and says, 'Zainab, first the Hollanders made me crazy, and now they want to burn me and throw my ashes into the sea. Please, Zainab, save me!'" No matter how much I tried to reassure her that this wasn't so, she was in a panic. I once saw her dash to Reception, screaming that she had seen an asylum seeker who resembled Kadhem. She couldn't get a good view of him because he was running, so she assumed it was Kadhem running away, so as not to be burned. She started to see this fleeing Kadhem on a nightly basis.

Anneke from Social Services tried to reassure her that Kadhem's body had been dealt with appropriately. That it had been treated with the utmost respect, but that she simply couldn't tell her where it was because Zainab was not a relative. But this did not help. Until her last day in the ASC, Zainab went to Social Services every day. She did not stand in the doorway, because there she would be sent away, but at the glass partition, and waited there for as long as it took for a staffer to look up at her and mouth the words: "No body today." Then she would leave, and go about her daily business. She made sure every asylum seeker knew that there was once an asylum seeker named Kadhem who had gone crazy and killed himself, and that no one knew what had become of his remains.

49

Perhaps the most difficult thing about recounting life in the ASC is to make time progress, because time seemed to stand still there, like a swamp filled with poisonous insects and swollen cadavers. How often did I walk through the building with the idea that it was still my first day, a day that simply lasted longer than other days. And when I tell about the other asylum seekers, I sometimes lose track of when I met them and when we parted ways.

At the end of the hallway in Blue there was a window. I often stood there looking out at the trees. I watched the buds appear on the branches, the leaves turn green and get wet and eventually change color and fall off—without actually seeing them. Yelena once came over and asked what I was looking at.

"Over there."

"Over where?"

"There." I pointed off in the distance.

"You probably don't realize you've gone crazy," she said. "If you get a residence permit, the first thing you need to do is go to a psychiatrist. You know, I'm starting to go crazy here, too." She emphasized the word "too."

"Looking out there is the only way *not* to go crazy," I said. She thumped my chest with her fist, said something in Russian, smiled, and went off to her room.

During my first six months, I was afraid to talk to anyone who had been in the ASC for more than three years.
I was terrified that their fate would be mine as well.
These were strong men and women, who used to be
laborers, soldiers, rebels, engineers, doctors, scientists,
and so on. After their third year, for some reason, they
began to lose control over themselves. It always fright-
ens me to see pleasant, calm asylum seekers suddenly
become someone else.

I remember a Russian asylum seeker with red hair and
freckles, who we called the Red Russian. Rumor had it
that he was a professional weapons manufacturer. He
was assigned a room with two Chechens and an Armenian, because they all spoke Russian. Sometimes I saw
him with bottles of alcohol he'd bought, and they did
not appear to be the cheap brands either. One day he
asked me in his Russian English if I knew of a pool hall
in the neighborhood. This way we got on greeting terms.
Every now and again he would ask after "that Russian
girl"—Yelena—whom he never talked to, which struck
me as strange, seeing as asylum seekers with the same
language always talked to each other. One day I saw the
Red Russian rubbing his back against the wall. I thought
he had an itch, but Sayid told me he had developed a
pathological fear of being stalked, and was terrified
that there was someone behind him. Children began to
run away when they saw him. In his lucid moments he
tried to reassure them, but this was futile, because the
mothers had already told the children that the Red Russian had gone crazy. Back when Firaas was still living
there, he would laugh when he saw him, and whine in
mock pity, "Oh, poor Red Russian, he requested asylum
in the wrong country. In Iraq, he would not only get

political asylum, but a weapons factory, too, and a few thousand men to work for him."

Speaking of Firaas, he was the one who showed me that it was possible to have contact with Dutch people outside the ASC. At a certain point I got curious as to what he did in all those hours he spent outside the center. So he took me to the home of a woman in her forties, who lived there with three large dogs. She was very friendly. I sat down on the sofa. She noticed that the TV was still on, apologized, and switched it off. I never could figure out why Dutch people apologized and turned off the TV when they had company. She offered me something to drink.

"Tea," I said. She started listing off all the kinds of tea she had. I said that regular black tea would be fine, with sugar, at which she listed off all the kinds of black tea she had, and how many kinds of sugar. It was like being in a specialty food shop.

While she was off making the tea, the three large dogs licked me incessantly. I was covered in saliva. The woman came in with the tea. When I tried to shoo the dogs away, the woman smiled and said they were very sweet dogs and would not bite. I didn't dare tell her that I thought their saliva was disgusting, especially on my face, because I didn't want to insult her. Firaas had obviously been here often. He left the room for a bit, and then came back. Then the woman left for a bit, and came back. She spoke to Firaas exactly the way she talked to her dogs.

"You've left the upstairs light on again. Electricity costs money, you know. It's not free, like in the asylum center." She looked at me, switched back to being friendly, and asked why I chose to come to the Netherlands. I gave her a short answer, because Firaas had told me that the Dutch prefer this. When she returned to the kitchen, I grabbed the chance to ask Firaas to open a window, as the dog smell was overpowering. I said it quickly in Arabic, so as not to have to ask her directly, or insinuate that her house stank. Firaas opened the window, but when the woman saw it, she scolded him—just as before, like talking to a dog—that he must close the window at once. "Heating costs money. It's not free, like in the ASC." I drank my tea, which tasted like dog drool, got up and thanked her, and said goodbye to the woman and her three dogs. Cycling back to the ASC, I was grateful to breathe fresh air again.

Firaas caught up with me. "I'll go back to the camp with you," he said. I asked why he didn't stay any longer. "You know, sometimes you have to choose: either sit like a dog in that house, or like an asylum seeker in the camp." He roared with laughter and slapped his handlebars.

"You're not even the first dog there, but the fourth," I said. Now he slapped his handlebars with both hands, and nearly fell off his bike.

"Believe me, Samir, sometimes I have to take a break as Dog Number 4, to keep from going crazy." He glanced over at me. "There's room for a fifth dog. If you want, I'll reserve the place for you."

50

I became addicted to *lekkerbekjes*, batter-fried fish, and this also gave me something to do outside the ASC. The fish stall was run by a man, a younger guy, and two girls.

One day I was standing in line and the girl in the stall called out: "Who's next?" A silly question, because we were standing in line and naturally the person in front was next.

"Me," I shouted from the back, as a joke, but a few annoyed faces turned to me, as though I'd meant it seriously.

"Sorry, mister, you've only just got here," the girl said, irritated. I left the line. Her surly attitude was enough to put me off lekkerbekjes for good.

As I walked off, another girl started to speak to me.

"You've lost interest in fish, I bet." She had seen what had happened.

"Kind of," I said.

"We Dutch have no sense of humor, you know," she said, walking with me across the market. "Where are you from?"

"From the ASC," I said.

"I meant, which country."

"Yes, the ASC. My country is one huge ASC, home to millions of asylum seekers."

She was twenty-five, pretty, and seemed to be the most easygoing girl in the world, because within five minutes she repeated the word *okay* at least five times, which is one okay per minute. The person who shared his life with her would hear so many okays that he could skate on them, swim in them, sleep on them, and wake up in them. She talked and I nodded, pretending to listen, but thinking of that one golden okay that would lead me to her body, which was no doubt far tastier than a lekkerbekje. She smiled as though she were watching a play she'd read beforehand and knew it would only get better. Her name was Maddalena, an Italian name her parents had chosen, she said, because they had met in Italy. So alongside Da Vinci, Dante Alighieri, Michelangelo, and pizza, I thought, here was yet another reason justifying Italy's existence. She didn't ask any more about the ASC or Iraq and that was fine with me. Because discussions about those two subjects never ended well. She asked me about Malaysia, Vietnam, and Thailand. Countries I had been to and where she wanted to go. We walked and talked, and it clicked between us, better than sugar and tea, or sauna and heat. Then she pointed to a window on the third floor of an apartment building.

"That's where I live," she said. I asked if I could drink tea at her place.

"Okay," she said. "Tonight at eight o'clock is good."

I walked back to the ASC and felt that Maddalena had performed the best volunteer work ever, and that the lekkerbekje was surely the most delicious one I had almost eaten. I mustn't sell myself short and think that an asylum seeker couldn't hook up with a Dutch woman outside the ASC. Maddalena was beautiful and friendly and she always said okay. And I would drink tea in her apartment at eight o'clock that evening.

No one at the ASC believed it. That a chance meeting

would lead to friendship and culminate in an invitation to a Dutch woman's home. Walid claimed that she was either a hash addict, a whore, or just plain crazy. At six o'clock I took a long shower, shaved my face and armpits, and trimmed my pubic hair. I brushed my teeth at least six times and went from room to room looking for an iron. From one person I borrowed a gold chain, from another, a silver ring. Toby, a perfume thief, offered me two kinds, one of which I sprayed all over my body and the other onto my clothes, and I searched high and low until I found dress shoes my size. For the first and the last time, I went to Reception not as an asylum seeker, but as someone who had a date.

"Aspirin?" asked Rik, the receptionist.

"Condoms, please. Do I look like someone with a headache?"

"How should I know? You always ask for aspirin."

"From now on, no more aspirin, only condoms."

"Who's the lucky girl?"

"A Hollander," I answered proudly.

"Really? Then maybe you should take some aspirin with you after all," he said empathically.

"Not necessary," I said, and off I went to my date with the three condoms distributed over various pockets, so that one would always be within reach when things got exciting.

At the apartment building I looked up at the church clock. Twenty past seven. I rang the bell.

"Who's there?"

"Samir."

"I thought we said eight o'clock," she replied brusquely. "Hang on." I stood there. A man with a dog walked by, and I told him I had a date at eight o'clock, but that I was a little early. A woman peered at me from a window across the street, and I called to her that I had a date at eight o'clock, but was too early. Another neighbor asked the first one what that asylum seeker was doing down there, and she told her I had an appointment at eight. Gosh, I thought, make a date with a Dutch girl and you get to meet the entire neighborhood. At eight o'clock sharp the door opened and many pairs of eyes followed me inside.

I walked up the stairs and Maddalena offered me a cold hand. Not a single okay passed over her lips. She made tea.

"I wanted to call you to reschedule," she said, "but I didn't have your number."

"That's okay," I said. Instead of listening to her okays I started saying okay myself.

"I'll leave as soon as we've had our tea, if that's okay. Or should I go now?"

"No, no, drink your tea first." She bit her nails and snapped at a little white dog in a basket who wasn't doing anything wrong. She tried to turn off the TV with the remote control, but it was already off, and when it went on she swore and switched it off again. If the dog and the television were having such a hard time of it, imagine the trouble I'd be in if the tea took too long, so I drank it in quick little sips, even though it was still quite hot. I said "okay" after "okay" until the tea was finished and I was relieved to be back outside. I had a headache, and the forty-minute wait and the twenty minutes in her apartment had worn me out. I hadn't an ounce of energy left, and barely made it back to Reception. I took the three condoms out of my various pockets and laid them on the counter.

"Didn't need them?" Rik said, and without asking he slid me two aspirin.

"Could you do me a favor? I'm too tired to look for someone to come and get me extra ones for later. Could I please have four more, two under John's name and two under Zainab's? It's an emergency."

"Gotcha," Rik said as he gave me four more tablets. "But don't take them all at once, and this is just between us, okay?"

I walked to room O-139 and had a think. If "okay" in the Netherlands could turn a condom into an aspirin, what would "not okay" do?

"What's the matter? Are you getting deported?" Fettah asked. "You're so pale."

"No, worse than that," I whispered. "I had a date with a Dutch girl."

51

I often sat at the window, staring outside. *Outside* seemed far away: that world beyond the iron fence surrounding the ASC, and even further away, another world where I might resume my life. Sometimes at night I would stand at the glass partition of the closed Social Services office and stare through at the computers that had tamed me and had turned me into an impotent inmate in an open prison. This feeling made me lose my sense of self-worth and my faith in many precious things like love, harmony, peace of mind, and the future. Little by little I discovered that anger and aggression had welled up inside me, and that sometimes, for no reason, I would feel like screaming or picking a fight. It took all my energy to suppress that anger and aggression in a building bursting with people in the same situation, and without a sliver of privacy. As a result, I trudged rather than walked. I could barely put one foot in front of the other. It was like I was carrying fifty kilos of tedium on my shoulders. Tedium that lasted not for minutes or hours, but for years and years. Everything was tedious. The walls, the corridors, the windows, the ceilings, the stairs. Most tedious of all was the building itself, which was not a residence, nor a hotel, a jail, compulsory rehab, or a hospital. You had to live there, you weren't allowed to do anything, but you had to stay normal. And if you saw how many of the other occupants were thieves, criminals, and liars, you would understand why the Dutch people did not call it a refugee center, but an asylum center. All sorts of folks who had no business in the Netherlands were sent there: illegal immigrants who had been arrested for some crime or other, for instance, and then requested asylum got sent to the ASC. I remember an African guy who had come to the Netherlands to study. He had punched his Dutch girlfriend in an argument, but to keep from getting deported he requested asylum and wound up in our ASC. There were others who had come to the Netherlands as tourists, and for one reason or another decided not to return. They, too, landed in the ASC. Or men from exotic climes, who had married a Dutch woman and then got divorced, but instead of returning would ask for asylum. Among this mixed bag and the bona fide refugees we were expected to live, wait, and stay normal.

Time. At first, an asylum seeker counts the days in the ASC, and when he gets tired of that he counts the weeks, the months, and eventually the years. There were two ways to deal with time: forget it entirely, or keep strict track of it. Whenever I bumped into Jamal or Najat, I would ask the age of their son Milaad to be reminded of how long I had been in the ASC. "You always ask how old Milaad is, but you never come to his birthday party," Najat said. So I started buying gifts and visiting Milaad on his birthday. No one knew it was actually not a party at all for me, but a depressing day, because it meant another year had gone by without being able to get on with my life.

It was somewhere in the course of the fourth year of the asylum procedure that I received the first letter pertaining to my asylum request. I remember the envelope. The logo in the upper left-hand corner was a blindfolded woman holding a scale. In the envelope was a letter of rejection. It said I was to leave the Netherlands within twenty-eight days.

I had seen plenty of these letters for other people, its message expressed in the same worn-out terms, but these twenty-eight days were *mine*. I wondered what had made the IND decide on twenty-eight days. Why not something more logical, like twenty or thirty or thirty-five? To this day, this choice perplexes me. Is this the exact number of days you need to walk or bike to the Dutch border? In another sense I thought it was laughable, because I wanted nothing more than to leave the Netherlands, but had discovered first-hand how impossible that was.

I took my letter to Sagal, the Somali woman who worked at Social Services and had once been an asylum seeker herself, and asked her why asylum seekers were made to wait years and years for this letter, which the IND knew they would send sooner or later. Sagal said that it was because there were so many asylum seekers, and that the IND took each and every dossier seriously, and studied it thoroughly, as one did in the Netherlands, before making their decision. I told Sagal I did not believe this. Because I knew that some asylum seekers were genuine political refugees, and they got that same hackneyed answer, while others, having hired an expensive lawyer or because of government errors, did get residency status even though they did not even come from the country they said they did. I asked her if she remembered Daoud, a Sudanese professor who suspected his asylum request was not taken seriously, despite the obvious political problems in his country. He went crazy when he heard that Djibril—a young asylum seeker who said he was from Sudan but really came from Ghana and had filed for asylum under a false name—had been given political asylum.

I also told Sagal that the Netherlands had once ruled over all of Indonesia, and all of Suriname and the Antilles, in the days before computers existed. Instead of a few thousand asylum seekers, they managed to control millions of people. Surely some semblance of efficiency was possible now? I told her I believed our being made to wait in the ASC for years and years was intended as a deterrent, as a kind of wall to keep even more people from trying to get into the system, because every time an asylum seeker got a residence permit and moved on, another one would come and take his place. But if he stayed, no new ones would come. Simple logic. Sagal looked at me attentively. If she hadn't worked for Social Services, would she have nodded in agreement?

Then I started the twenty-eight-day countdown. Maybe the Foreigners' Police would come knocking on the door of O-139. My bag was already packed. But the twenty-eight days came and went, and nothing happened.

Much later, my case was brought to court, because my lawyer had appealed the IND's decision. The appeal itself was a kind of cliché. I had to go to Amsterdam. I was overjoyed. Finally, I would see someone who could determine my fate. I would look into that person's eyes, I could say something to him, and he to me, instead of those letters that take years to deliver. It didn't even matter to me whether the answer was yes or no—just the thought of standing face-to-face with a judge gave me a good feeling.

In the end, I went to court twice. The first time, I

reported punctually, even early, but my lawyer had not arrived yet. When I asked the lady at the counter if I should wait any longer, she looked at the sheet of paper before her.

"Mr. Karim? Oh, your lawyer is sick. You can confer with the judge about what to do now." The lawyer had my telephone number—couldn't he have called me? There was indeed a judge and someone from the public prosecutor's office in the courtroom, but without a lawyer there was no point in hearing the case. So off I went, empty-handed. Before returning to the ASC I went to Dam Square and watched pigeons steal French fries from tourists, and wandered the streets of Amsterdam until it was time to catch the last train back.

Of course I had to wait again for a new court date, and when it did come, that too ended in disappointment. Maybe I shouldn't have got my hopes up. This time, my lawyer was there and I was told I could speak, but before I even got going, the sitting had been adjourned and there I was outside again with the same unsatisfied feeling, because no one would listen to my story.

I don't remember exactly when I received the letter saying that my request had been definitively rejected. Over the course of those nine years I amassed an Aldi shopping bag full of letters from the IND and the Ministry of Justice. I've still got them stashed somewhere in my attic. If I can face it one day, I'll go up and find that bag. But first I have to get on with my story, otherwise I'll get bogged down in telling you about irrelevant paperwork. So now that my case had been dismissed, there were no more legal avenues to be followed. I continued to receive letters instructing me to leave the country within twenty-eight days. In retrospect I think these letters

52

When Milaad got even older, and began to understand the ways of the ASC, our exchange went as follows: "Hey, Milaad, how old are you?" Rather than answering my question, he told me what I really wanted to know.

"Another three months and four days, and you'll have been here seven years."

After Milaad's birthday party I sat on my bed and looked at my fingers.

"You've still got all ten," said Walid, my roommate. He did not realize I wasn't counting my fingers, but studying my fingerprints. I inspected the minuscule lines and grooves that had got me sent from Germany back to Holland, and that had pushed Kadhem to suicide.

For a while I stared at them, and then at the ceiling, musing that Europe had become so small that it fit into a computer, and that it was impossible to move about in it freely. Still, despair did not have me completely in its grip, because as soon as I thought of Saddam Hussein, the ASC suddenly felt less awful. And that at least I didn't have to sleep in mosquito-infested parks and hide myself from the police all day long, like in Vietnam, Thailand, Malaysia, and Cambodia. That autumn, a spark of hope flashed through me when I heard about an asylum seeker who went to Norway and was not sent back.

Rami, who was from Algeria but requested asylum as a Libyan, hoping this might boost his chances of getting a residence permit, misplaced his W-document during the first year of his asylum procedure. For the next two years, they would not renew his W-document because he couldn't produce the original one. A few years later, when they did give him a new document, he came across the original among all his papers. This was a stroke of luck. He had his first and last W-document, meaning he could prove he had been waiting for an answer for eight years. Word had it that the Norwegians granted him asylum based on those two documents. So Norway apparently did not follow the "port of arrival" rule. Through the grapevine I heard that Norway's asylum policies were totally different to those in the Netherlands. They didn't cram hundreds of people into a single building, the Foreigners' Police were more friendly, Social Services were easy-going, sick people received proper care. Rami had met asylum seekers who had started in the Netherlands and were let into Norway without their fingerprints being checked. Traveling without a false passport, however, was impossible.

My quest for a forged passport took me back to Amsterdam. A Dutch passport with a foreign surname cost eight hundred euros, plus another two hundred to doctor the photo. But to buy a passport from someone you knew personally, a drug addict perhaps, would only cost maybe a hundred and fifty, plus the price of that person getting a replacement passport from City Hall. I looked into buses to Norway, and learned it cost a hundred euros to get to Oslo.

I wrote *Oslo* on a sheet of paper and hung it next to my bed. I looked at it before going to sleep. The word *Oslo* had become a window that allowed me to look into another world. My plan was to find work, earn some money, buy the passport, and take a Eurolines bus from Groningen.

53

A few weeks later I found illegal work in a shawarma joint run by an Egyptian named Hamdi. It was my first job where I was paid by the hour. Before coming to the Netherlands I had always worked for a weekly or monthly wage, and in the ASC the concept of "hour" had lost its meaning altogether. But now I was starting to discover that hours outside the ASC were worth something. The shawarma joint had three doors: the front entrance for customers, a back door for garbage, and a secret exit for the illegal workers. Via a cellar you came to a small corridor with a stairway that led to the apartment above the restaurant. There was a rusty bell, and if it rang we had to hurry through that secret passage, change into clean clothes and go outside. On weekends two Dutch girls waited tables. Hamdi would get jealous if he caught us talking to them. He didn't say so outright, but whenever he saw us conversing, Hamdi would yell that the tables needed cleaning, or some such command. I washed dishes, made salads, and if it was busy I'd clear tables, which was usually the girls' job. The passageway between the kitchen and the restaurant wasn't wide enough for two people. You had to squeeze past each other, which the other kitchen staff used as an excuse to touch the girls' backsides. Susanne didn't catch on and if someone grazed her butt she would say: "Oh, this hallway's so narrow, isn't it." The other girl was named Kathleen. Every time she got felt up she would turn and say: "Don't you have roving fingers?" or "You did that on purpose!"

The kitchen was filthy. There was a big, rusty ventilator hood that made more noise than a Boeing 747, and if it was turned off, the kitchen would fill with smoke and the smell of rancid, burnt oil because Hamdi was cheap and only refreshed the cooking oil when the food got discolored. After a four-hour shift, I would cough for at least another eight hours. The floor was permanently wet.

We were paid two euros per hour. Hamdi had his own unique method of counting our illegal work-hours. On weekends there were three of us, during the week just one or two, and on holidays five or six. We arrived late in the evening and had to wait until it got busy. Only then did our shift officially start. So the first and last hours usually didn't get counted, even though you were done only when the last drunkard left the snack bar. Working from nine in the evening until four in the morning, minus the first and last hour, added up to five paid hours. Five times two euros was ten euros. Even though it was a pittance, for us asylum seekers it was an enormous sum. We had to make ends meet on the weekly allowance they gave us at the ASC and we weren't supposed to take outside work.

Hamdi also had his own way of dealing with the police. Sometimes one or two police officers would come in for takeaway. Hamdi would strut right over to take their order, without giving them or the other customers the feeling that they were cutting in. Hamdi personally packed up the food, chatted amiably with them, and settled the bill. In the takeaway bag was not only their order, but also drinks and straws and extra napkins, and the bill was always less than half of what it should be.

And although at the time I was very upset at getting fired, I am now grateful to that one Dutch guy, a weekend regular during the three months I worked there. He was in his early twenties and one evening while placing his order he asked: "Where's the Negro?" He meant Kevin, a Ghanaian fellow from the ASC.

"He's free today, because it's not so busy," I said.

"Do you have to put it that way?" his girlfriend said to him. I didn't realize she was referring to the word "Negro."

"But he's black."

"Can't you mention him without specifying his color?"

The guy chuckled uncomfortably, because he was drunk. "You're right, babe, I shouldn't call him that." When they paid and got up to leave, he called over to me. Hamdi was within earshot. "Sorry about that, I shouldn't have said Negro, but I'm a little drunk." This is how I discovered that Dutch people are allergic to certain words. Hamdi walked them to the door, said goodbye with a big smile, and then called me into the kitchen.

"Don't you know that Dutch people consider the word Negro hurtful? They're correct and sensitive people, you know." This caught me by surprise, because it wasn't me who had used the word, but the customer; and his girlfriend was the one who protested, not me. I tried to explain this to Hamdi, but I couldn't get a word in edgewise.

"Please, Samir, smile at the customers, listen to them, do what they ask, but don't converse with them. The customer is always right." He told me to get back to making salads. At four thirty in the morning he gave me fifteen euros and when I was at the door he said amiably: "Listen, you don't have to come back. And tell

Kevin he doesn't have to come back either." I didn't know how I was going to explain to Kevin that he'd lost his job because a sensitive Dutch girl was allergic to the word *Negro*.

Not long after that, Yelena returned to the ASC.

54

Yelena seemed tired and sad. I assumed Maarten had kicked her out of his house and that she had no choice but to return to the ASC, from a house with just one other person to a building with more than five hundred. The first day she sent me to Reception to get her some aspirin. I did, and right away she asked me to go get her two more. I told her they wouldn't do that.

"Just say they're for Yelena in O-124," she said, as if her name were a magic password for aspirin. Instead, I commandeered another asylum seeker to fetch two aspirins in his name, and then brought them to her with a glass of water.

"Did you say they were for me?"

"Of course, otherwise they wouldn't have given them."

"See? I told you so." After the affair with Maarten, and the headache from the affair with Maarten, Yelena needed to talk. The reason for this, as I understood it, was that she hadn't talked much since meeting Maarten because he, like so many Dutch people, said things only once and only wanted to hear things once.

Yelena's analysis of Dutch people was comprehensive, varied, and amusing. They do not exaggerate, she said, and are not quick to laugh. A joke has to be strong, logical, and catchy just to get a smile out of them, and if you repeat a joke to get them to laugh, they become irritated.

Yelena did not understand why Dutch people, even if they were sitting in a group together, always spoke

English if there was one non-Dutch speaker among them, or someone who couldn't keep up with the conversation. But the worst was that the Dutch people could smother a person's hope. If the weather was bad, they did not say: "Soon the sun will come out again," but: "This is going to last a good two and a half months." For any given problem, they had enough information not to find a solution, but to be better informed about the problem itself, so that a minor issue could be turned into serious trouble. Another irritation was that if you spent the whole day cooking, people would comment the whole time about how nice it smelled, but during the meal they talked about everything under the sun except the food and how good it tasted.

Dutch people with children had completely lost touch with reality, because when it was Maarten's birthday and his two sisters dropped by with their children, one of them changed her 18-month-old son's diaper in the middle of the living room full of guests. It took three days to get rid of the smell.

Yelena kept saying that Maarten was thrifty when he was in love, and a tightwad when he wasn't. His family was stingy, too, and his neighbors and friends and colleagues, and even his cat. The Dutch were a stingy folk, according to Yelena, so she was surprised they gave asylum seekers free room and board and aspirin and condoms. On the other hand, Yelena said, they were the most honest and harmless people around. She liked the fact that everything was well-organized, but abhorred their taste in clothing. They had only one or two kinds of perfume, not to spray, but to look at on their bathroom counter.

"The ASC is better," she sighed. It had been her own choice to return.

We resumed our walks to the sea, and she talked about Maarten and about Maarten's family, Maarten's neighbors, Maarten's colleagues, Maarten's cat, Maarten's photo albums from his birth to age twenty-eight, and Maarten's psychological problems that started when he was twelve, when his parents got divorced.

Talking about Maarten also exposed her own self-doubts. Was she pretty? Was she cut out for a relationship? Was he the right guy? She missed sex. She had tried everything: with make-up, without make-up; short skirt, long dress; with lingerie, without lingerie. But Maarten did not respond. She didn't dare tell him she wanted to make love, because she felt that her looks should be enough. I could certainly go along with that.

"Once, I told Maarten not to come into the bedroom for half an hour, because I had a surprise for him." She had thought long and hard about it; the surprise should be something that would melt the ice that had formed between them. After endless discussions with Maarten about philosophical problems and social problems and economic problems and mental problems, it was now time for sex. So half an hour later Maarten opened the bedroom door. Yelena lay naked on the bed, surrounded by hundreds of tea lights. She had opened the two windows all the way, as if to say: "Warm me! Burn me! Fuck me!" I nodded with difficulty, because all the while I was fantasizing that I was Maarten, and that Yelena was surrounded not by policemen and asylum seekers, but tiny candles.

All I could squeeze out was: "And ...?"

"And what?"

"Did he do anything with you?"

"No." She turned sour. "He just glared at the open windows. The cold draft made the candles flicker."

"And then he jumped on top of you, to warm you up?"

"Not me. The windows. He shut them and said that this all cost heaps of money. That is was three below zero outside and now the bedroom wasn't eighteen degrees anymore, and the furnace would have to heat the place up again, and that gas wasn't cheap in the Netherlands, like it is in Russia. He started in about the gas trade between Russia and Europe, and how the Dutch government did its best to keep the cost of heating for ordinary people like him affordable. When he saw that I had wrapped myself up in the blanket, he said, 'But it really was a nice surprise, to convince me that Russians can take the cold better than the Dutch.' Then he blew out all the candles, because not only our house, but the whole neighborhood could go up in flames."

"And then?"

"And then he explained that the houses—"

"I meant, did he do anything with you?"

"Of course not. If he had, I wouldn't have come back here."

Yelena talked, and I could barely concentrate on what she said, because inside, I was on fire. If I kept listening, smoke would start pouring out of my nostrils. We walked back from the sea and I thought that Yelena was not only beautiful, but funny and romantic, and that she truly followed her feelings, and not just the promise of a residence permit.

When we arrived back at the ASC, she suddenly turned and looked straight at me.

"I'll go in first," she said, and then uttered the most romantic thing a beautiful woman had ever said to me in my whole life: "You go get condoms from Reception and come to O-124." She shook her blonde curls onto her shoulders and sauntered to the entrance.

I wanted to run after her. Her beauty had devoured my last ounce of patience.

"Condoms," I panted at Reception. My trembling hand grabbed the strip of three foil packets and I walked into the ASC, which Yelena had instantly transformed into paradise. I was so flustered that I forgot to put them in my pocket, so that before I reached the orange wing, all of Orange, Green, Blue, and Yellow knew that Yelena had walked into the ASC alone, and that I was trotting after her holding three condoms. I decided to first take a shower. I hurried to my room and put the condoms on my bed.

"Aha, I see you got a residence permit," joked Fouad.

"Not one, but three," I replied.

I went to the shower rooms with my underwear, towel, shampoo, and condoms, and was finished within four minutes. So as not to lose any time, I wrapped the towel around my waist, grasped the condoms firmly in my hand, and went straight to room O-124. Yelena opened the door and saw me standing there, the water still dripping onto the floor in the hallway. I still see everything happen in a slow-motion replay. She looked at the towel and at my hands, then raised her eyes to my face. Her glance held mine for no more than a second. Then she looked at the wall behind me and shouted a single word in her strong Russian accent. A word that was worse than deportation.

"Loser."

She slammed the door.

I turned in my puddle of water and saw three Afghans, two Chechens, an Iranian, a Turk, four Armenians, one Chinese man, seven Iraqis, and at least ten Africans standing there. Water dripped from my chest hairs.

Going to bed with me was the last thing in the world Yelena was planning to do, this much was now clear.

"And now? Now I have to clean up again!" Belsi griped, who was already mopping up the trail of water leading from the showers to room O-124.

"Don't worry, man, everything is the same," John said. "Here, for five euros you can have a day pass, take it to Amsterdam, the ladies behind the train station are much prettier than that Russian nut case." I shuffled back to the shower room, threw the condoms into the wastebasket, and punished myself for my vain hope and stupid behavior by taking an ice-cold shower.

Then I lay down on my own bed instead of the one in O-124, but the shame and the missed chance kept me from sleeping. An hour later there was a soft knocking at the door. I hoped it was Yelena, because this was just the way she knocked.

But instead of Yelena, I saw Hatim, the blind asylum seeker with the sharpest ears in the entire ASC.

"Hood evening," he said.

"Good evening," I replied.

"Is it true, what I heard?"

"What did you hear?"

"That you got three condoms from Reception, and that you took a shower for four minutes and then had sex with the Russian woman in O-124? But why didn't I hear anything? It was so quiet in her room, there couldn't have been anything going on. Or did you take her somewhere else?" His blind eyes rolled every which way, as though I was a mosquito flying around inside his head.

"I don't know for how long I showered, but the part about the three condoms is correct."

"And where did they end up, the condoms? In the right place?"

"No. In the garbage can."

"What a pity." He turned and said, "I thought to myself: Why don't I hear anything in O-124, maybe nothing happened. Now I understand!"

He walked off, and from my bed I could hear the tapping of his cane die out as he disappeared down the hallway.

55

Hatim was from Kuwait. He was blind, but he knew more about the goings-on in the ASC than even Sayid did.

Hatim was the barometer of my voice. "You sound sad," he might say. Then I would be careful not to let myself sink into the quicksand of melancholy, and would go for a walk somewhere outside the ASC. If he said I was quiet, I would go straight to the canteen to chat with the others. Even if I had crashed in a corner somewhere, completely drained from the deadly monotony of life in the ASC, I could hear Hatim's cane coming toward me, as though he knew exactly where I was sitting. He would find my shoes with the tip of his cane, and feel around them.

"These are your shoes. Are you there too? Why so quiet?"

"I'm fed up with this place."

"You've got two eyes, don't you?"

"And glasses," I said.

"Then go outside. Look at the trees, at the waves. What are you doing here, man? Go into town and look at the women!" I always took his advice.

Being blind, Hatim had his own room. I often knocked on his door to ask if I could pick anything up for him at the market. He would open the door and say, "Why are you pounding like that? I'm blind, not deaf." No matter how softly I knocked, this was always his response. I started knocking so quietly that I couldn't even hear it myself, but he heard it and said, "Coming!" Once I told him his television was on with the sound turned off. I thought he didn't realize it, because, after all, he could not see.

"The volume's on low," he said. When Social Services arranged for him to have a satellite dish so he could listen to Arabic TV series, he praised the Dutch people for their helpfulness. "I would like to be able to see for just an hour, so I could see what they look like. I'm sure they're as beautiful as angels."

When Hatim had just arrived at the ASC, Van 't Zijde told him he didn't have to report unless he wanted to. Hatim was so pleased with the choice that he chose to report. Maybe to prove that he could. When he reported, Hatim always looked cheerful, because then he had something to do.

Whenever the others heard the ticking of his cane on the floor, they would tell him where the queue was. And he would answer, "I know, I know," and join at the back. He would feel the feet or the back of the person in front of him, and sometimes their butt. So the women and girls always jumped out of line whenever they saw Hatim coming, meaning he kept shuffling forward until he reached the counter. Then he would bend his head forward and say through the little window, "Hood morning, man at reporting" and slide his W-document through the window and smile. When the staff member said, "Here you are," Hatim's hand, which looked like a girl's hand, would reach forward, take the document, and he would say "thank you" and shuffle off. One Iranian asylum seeker, Talib, would always try to position himself in front of Hatim in line, and let his butt press up against Hatim's cane. He would wriggle his buttocks up and down, left and right, until he touched the cane, and then would exclaim, "Aiiii!" and tell Hatim to watch out. "Man, you just pushed your cane up my butt."

"Sorry, sorry."

"Never mind, I kind of like it. But next time take it a little slower, otherwise it hurts." The other asylum seekers in line did their best not to fall over in silent laughter.

Once the official behind the window demanded to know why it was so restless in line.

"Sir!" called Talib. "I have been standing here approximately eighteen and a half minutes, and since the line hasn't moved, I fell asleep. Standing, like a horse. And then something hard got pushed into my butt. Maybe it's kind of nice, you know. I turned around and saw that this blind man had rammed his cane into my butt. Four and a half centimeters deep!" Talib said this in a theatrical manner, as though it really did hurt.

"Maybe you shouldn't fall asleep in line next time," the man said.

"Certainly, sir, as long as you don't fall asleep at your computer."

Sometimes Talib would say, "Please, Hatim, we've been standing here for so long and I'd like to get this line moving, would you do me a favor and stick your cane into my butt?" He always said this in Dutch, which he spoke quite well, so that all the asylum seekers could hear, understand, and laugh.

Hatim was forty or forty-five years old. He was an Iraqi who had grown up in Kuwait, where Iraqis are called "al-Bidun," or "those without," which boils down to "without Kuwaiti nationality." Often they had lived in Kuwait for generations, but were never given nationality because they were originally Iraqis. Hatim's grandparents came from Iraq, but he himself had never set foot there.

I have to interrupt myself here for a moment. It is important to know that when a war breaks out somewhere, the first asylum seekers to arrive are those furthest from the conflict. They can be, for instance, refugees who have lived in another European country, but were not content there and grasped the opportunity to make a new start elsewhere. Only much later do the genuine refugees from the war zone arrive. But by then they have been robbed of their chances at asylum.

Part of what makes this strange situation possible is that the IND checks an asylum seeker's dialect to confirm where he or she comes from, but never checks how long ago they left their homeland. And this was Hatim's good fortune. Before America's war in Iraq began in 2003, he fled from Kuwait to the Netherlands and ended up in our ASC. He requested asylum as an Iraqi from Basra, a city near the Kuwait-Iraq border.

When Hatim walked through the halls of the ASC, he often took someone's hand so they could lead him. Of course he preferred the hand of a woman or girl. When Saskia started her internship at Social Services and shook his hand to introduce herself, Hatim was in seventh heaven. He asked me to describe her, wanting to know every detail from head to toe. But then instead of letting me describe her, he asked specific questions.

"Does she have a nice round ass?"

"Yes," I said.

"Is it sexy?"

"Sure is."

"Are her breasts large enough for a penis to fit between them?"

"Oh, yes."

"Does she have a long, slender neck?"

"Yes."

"And soft lips?"

"That's right."

I went on to describe her. But upon arriving at her hands, he said, "You don't have to tell me about her hands. I've seen them."

"Seen them?"

"Not the way you have," he said. "But when she shook my hand, I could immediately imagine what they looked like." I started to wonder if Hatim really was blind after all, that maybe he was pretending to be, just for the asylum case. Maybe he was only asking me to describe Saskia in order to keep up appearances. I had to confirm every question he asked. When I asked him how he knew all these things, he said, "Once you've touched the hand of a woman, you can see her whole body." Hatim saw with his hands. That explained why he turned down my offer a few days earlier to take him somewhere. He wanted to stay put, because Kristi, the African tigress, was picking up her son from school. "Don't worry, I'll wait," he said, shooing me away. "Go on, otherwise you'll be late."

"Late for what? I've got nothing to do and nowhere to go."

"Weren't you off somewhere? Get along now." He repeated the shooing gesture again, faster. So I left. Fifteen minutes later I saw him walking hand in hand with Kristi. Later, I asked him to describe her, just from having held her hand, and he did, as though he'd seen her for real.

"Oh, that Kristi ... Her hand alone is warmer than the radiator in my room. What must the rest of her body be like ..."

Before Tamara (the young woman who had let me peek in the general's dossier) left her job, Hatim told me that she had the sexiest voice around. I started to pay attention, and he was right. If I closed my eyes while she spoke, I could tell how pure her voice was.

Tamara left before I could say goodbye to her. I heard she'd gone to Australia, where her sister lived, and might well stay there, because she had bought a one-way ticket. Maybe she is still there now.

Most of the men in the ASC became jealous whenever they saw Hatim waiting like a spider for the hand of a girl or a woman, because for him, that was sex. Talib said that if simply touching a hand was sex for Hatim then he had made love to pretty much all the females in the ASC.

Next door to Hatim was O-75, home to three Chinese men who kept very much to themselves. They spoke to no one, neither to the other asylum seekers nor to the volunteers, and if anyone else happened to be nearby, they did not speak to one another either. The door to their room was always shut, no one ever saw them in the kitchen or the laundry room, and they never went to Reception to ask for mail.

Before I knew all this, I greeted one of them in passing. He looked at me.

"What?" he said.

"Hello," I said, because I thought maybe he hadn't understood my "good morning."

"What?"

His face was filled with question marks. Maybe he didn't realize I was greeting him, and thought I might have asked him something. I shrugged my shoulders and went on my way, but later I heard him talking in good

English to someone from Social Services. Sayid told me he had had the exact same experience. None of the asylum seekers had any luck breaking the ice with the Chinese men: their response was invariably "What?" and so they became known as What 1, What 2, and What 3.

Hatim once came up to me in the social hall, where I was having a cup of tea with Talib at the bar.

"What's happened to What 2 and 3?" he asked me.

"How so?"

"Well, they all used to sleep in the room next to mine, but now only What 1 is left."

"You're mistaken, they're all still there, you just can't see them."

"I'm telling you, What 2 and What 3 are gone. Only What 1 is left. His bed is on the far side of the room, not against my wall." We went back and forth on this, but I couldn't convince him, nor he me. Talib, of course, became curious and, as it turned out, Hatim was right. There was only one Chinese man left in O-75. He would report for himself and the other two at different times. The Dutch officials behind the counter had no idea they saw the same Chinese guy three times a day.

Now that Talib had figured it out, more and more people got wind of it, and before long it was an open secret in the ASC. Everyone was impressed with how What 1, What 2, and What 3 had pulled the wool over the Hollanders' eyes. There was only one What in that room: he would go report for himself, return to his room, change clothes and report two hours later for his friend, and then again another two hours later.

"Just listen," Hatim whispered to me and Talib, when we were in his room. "Now What 1 is opening What 3's cupboard. Do you hear it?" Talib and I went out into the hallway and sure enough, a few minutes later What 3, who always wore a green cap, came out of the room. We followed him and saw him join the line to report.

Talib grinned at me. "It's the Hollanders who are blind, not Hatim!"

"They're clever, those Chinese," I said. I almost added that they weren't only clever, but fearless, but when I saw how robotically the official took the man's pass without even looking at it, I concluded that fearlessness was not necessary. I could even report as Yelena and get away with it.

Just as God created What 1, What 2, and What 3 so that they would be relieved of reporting, Talib relieved me and many other asylum seekers from the deadly doldrums of the ASC.

I spent my days reporting and waiting, reporting and waiting, reporting and waiting. Now and then, something would suddenly snap in me and I would have the urgent need for change. Kind of like what happens with a caged animal: he'll be calm for a long time, but suddenly he'll fly into a rage, roar, and sink his teeth into the bars. Sometimes I jumped and roared, but before I bit myself, I would go and find Talib, so that he could calm me down.

56

I haven't talked about Talib much until now, but he was important to me. He had an ugly, scarred face. His skin showed signs not only of acne, but of burn wounds and torture. Whenever Saddam Hussein felt the power slipping through his fingers, he would order punishments whose physical effects were clearly visible, like chopping off an ear, a hand, or part of the nose. Talib lost his right ear because he had deserted the army. The second time he deserted, he lost part of his nose. And because a third desertion would have cost him his head, he fled the country. He smuggled a statute book with him, which spelled out all the cases for which ears and noses were to be cut off, or the death sentence applied, as proof for the IND. Other asylum seekers assumed this would assure him of quick approval of his asylum request—within a year or two—because his body was hard proof of the dangers he was exposed to in Iraq. But Talib had been in the ASC for longer than I had. Even so, he never looked morose and never had conflicts. Zainab shortened the trousers he bought at the thrift store, but her work of taking them in at the waist was not so successful, so he always looked fat, even though he wasn't, and it certainly didn't tally with his sunken cheeks.

Talib could make any situation theatrical—not for the sake of melodrama, but simply to have a good laugh. He was from the south of Iraq, a region known for its many folk poets. He always had a pen and paper handy, and you often saw him stop to jot something down. Sometimes he would work for weeks on a single poem. They were most beautiful when he recited them out loud. Whenever he was finished with a poem, he would discard the paper it was written on, because he knew it by heart.

Talib tried not to stick out, and although he spoke better Dutch than most of the other asylum seekers, he chose not to use it that often in his contact with the Dutch staffers. Sometimes he brought me with him to translate, even though his Dutch was better than mine. When I asked him why, he said, "If you speak their language, then the Hollanders know you know what's allowed and what's not, so you're more likely to be punished if you break the rules."

Talib worked as a cleaner at the ASC for twenty-five euros a week. As soon as he had fifty euros, he would go to the whores and come back broke, only to work another two weeks and then go back to the whores again.

When I asked why he did this, he said, "Here in the ASC you can either spend years waiting for the IND, or two weeks for the whores. It's a shorter wait, and more fun."

After I was fired from my job at the shawarma joint, I went in search of other work to save money to get me to Norway, but without success. Sometimes I would bike around the neighborhood and ask for work. Other times I would stop at a building site or an industrial park, and everywhere they told me the same thing: that I should go to an employment bureau. But there, they wanted your social security number, which of course I didn't have. Having only the time and the energy to work was not enough.

One day, something happened at the ASC that would make my stay there even more difficult, and made me realize that I had to get out of there before things got even worse. Hafed was an asylum seeker from Ahvaz, an Iranian town where they speak both Farsi and the southern Iraqi dialect, but he requested asylum in the Netherlands as an Iraqi. Because of this shared dialect they didn't find out he wasn't Iraqi at all. I had a good laugh about this, especially when I read the transcripts of his first and second interviews. He had made some pretty glaring mistakes about Iraq that the IND officer didn't catch. For example, he had given the location of Chibayish incorrectly, and said that Saddam Hussein had drained and burned the swamps in the region because they were infested with mosquitoes, not because it was full of Shi'ites in hiding.

His wife and daughter had arrived in the Netherlands via Italy a few months before Hafed, who came later via Germany. Because the Germans had intercepted him on his way to the Netherlands, he was forced to request asylum there, and they took his fingerprints. The Germans sent him onward to the asylum facility, but he continued on to Holland. Now the family was living in the ASC, and his wife was expecting their second child. But when the Dutch authorities discovered that he had given his fingerprints in Germany, they said he had to go back there. I often saw people get sent back to another Schengen country, or to their country of origin, but Hafed's expulsion to Germany stuck in my mind.

His second daughter had just been born. She was maybe two weeks old. His elder daughter, who was six or seven years old, had a blood disorder. We all thought that this would be a reason not to repatriate them. Or at least not right away. We advised Hafed to go to the church, but they were not in the position to offer him any assistance, and he had to wait. Hafed did not know where to go, and of course he didn't want to leave his newborn child behind. So when the Foreigners' Police came for him, they found him in room Y-07.

The three burly policemen wore huge boots, which made the men look even bigger. They came into the building via Reception, walked down the hall, and took the stairs to Yellow, as though they knew exactly where to find Y-07. They didn't only smile at the children, as they usually did, but at everyone. Maybe they wanted to show that they were on their way to do something they didn't agree with, but had no choice. They knocked at Y-07, and the little girl opened the door. When she saw the three policemen with their pistols and handcuffs, she froze.

"Is your father here?" one of the policeman asked in a friendly voice. The girl just stood there looking at them. Hafed came to the door, smiled at his daughter, and said he was going to report and would be right back. He followed the policeman in his slippers, perhaps so as not to alarm his daughter. But the girl followed him, and when they walked past Reception and out the front door, she knew they were going to take him away.

She started to scream, "*Baba, baba!*" and ran toward them. Hafed turned to her, smiling. She took his hand, but he pushed it away, opened the door to the police car himself, and got in. Maybe so that the policeman wouldn't have to do it, which would have frightened the girl even more. The car drove off. Her voice echoed over the forecourt.

"*Baba!*" She ran after the car until it disappeared around the corner. Then she ran to Yellow. When I got to room Y-07, I saw his wife lying on the bed.

"They've taken him away," she said. I knew I couldn't stay here any longer.

57

I had to find work in order to earn some money to reach Oslo, so I was glad when Talib said he had found something for me, and that it paid as much as fifty euros a day.

"In a month you'll have enough to get to Oslo," he said. We cycled to an industrial zone outside the city. There, we were met by a Dutch guy who brought us to a huge warehouse where three asylum seekers were opening boxes with utility knives and removing canisters of powdered baby formula, truckloads full, originally from Denmark. They rubbed off the expired sell-by date with cotton balls and cleaning fluid. Then they put the canisters on a conveyor belt, where a machine stamped a fresh new date onto them. From the lettering on the boxes I guessed that the canisters were going to be sold in Russia, or another country where they used Cyrillic writing.

"Eight hours a day for fifty euros. Twice that on weekends," the man said in English, after asking me if I lived in the ASC and whether I had Dutch friends outside the ASC, to which I answered that I did not.

"I can't do this work," I said to Talib in Arabic. "This milk formula has expired, kids could die from it."

"No, man, it's not poison. It's just a little past its sell-by date."

"I won't do it."

"Everything okay?" the man asked Talib.

"Yes, sure, but he can't work here, because he's allergic to the stuff we use to rub off the date."

"Then he can go to the other end and seal the boxes," the man said. But I didn't want to do that either so I left that place full of trucks and forklifts, where Talib earned enough to go to the whores every day. For days I didn't know what to do about it, and did nothing. I still feel guilty. Going to the police would have meant jail, and going to Social Services nearly the same thing, but looking back on it, I could have called a newspaper or the radio to inform them about the scheme. The babies who were fed that formula are now seventeen years old, and sometimes I still worry that they got sick from it. When I once said to Talib that what they were doing was criminal, he said: "What are you talking about? Do you think the Dutch don't know what all those Polish trucks are doing there? They just pretend not to. But, oh, they'd be up in arms if the stuff ever got sold in the Netherlands."

Soon thereafter, Talib came to say he had found me another job. We cycled for an hour and arrived at a large cattle farm, with which Talib seemed to be well acquainted.

"What now? Are we going to milk cows? I can't do that," I said.

"Just be patient ..." Talib said. We passed a shed, where a tile mounted on the door was inscribed with the opening lines from a Dutch poem:

waarde vriend het is hier prachtig
de koeien zijn ontroerend drachtig*

---

* 'it's stunning here, dear friend / the cows so poignantly with young' (Bergman, 1960)

Talib approached the farmer, who was feeding the cows. The farmer talked to the animals and occasionally stroked them on the head. The cows seemed to understand him. He shook Talib's hand, introduced himself to me as Daan Hondenveld, and led us to the kitchen. We drank tea and the man asked me in English if I understood that the work I was going to do was volunteer work.

"I'm not paying you guys a cent," he said with a wink. I looked questioningly at Talib, who nodded elaborately. After the tea, we followed the farmer to a greenhouse behind the cowshed. It was brightly lit and was full of knee-high plants.

"Have a good one," he said, and left us to it.

"Fifty euros, man," Talib said. "Per day. Sometimes for just three or four hours."

"What do we have to do?"

"Just check every stalk and leaf." He could see my hesitation. "It's for medicine."

"Do you think I'm crazy? I recognize these leaves. From Bob Marley's clothes. This is marijuana." This was also work I could not do, it didn't feel right.

Talib took me to the farmer and told him I had allergies. Farmer Daan wanted to give me twenty euros but I refused and thanked him for the opportunity.

"I do have other work," he said, and took me to a large shed and asked me if I could clear it out and clean it.

"Volunteer?" I asked. Farmer Daan laughed.

"Twelve euros an hour."

"How much??"

"Too little?"

"No, not at all." Cleaning at the ASC brought in twenty-five euros a week, working in Hamdi's shawarma place paid ten euros a night, and here, among the cows, I'd get twelve euros an hour? When I was done with the shed he asked me to feed the cows and shovel away the dung. This was a job I could look forward to.

Farmer Daan was forever calling out: "Break time!" Whereupon we would drink coffee and then resume working until the next time he called out "Break time!" for a sandwich or tea. He did not deduct the breaks from our hours. Talib worked in the greenhouse, and I was given all sorts of odd jobs to do, and he never checked whether or not we were doing it properly or fast enough. He whistled and sang pop songs by singers called Ronnie Tober or Ramses Shaffy. In his house there were lots of photos of cows, and two of his wife, who we never saw. She wore black and white clothes in the picture and looked a little bit like a cow herself. Maybe that's why he married her. Or maybe she was once a woman, but after living with him on the farm for a while she turned into a cow, which would explain why we never saw her. Once, on a rainy day, Daan showed us a video of the first time his cows got let out of the barn after the winter. We saw how they leapt and danced about. Farmer Daan had the remote control, and kept repeating that bit, so we could see how delirious the cows were to be outside. The cows were happy with spring and Farmer Daan was happy with his home movies, but Talib and I were happiest of all, because he was paying us to watch home videos.

One day I saw him talking to one of his cows, and was shocked when it nodded. She appeared to understand what he said, as though he wasn't a man, but a steer.

"You see?" said Farmer Daan. "If you really listen to a cow, she'll listen to you too. Understand them, and they'll understand you back."

Flabbergasted, I carried on pitching hay, and secretly

58

After a while I had scraped together enough money to buy a forged passport with a Turkish name and a bus ticket to Norway. In Groningen I boarded a Euroline bus to Germany. After about an hour, a Dutch customs agent got on and shined his flashlight on everyone's passports, mine included, and let us pass. I transferred to another bus to Copenhagen. Before the bus drove onto the ferry, a Danish official, having looked at my passport, asked me to get out. Then he searched my bag, found nothing suspicious and let me get back in. There were no more checks until we got to Oslo.

Once in Oslo, I walked over to a secluded spot and threw away everything I had in my bag that would show I came from the Netherlands. Even the bag itself had a Dutch slogan printed on it, so I threw that away, too. An hour and a half later, all I had on me was a forged pass-port and a pair of underpants. I didn't want to get rid of the passport, in case I was sent back. Maybe I'd need it, but what to do with it in the meantime? Finally, in a park I found an old tree with exposed roots, and I buried the passport in the in-between space. Then I walked through Oslo's streets until I encountered a policeman. I told him I wanted to request asylum.

The memories of the ride in the Norwegian police car are sweet. The female officer asked me in English if I was hungry. I nodded, so they drove to a McDonald's. They bought me a meal and allowed me to sit there and eat it before taking me to the reception facility. McDonald's might not be so wholesome, but at that moment this Big Mac was the healthiest food ever, because it allowed my soul to believe in humanity again. The place they brought me to was clean and tidy. I was given a room to myself, and because I had repeatedly put glue on my fingers to make my fingerprints unrecognizable they thought there was something wrong with my hands and sent me to a different facility. There, a Norwegian guy spent an hour or two with my fingers, and two days later they told me I had come from the Netherlands, and had also tried to claim asylum in Germany. They asked if they should send me back to the Netherlands by the official procedure, or if I would prefer to return the way I had come. I chose the second option and was given a ticket to the border and a piece of paper stating they shouldn't detain me. I went back to the park in Oslo, where my fake passport was waiting for me under the large tree as though this was the most normal thing in the world.

I was detained in Germany anyway. I told them I had requested asylum there once before and that they had already sent me back to the Netherlands, and that I was en route to the Netherlands right now, but they did not believe me. They sent me back the official way, which meant my journey ended in a Dutch jail cell.

This time around was worse. Not because it was a cell, but because it was Europe. Now I realized I didn't stand a chance anywhere outside the Netherlands, and that my fingerprints made the Netherlands my entire world. And that the Netherlands gave me two choices: Saddam Hussein or the Immigration Department. It was like being given the choice of which death penalty you wanted: the electric chair or a lethal injection.

Something within me had died. Something that had rescued me from wars, disasters, and misery: hope. For the first time in my life, I felt completely hopeless and empty. Even if I swallowed oceans, mountains, forests, rivers, and deserts, I would remain empty.

I also discovered that I had become submissive. Not out of fear of reprisals, but because it felt like I didn't deserve my life, and that I should despise myself for it.

When they let me back outside with a train ticket to the ASC and a letter saying I had been sent back from Germany, I felt a complete lack of will. Everything around me had lost its meaning.

"Watch out!" a woman shouted. I was just about to cross the tram tracks when the tram's bell rang.

"Be careful!" someone else said.

It had started to rain. I saw people running for cover, but I looked up at that dripping gray expanse. I thought of the sky. Not this sky, but the faraway skies of Iraq.

59

The same ASC. The same Reception, the same Social Services, the same counter to report at.

"Well, look who we have here," Anneke said with a smile. "Would you like to report?" She looked at the piece of paper I gave her and then in the computer, and told me I could have my old room back, O-139. I went to the storeroom for two blankets, three sheets, a towel, a pillow, and a pillowcase, but Jade Bakker, who worked there, looked in her computer and said I still had two blankets, three sheets, a towel, a pillow, and a pillowcase in my possession. I went to O-139 to ask what had happened to my two blankets, three sheets, towel, pillow, and pillowcase. My old roommates were gone, replaced by new ones. Even the once-empty fourth bed was now occupied. I asked my new roommates where my two blankets, three sheets, towel, pillow, and pillowcase were, but they said they had no idea, Social Services must have taken them. I went back to Social Services, where Aiden told me that if they had taken my two blankets, three sheets, towel, pillow, and pillowcase from my room, they would have brought them to the storeroom. And so I ended up back with Jade Bakker, who said that the two blankets, three sheets, towel, pillow, and pillowcase might well have been brought back to the storeroom, but this hadn't been fed into the computer. And because Jade Bakker complied with the storeroom's computer and not the storeroom itself, I returned to O-139 without two blankets, three sheets, a towel, a pillow, or a pillowcase, and lay down on my bare mattress.

I slept for hours and hours, and when I woke up it was dark. I turned on the light and saw my three roommates sleeping. No one snored. I turned off the light, felt around for my socks and shoes, and left the room. The halls were empty as I walked to the kitchen, hoping to find someone there to borrow some tea from. There, I saw Yelena.

"It's you!" she exclaimed, and ran up and gave me a hug. She started crying, which surprised me. "You're so thin," she sobbed. She made tea and invited me back to her room. She left the door open to make it clear this was purely a social visit.

Even though I had been gone for quite some time, she did not ask where I had been. She only wanted to tell me what had been going on with her. Just listening to Yelena's chatter recharged my spirit. Imagine being stranded in the desert, dying of thirst. And suddenly you hear the sound of water at an oasis. Yelena's voice was that water, and the oasis was Yelena herself. I loved her, not as a woman, but as life. And maybe my love for her could help restore my love for myself and for my own life.

Her room was tidy. Above her bed was a photo of a young man. You could tell in an instant he was a criminal. As though she could read my thoughts, she said, "He's so sweet. The sweetest guy I've ever met in my life." His name was Sufyan. The strange thing was that Sufyan always came to the ASC to visit Yelena, never the other way around. "He still lives at home," Yelena explained. His parents were traditional Muslims, and she hadn't been introduced to them yet. Yelena didn't mind, because she was in love and that was all that counted.

One day Sufyan showed up in the orange wing. He was smaller than Yelena, and he wore rings and gold chains and looked exactly like he did in the picture: hostile and belligerent. Whenever he was in the ASC, Yelena's world was room O-124. She would dash back and forth between her room and the kitchen or the bathroom. So, suddenly there were two Yelenas: one with Sufyan and one without, and you could tell which one she was by the way she walked through the halls. Once I saw Sufyan get out of a new BMW and wondered why, if he could afford such a fancy car, he didn't just take Yelena to a hotel.

Like I said, my former roommates had all disappeared. Fouad had been transferred to a different ASC, no one knew what happened to The Fourth, and when I asked what had happened to Walid, the answer was that he had gone "AWOL." I took this to mean he had an infectious disease, but the staffer laughed when I asked if it was fatal. "Absent Without Leave," she explained. He had disappeared after receiving a letter from the IND saying he would be deported within twenty-eight days.

Soon thereafter, Sayid showed up with a bag containing two blankets, three sheets, a towel, a pillow, and a pillowcase, which he had gotten from someone else who had gone AWOL. He said I could have them for one euro per item.

My three new roommates were all very different. Salih talked incessantly, even in his sleep. Fortunately the volume of his voice was low, even when he slept, which was less irritating than the old roommates' snoring.

The second one was Alaa, a man of few words, and the third was Malik, the most inscrutable asylum seeker I met during those nine years. It turned out he'd been living in the ASC longer than me, and had only just changed rooms. I was surprised I'd never bumped into him before. He seemed to know something about everything, and his information, like him, was always positive and unbiased. I thank Fate for allowing me to meet him. He was chubby and hairy, and had a large head on a sturdy neck. Of all the asylum seekers, he had the most respect for the Dutch. He loved the Netherlands even more than many Dutch people did. He was open-minded and spoke gladly about anything, except about himself: then he was quiet and closed. What had he studied? How old was he? How did he get to Holland? Was Malik his real name? He had bought a record player, and when he was alone in the room he would play classical music. As soon as one of us came in, he would immediately ask if the music bothered us, and then quickly turn it off.

There are people in this world who do not attract attention, who live without causing a fuss or irritation. Malik was one of these people. He always reported during the last ten minutes before the counter closed, because there wasn't so long a wait, and he was never afraid he'd forget. He would also wait to use the kitchen until everyone else was finished, even though this meant eating very late. Alaa and Salih respected Malik. If one of them said something contentious, Malik would not protest or argue, unless asked directly for his opinion.

"Look how the Hollanders let us rot here in this place without giving us a residence permit," Salih said to Malik one day. "What do you think of that?"

Malik scratched his head. "Just look around you. Isn't it a miracle …?" Malik checked whether Salih was listening, and continued: "Look how many kinds of people live here, how many nationalities, how many traditions, languages, religions, how much aggression and homesickness. All in a single building. We share the showers, use the same toilets. Without any problem. And there's medical care and social services and lessons in road safety. The Hollanders' job is to make life here more tolerable. Isn't that a miracle? In Iraq we spoke the same language, had the same traditions, and ate the same food, but never had social services or road safety courses. No Iraqi ever got a lawyer, but here all Iraqis have a lawyer and health insurance, even if they don't have papers. Do you know how much this place costs each Dutch person?" At which point Malik felt he had been talking too long, and stopped.

"But why don't they give us asylum, like in Spain or Italy?" asked Salih. "There, they practically hand out residence permits."

"Because the Dutch don't want to just give you a residence permit, but also a life. A place to live, the chance to study, welfare until you no longer need to rely on the system. In Italy and Spain you just get that piece of paper and they say: off you go, you're on your own. There's a Chinese proverb: *Give a man a fish, and you feed him for a day. Teach a man to fish, and you feed him for a lifetime.* Well, it's true, and that's what the Dutch do."

"Man, the Hollanders prefer liars," Salih countered. "Take Firaas. He got everything by lying. But you, the honest one, you get nothing, even though you're obviously a political refugee."

"But Salih, think about it, there are more than five hundred asylum seekers living here. How on earth are the Dutch supposed to know who is honest and who isn't? They have humanity, and because they respect all men they give everyone a chance to live in this building. If by magic they could know for sure which of us is a political refugee—and you can count them on one hand—they would give them political asylum that very day and send back the rest. But since it's impossible to identify those few political refugees, more than five hundred people get the benefit of the doubt."

That's how Malik talked. And because he was an asylum seeker like us, it made him credible. Salih enjoyed debating with Malik, sometimes just to have something to do. For me, this discussion was important because it showed me the humanity in a situation that had cost me my own humanity.

Salih and his brother had come to the Netherlands nine years earlier. They each told the immigration officials the same story about the troubles in Iraq, and were both fleeing for the same reason. They arrived in the Netherlands together, even with the same smuggler, but their dossiers ended up with two different civil servants. Salih's brother got a residence permit after eight years, but not Salih. Every night before we turned out the light we listened to Salih's monologue and his carping about it. Why he still didn't have his residence permit? According to him it had already been approved, only it hadn't been sent yet. Why did his brother get one, while he, Salih, still had to wait? When his brother came to visit, Salih seemed more annoyed than glad.

Sometimes he would show us the transcripts of his and his brother's hearings, so we could compare them. "Do you get it?" he asked Malik, handing him both transcripts. "Read them. They're identical." Malik took the transcripts, which he had read many times before, and pretended to study them.

"Maybe because your dossier and your brother's went to two different civil servants. You were both older than eighteen, so they regard you as two separate cases."

"But that's unfair. That the same story is good enough for a residence permit for one, but not the other."

"Civil servants are people, not machines. If you both went to different doctors with a headache, you might each get prescribed different medicine." This seemed to satisfy Salih, and we heard no more of his bellyaching that night, but the next day, at the same time, just before the light went out, Salih would repeat his lament, get out both transcripts, and Malik would look through them again as if for the first time, and explain it anew, substituting a headache with a sore throat. While Malik only changed the example, Salih himself changed. He became angrier, at the immigration officials, at himself and his fate, at his brother.

I thought of Malik, how tedious it was that every evening such a wonderful person, with his collection of classical albums, had to repeat the same explanation to Salih, and how every evening he studiously compared the same transcripts. I was afraid that one day Malik would change, or give up, but every evening when I heard his friendly voice I believed, albeit briefly, that even in this place a human being could stay a human being. Until the lights went out. And then I thought: but for how long?

60

Malik did not change. Salih got angrier. Alaa became even quieter. And I felt myself change. I had become more wary of the Dutch.

The tidy, quiet, clean-swept streets, the correctness and the never-ending rules. The staffers at Reception and Social Services, who had the power to send you to a cell they had never seen, could not get their head around the fact that asylum seekers might be afraid of them. They were people, too—no reason to be afraid, surely? It irritated them. And then you had the civil servants from the IND and the Ministry of Justice, who decided whether you could get on with your life, and where, and when. I started to imagine that there were no normal people living outside the ASC, just civil servants, and it annoyed me to meet people outside who were actually nice.

I pretended to be normal whenever there was a Dutch person around. That I was not crazy and on my guard. But it felt like there was someone else inside my body who was keeping all my thoughts and feelings in check. I got into angry conflicts with the other me, and after a while I stopped wanting to play-act, and just be myself. But if I didn't act normal, I was crazy, which took the ASC staffers by surprise, because they were used to seeing me act normal. This disjunction was torture for my soul.

I still have vivid memories of the day I went calmly to the back door, thinking it wasn't eight o'clock yet and the door would still be open. But when I got there and realized it was locked I started banging on it with all my might, until blood dripped from my fists and I broke one of my fingers. Exactly what I had feared at the beginning had come true: I had become someone else.

The only thing that could calm me down was to leave the building. So I bought a raincoat and a Thermos, and went outside first thing in the morning. I spent the day pretending I didn't really live in the ASC. As soon as I got out of town, I felt better. I discovered a small lake with lots of water birds and a concrete birdwatching hut among the bushes. I would spend hours there, and when it got chilly, I'd return to the ASC.

If Sufyan was absent for a while, Yelena would invite me to her room for tea, and tell me how happy she was with him and would fantasize about their future together. What Sufyan wanted with her, or with himself, she didn't say. It wasn't clear to any of us whether he was only interested in her body, or also in her heart. But Yelena did not want to go into that.

After a few months, it was clear things were not going well between them. Hatim asked me why Sufyan no longer made love to the Russian girl, but only picked fights with her. I didn't know either why she looked so bedraggled, until Sayid told me he had heard from the Chechen woman Bogdana that Yelena was pregnant, and that Sufyan did not want the child. So now we knew what was behind the noise coming from O-124, and why Sufyan slammed the door behind him so often.

One day Sufyan was screaming so loudly in O-124 that

lots of asylum seekers came out to fry an egg, prepare a salad, or make tea. The kitchen was full of asylum seekers, who were not there to fill their stomachs, but their ears.

What I later heard from Yelena was that Sufyan did not want a child with her, and that she had to get rid of it, even after she told him he didn't have to have an active role as a father. He threatened her, so she went to Social Services. They told her that if she wanted to keep the child, it was her choice and not his. They would protect her and transfer her to a different ASC. She could also file charges with the police. Yelena started packing her things in secret, so she could be transferred quietly, but suddenly she disappeared for a few days. After she returned, the nurses from the clinic came by regularly to check on her. Sufyan seemed to be out of her life, although his photo still hung above her bed. I bought a blender at the thrift store and a bag of fruit at the market, and even though I knew she didn't care, I thought she could use the vitamins and went to her room to make her a fruit shake. I could tell something about her was absent, but couldn't put my finger on it. She no longer talked about Sufyan, but about having had an abortion and how she regretted it. She suffered from insomnia, so Social Services gave her a new room in Blue. But she couldn't sleep there, either.

She would often come by our room and ask Malik to put on some Chopin. She explained to Salih that he was a Polish composer, and that when he died they put his heart in a pillar in a church in Warsaw. She had seen it on a family visit there when she was eleven.

After a while, Yelena started perking up, especially after seeing a psychologist Annelies Vos had arranged for her. Then she stopped visiting us in O-139, because Sufyan was back in the picture. She avoided talking about him with me.

About three months later, Sayid confided in me that he had heard from the Chechen woman Bogdana that Yelena was pregnant again, and did not want Sufyan to find out. The news spread through the ASC until the only one who didn't know was Sufyan himself. Before her belly started to grow, Yelena disappeared again. She did not say goodbye to anyone, nor did anyone know where she had gone.

61

During my fifth year in the ASC it looked like there would be a war between America and Iraq, near the Kuwaiti border. Then something surprising happened: the IND decided that every Iraqi from the south of the country could reapply for asylum. Since that's where I was born, I also received a letter to this effect. I reread my first and second interviews, because I assumed my new request would have to tally with my original story. But several Iraqis who had had their new interview came back and said that wasn't the case at all. Now the IND wasn't interested in why you fled, or your problems with the regime. No: this time the asylum seeker had to provide accurate information about his town, city, or province. One man was even allowed to phone his family there to be sure that the information was correct, and to ask if anything had changed in the meantime. The IND wanted to know exactly how many people lived there, which religions were represented, what the connection was with Saddam Hussein, and how many offices the Ba'ath Party and the army had. But the craziest part was that the asylum seekers were told their request would be processed within three months. I heard that some were invited back for a second interview, this time with an English interpreter present. I didn't believe the gossip that this was a back door for the Americans to gather inside information to aid their war effort. But when my turn came, this proved to be entirely true.

The IND official read my personal data out loud and informed me that this interview would be different from the first two.

"In what way?" I asked.

"You'll see," he said. He laid a large map of Iraq on the table and asked me to point to where I was born, and marked it with an X. That was a village close to the city of Nadjaf. I told him we then moved to Baghdad. He asked which bank of the Tigris, Rusafa, or Karkh, and marked that with another X. Then I told him I studied in Erbil, Kurdistan: another X. He said there was a chance I would be invited for a second interview, and started asking me questions that had nothing to do with my refugee status, which made me suspect that the grapevine was right. I asked him what these questions were for, and he replied that I just had to answer him.

"Sorry, but I'm an asylum seeker, not a spy," I said. "My fatherland is on the brink of war, and you're asking me things that have nothing to do with my being a refugee, but about the country itself. And if they do have something to do with my request, why didn't they ask this back in 1998?" He stopped typing and looked at me. I told him I wanted him to make a detailed record of this exchange.

"I'll record what I want," he said.

"But in 1998 the IND took down everything I said, including the misunderstandings," I said to him in Dutch, "and thanks to that I've been stuck in an ASC for years now. Why suddenly so different? If an asylum seeker's answers aren't important, what is?" The interpreter listened quietly.

"Listen, you're not here to tell me how to do my job."

"Sorry, sir, but aren't my problems in Iraq your job? Ask me questions about that, then."

"Listen," he repeated, this time angrily. "I'll say it one more time. You're here to answer my questions. You should know that without this interview, you have no right to return to the ASC. You may not return to your old asylum request. You signed a paper stating you want to cooperate on a new request. I'll give you a fifteen-minute break. Have a cup of coffee and think about whether you want to continue this interview or not."

I did not think about anything in those fifteen minutes, I just drank the coffee. After exactly fifteen minutes the man came up to the coffee machine.

"And?"

"I refuse."

"Why?"

"I do not wish to give information about Iraq when the country is almost at war. I only want to talk to the IND about the reason I fled Iraq, and my problems with the Iraqi government and with Saddam Hussein. I have no problems with Iraq itself. Nor do the thousands of generations that came before me." I told him I thought the IND was a terrorist organization, because it had kept me cooped up in an ASC for years and did not take my asylum request seriously.

I said all this to the IND official. Maybe it wasn't so courteous, but after years of waiting, and with war looming and my family in danger, nothing else mattered, not even courtesy or fear of the IND. The official wrote in his report that I regarded the IND as a terrorist organization, and therefore refused to conclude the interview. He printed it out and asked me to sign it.

I did not do the same as back in 1998. I read it first. I told him he did not take down everything I had said. He replied that he did not use his own words, but mine. I said that that was correct, but that he had left many things out.

"I don't want to argue any longer," he said. "First you refuse to cooperate with the interview, and now you don't want to round it off." Not signing would mean the interview had not been completed and I could not return to the ASC. He said I should take the matter up with my lawyer.

After I signed, the official handed me a copy, as they are meant to do. He left me in a waiting room, where I met an asylum seeker from Aimara in southern Iraq, whose interview lasted five hours. After such a long interview, he expected to receive a positive answer from the IND.

I certainly did not expect the same. But I was relieved to discover I hadn't lost myself entirely, and was still strong enough to refuse to go along with these games. I still had some spirit left in me, even though I had to dredge it up from deep down. A couple of hours later I sat, relieved, in the train back to the ASC.

62

Daytime was the hardest part about living in the ASC. I never knew what to do with myself. The days began and ended in the hallways, not just for me, but for hundreds of us.

During my first two years, I immersed myself in the Dutch language, because if the ASC was a prison, then the language was a latchkey. The key that would open the door to the Netherlands, to the Dutch people, to life on the outside. I soon discovered, however, that if you spoke English you would always get an explanation for things, but if you spoke Dutch you'd get asked things like: Why are you here? What do you do here? Why don't you leave, if you don't like it?

The Dutch language did not open the door to the Netherlands itself, but rather to the local public library. I started going there in the morning to read. Not because I'm such a fanatic reader, but because I didn't like being in the ASC. The library was tidy and quiet and had a pleasant atmosphere. The place where they kept books was better cared for than the place where they kept refugees. And why not: when you opened a book, you saw nice, quiet words, and when you opened an asylum seeker, you found only a tangle of noisy problems.

I started in the children's section, for beginner readers. I sat down at a table, opened a book, and read. Whenever I came across a word I didn't know, I would look it up in my dictionary and jot it down in my notebook. The librarians were friendly and helpful.

I remember once sitting there reading a book called *Frog is Frog*. Suddenly, I heard a small voice next to me.

"Mister?" I looked up and saw a girl of about six, with glasses that covered half her face. She handed me a book. "This one is even better," she said. It was *Frog is in Love*. And sure enough, it was a good book.

After I had read all the children's books, even Miffy, I went upstairs to the adult section, where I needed my dictionary more often. The library transformed me.

One day one of the librarians said that if I wanted to, I could take a book back with me to the ASC. I didn't dare admit to not having a library card, or ask how she knew I lived in the ASC.

"I'm going on vacation for three weeks," she said. "You can borrow my card."

Her trust made a deep impression on me. She never did ask for her card back. A few months later I saw her in town, walking with a man and a child, and I tried to greet her, but she ignored me. I didn't really mind, because her library card was in my pocket. By then I was used to the fact that if I knew a Dutch person from his workplace, he would ignore me if I saw him on the street, and if I knew someone from his private life, he would pretend not to know me at his workplace.

But the person within the ASC who changed the most, and the most unexpectedly, was Zainab. Zainab no longer walked, she biked. For this woman from the south of Iraq, with all her traditions, this was equivalent to a political commentator in a burka praising a far-right party. At first we thought it would be impossible for Zainab to learn to ride a bike, but she did it. She was extra motivated when she saw Parishad, the Afghan woman with her many layers of Islamic clothing, on a bicycle. If even Parishad could learn, Zainab said, then so could she. When Patrick Schepenmaker heard this, he said he would give her his mother's bicycle because she couldn't ride it anymore. So a few weeks later, Patrick arrived with a really nice granny bike with a light up front and a light on the back and a chain lock, and Zainab was pleased as punch. She was probably even happier with her bike than she would have been with a residence permit.

Fatima, who was such a good cook, complained that no bicycle would be able to carry her weight, otherwise she'd have learned long ago. But she changed too. She no longer prepared snacks for Social Services and the volunteers, because they could not give her a residence permit in return. So she started taking her snacks to church on Sundays. Instead of waiting for an answer from the IND or the Ministry of Justice, she waited for Jens van Munster. She would often take others with her to translate, so that Jens van Munster would know exactly what she wanted. She told him her knees and her back hurt, and that her heart was weak and her intestines did not function properly, and for this reason she really needed a residence permit. But Jens van Munster never gave her the letter she so yearned for. She tried to get me to go with her, but after the incident with Abdulwahid, I never set foot in another church in the Netherlands. Just as the IND cured me of my belief in Europe, Jens van Munster cured me of my belief in Jesus as a savior, even though my respect for Jesus as a person, like Nelson Mandela and Gandhi, has never wavered.

Jens van Munster still came to the ASC every month and parked his car in front of the gate, and said that

Jesus was salvation, not a residence permit. He dealt out books to the asylum seekers, and the three gray-haired women gave toys and chocolate to the children. Sometimes, if it was too cold out, he would come inside. But then he did not talk to the adults, he only played with the children. He did not pass out books either, and avoided Abdulwahid.

It was around this time that Abdulwahid caused his biggest fuss ever, and then vanished. One day he was walking in town wearing his Yemenite clothes, and was approached by a few men who had come from London to suss out the situation of Dutch asylum seekers. Visitors from outside were only let into the ASC if they were guests of a resident, and then only until eight at night. So Abdulwahid invited them in. They had long beards, smiled constantly, and spoke fluent classical Arabic. Having convened in the social hall, they started handing out Qur'ans and books in Arabic about Islam. In no time, they were surrounded by Social Services personnel and officers from the Foreigners' Police, as though war was about to break out. They asked the four men to leave the building, but Abdulwahid said he had the right to invite people to the ASC, and that they were his guests. Patrick Schepenmaker said that it was strictly forbidden to hand out books, to which Abdulwahid replied that "the man from the church" passed out Bibles and books about Christianity. Patrick said they only did so outside the ASC, not in the building. Abdulwahid talked and Social Services talked and the Foreigners' Police watched. Then the four men said to Abdulwahid not to make a big deal out of it, and that they could just as well hand out the books outside, where the preacher handed out his Bibles and books. So outside everyone went. There, where Jens van Munster always parked his car to hand out books, the four men had to show their English passports and were asked to leave. Abdulwahid lost his patience, but the four men calmed him down in Arabic and then left. Many other asylum seekers were so angry that everyone who had received a book from Jens van Munster threw it out their window, until the forecourt was littered with little green Bibles. Social Services spent all day going from door to door to say that it was forbidden to throw books out the window.

The four men were staying in a hotel in town. Abdulwahid told me they could perhaps help me get to Malaysia if I wanted, or Australia or Canada, places where they didn't check your fingerprints. So I went to the hotel with him. They listened to my story and said they could help me by paying for a lawyer, but not right away, because in every ASC they visited there were people who had been waiting for years, including families with children or sick people, and these cases would be given priority. One of them offered me a book that would teach me to have patience in the ASC. I said I had already read a lot about Islam, but I preferred poetry. There were, he said, plenty of bookstores in London that sold Arabic literature, so I made a list for him, and a month and a half later I received a package with the titles I had asked for, as well as a few pamphlets about Islam.

Abdulwahid said goodbye to everyone in the ASC. First all the asylum seekers. Anyone he did not bump into in the hallway, he visited personally. After that, the Foreigners' Police, the volunteers, the storeroom attendant, the health clinic, and the receptionists.

"Abdulwahid going London," he said to everyone. He turned in his bank card and his W-document, and I walked him to the hotel where the four men were waiting for him.

"Are they taking you with them?" I asked.

"It's a little bit trickier than that. I'm going to France first, then to London."

I truly regretted Abdulwahid leaving the ASC. I have traveled all over the world, and know from experience how small the chance is that you will meet as genuine a person as Abdulwahid. A man afraid of only one thing: his conscience.

After that, everything returned to normal in the ASC, as though nothing had happened. Abdulsalaam stood at Reception and asked Zainab, "No mail today?"

"No, and no body either," Zainab replied. Rik assured Abdulsalaam that there really was no mail, and gave Zainab a stern look to get her to go away. When she finally did, he heaved a deep sigh.

"Are you okay?" I asked him.

"That woman, the Iraqi lady in black, what was her name again? Oh yeah, Zaynaap. She was here today for the third time, asking about Kadhem's body. I don't know how to get it through to her that we are an asylum center, not a cemetery."

I smiled, and when he gave me a questioning look, I said, "Maybe this *is* a cemetery, but one where the bodies are still alive."

63

After Abdulwahid left for London, I got a phone call from my father. It was the first time he had phoned me. He spoke softly, and struggled to breathe.

"Come to Jordan, Samir," his tired voice said. "I want to say goodbye to you. My time has come. It will be this month, or next."

His call was a shock. I knew my father suffered from heart ailments, but did not realize how serious it was. The few times I had spoken with my siblings—not so often, because I didn't have much to say and it was horribly expensive—no one had ever mentioned his precarious health. I went to Social Services and told Annelies Vos I needed a travel document to go to Jordan to see my father before he died. Even if that meant I could not return to the Netherlands, then so be it. Annelies said an asylum seeker could only get a travel document if he already had a residence permit. I asked Wim from the volunteer organization VVN if he could help me. He called the IND and explained my situation, but was told that a travel document was impossible without a residence permit. I refused to believe this. I went to the head office of the IND myself, but the receptionist would not let me in without an appointment. So I called, gave my particulars and said that I needed an appointment, preferring to explain my situation in person, but they said the VVN had already phoned and the answer was no, I could not get a travel document.

The next day I tried in person again, this time with a different receptionist, but got the same answer. An appointment was out of the question. I begged her to let me in, but she was unyielding. When I refused to leave, she called the police. Two officers came and said I had to leave, but I told them I would only go after I had explained my predicament to an IND functionary in person. This landed me in a police car, my hands cuffed behind my back. They brought me to the train station, but I said I would go straight back to the IND, and when I did just that, they took me to the police station and put me in a cell for six hours.

I returned to the ASC, borrowed money from everyone I knew, and when I had collected €550 I bought a passport. I went in search of someone who could doctor the photo, but before the passport was ready, my father had died.

I reported at the counter the next day.

"You didn't report last time," the woman behind the window said.

"My father died."

"You still have to report. No pocket money for three weeks." She entered her punishment in the computer.

Then she confiscated my W-document and made me stand in the corner until five o'clock.

That woman thought she could hurt me. What she did not know was that the person standing before her was a cadaver.

64

The next time I asked Milaad how old he was, he answered, "Almost seven." So I had been in this building for nearly seven years, and this little boy had been here his whole life.

"Where are you from?" I asked him.

"The ASC," he said.

His mother called from the kitchen, "Either tell him you're Iraqi like your father, or Tunisian like your mother. The ASC is a building, not a country."

I decided to accept the fact that I would be living in the ASC for an indeterminate time. That it was my home, my country. This was better than harboring expectations. Expectations will destroy an asylum seeker. Dutch people are not dangerous, except if you have hope and the expectation that you might get something from them.

I couldn't sleep properly anymore, but never really woke up either, and I would often get stuck in that hazy no-man's-land in between the two. I got up with a headache, and paced the halls in an attempt to make myself tired, but after a few minutes my muscles would protest. It was not life-threatening, because lots of longterm asylum seekers suffered from the same thing, but it was vexing all the same. Albertina, who taught Dutch lessons, suggested trying yoga, and gave me the address of a yoga center in town. Fortunately you did not need official papers to sign up, but lessons cost ten euros, so I only attended the free trial session. I did find a book on meditation at the thrift store, but instead of bringing me peace, it reminded me how much stress there is in a place housing five hundred people.

The illustrations in the yoga book showed a woman meditating in a large open space, a man at the foot of a waterfall in the jungle among colorful tropical birds, and a group of people walking along a beach. There was not a single picture of a person meditating surrounded by five hundred asylum seekers.

I discovered that in an ASC you learned the opposite of meditation. In another book I read about stress and its effect on children who grew up in a stressful household. Some children had been born in the ASC, and every child inside the center had seen violence between aggressive asylum seekers and the Foreigners' Police with their own eyes. And if they hadn't seen with their own eyes that some asylum seekers hung themselves, starved themselves, or set themselves on fire, then they surely knew about it.

My first approach to meditation, and getting back in touch with my body, was to learn to concentrate. I decided to pursue this goal of clearing my mind by concentrating on nothing at all. This was impossible in room O-139, so I went to the window at the end of the hall. I stood there staring outside at a branch, until that branch itself became my thoughts. Once, when I was busy staring at the branch, Salih came up and waved his hands in front of my face. I was determined to ignore him, and only to focus on the branch.

"Have you gone blind?" he asked.

"No, man, I'm trying to learn concentration," I replied.

"What?"

"Con-cen-tra-tion," I enunciated, purposely not looking at him, so that he would leave me in peace.

"Oh, concentration. So you're learning concentration."

He went off, and came back a little while later.

"You still learning ... What was it, again?"

"Concentration."

"Yeah, yeah. And? Is it working?"

"Not yet." Off he went again, and brought Habib back with him. They were laughing.

"Look at him. He's learning ... eh, you're learning concentration, right?" I nodded. "Cool."

And so went my first attempt. It ended up being not an exercise in concentration, but in irritation. I was irritated all the time anyway, but at that moment it hit me how irritating this all was. Dancing the tango with a hyperactive monkey or a depressed gorilla would be easier than meditating among asylum seekers. I bought some more books on yoga and meditation at the thrift store, and buying these books itself became yoga, and reading them meditation. But then one day I bought some old fountain pens from a woman at the flea market. She wanted five euros for them at first, but when I gave her my most pathetic look and told her I was from the ASC, she gave them to me for two euros. I bought a bottle of ink and started repairing the pens in my room. For the other asylum seekers, repairing a pen was easier to grasp than meditation or yoga. While I was busy with my pens, the others left me in peace.

I would disassemble the fountain pen, clean it thoroughly, and file, scrape, and buff it until it wrote like melted butter. I did all this deliberately and with the utmost concentration. At first, every noise and sound within earshot—a yell, or even footsteps or an opening door—would disrupt my concentration, but after a while, I could shut it all out, and focus on the pen.

This was my escape from the ASC. It enabled me to forget, just briefly, the years of waiting and the utter hopelessness of that place. I was not the only one who, in one way or another, sought refuge from the endless wait.

There were, for example, four young men from Armenia, Chechnya, Congo, and Iraq who had met in the ASC. On weekends they would dress up, polish their shoes, and go out. Not to church, even though they always came back with smiles on their face. No one had the faintest idea where they went.

65

One of these was a guy named Zako. He once asked to borrow money from me. I gave him everything I had at that moment, eighteen euros. When he thanked me, I asked where he and the other three always went, dressed up so smartly.

"To the museum of living fine arts," he said, laughing. "Want to join us sometime?"

"Sure," I said. "Do I need to get dressed up, too?"

"Not necessary. But you never know when one of the paintings will want to talk to you, or drink tea. Then you should be dressed properly."

We took the train to Amsterdam, got out at Central Station, and walked for a bit, until Zako said we had reached the museum. He pointed to a scantily-clad young woman in a window. So that's where they went: to the red light district, every week if they had enough money for the train. If they could, they would have gone every day.

"Just look at that painting. She's smiling at us," Zako said, pointing at a brunette in neon-yellow lingerie.

"Why do you call her a painting?" I asked.

"If you have enough money, you can pay her and fuck her. That makes her a whore. But if you're an asylum seeker and don't have the money, then you can only look, and then she's a living work of art."

Everyone there had their own method for making time go by. Mushtaak, for instance, often went into town dressed as a tourist, with a camera around his neck and a map of Rome he had bought at the thrift store. He wanted people outside the ASC to think of him as a tourist, not an asylum seeker. However, Mushtaak was oblivious to the fact that a tourist usually carries a map of the city he is presently in, not a random city elsewhere. When confronted with this, he protested, "You're an asylum seeker! Have you ever been a tourist, that you're such an expert on how a tourist is supposed to look?" In town, he chatted up every woman he encountered, telling them he was a tourist from Rome. He would ask the women if he could take their picture. As soon as the film roll was full, he would get it developed: thirty-six women per roll. He pasted the pictures into an album he got at the thrift store, and whenever anyone dropped by for a visit, he would take out an album, with the year the pictures were taken written on the front.

"These were my sweethearts that year," he would say proudly. "This one liked cuddling, this one was a great kisser, this one gave a terrific blow job ..."

This was Mushtaak's way of escaping from the ASC.

Ghali, Mushtaak's roommate, escaped by studying the photos and listening to Mushtaak tell about his sweethearts. Zainab killed time with cooking and sewing. Abdulsalaam by waiting for the mail. Everyone figured out what worked best for them. The only one who did not have any special technique for passing time in the ASC was Baback, the Iranian asylum seeker who was such an incredible actor, because he had long made the ASC his home, his city, his country, his world.

66

My exercises in concentration with the fountain pens came to an end when they dragged Alaa, our drug-addicted roommate, into the ASC bleeding. They had found him on the front steps. No one called the police, because they knew this would land Alaa in jail. Alaa's face was blue and he was groaning. Salih, Malik, and I gave him clean clothes and washed his own ragged clothes in two extra-hot machine cycles to get the stench out. The next day we took him to the clinic. There they determined he had broken a couple of ribs. Since the nurses refused to give him strong sedatives, we bought some hash and rolled him a few joints to lessen his pain and give us some rest in O-139. I tried—in vain—to get transferred to another room.

"That won't solve the problem," said Daphne Koster from Social Services. Daphne, it seemed, needed reminding that she worked at Social Services and that we were asylum seekers, and that she could do something for us, and not the other way around. She always smiled when you told her your problem, as though you were standing together at a petting zoo and chatting about the baby goats. She would nod, as if in agreement. "Interesting," she'd say next, and then look at you, expecting you to come up with the solution yourself. The frustrating part was that although Daphne's mouth told us we were right, her computer did not. Because when I explained the situation in O-139 she said, "Interesting,"

"That's clear," and "How annoying." I knew there were three single rooms free, and I said that I knew they were reserved for gay men or single women but if I could have one of those rooms, I would vacate it the minute they needed it for someone else.

"Interesting idea," she said. She looked in her computer and saw that there were indeed three single rooms free in Green, but that unfortunately I couldn't have one of them. Rules are rules.

Life with Alaa became increasingly unbearable, because he stopped brushing his teeth. And since he did not have a residence permit, it was hard to get him an appointment with a dentist. Aside from smelling bad, he moaned incessantly from toothache. Day and night. Finally, Salih came up with a solution. Alaa was counting the small change he had begged on the streets, and Salih waved a fifty-euro bill in front of him. Alaa leapt up like a dog to snatch the bill, but Salih quickly stuck it back in his wallet. He told Alaa he could only have it if he went to Social Services and said he was gay, so he would get transferred out of our room.

"Give me five euros now, and the rest when I get the room," Alaa said.

"No way," Salih replied. "You can have the fifty euros when you come back here with the room key in your hand."

It took a week, but eventually Alaa returned with the key to a single room. Salih made him first pack up his belongings, move to the new room, and turn in the key to O-139 at Social Services. The drugs had changed Alaa from a nice guy into a dog that obeyed its master's orders.

Alaa's place in our room remained free for the rest of our time in the ASC. The reason for this was not clear, but I heard along the grapevine that there were fewer new asylum seekers. Alaa continued to knock at our door, but we told him his bed was in G-07, and we regularly escorted him to Reception, because he had lost his key again.

67

At the supermarket one day I saw a newspaper clipping on the bulletin board for an animal shelter. The newspaper ran photos of dogs and cats up for adoption, in a last-ditch effort to find owners before the animal got put down, because the time limit for shelter pets was three years. I looked at the photos of my four-footed fellow asylum seekers and decided to pay them a visit. I took the clipping off the bulletin board and cycled to the shelter. Their Reception had no walkie-talkies, no alarm buttons, no telephones, no pigeonholes, no computer monitors.

"Are you looking for a cat or a dog?" a woman asked.

"I've come for this one," I said, showing her the advertisement.

"Ah, Tutu. He's right over here. Come with me." She enthusiastically led me down a corridor lined with cages. Some of the dogs slept, some lay in a corner with their eyes open, others stood wagging their tail, in the hope I might be their ticket out of the shelter.

As a boy I spent six years riding a donkey to school. Upon arriving, I would let the donkey roam free. But he never ate from anyone else's orchard, he did not even sleep in the shadow of someone else's tree. And at twelve o'clock sharp, when school let out, he got up and stood waiting for me. Animals were always part of our family. We never ate the meat of our own animals. In this Dutch pet shelter I had the sensation that after all my years in the ASC I understood the animals, and they me, because we carried the same burden on our shoulders: waiting.

"This is Tutu," she said. "He got a bit too big for the family who had taken him as a puppy. He's very good-natured and loyal, but a little clumsy." She opened his cage and called him. "He's four and a half. In two weeks he'll have been here for three years. If he's not adopted by then ..." she said, looking at me. "You might be his last chance."

"Can I take him for a walk?" I asked.

"Of course," she said, handing me a leash. "He can get a little over-enthusiastic and might not listen, but really he's incredibly sweet and well-behaved." I attached Tutu's leash and took him outside. Because the woman did not ask for my ID card or even my name, I felt I could let Tutu free so he could run away. He would find a new home on his own more easily than through the Dutch bureaucratic system.

I unclipped the leash and shouted "Go!" but instead of running away he looked at my hand. I picked up a stick and threw it. He ran after it and brought it back.

"Go, Tutu! You're free," I shouted at him. "You'll be dead in two weeks if you don't go now!" But he just stood there looking at the stick in my hand, his tongue hanging out, his head cocked to one side. I threw the stick as far as I could. If I'd had the strength, I'd have thrown it over the horizon. Tutu kept fetching the stick and bringing it back.

At a quarter to five we were back at the shelter.

"I thought Tutu had escaped," the woman said.

"I hoped so, but he sure is a well-behaved dog."

"So you'll take him?"

"I wish I could, but they don't allow pets in the ASC."

When the woman heard this, her expression told me she was annoyed she'd wasted her time on me.

"Well, hang the ad back up in the supermarket. Who knows, maybe a real owner will show up in time ..."

I decided to write an advertisement for myself, just like for the shelter animals. Instead of "pet of the month" at the top, I wrote "asylum seeker of the century." I copied the text from the newspaper clipping, and only changed the length of my stay in the shelter.

A few days later my telephone rang. It was a woman with an old-sounding voice. She had seen my advertisement and said she'd like to meet me. When we met, I realized she wasn't a day over thirty. My ad was cute, she said, and that's why, after a certain hesitation, she decided to a call. She was somewhat reserved, because after all, asylum seekers couldn't be trusted. And there, she had a point: often all an asylum seeker wants from a blond woman is a residence permit, money, and a passport. I also wanted a residence permit, money, and a passport, but from her I wanted something very different. She was simply pleasant to be with, and we had a good time together.

"I like you," I said to her one day.

"Do you like me, or the Dutch passport?" she asked.

A month later I said, "I'm crazy about you."

"Are you crazy about me, or the Dutch passport?"

Another few weeks went by.

"I'm in love with you," I said.

"With me, or with the Dutch passport?"

She seemed only to want to see me as an asylum seeker, not as a person.

One day it was raining hard. We bumped into each other in town, and she invited me home with her. She got out of her wet clothes and told me to do the same, otherwise I'd catch cold. I sat awkwardly on her sofa in my boxer shorts and T-shirt. But we were having a good time, and when I tried to kiss her, she said, "Do you want to kiss me, or the Dutch passport?"

It was a scene you would only see in a film. We kissed. She took off her clothes and tossed them onto a chair. She smiled at me.

"Do you want to fuck me?" she asked mischievously, as though we were really only planning to do yoga on her bed.

"No," I said, "but I do want to fuck the Dutch passport." Keeping her eyes fixed on mine, she reached into the nightstand drawer and took out the world's most coveted passport: a condom.

When I phoned the following weekend to make a date, she said it would be better if we met in town.

"Maybe we shouldn't see each other anymore," she said in the park. "I'm starting to like you and am afraid I'm falling in love."

I never saw her again.

68

So now I'll tell you about my last year in the ASC. Not because that's where we've arrived, but because it's where I *want* to arrive. I hadn't planned on sharing so many anecdotes, but the hundreds of people I met in the ASC seemed to need me to tell their stories. And many other asylum seekers still call out to me in my mind, asking me to share their story as well.

Like Abbas, the Iranian who had come to the Netherlands from Germany with his family. His two daughters were still minors at that time. He was sent back to Germany after a few months, but once his daughters turned eighteen they were told they could apply for asylum independently of their parents, which they did. I will never forget how Abbas's face went pale when he learned that his asylum request cost him his daughters.

Or Gustave from Burundi, who went from hallway to hallway on his crutches while he waited for a residence permit that might allow him someday to walk with a prosthesis instead of on just one leg.

Or Zalmai from Afghanistan, whose wife and children were waiting in Russia for him to get a residence permit, so they could be reunited.

Or Lubna from Syria, with her handicapped son Ziaad, who was anxious to be reunited with her husband, who was stuck in Turkey.

But I can't. My energy is used up. So I'll jump to my last year.

Jamal invited me to his room for Milaad's 9th birthday. Najat had bought a cake with a big 9 on it, and taped a sheet of paper on the door with a bright yellow sun, also with a 9 on it. The room was packed with asylum seekers. Not wanting the asylum issue to overshadow Milaad's birthday party, they just exchanged arrival dates, saying, "I came three years before you were born," or: "I came here when you were two." When it was my turn, and I said I arrived on exactly the same day he was born, everyone laughed. They thought I was making a joke. I laughed, too, and told them it was true, but no one believed me. Maybe because in the ASC jokes are better than reality.

69

Shortly before Milaad's birthday, the ASC woke up to news that no one dared believe at first. Rumor had it that the government had issued a general pardon for all asylum seekers. All asylum seekers. Exactly what this meant, no one knew, and no one believed it would actually apply to them. Talib started spreading a joke that there was a General named Pardon, who had gone through all the IND dossiers and decided to give everyone a residence permit, no matter what was in their file. A kind of military coup. For many ignorant people, this was a way to make sense of it. Social Services, the VVN, and even Reception began explaining what the general pardon meant: that asylum seekers whose procedure predated April 1, 2001, and who had still not received a definitive answer and could not be repatriated, would be given a residence permit. On the condition that the person did not have a criminal record and had been in the Netherlands continuously from that date onwards. The reason for this general pardon was that a new Aliens Act went into effect on April 1, 2001, and the Dutch government wanted to start with a clean slate.

People started lining up to ask if the new law applied to them. For some of them it was a drama. João, an asylum seeker from Angola, had had his first interview on April 2, 2001.

"Look," he said to Wim from the VVN. "I arrived on

March 28, so *before* April 1, but they only took my first interview on the 2nd. Please, call the IND and say I should also have the general pardon." But Wim, who had years of experience, told João the IND knew exactly where to look, and he would hear from them in due time. "Listen, that's no good," João said. "I've been waiting here for years, and because they registered me just one day after April 1, I won't get the general pardon. That's absurd!"

"Call your lawyer. He should be able to do something."

"I've been trying all day to call him, but his secretary said exactly what you just did. I wanted to speak to him personally, but he didn't have time, or was in court."

The line was long, and Wim told him to come back the next day. João wandered through the ASC with all his papers, relating his situation in English, Dutch, or Portuguese to everyone he encountered. I heard that Wim did call the IND for him, and that João had actually arrived in the Netherlands on April 2, but he kept making his rounds with the bag full of papers because even if he didn't arrive on March 28, the whole thing was totally unfair.

Claudinho, another Angolan, went to Wim to say that João was getting close to the edge, and suggested Wim tell him the IND wouldn't make a fuss about just one day, but Wim did not want to give him false hope. Claudinho went to Social Services with the same request, and got the same answer.

The IND did not give João a residence permit. There were many other asylum seekers who suffered the same fate, because they had arrived weeks or months after April 1, but that was no comfort to João, for whom getting a residence permit or not had been a matter of hours.

70

Because I had left the Netherlands twice during my time here, when I went to Germany and was sent back, I did not qualify for the general pardon. It looked like I was destined to spend the rest of my days in the ASC, or at least until Iraq was safe enough to return to.

To be honest, I didn't really mind not getting a residence permit. It would be like massaging a dead body. I did, however, realize that the Dutch were not so perfect after all, with all their rules and computers, because there were some glaring mistakes.

It wasn't the first time. I remember a man named Mohammed Abdullah who lived in the ASC and was given a residence permit. The name was correct, but it was the wrong man. Apparently, the residence permit was intended for a different Mohammed Abdullah, in another ASC. But our Mohammed Abdullah was given residency, even though he had only been in the Netherlands a couple of months, and of course things never went that quickly. We joked that the original Mohammed Abdullah was waiting not only for himself but on behalf of every Mohammed Abdullah in all the ASCs throughout the Netherlands.

But with the general pardon, even worse mistakes were made.

Amadi, a Somali asylum seeker who had committed suicide a few years earlier, received a letter saying he'd been given a residence permit. So some asylum seekers had arrived in the Netherlands a day too late and did not get residency, while others were given it years after their death. For Talib, this was obvious: "Of course an asylum seeker needs a residence permit in heaven! That's why the IND sent the letter to Amadi. So he doesn't get kicked out."

Walid, my roommate for the first few years there, had long since fled to London, but we called him right away when he received his letter about the general pardon.

Mail came for various asylum seekers every day, but none came for Abdulsalaam. Now he was certain the IND had forgotten him. He inquired at Reception several times a day if there was mail for him. He asked Anneke and Patrick and Hilda and Daphne and Aiden why he did not receive a letter. And no matter how often Wim repeated that 'general pardon' was not a person, and therefore had no telephone number, Abdulsalaam kept on asking for it. Even the cashier at the nearby Aldi, who by now had known him for years, asked him if he had received his letter yet.

Every time another asylum seeker got his letter, Abdulsalaam would rush to Reception.

"The man in O-30 got a letter. Surely there's one for me, too?" The answer was always: No.

Zainab asked everyone who spoke Arabic the meaning of 'general pardon.' She invariably ended up with me, and I simplified it for her.

"You know how in Iraq, on Saddam Hussein's birthday, prisoners are let out of jail and deserters are allowed to return to the army? That's Saddam Hussein's general pardon. Now, the IND has said that anyone who arrived before April 1, 2001, can have that kind of general pardon. There are twenty-six thousand." Zainab's eyes opened wide. I thought she understood.

"So many? I thought we were the only ones, in this building …"

Not long thereafter, Zainab received the letter with her general pardon. Three months later she took her travel document to the Canadian embassy, along with the invitation from her brother in Quebec, and within a month she had a visa for Canada. Salih and I brought her by train to Schiphol airport. She had only one small carry-on. She had given her pots and plates, from which we had eaten all those years, and her sewing machine that had mended, taken in, and let out our clothes, to a Yemeni woman.

"Does this train really go to the airport?" she asked Salih.

"Yes, it does. Hundred percent sure."

A little while later she looked over at me. "It does go to the airport, right?"

"Absolutely."

When the conductor came, she asked me (even though she could have done it herself) to check with him if this train really did go to the airport.

"Next stop," he said. After eleven and a half years, Zainab could hardly believe she was sitting in the right train, and asked us every two minutes to reassure her.

The train stopped at Schiphol, and the escalator brought us up to the departures hall. We helped Zainab check in, and gave her her boarding pass. When she joined the line for passport control, we asked one of the other passengers to help her get to the right gate. Just before saying goodbye, she said, "And that poor Kadhem. Where oh where is his body?" She gave me an envelope containing the €118 she had withdrawn with his bank card before he committed suicide. She asked me to save it to use to send his body back to Iraq, in case the Dutch released his body and hadn't burnt it. I tried to give it back to her, but she refused.

I still have that envelope with the €118 in it.

She stood in line holding her travel document, and when it was her turn, she reached into her carry-on and brought out the bag with all the papers from the IND and the Justice Ministry. We couldn't shout to her that she didn't need them anymore, and later we saw her following the woman we had asked to assist her. She disappeared into the departures hall, still in her black clothes.

71

The ASC slowly emptied out. The departure of Kristi, that marvellous African woman, left the greatest void. She moved in with her boyfriend, a man covered in tattoos. A little while later, I bumped into them in town with her son Jimmy, who, you will recall, was supposed to call me "Daddy" when I picked him up from primary school. Kristi and the man were walking hand in hand, and she was very pregnant. Jimmy had grown into a lanky teenager, sports cap tilted to one side. He looked up at me and winked as he gestured at the tattooed man with his thumb, as though to say, "I don't call him Daddy, either."

"Who pumped you up?" I called out to her. She laughed that loud laugh of hers.

"My general pardon's prick!" she answered pointing proudly to the man, who smiled. That was the last time I saw her.

I once heard that Zako was looking for me, because he had news. It was about Yelena. He told me he had seen her in one of those windows in the red light district. We went there together, but now it was a different woman.

"That Russian girl was here yesterday, I swear it," Zako said. I went back a few days in a row, and sure enough, I saw her. I buried myself among the tourists, so I could pass the window a few times up close without her noticing me. There she was, with that same dreamy look, even behind the window. That look was the only thing that hadn't changed. Yelena. The woman who spread life through the orange hallways the minute she stepped out of O-124. Some people are beautiful. Their presence alone makes life bearable. But now she evoked something else in me: intense pity. Not only for her, but for beauty itself, and for me. I felt a lump in my throat when I thought back on what she had meant to me all that time ago. The same beauty that transported me to heaven was now for sale behind a window.

I considered going up to her, but was afraid it would humiliate her. I walked toward Central Station, turned back halfway to talk to her after all, but then turned around again. Every time I got close to her window, I decided against it and turned back.

She is the only person I met in the ASC who I would like to see again. Sometimes, when the snow falls at night for the first time and turns the darkness into white, I get a warm feeling inside because Yelena appears briefly in my mind before vanishing again.

72

About seventy asylum seekers who did not fall under the general pardon were left in the ASC. For years, it was a place of waiting and wailing, silence and screams, birth and death, suffering and succor—and now, strangely enough, it seemed incapable of near-emptiness. But it was. The emptiness was unbearable. The quiet in the rooms was hell. I have never experienced such a wretched feeling of loneliness and abandonment as in that desolate place. Every morning, I had to adjust anew to the deafening silence. Sometimes the silence was so overwhelming I couldn't really tell if I was asleep or awake.

When my roommates Malik and Salih got their residence permits under the general pardon, they both were also given a place to live. Salih in Groningen, Malik in a village in South-Holland. I stayed behind alone in O-139. Finally, a room to myself: this, too, was a kind of general pardon. But I found out I no longer slept as soundly as I once did. Something inside me always stayed awake. I used to think that this was because I had to share a room with others, but apparently that wasn't it. It was because I shared my inner mind with others: with Reception, the IND, the Foreigners' Police, Social Services, and all those other asylum seekers.

In the end, I too fell under the general pardon. Don't ask how, I still don't really know myself. It doesn't matter, because it proved that my asylum request had never really been taken seriously. I had seen so many mistakes already that it was hard to take the IND's decision seriously either.

I couldn't get to sleep, my last night in O-139. So I paced through Yellow with its yellow walls, Blue with its blue walls, Green with its green walls, and Orange with its orange walls, from wing to wing, over and over, until the colors of the walls all faded and became gray. Everywhere I went was accompanied by memories and feelings. Every brick was a piece of history. On that last night, the building made me think of a sinking ship. I heard a violin coming from O-101. It was Levon, the Armenian. I stood outside listening, as I always did when he played, but this time I knocked on the door when he finished and asked the name of the piece.

"*Dle Yaman*," he said, and wrote it down for me. He promised to play it for me as often as I wanted, but I told him I would be leaving the next day.

Before I left, I returned the two blankets, three sheets, towel, pillow, and pillowcase to the storeroom, and brought the receipt to Social Services, where Anneke gave me a day pass for the train and wished me a good life.

I went back to O-139. I had packed my things in a bag Abdulwahid had left behind when he went to London. I picked it up and looked out the window one last time. I opened the door, took one last glance around the room, and left the ASC by the back door.

"Samir, Samir, wait!" someone shouted. I turned and saw Abdulsalaam. "I was just at Reception and they told me that even you got a letter. But not me," he said. "Do you think I'll ever get one?"

How I wished I could give him an answer.

73

As I walked from the ASC to the train station I thought: what now, after nine years of marking time in that place? I looked in wonder at the world around me. Now that I no longer belonged to that building, it was as though I had been shut up in a sealed basement all those years. Rather than becoming open and larger, the world appeared treacherous and less trustworthy.

I had changed, both physically and mentally. Social Services knew Samir, as did the receptionists, the Foreigners' Police, and the IND. But I did not. And I had to get to know him so I could get on with my life.

A young mother, also on her way to the station, was pushing twins in a baby carriage. It was a positive, hopeful sign in those first minutes free of the ASC. The woman was carrying a handbag and a heavy suitcase. I offered to help and she nodded. At the station, she looked up at the departures board.

"Shit," she said, irritated. "Fifteen minutes' delay." I laughed out loud. She gave me a questioning look.

"I've just had a delay too. Nine years. In that building," I said, pointing to the orange wing of the ASC, still just visible in the distance. The woman smiled. If I hadn't carried her bag for her, she'd probably have thought I was crazy.

Maybe I was.

Abbreviations:

DUTCH	AZC	asielzoekerscentrum
ENGLISH	ASC	asylum (seekers') center[1]
DUTCH	IND	Immigratie- en Naturalisatiedienst
ENGLISH	IND	Immigration & Naturalization Service[2]
DUTCH	OC	Ontvangstcentrum
ENGLISH	RC	reception center[3]
DUTCH	COA	Centraal Orgaan opvang asielzoekers
ENGLISH	COA	Central Agency for the Reception of Asylum Seekers[4]
DUTCH	VVN	Vereniging VluchtelingenWerk Nederland
ENGLISH	VVN	Dutch Council for Refugees[5]

1 Residents of the asylum centers usually live with five to eight people in housing units. Each housing unit has a number of bedrooms and a shared living room, kitchen, and sanitary facilities. Residents are responsible for keeping their living environment in order. In a center the residents take care of themselves as much as possible. On average, there are about forty different nationalities in an asylum center.

2 When you apply for asylum in the Netherlands, you are asking the Dutch Government officially for a residence permit. You need this permit to be allowed to live in the Netherlands. First, you must register as an asylum seeker

in the village of Ter Apel. There, you usually also sign your asylum application. You will also find out when and where your asylum procedure will start. During that procedure, the Immigration and Naturalization Service (IND) will assess whether or not you get a residence permit.

3 Upon arrival in the Netherlands, asylum seekers often have no more possessions than the clothes they wear. The COA assists and accommodates them. The reception comprises shelter, pocket money, and access to basic services such as health care. This is laid down in the Regulation for Provisions for Asylum Seekers and other categories of foreign nationals. There are different types of reception centers. Where an asylum seeker lives depends on the phase of the asylum procedure.

4 The COA is responsible for the reception of asylum seekers and supports them in preparing for a future in the Netherlands or elsewhere. In doing so they closely collaborate with other organizations in the chain, for instance the Immigration and Naturalization Service (IND), the Royal Netherlands Marechaussee, and the Repatriation and Departure Service (DT&V). Each of these partners has its own tasks and responsibilities.

5 The Dutch Council for Refugees is an independent organization that acts in the best interests of refugees and asylum seekers in the Netherlands. Their employees and many volunteers commit themselves to the protection of asylum seekers and refugees by providing personal support and representing their interests at their admission, reception, and social participation. Their work is based on the Universal Declaration of Human Rights.

On the Design

As book design is an integral part of the reading experience, we would like to acknowledge the work of those who shaped the form in which the story is housed.

Tessa van der Waals (Netherlands) is responsible for the cover design, cover typography, and art direction of all World Editions books. She works in the internationally renowned tradition of Dutch Design. Her bright and powerful visual aesthetic maintains a harmony between image and typography and captures the unique atmosphere of each book. She works closely with internationally celebrated photographers, artists, and letter designers. Her work has frequently been awarded prizes for Best Dutch Book Design.

The font on the cover is called Mississippi. It is a gradient font, meaning that it dynamically increases and decreases letter height to control the rhythm of words, and this cover design features its first use. The Mississippi typeface is inspired by the aesthetics of mid-20th century America, with its Blues music, endless highways, and bold advertising. It is designed by Nikola Djurek and published by the Dutch type foundry Typotheque. The drawing of the teetering man on the cover is based on the physiognomy of the author Rodaan Al Galidi and was created by Annemarie van Haeringen (Netherlands), an internationally renowned Dutch illustrator.

The cover has been edited by lithographer Bert van der Horst of BFC Graphics (Netherlands).

Suzan Beijer (Netherlands) is responsible for the typography and careful interior book design of all World Editions titles.

The text on the inside covers and the press quotes are set in Circular, designed by Laurenz Brunner (Switzerland) and published by Swiss type foundry Lineto.

All World Editions books are set in the typeface Dolly, specifically designed for book typography. Dolly creates a warm page image perfect for an enjoyable reading experience. This typeface is designed by Underware, a European collective formed by Bas Jacobs (Netherlands), Akiem Helmling (Germany), and Sami Kortemäki (Finland). Underware are also the creators of the World Editions logo, which meets the design requirement that 'a strong shape can always be drawn with a toe in the sand.'